KT-227-057

The
DISH

STELLA NEWMAN

headline
review

Copyright © 2015 Stella Newman

The right of Stella Newman to be identified as the
Author of the Work has been asserted by her in accordance
with the Copyright, Designs and Patents Act 1988.

Extract from 'The Love Song of J. Alfred Prufrock' taken from *Collected Poems 1909–1962*
© Estate of T. S. Eliot and reprinted by permission of Faber and Faber Ltd.

First published in Great Britain in 2015 by
HEADLINE REVIEW
An imprint of HEADLINE PUBLISHING GROUP

First published in paperback in 2015 by
HEADLINE REVIEW

1

Apart from any use permitted under UK copyright law, this
publication may only be reproduced, stored, or transmitted, in any form,
or by any means, with prior permission in writing of the publishers or,
in the case of reprographic production, in accordance with the terms of licences
issued by the Copyright Licensing Agency.

All characters in this publication are fictitious and any resemblance
to real persons, living or dead, is purely coincidental.

Cataloguing in Publication Data is available from the British Library

ISBN 978 1 4722 2007 3

Typeset in Garamond by Palimpsest Book Production Ltd, Falkirk, Stirlingshire
Printed and bound in Great Britain by Clays Ltd, St Ives plc

Headline's policy is to use papers that are natural, renewable and recyclable
products and made from wood grown in well-managed forests and other controlled
sources. The logging and manufacturing processes are expected to conform to the
environmental regulations of the country of origin.

HEADLINE PUBLISHING GROUP
An Hachette UK Company
Carmelite House
50 Victoria Embankment
London EC4Y 0DZ

www.headline.co.uk
www.hachette.co.uk

To my sister, with love

'An ounce of loyalty is worth a pound of cleverness'

— Elbert Hubbard

Four Years Ago

The DISH

Stella Newman studied English at Sussex University, then went on to work in advertising, at the BBC and then as a professional food taster. She is now a full-time writer, based in London, and has written three novels: *Pear Shaped*, *Leftovers* and *The Dish*, as well as the festive e-short story, *A Pear Shaped Christmas*. She blogs about restaurants, food and writing at www.stellanewmansblog.wordpress.com and you can follow her on twitter @stellanewman.

Bromley Libraries

30128 80204 265 8

Also by Stella Newman

Pear Shaped
Leftovers
A Pear Shaped Christmas (short story)

To: Roger Harris@The Voice
From: Laura Harwall@Bean To Cup
Subject: Sub-editing work

Dear Roger,

I hope this email finds you well.

I'm sure you won't remember me – it's been so long – but I'm Laura Parker, Jane Parker's youngest daughter. (Harwall is/was my married name, but I'm just starting to change everything back.)

I have such vivid memories of you from the times we used to visit Mum in her office when you were still based in Fleet Street. Mum would try to make us sit quietly and behave – fat chance! Jess and I would come and pester you for Jelly Babies. You were probably trying to file copy on the Falklands but you always made time for us and even put up with my sister's atrocious manners. Did you *really* like the green Jelly Babies best or did you just pretend to so that Jess and I could eat all the red and black ones?

Anyway, twenty-five years on and here I am pestering you again. The reason I'm writing is because I'm moving back to London and I wondered if there were any sub-editing jobs going at your place? I'm a huge fan of *The Voice*. You launched just as I moved up North, and I find it so heartening that while other magazines have haemorrhaged readers, your ABCs go from strength to strength. Your journalists are the only ones I truly trust, and I've come to realise that trust – above all else – is what matters.

A bit about my background: after graduating in English and Spanish, I spent the majority of my twenties working for Union

Roasters, then left to help launch Bean To Cup. For the last three years I've been running our (now) five award-winning branches. While at uni I worked every summer as a sub at the *Manchester Evening News*. I have full secretarial skills as well as shorthand (Mum insisted). In addition I speak pretty fluent French (Dad now lives in Paris, Jess dragged him out there to be full-time babysitter to her twins. She heads up the equities trading desk for Paribanque, can you believe?)

In terms of subbing, I'm more than happy to do late shifts, nights, freelance – anything you have going. I'm a fast learner, very flexible with my hours and am available to start as soon as possible.

Looking forward to hearing back from you.

All the best,

Laura Parker

To: Laura Harwall@Bean To Cup
From: Sandra Milton@The Voice
Subject: re: Sub-editing work

Dear Mrs Harwall,

With regards to your recent enquiry, I regret to inform you we have no vacancies at this time. In addition, as your experience in newspapers was almost a decade ago, may I suggest that if you are indeed serious about re-entering the sub-editing profession, you gain some further experience? Perhaps apply for the course at Cardiff or City, if you are such a fast learner?

Yours sincerely

Ms Milton

To: Laura Harwall@Bean To Cup
From: Roger Harris@The Voice
Subject: My goodness!

Laura Parker, what an absolute delight to hear from you!

Of course I remember you. How could I forget the Parker sisters? Jess was the first eight-year-old girl (and come to think of it the last) who assured me she'd be the next female prime minister and that she'd teach Maggie a thing or two. And you, Laura – I've never seen anyone attack a Jelly Baby with such precision and delight, always the red ones, head first, one decisive bite: then a slow demolition of the rest, limb by limb. Graceful, methodical and with the mouth of a killer.

The ever-efficient Sandra managed to reply before I noticed your message. (If you ever need a henchman, Sandra's your woman. She's worked for me for ten years and still scares me slightly! No matter: she runs the office with Teutonic efficiency, leaving the rest of us to get on with the words.)

I'm terribly sorry to hear your marriage didn't work out. Been there myself. Still, your mother always used to say you were a brave little thing. I remember when you split your head open on a bumper car pole at the Hampstead Easter fair shortly after Jane started working for me. She told us you'd taken it all in your stride until you realised your sister had eaten your Cadbury's Creme Egg while you'd been having your stitches sewn, then all hell broke loose.

Unfortunately, as Sandra notes we have no vacancies in subs (though don't worry about a course – the laws of grammar haven't changed much recently). We run a supremely lean, post-financial crisis ship here – eleven full-time staff, the rest freelance. There is one vacancy – though I only mention it because we were about to advertise. It's far too junior and the pay won't be in line with your current salary. In fact I'm sure it's of no interest whatsoever. Regardless, I am looking for someone to replace my PA Maureen, who's retiring at the age of 132 – or so she'd have us believe!

Anyway, as I said, far too unchallenging for a girl with your manifold abilities, I'm probably insulting you even mentioning it.

I do hope, divorce aside, life is treating you well enough. Send my best to your father and sister, and if by any remote chance you are interested in applying, send me your CV and perhaps we can talk through the role in greater detail on the phone?

Warmest regards,

Roger

PS Yes of course I like the green ones best!

To: Jess, Dad
From: Laura
Subject: Life . . .

Quick update: I've officially filed for divorce as Tom's too cheap to pay the court fees. I discussed with my lawyer what grounds to file on – adultery being the obvious one – but Tom *still* claims he and Tess have only just started seeing each other, even though he's moved in with her. He thinks he's such a good liar but at least now I know the signs (i.e. opening his mouth/forming words.)

We've settled on 'Unreasonable Behaviour'. Shagging his colleague/my friend and lying about it for 13 months? Unreasonable just about covers it.

I haven't seen *her* since my birthday, when she bought me that silver Friendship bracelet. Presumably Accessorize were all out of Lying Two-Faced Slapper bracelets. I'm not sure why I judge her quite so harshly. I suppose you expect better from another woman. Well, the two of them deserve each other, and now I know never to trust anyone ever again.

Regardless. I think I've found a job in London, as PA to Roger Harris. He now edits a brilliant monthly magazine, *The Voice* – it's like a cross between *Private Eye* and *The New Yorker* – funny, sharp and honest. Also, I've spoken to Rachel and I'm going to rent her spare room. She's hardly ever there and I can have it for £350 a month – a total bargain for Maida Vale.

X

PS I'm not going to make it over for my birthday – think I'm going to lie low, so please could you send me some more of that fig jam? It's perfect – not too sweet, and has great little chunks of fruit in it.

To: Laura, Dad
From: Jess
Subject: HOLD IT!

Laura, you're making a VERY BIG MISTAKE. Don't EVER take a pay cut. And DON'T run away from your problems.

Also I think you should freeze your eggs. Fertility goes OFF A CLIFF after 30. One of my team has just frozen hers at 26 – a hugely sensible, forward-thinking move. Be pro-active! Charles and I could give you some money towards it, for a birthday present, if you like?

To: Jess, Dad
From: Laura
Subject: Please stop talking to me in capitals!

Jess. I'm lucky to be offered a job *at all* in the current climate. Besides, it's only an interim move while I sort my life out.

PS Thank you, and your husband, for offering to invest in my ovaries, but I'd much rather you bought me the new Nigel Slater if it's all the same?

To: Laura, Jess
From: Dad
Subject: re: Life . . .

Girls, don't squabble, please.

L – sounds interesting re Roger Harris. Your mother always rated him, although Jess may have a point, I'm not sure you should take a pay cut. You won't be able to afford the same lifestyle in London doing a secretarial job. And what about your friends, aren't they all up in Manchester now?

PS What is this Grindr thing? Can I do it on my BlackBerry?

To: Dad
From: Laura
Subject: re: Life . . .

Unfortunately most of my friends up here are mine *and* Tom's. They're politely sitting on the fence, and while I fully appreciate that no one wants to be involved in the drama (least of all me) it makes for a pretty lonely time up here regardless.

As for lifestyle, all I spend money on nowadays is food, and London's full of good, cheap places to eat.

PS Stay away from Grindr, Dad, it's really not your thing.

To: Laura
From: Jess
Subject: Important!

I've considered it overnight and I definitely don't think you should take this *secretary* job. I thought you were going to do freelance *subbing* while you found a proper job? It's essential to maintain your salary level. Believe me, I know all about these things: once you take a pay cut/step down from a career path it's almost IMPOSSIBLE to get back up again. I saw a CV the other day – bright woman who'd taken a year off to do some whole *Eat, Pray, Love* thing – and I just thought: flaky hippy.

Now would be the right time to return to a blue chip – apply to Nestlé or Kenco. The hot bevs market is virtually recession proof.

Laura: you've worked hard, you're smart and you're at a VITAL stage in your career trajectory. Don't under-deliver on your potential! Mum would have said the same.

To: Jess
From: Laura
Subject: Let me explain . . .

Jess, last December while I was laid up with flu, Tom went to New York (with Tess) for their 'annual marketing conference'.

YOUR BARCLAYS BANK ACCOUNT STATEMENT

CURRENT ACCOUNT

YOUR TRANSACTIONS

Date	Description	Money out
14/12	Agent Provocateur	£230
	The Mercer Bar	£78
	Duane Reade	£3.88
15/12	Tiffany & Co	£3200
	Starbucks JFK Int'l	£4.23

I don't need to spell out the punchline, but . . . last Christmas Tom bought me a WH Smith pocket diary and a griddle pan. Even though there are moments when I can sort of laugh at all this, these moments are brief. For the most part, my heart is broken. There are days when it is all I can do to get out of bed. Washing my hair feels like climbing a mountain. My heart literally aches. I feel humiliated every time I see any of our mutual friends. I need to leave this town and these memories behind.

Mum wouldn't have said the same as you. She'd have said life is precious and life is brief and if you're not happy – change something.

Much love,

Your flaky hippy sister
x

To: Laura
From: Jess
Subject: No, let *me* explain!

Clearly you are in the 'Frustration/Anger' phase of the Kübler-Ross change curve. Understandable, but why not take this opportunity to focus your energies on your career? Do not let yourself be DERAILED by this bump in the road!

To: Jess
From: Laura
Subject: Let me explain further . . .

Did Mrs Kübler-Ross find a bunch of filthy sex texts on Mr Kübler-Ross's iPhone? I very much doubt it.

Yes, it is a bump in the road. It's a big old bump. But don't worry, I'm on the case.

To: Roger Harris
From: Laura Harwall
Subject: OK . . .

I've thought about it. I'm in. When can I start?

PS Doesn't everyone eat the head of the Jelly Baby first?

Today

I

'Parker, can I borrow you a minute?'

'Let me just grab a napkin, Roger . . .' I say, cradling the phone under my neck while I attempt to keep my burrito in check with one hand: impossible – it's too heavy and too precarious.

'Sorry! I didn't realise you were having lunch, it can wait.'

'It's fine,' I say, although invariably I say *it's fine,* when I mean *it's not.* That very next bite of burrito would have had every single component lined up in a row: rice, beans, slow-braised pork, salsa, sour cream, guacamole and a few shreds of cheese. I'm no mathlete but I reckon the probability of having full-house distribution of all seven components in one mouthful is slim. In fact it's rare, and now I've put the burrito down all order is lost.

Roger's office is chaotic as usual, his floor stacked with back copies of *The Voice,* his walls papered with layouts for March's issue. His desk is an avalanche waiting to happen – books, journals, golf balls and empty packets of McCoys – watched over from the corner by a life-sized cardboard cut-out of Joanna Lumley in full Patsy get-up: beehive, shades, bottle of Stoly. Azeem, our digital editor, gave her to Roger for his 60th and she's a gift that keeps on giving.

Sandra tries to make Roger tidy up in here once a week, but trying to keep this space in order is like slagging off Justin Bieber on Twitter, then attempting to hold back an army of inflamed online Beliebers with your bare fingers: futile. My day job is still being Roger's PA so theoretically desk tidying is my responsibility. It certainly isn't Sandra's, she's Managing Editor*, far* more senior and important than me. But then Sandra's not a normal Managing Editor. No: Sandra is a ferociously cold fifty-five year old who dip-dyes her hair hot pink to prove she has a personality. After a particularly unpleasant run-in with her, Azeem suggested that Sandra's heart was a small pebble she'd found on Farringdon Road, which she'd taken back to the office and shrink-wrapped in plastic with her precious laminating machine. He's re-christened her The Laminator.

Sandra, meanwhile, has created her own nickname (bad form, surely, like laughing at your own jokes?). In an effort to prove to everyone at work that she's closer to Roger than the rest of us – Sandra calls herself Roger's 'Office Wife'. That's fine: OW suits Sandra just fine – as does ROW. Roger probably won't marry again and certainly won't marry Sandra, but Roger is kind and so he let's her keep the nickname. And life is way too short to argue about who tidies Roger's office, so she can keep that job too.

'Parker – have a seat.'

'Chance would be a fine thing,' I say, removing a brass trophy from last month's Press Awards from the chair.

'Is that yours or mine?'

'Mine,' I say, reading the plaque: *Best Features Review – Arts & Leisure.* 'But I can't do much with it. I'll leave it in here.'

'Nonsense, you should be proud of it. Use it as a paperweight?'

It'll only antagonise Sandra, I think, as I cradle it in my lap. Still, I am proud of it, very much so.

'What are you looking for?' I say, as Roger pushes a pile of papers to one side, then starts shuffling through another.

'Something you'll like! Something with your name all over it.'

He doesn't mean that literally. Nothing has my name on it, not when it comes to my *other* job. When I started writing our restaurant column, The Dish, after Fergus Kaye's meltdown, Roger and I agreed the new column should be anonymous. Of course Jess sent me a long, ranty email telling me I was being a naive pushover and that I should always FIGHT FOR FULL CREDIT and INSIST IT'S UNDER THE LAURA PARKER BYLINE.

But Jess was wrong. Food critics aren't like other critics: when our film critic, Henry, sees a film it's the same film our readers will see. You don't see Spielberg running round backstage at the Odeon re-shooting a happy ending just for Henry. But with food it's a different story. A food critic whose face is known will never have the same experience as the average reader. On the rare occasions I ate out with Fergus and Roger, we'd be seated at the best table, and the chefs would send over Fergus-shaped treats: extra foie gras, free champagne. The pen is mightier than the sword (and the rolling pin.). No – the only way you can do this job properly is if *no one* knows your name.

'A friend at *The Times* sent it to me on the sly,' says Roger, handing me a cream A5 card with gold foil edging. 'Obviously we're not welcome after last time . . . So all the more reason to go!'

If he wasn't nearly thirty years older than me, I'd have a proper boss-crush on Roger. He's bald, stout and looks his age: 62. If you didn't know him you'd think he was a retired geography teacher who'd been kept awake three nights in a row with root-canal problems: not standard crush material. But Roger is a brilliant journalist – fearless, sharp and compassionate. Also, he saved me from my old life. And more than anything, he makes every day in this office fun.

'What do you think?' he says, leaning forward on his elbows. 'Have you got to the bit about the sexy-punk aesthetic?'

'Hold on . . . I'm counting the number of times they've used the word *exquisite*.'

'And what a dreadful name!'

'*LuxEris* – sounds like a cross between an exotic dancer and a hybrid.'

'Perhaps I should have christened Gemma that . . .'

'Oh dear – what's she up to now?'

'Threatening to go to Thailand for three months with some chap she met online five minutes ago. Her mother's on the verge of having her locked up. Bet you never gave your parents this much grief.'

'I'm just glad the Internet didn't exist when I was nineteen,' I say. 'Besides, Mum would have banged me to rights.'

'True, Jane would have. I suppose Elizabeth and I both spoiled Gemma . . . guilt. Still, I can't understand where she gets this stubborn, rebellious streak from.'

'Oooh, stubborn and rebellious – I couldn't possibly imagine! Are you sure she's not adopted?'

He sits back in his chair and laughs. 'OK, she probably is mine. So then: what do you reckon – make this the main review for April?'

'You're quite sure you're happy for me to—'

'Both barrels, Laura. Besides, it might actually be good.'

I snort my response.

'So what's the diary looking like?' he asks.

'I'm doing a noodle place tomorrow and an Italian pop-up on Wednesday – Thursday?'

'There is one condition though.'

'Go on . . .'

'I'm coming with.'

2

Roger hardly ever comes with me when I review a restaurant. Partly because he's too busy meeting power-list types, in clubrooms women are forbidden to enter if they've ever owned a pair of trousers. Partly because he has cholesterol problems, and partly because if we ate out together more, he'd blow my cover.

I'm delighted he's coming though, and looking at this press release again back at home, I can see why:

Ivan Marekov and Erek Van der Velten are proud to announce the opening of LuxEris – their extraordinary new haute-casual dining experience. The visionary restaurateurs bring their unique brand of gourmet cuisine + sexy fun back to the capital, taking possession of the basement of The Needle – the 7th tallest building in the Square Mile.

LuxEris marks the dynamic duo's first joint venture with Executive Head Chef Jonn Zavragin who will oversee the kitchen team and an eclectic menu of global small plates. Diners at the 300-cover venue will enjoy exquisite industri-glam interiors by Ardaskian and signature cocktails curated by Denmark's legendary mixologist, Nils Iversen.

'Our philosophy of regional, seasonal, cutting-edge, luxury ingredients has found the perfect match with Jonn's uniquely exquisite sexy punk-aesthetic. Where better to combine our dynamic visions than London – capital of street food, edge and glamour?' says Marekov.

'The concept of what defines Modern Luxury in the 21st Century is at the core of our brand's DNA,' adds Van der Velten. 'And Eris is the ninth biggest planet in our solar system. We couldn't think of a more fitting name for our ninth branded baby.'

'Food is the new rock 'n' roll,' says Zavragin. 'I can't wait to take it to the next level in the city that brought us The Clash and the Sex Pistols.'

We look forward to welcoming you to the new shining star in the VanRek™ portfolio.

Additional info:

The VanRek™ brand operates eight upscale eateries globally: Abu Dhabi, Beijing, Beverly Hills, Dubai, Hong Kong, Moscow, Las Vegas and London.

VanRek's™ first UK brand extension, the high-end burger and cocktail joint, Carnivacious, launched in Chelsea in Autumn 2013, to five-star reviews.

Press enquiries – Petronella at Gilded PR

Five-star reviews, my arse! I gave it two – out of twenty – and only because the waiter was trying so hard. £45 for a burger, £8 extra for truffle fries? Mind you, they could have charged double and no one would have blinked an eyelid – no one in that place could move a single facial muscle.

The only critic who did give their last restaurant a glowing review was Petronella's boyfriend, good ol' Fergus Kaye, in the *Daily Metro*: a thousand-word rave about the beautiful front-of-house girls. Of course they were beautiful, VanRek™ only ever employs models as waiting staff. Judging from their raw floppy patties, I suspect their chefs might be models too, or actresses; anything but actual chefs.

LuxEris sounds exactly like the sort of place my flatmate would like. Amber is deeply glamorous, and utterly peculiar about food. One week she's hard-core vegan, eating cashew cheese and mainlining liquid kale, the next she's filled the fridge with grass-fed steaks and will sigh loudly if I try to introduce a packet of sausages that didn't cost £14. When I first moved in she had a total freak-out after I left a carton of eggs and some tomatoes tucked on the kitchen counter. I tried to explain that putting them in the fridge does them no good – but Amber *doesn't like looking at food* and it's her immaculate flat, we live by her OCD rules. Fair enough, cheap rent, and it meant I could still live in this great mansion block after I moved out of Rachel's spare room. So now I keep eggs and tomatoes on my bedside table and a basil plant by my window; makes me look like a weirdo, but it's not like I've had to explain myself to a constant stream of gentlemen callers these last three years.

On which note, I should text Russell back. He's in a pub near Marble Arch and wants to meet up later. If I don't see him tonight I won't see him till Sunday; but I don't want a late night on a Monday; besides I don't want to be the girl he calls after the pub – I need to establish healthy ground rules.

Amber's out with her boyfriend, so I take my computer and curl up on the sofa with a large glass of Malbec and Amber's miniature schnauzer, Annalex. Amber'd go mad if she saw me drinking red wine on her Winter Snow sofa (try telling Amber's interior designer it doesn't snow much in summer). Still, I'm pretty house trained – well, more so than Annalex. Poor dog is so confused about her identity (Amber insists on styling her as mini-Amber) – she's now on antidepressants and poops in protest at every new outfit.

Right: Google, let's see what you've got: 'chef Jonn Zavragin'. Looks like he should be playing lead guitar in Whitesnake. And what is it with chefs and crap tattoos?

Oh, but actually . . .

James Beard Award 2011 . . . Michelin star at 30 . . .

Impressive . . .

Executive Head Chef/Proprietor of The Big Z in Caesar's Palace and Jonn's in Chicago . . . new range of salsas, second biggest brand in the market . . . star of US hit show Jonn's Kitchen *. . . Married to the Victoria's Secret model, Consuela Fonesca . . . hobbies include playing guitar, listening to hip hop, collecting vintage Harley Davidsons.*

Far too much on his plate to be opening another restaurant, there'll be no quality control.

Right: Www.LuxerisLondon.co.uk . . . What *is* this music? Sounds like a porno.

LuxEris is . . . Senso-pleasure – Life-stylish – Eater-tainment

Ridicu-wank . . .

LuxEris operates a strictly no reservations policy . . .

I suppose that's marginally better than being put on hold for an hour, only to be told you can get a table at 4.30 p.m. in June 2023. Any reviews on TripAdvisor yet? Ah yes, a handful of five stars, all using the word exquisite, now who could possibly be behind those?

One more quick background check . . .

Eris (dwarf planet): 9th biggest body in the solar system, largest of all the dwarf planets . . .

Since when was Pluto only a dwarf planet? No one told me it had been demoted. Ooh, but look how tiny it is compared to Jupiter, Jupiter's gargantuan! Space is amazing! Space is distracting . . . Which planet's the closest to Earth again? Venus, that's right. How is it that I can remember the exact springiness of the focaccia in that tiny bakery in Lucca eleven years ago, but I can't remember basic science facts?

Eris (Greek mythology) – Daughter of Zeus and Hera . . .

That Zeus, what a player! He's fathered more love children than Hugh Grant. Ah, and Hera was his baby-mama *and* his sister: class. They should do a Jeremy Kyle Greek Gods special.

Eris . . . the Goddess of chaos, strife and discord . . .

Chaos, strife and discord? Did they not check that on Wikipedia first?

Surely that's just asking for trouble?

3

I'm not a morning person; not really a midday one either – I tend to be at my best any time after lunch. In Manchester we started work at 8 a.m. – and one of the countless terrific things about working for Roger is that we don't start till 10 a.m. – a luxury on a day like today.

Last night I went to a new Italian in Bermondsey with Sophie who lives opposite. She's the only person apart from Dad and Jess I've ever told about my column – partly because I trust her like family, and partly because she's the perfect dinner companion: she runs her own dessert company, adores food, and if I don't know the name of some obscure sea vegetable, she just might.

After supper (let down by fussy starters, deeply un-Italian) we came back for a bottle of wine at our local. We ended up laughing about whose ex was worse (hers = fat bloke who dumped her for being 'a big size 10'; mine = laziest adulterer in the North – he made it as far as one desk along).

Birdsong woke me at 6 a.m. but I rolled back into sleep and even though I didn't get up till 8.20 a.m. I still have time for my daily pilgrimage to Fabrizio's en route to the office. Fabrizio's is my favourite coffee shop in London, tucked away in an alley off Clerkenwell Road. The front area is a classic 1950s Italian coffee bar – Formica counter-top, beautiful shiny silver La Marzocco espresso machine, and amber glass jars of house-blend beans, ready to be ground. Then, hidden behind a small curtain at the back, is a cosy sitting area, just four wooden tables where Fabrizio plays jazz and blues and, very occasionally, early Donna Summer. In the basement he's installed a small roasting machine and sometimes he lets me roast a batch for old times' sake; sometimes I just stand there smelling the coffee.

I have begged Fabrizio to start selling breakfast of some description – pastries, bacon sandwiches – anything that when I'm hung-over can help break my fall into the day. I've talked him through the margins we used to make on snacks at Bean To Cup, but he just laughed, shook his head, and said, 'I don't need the fackin' aggravation, darlin'.' Sophie occasionally meets me here and recently she's been on a major sweet-talking offensive so I'm hopeful he might stock her cakes one day; but no food yet. So this morning I walk in and, like Norm from *Cheers,* am greeted with a hearty welcome and my usual: a warm double espresso, to go. 'Italians don't drink their coffee so bloody hot, Laura. You English, with your cappuccinos after dinner and cheese on your tuna pasta – fack me.'

As I take my coffee and head to the office, a line from a T. S. Eliot poem we studied at school comes to me: '*I have measured out my life with coffee spoons . . .* ' Mr Samson said in this sentence Eliot was 'trying to communicate the ennui so inherent in the modernist positioning'. At the time all I was thinking was the clock hand must be moving backwards. One poem, 130 lines long? Come back, haiku, all is forgiven.

I'm still not certain what that line meant – but I like it. It makes me think of my life over the past four years. I could measure those years out by my relationship with Fabrizio's coffee. Four years ago, I'd come into this café and be unable to make eye contact with Fabrizio. I could only look downwards, see downwards. Ordering a cappuccino with two sugars every morning, letting my tongue touch that chocolate dusted froth, was the one point of sweetness and comfort in my day.

And then one morning, about six months after I'd been back in London, I was sitting having a coffee in the back room. Fabrizio started playing 'Fly Me To The Moon' – a song my mum used to dance around the kitchen to with Jess and me when we were little. I remembered my mum's face – full of life – and I burst into tears. Fabrizio came rushing over to my table and gave me the longest hug, and I thought: *It's not true that Manchester is friendlier than London. No one's ever hugged me in a coffee shop up North.*

And ever since then, I have found myself crawling back into the world, taking pleasure in things, learning, rebuilding myself. And when Roger gave me my big break and I started writing The Dish,

I weaned myself off the anaesthetic froth of cappuccinos, off the two sugars, and on to flat whites, and then regular whites. And now I have lots of good things in my life, and I can start the day the way I used to back when I was happy – with this black, strong, almost poisonous liquid – and feel awakened. Feel excited again. Feel the thrill of what lies ahead.

The Voice is published on the first Tuesday of the month. Today is the last Thursday in February so we're sending March's pages to the printers now. The restaurants I'm visiting this week will run in April's mag. I've already written up Tuesday's noodle bar, and I'll do the Italian and LuxEris this weekend. The reviews then go to our lawyer, on to our subs who craft and double-check, then get typeset, photos dropped in and whoosh, off they go!

My final deadline is still nearly four weeks away but I like to file early. It's pretty much guaranteed the minute you fall behind – even by just one day – life will throw some Super Mario barrels in your path to trip you up. You'll find yourself scribbling copy the night before you go to print, with Sandra looming ready for the kill, like Donkey Kong in a floral wrap dress. I've only had to file up to the wire once in three years – an unplanned trip to Paris to help Dad look after Jess's twins. It is a situation to be avoided: at all costs.

It's now 6.30 p.m., but Roger's still immersed at his desk, so I'm sifting through letters to the editor regarding our back issues. Edgar Smyth from Kensington *violently disagrees* with Henry, our film critic, that Billy Wilder deserves the title *auteur* as 'Wilder's films do not represent a cohesive body of work like Hitchcock's do – only a hack would suggest otherwise'. Calm down, Edgar, it's only a movie . . .

Ah, one for me . . .

Dear The Dish,

I am a 73-year-old, retired GP from Sevenoaks, and, while I have trav-elled extensively, I have never made it as far as Korea. I must admit, it has never been on my shortlist. On the train up to town last month I read your review of Genwa and decided to take a chance. What a revelation – such intense flavours, and exactly how I'd imagined from your vivid descriptions. In particular I am taken with kimchee, which you might be interested to hear pairs exceptionally well with mature Cheddar. I wish I had discovered it earlier in my life; still, better late than never! Do keep up the good work.

Yours sincerely,

Michael Austin

That's the very best part of my job – when a reader discovers a great restaurant because of something I've written. And a kimchee and Cheddar combo? I reckon he's right: salty, sharp, spicy, crystalline . . . that's genius. Thank you, Dr Austin – you have won yourself a bottle of champagne, sent in by Edible PR, after I gave one of their client's openings seventeen stars. I always re-gift these gifts – as far as I'm concerned they amount to a belated bribe. Roger thinks I'm a goody two-shoes – he said if I wrote the review *after* I'd been sent a present, it would be a different matter. But still, I write what I write: I believe in razor-sharp boundaries.

And another for me . . .

Dear The Dish,

Your vocabulary is that of a five year old, raised by an illiterate lupine. You obviously know nothing about food or you would not review peasant fare: since when did a hamburger merit a write-up in a proper magazine? Go back to the second-rate student rag from whence you came. I'll be cancelling my subscription forthwith.

Yours in disgust,

An Ex-reader

Ah, adorable. Presumably by lupine you mean a wolf, not a flower – but either way, show me a wolf that can read and write and I'll quit my job and take it to Vegas. Illiterate lupine . . . well that, Ex-reader, is what I'd call 'tautology'– a word they taught me at Wolf School. I'd point that out to you *if* you'd been brave enough to put your real name and contact details on this letter . . . I wonder if it's secretly Fergus, or perhaps it's Sandra, writing with her left hand . . . Oh well, you can't please all of the people all of the time, I think, as I rip the letter in two and drop it in my bin.

6.40 p.m. . . . we should head off by 7 p.m. if we're going to avoid a queue at LuxEris. I pop my head round Roger's door and he holds up five fingers. Just enough time for me to make myself look presentable, so I head to the ladies' room.

Tom used to say I had many different faces. I could look *stern and unapproachable*, or *like a kid who's just broken something and hasn't yet told their mum*. With my glasses on *like a scientist*; with artful make-up *almost Danish*. Sometimes *sweet*, often *anxious*. But I just have one face: grey-green eyes, a smallish nose, regular, not very memorable features; no razor-sharp cheekbones, no Cara Delevingne signature eyebrows; nonetheless, an ideal face for staying under the radar. Even so, I try to tweak my look subtly every time I eat out. Front-of-house staff move around all the time, and I never want to take an unnecessary risk (though I draw the line at the fake moustache Dad sent me when I started the column). LuxEris is the most glamorous of the restaurants I've visited this week, so I let my hair down, sweep a thin layer of black liquid eyeliner over my lids, add another layer of mascara and some lip gloss and that's me, done.

Roger's still working but he beckons for me to sit while he finishes up. Now March's issue is being put to bed, the layouts that were plastered over these walls have come down. It'll be at least a week before April's plans go up, and this is my favourite week in our production schedule because Roger's walls are, once again, revealed. There are at least twenty frames hanging here but four in particular stand out. The first is a framed quote by an American writer, Elbert Hubbard, about whom Roger is writing a biography:

Editor: a person employed by a newspaper, whose business it is to separate the wheat from the chaff, and to see that the chaff is printed.

When I first saw that it confused me. I'm ashamed to admit I had to double-check that wheat is good and chaff bad, even though coffee beans produce chaff too. I didn't know Roger then, and I didn't understand why he'd have that up there – but he has it to remind him how *not* to do his job.

The second and third frames are photos: one of Roger in the Oval Office, shaking hands with Bill Clinton. And next to it, a photo of Roger when he still had hair, in the eighties, with one arm around Jim Henson, and the other around Miss Piggy. (She's wearing strapless pink taffeta and pearls, Go Piggy!)

And the final frame is another quote, just three sentences long, not exactly Shakespeare:

The Foxmore in Battersea is the perfect neighbourhood restaurant: delicious food, fantastic staff and a lovely relaxed dining room combine to make this a near-flawless experience. Let's start with the bread; in fact I'd happily start, middle and end with it. Served warm with caramelised onion butter, its springy texture and malty crust make you realise that man could live by bread alone – if only man could get a table here . . .

Not exactly Shakespeare, but they were the first sentences I wrote for Roger.

So now, even though he's made us late for dinner, and he's tetchy about last month's ad revenue, and when I finally do get him into a taxi he realises he's left his wallet on his desk so we're going to be even later, there is no one in this world I would rather work for, and I can't imagine there ever will be.

'Lombard Street – and would you mind going via St Paul's please?' Roger says to the driver.

He looks tired tonight.

'Rough day?' I ask.

'I could do with something life-affirming to look at, that's all.'

'Anything I can do to help?'

'My daughter's gone and booked a ticket to Thailand with this new chap . . . Anyway, let's not,' he says, tracing a raindrop down the window of the cab.

'Are you looking forward to the meal?'

'Intrigued. The *Telegraph* came on Tuesday – by all accounts you must visit the men's toilets.'

'I should have brought my fake moustache after all. Apparently they've had a nightmare with the team. Jonn Zavragin's had to chuck money at one of his old boys to run the kitchen; I bet he hasn't even done one shift there himself.'

'Jonn with two "n"s – do you think he added the extra "n" to make himself sound more rock 'n' roll?'

'It's like buying a Porsche, isn't it?' I say. 'It's just a penis extension for your name.'

'Ah, now that's more like it!' Roger's face lights up as we drive past the cathedral. 'Fifteen years and forty million pounds to restore it to glory.'

I let out a whistle. Though actually LuxEris's launch budget is apparently £8 million, a million on silverware alone. Hope they've installed some metal detectors on their exit doors.

'Majestic, is it not?' he says.

It is utterly beautiful.

'St Paul: Patron Saint of London, Patron Saint of Writers and the Press . . . not what you'd call a feminist though,' says Roger.

'No?'

'*I do not permit a woman to teach or to have authority over a man, she must be silent.*'

'Good luck with that! Oh my goodness, don't tell me that's the queue?'

A line of at least forty extends from the base of The Needle, the most hulking new skyscraper in town. As we pay, the cabbie gives us a look as if to say: *who'd be mad enough to wait outside on a filthy February night? Sucker born every minute.* More like every thirty seconds judging by the length of this queue.

We take our place at the back, pulling our coats tight against the drizzle. After a moment, Roger turns his head sharply to the left, like a startled sparrow. 'Is that racket coming from these paving stones?'

'Built-in speakers!' I say, pointing to the concrete blocks at the base of the building.

'Laura, I don't mean to start off on the wrong foot, but do you think, if we are going to be queuing for some time, we might ask them to play a little Vivaldi? Some Doris Day?'

'I thought you were a huge Jay-Z fan.'

'I like that one he did with Alicia Keys. I just don't like this one. "99 Problems" . . . *bitch* this, *bitch* that . . . He's like the St Paul of rappers.' In front of us, a couple of shiny-faced suits nod along meaningfully, like they're straight out of Bed-Stuy, rather than Bed-Ales. 'How long do you think this queue will actually be?'

It doesn't seem to be moving much. 'An hour? Why?'

He looks at his watch. 'We could come back tomorrow at 6 p.m. That might be better?'

'Whatever you prefer.'

'Ah no. That won't work. I've got an Ocado delivery booked for 8 p.m. Sod it – we're here now.'

Ocado: meet the course of history.

It is past midnight by the time we finally emerge from the Hades-like bowels of LuxEris. I have never seen Roger as angry, or as funny, as he has been tonight. Over the last five hours, we have witnessed greed, sloth, gluttony, wrath, envy, nausea, a small fire and a row of golden toilets with breasts.

'I don't think I can do it,' I say, gulping down a lungful of sweet, polluted London air. 'It feels like too much.'

'That's why you must!'

'But I can't do it without going to town.'

'That's what I pay you for.' He takes his own deep breath of relief, then shakes his head rapidly as if trying to rid himself of the horror. 'Have you written April's other two reviews yet?'

'Noodles are done, I'm doing the Italian this weekend.'

'Drop the noodles . . .'

'And just run this?'

'Maximum impact. We'll increase it from a single to a double-page spread, stick the lav in the middle. Take whatever word count you need, but nail them.'

'Sorry, Roger, I think I developed tinnitus in there – could you say that again?'

'I said: nail them.'

I go home and I write and I write, fuelled by outrage and coffee, until 4 a.m. when I realise the hot flush I'm experiencing is neither a caffeine overdose, nor excitement at how brilliant my piece is, but a symptom of the onset of mild food poisoning. I creep to the kitchen for a glass of water, keeping the light off so as not to wake Annalex from her sleeping-pill-induced slumber. I end up sitting on the toilet floor, shivering, sweating and sitting vigil.

I slowly sip water, waiting, waiting.

Nothing happens.

And still nothing.

This is the icing on the cake, or the nail in the coffin – the nail in the icing, quite frankly. I rest my arm and then my head on the toilet seat and pray for sleep or vomit, whichever comes first.

The thing is, my review should be entertaining – I hope – but it'll be entertaining in a rude way – and it's easy to write like that when a restaurant is so unremittingly awful. But that's not the reason I do this job – truly it isn't. I'm so much happier when I can write positively about places doing good things . . . So tired . . .

Please just let me be sick, this acidic hum is exhausting. I wish this had happened while I was still at LuxEris, I can think of nothing more fitting for those toilets than yacking on them. What is wrong with this world, that someone would design a toilet that resembled a naked goddess Venus and cover the whole thing in gold leaf?

Oh no, oh no . . . here it comes, here it comes . . . yes? No, it's gone again. Bloody cauliflower panna cotta. Or maybe it was those eels? They tasted like a cup of sewage left out in a heatwave.

Oh God, take a deep breath. Sip some water. More water.

OK, I think it's subsiding. 6.02 a.m.

The minute I lie back down I feel a wave of nausea rise up so violently, I rush back to the bathroom – but by the time I'm poised over the toilet it's disappeared again, another false alarm. This pattern repeats itself every ten minutes until 8.00 a.m. when I decide to chance a cup of black tea with honey, which seems to do some good.

I send Roger a text asking if he's been feeling unwell – he sends back:

Only an inflamed bile duct! Don't come in if you're sick, Laura!

I crawl back into bed and manage two hours of fitful sleep, then wake up and reread my review. I get as far as point 94:

To be clear: I don't pay to leave my coat in a restaurant, I don't pay to pee and I don't pay for tap water.

And remember I wanted to Google those toilets . . . £5,100 for the pan? Gold-leaf seat – £2,200? £300 extra for the flush?

Seven thousand, six hundred pounds on a toilet is obscene, it is beyond vulgar, it is plain wrong. I start typing again, fingers powered by the last savage bursts of outrage:

Eating out should not be this hard. Eating out is meant to be sociable, pleasurable and fun. Everything that is wrong with the London dining scene is on the menu here: rudeness, arrogance, greed, pretension, joyless ostentation, vulgarity and a total lack of true hospitality.

You don't care what people want to eat, how they want to eat it or whether they have to shout over your deafening music in order to have a conversation: all you care about is money.

One last spell check . . . My finger hovers over the mouse. Is this final part too brutal?

LuxEris: Your name, your pricing and everything you stand for is preposterous. This is not 'Eatertainment': this is punishment. Stop referring to your restaurant as a brand – it's an insult to McDonald's.

What did Roger say again? *Nail them.*
I press send.
Job done.

4

Roger is already at lunch by the time I make it in at noon. Sandra gives me a filthy look; more filthy than the fact I'm two hours late deserves. Roger must have told her he's pleased with the piece.

Ah yes! He's left a Post-it note on my screen saying 'Withering Heights' and there's an email in my inbox:

> *Have told planning you need double the normal space. I'll ponder the headline with Kiki (Bad Things Happen in Basements? The Kitchen Stinks?). Have forwarded to Legal. Terrific job.*

The more I think about it, the more I wonder whether I should reference the Jay-Z track in my first line; a lot of readers might not know the original . . . Best thing to do when I'm not sure about something is to email the family: Jess likes Celine Dion – she actually does, and Dad likes Gilbert and Sullivan – so let's see if either picks up on it.

Azeem heads over to my desk. 'I'm going down Leather Lane,' he says, taking his wallet out. 'Halves on a red chicken curry and a pad Thai? I owe you, don't I?'

'No curry . . .' I say, as a little acid reflux makes itself known in my throat.

'Fish and chips?'

'Honestly, Azeem, if I eat anything—'

'Are you dying?'

'Just staying away from solids.'

'They could blend it into a fish and chip smoothie? Very Heston.'

'Azeem!'

'Ah,' he says, looking at me with vague concern. 'You do look a bit green. Does this mean you're not coming down The Betsey later?'

'Going straight home,' I say. I still look and feel dreadful; maybe I should sue LuxEris for ruining my Friday night? Those guys could totally afford to pay me compensation. At the very least they should buy me a butt naked toilet that resembles Jon Hamm – now *that* would be worth £7,600 of anyone's money. Jon Hamm: now there's a man who does not need to add an extra N on his Jon. Though hang on a minute, he does have an extra M on his ham . . .

'Oh shit,' says Azeem, looking genuinely alarmed. 'Does this mean you're not doing Cake Run?'

'Come on, Az, you could do it?'

'Get Kiki on the case – I'll forget who's ordered what.'

'And that's why I created this spreadsheet,' I say, grabbing his sleeve as he tries to escape.

In an attempt to stave off boredom, I have set up colourful charts and systems for every possible function in this office. Azeem squints at my screen in confusion. 'That looks epically complicated.'

'It's perfectly straightforward, working down from the third floor, the ad guys like to splurge; last week they had salted caramel financiers. Subs and planners – more modest: brownies or giant cookies, then steer Roger towards something fruit-based – perhaps a strawberry tart?'

He leans in for a closer look. 'What no Laminator?'

'She claims not to indulge,' I say, dropping my voice, even though she's currently upstairs. 'But leave a cranberry streusel flapjack within a five-metre radius and it'll be gone in sixty seconds. Do me a favour . . .' I take two pound coins from my wallet. 'Buy her one anonymously; it couldn't make her more sour, could it?'

To: Laura
From: Dad
Subject: re: My review – what do you think?

I've read the piece – My goodness, sounds awful – they thoroughly deserve every word, and I loved the bit about the cold hot dog.

Any nice plans for the weekend? Munchkin Number One has become obsessed with Degas's *La Classe de Danse* so we're off to the Musée d'Orsay tomorrow to study it. She wants green sashes like in the painting for their ballet performance. Meanwhile all Munchkin 2 wants to do is watch *Despicable Me*. Again.

To: Dad
From: Laura
Subject: re: My review – what do you think?

Tell Milly if she watches it one more time, she'll turn into a minion.

Saturday – possibly helping Soph at farmers' market – then not much. Skype at 4? Sunday, I have a date with that guy, Russell.

To: Laura
From: Jess
Subject: Quelle horreur!

Good piece. £9.50 for a bread basket? The French wouldn't stand for such nonsense. But is it wise to admit you visited the men's toilet? Won't that make you appear grubby?

Jess has such insane reactions sometimes, it makes me laugh.

To: Jess
From: Laura
Subject: re: Quelle horreur!

No one will think I'm the town bike. Most of my readers are under the impression I'm a man anyway.

To: Laura
From: Jess
Subject: God is in the detail . . .

Well then, Clever Clogs, I'm afraid you'll need to rethink this section:

> *10. I don't care if the world's most famous 'starchitect' did design your tables – they don't work as tables. Their unique multi-faceted corners stab you, uniquely, in the hips.*
> *11. Plus they wobble.*
> *12. And they're rammed too close together.*
> *13. I'm 5'7" – no giant – yet my knees were hitting the underside – so please make your table legs taller.*
> *14. Or your chair legs shorter.*

To: Jess
From: Laura
Subject: Er, why?

What's the problem exactly?

To: Laura
From: Jess
Subject: Er, because

You talk about your height, and 5'7" doesn't sound like a man's height.

To: Jess
From: Laura
Subject: I am the same height as Tom Cruise, so there!

I've double-checked and the star of *Top Gun* is 5'7".

To: Laura
From: Jess
Subject: Seriously

Have you nothing better to do with your time?

To: Jess
From: Laura
Subject: No, actually.

We've just put March's issue to bed, and everyone else has gone down the pub – and I would have too, if I wasn't feeling nauseous.

To: Laura
From: Jess
Subject: Good grief

Pub at 3.30 on a work day? You media folk still live in the '80s.
   As for your review – next time if you don't actually want my opinion don't ask for it!!!

PS Can you buy me four packets of Parmesan biscuits from Flour Palace for next Saturday? My Eurostar gets in as per the attached agenda. I will have 90 minutes; need to be at Kensington Roof Gardens for drinks with European Heads of Trading at 5.30 p.m. so be on time!

To: Jess
From: Laura
Subject: re: Good grief

Have a great weekend, Jess. Love to the girls. L xx

Way too weak to take her on this afternoon. On which note . . .

To: Sophie
From: Laura
Subject: Tomorrow . . .

Are you doing farmers' market? If so, I probably shouldn't work the stall – meal from hell last night and now food poisoned. I could still drive the van, but might need to wear Hong Kong style bird flu mask to avoid infecting your brownies.

To: Laura
From: Sophie
Subject: re: Tomorrow . . .

Shit, forgot to tell you! Going up to Sheffield to see Will – first weekend off in five months! Was going to leave new Battenberg flavour trial outside your door this afternoon – should I leave chicken soup instead?

To: Sophie
From: Laura
Subject: Don't worry

I'm pretty much nil by mouth, so planning on being in bed by 8.30 p.m. Need to be fully recovered for Sunday; made it past the date three bump, who knows? Russell and I may even make it through date four . . .

To: Laura
From: Sophie
Subject: Yay, date four!

You'll be fine. Make sure you do something fun on Saturday. *Game of Thrones* on your own does not count.

To: Sophie
From: Laura
Subject: GoT

You wouldn't say that if you'd seen season three, episode nine
x

When I first moved back to London, Saturdays were savage. I used to forge myself military-style routines to battle those endless hours: walk and shop and clean and tidy; cook, read book, nails, wash and sleep. Days so full but my God, they felt empty.

Four years on and I'm no longer lonely, well, no more so than the next person. I've come to value my freedom. This morning I had a lie-in, then brewed a pot of coffee from Caconde in Brazil. The rich, chocolatey smell filled the flat like sunshine. As I was drinking it I noticed Annalex looking at me forlornly, so I took her for a walk along the canal, over to Regent's Park. She made a beeline for the snowdrops – they're toxic for dogs – and I wondered if it wasn't a cry for help, so just in case, I gave her some extra Chewdles when we stopped for a break on a bench. Sitting next to us was an old couple feeding the ducks. They were holding hands and wearing matching scarlet hats: those hats really stood out against the grey sky.

On my way home I detoured via The Sea Shell because I missed out on fish and chips yesterday, but when I walked in the smell of deep fat frying made me feel peaky. Instead, I went home and made fusilli with butter and peas – simple but comforting. Then I Skyped

Dad and Jess, had a bath and watched *Game of Thrones* – the dragons! The blood! I meant to watch only one episode but it was so exciting, I just had to keep going.

And Sophie says sometimes she worries I'm avoiding life, but I disagree entirely, I am living it. Why would I give up my freedom just to have any old man? Of course there are nights, like tonight, when I lie in the bath until the water's run cold, my toes resting on the taps, and I dream about the sort of love you only see in the movies: a love like in *The Notebook*. But that sort of love is a fantasy. It doesn't exist in the real world.

I'm not saying there are no good men out there – of course there are, and if one came along, terrific. But he'd better be terrific or there's no point. And Russell? It might be Russell. Three dates in is far too early to tell, isn't it?

When I get into bed tonight I have the strangest sensation, a tightness in my abdomen. It might be the return of the dodgy eels. But I don't think so. It feels more like nerves, adrenalin, anticipation. A feeling that something's about to happen, my life is about to change.

5

I wouldn't have been so late this morning if Amber hadn't been hogging the bathroom, performing a 'dry oil sub-dermal scrub'. Still, I've managed to make myself look presentable in seven minutes. If I hadn't wasted another five working out whether it was going to rain, I'd have been on time. I wouldn't have had to race for the bus, and I wouldn't now be standing here, sweaty, and without an umbrella in the drizzle. Though I'm not sure it matters – I'm outside No.1 Columbia Road, but Russell isn't.

It's 10.03 a.m. I'm sure we said 9.30 a.m? Start at the flower market, then head to St John for the legendary bacon sandwich; cinema for the new Ridley Scott and then a curry. My perfect day.

I check my phone. No text.

Is that him, walking along, hands stuffed in his raincoat pockets, looking panicked? Why can't I remember exactly what he looks like? When I think of him – do I think of him? – I just remember the profile photos from Tinder: one where he's snowboarding and you can't see his face. One at his daughter's fifth birthday party – he looks happy in that one, twinkly brown eyes, neat smile. And then a photo of him riding a mountain bike.

No, that's not him . . . Where *is* he?

Jess would approve of Russell, I'm sure. On paper, he ticks lots of boxes:

- Highly respectable job (software; something to do with vertical interfaces? I still can't compute)
- Sporty (running, footy)
- Does not play PlayStation (thinks it's for kids: correct!)
- Is tall (six foot)

Tick, tick, tick tick. Lots of annoying ticks . . .

No, that's harsh. He's an all-round strong 7/10. And I do think he has potential, I do. We have a lot in common: an ex-spouse who couldn't keep their pants on. He understands what it's like to go through that. What else? We both hate liquorice. We both like parks . . .

Hold on . . . is that . . . no, still not him. He's always been on time before today. Ah, perhaps that's why I like him. Because he's still here. Because he's the only man since Tom who I've had more than three dates with; turning up — that's all it takes!

Ah, finally! 10.09 a.m. He looks stressed, I'll give him a break.

'Laura, sorry,' he says, pulling me close for a kiss.

'Goodness, heavy night?' I say, smelling the vodka leaking from his pores.

'Just a few drinks,' he says, scratching his chin and looking over my shoulder towards the market. 'Christ, it's busy. Anywhere we can get a quick bite to eat before we do this flower thing?'

'I thought we'd do twenty minutes of the market, then grab a bacon sandwich? They stop serving at eleven a.m.'

'Is there anything round here I could have in the meantime? I'll still have the sandwich, but I need a little something.'

He does look rough, bless him. It must be hard, adjusting to this new way of life, juggling being a dad with being a newly single man.

'There's a bagel place up there, a cheese shop on Ezra Street . . . there's Lee's — they do amazing seafood, probably a little early in the . . .'

'Seafood's good, if I can get a Bloody Mary chaser?' he says, flashing a sheepish smile.

'You want to go to the pub?'

'Hair of the dog.'

'All right. The one up the top's the nicest.'

We slowly pick our way through the crowds of people balancing bunches of tulips and miniature lemon trees; terracotta urns and trays of rosemary plants.

'The fried prawns and calamari are delicious,' I say, as we queue at the window and the smell of the seaside drifts over us.

'Cockles! I haven't had them for years! Used to eat them out of a jar when I was a kid. You're not a fan?'

'You go for it.' Just don't expect me to eat any of them.

'How's Lilly getting on?' I say, as he stabs his wooden fork into the white polystyrene cup and fishes out a rubbery grey splodge.

'Mmm . . . difficult week,' he says, shaking his head. 'Becky wants her all of Christmas but I don't think that's fair. It's been getting me down.'

'That's why you've turned to drink?' I say, smiling.

'Huh?'

'Nothing, just the hangover . . . the pub . . .'

'I should buy you some flowers, shouldn't I?'

'There's no need, I'm happy just looking at them.'

He darts towards the nearest vendor who's bellowing, 'TWO FOR A FIVER, TWO FOR A FIVER,' and returns a moment later with two bunches of slightly droopy pale pink roses, which he hands over as if they're his tracksuit that needs washing.

'Thank you!' I say, moving to kiss him. Our lips touch, but he goes in for the full snog and ends up licking the outside of my mouth with a vinegar-tipped tongue.

'Let's grab that drink,' I say, steering him towards the pub.

'Right, Bloody Mary and . . . ?'

'I'll have a Diet Coke.'

'Don't make me drink on my own, Laura, I'll look like an alcoholic!'

'It's ten a.m.'

'Gin and tonic? A single?'

'Oh go on then. But can we drink it quickly?'

'Yes, sir!'

We move to the corner table and he settles down with his arm around me. I readjust myself into his body; I can never seem to get quite the right angle with Russell, he's lean and bony, all those half marathons. That's definitely something we do *not* have in common.

'So you've booked the tickets?' he says, absently kissing the top of my head.

'Yup, three fifteen p.m. trailer, loads of time. Are you going to fall asleep in it? You look knackered.'

'I'll be fine, as long as there's a car chase.'

'So where were you last night, anyway, that you're this hung-over?' I say, running my finger down his unshaven cheek. The stubble quite suits him.

'Huh?'

'Did you go out locally?'

'Yeah, yeah.'

'With the boys?'

'What?'

'Were you out with the boys, after football?'

'Oh. No.'

Oh no.

'Oh. I thought you were playing football yesterday?'

'Yeah, I did, I just ended up meeting up with a friend.'

'A friend?'

'Just a friend.'

Just a friend.

My stomach flips. I have been here before.

Those three little words are a sign: a sign that means: don't ask who.

'Who?'

'Why?'

Answering a question with a question. That's another sign.

'I'm curious,' I say.

' . . . A friend I met recently.'

'A girl?'

He nods and shifts in his chair. Oh please don't make me Paxman this out of you.

'Was she a girl you met on Tinder?'

He leans forward and puts his hand on his glass and rests it there, then turns to look at me with a face that says *there's no point in trying to style this out, is there?*

'Ah,' I say, though it comes out more like 'ouch'.

'Don't be like that, Laura, it's not a big thing.'

41

'Be like what?'

'You look so . . .'

'No, I'm not anything. But just to be absolutely clear, was it a date?'

He pauses before nodding.

'A first date?' I say, feeling my temper rise.

'Laura, I think you're lovely.'

Yes. I think I'm OK too.

'The thing is . . .' He takes a deep breath and sighs with the exhaustion of it all. 'It's only been six months since I broke up with Becky. I'm just finding my feet again.'

Your feet or your dick?

'You understand what it's like,' he says, swiftly changing gear from *caught in the act* to *we're on the same side*.

'I understand what *what* is like?' I say.

'Divorce. Splitting up from your other half.'

'Right.'

'It's not easy.'

'Yes, I do vaguely recall that.'

He nods and takes another slow sip.

'Are you about to say something else, Russell?'

'Like what?'

'You were saying, "It's not easy getting divorced . . ."'

'My point is, *you'll* understand why I don't want to rush things . . .'

He means rush things emotionally; he was certainly in a rush physically last time we met.

'But I genuinely do think you're very attractive,' he says. 'I'd like to see where this goes.'

I can tell you where this goes: nowhere.

'Laura, you said yourself you weren't ready for anything for ages after you broke up with Tom.'

'I did say that, Russell, that is true.'

'So then . . .'

I pause while I try to formulate my thought, to make it sound as unemotional as possible; I fail. 'When I broke up with Tom I wasn't ready for anything *so I didn't go round shagging more than one*

42

person at a time. I was *acutely* aware that I didn't want to be on the giving *or* receiving end of that. I wasn't prepared to muck anyone about.'

'Exactly, and I don't want to muck *you* about, which is why I'm telling you the truth now. I could have lied.'

'You're doing me a favour by telling me you're shagging other women?'

'What? How am I meant to win in this conversation?'

There are definitely no winners in this conversation.

'If I wouldn't put up with an unfaithful husband, why would I put up with it from you?' I say, trying hard to keep my voice low but hearing it get louder nonetheless.

'OK! Fine, sorry. I didn't realise you'd feel this way. I must have misread the signals. I thought you'd understand, that's all.'

'But I do understand. I understand perfectly.' I stand up and nod. 'Thanks for the gin.' I gather up the flowers, drain the last of my glass and head for the door, trying to ignore the stares of the hipsters next to us.

Well, we didn't make it through date four after all. I storm through the back streets towards St John. Why did I bring these manky old flowers with me anyway? I should have flung them onto the table like a proper diva.

Being honest with me . . . Jesus, what is *wrong* with these men? Do they think they can get away with anything, as long as they do it in plain sight? That's almost as bad as hiding it. I should never have let him have a third date. I *knew* it, I should have trusted my gut when he claimed he didn't have money for a cab home and could he crash at mine. Another lie!

Right – bacon sandwich, then home to watch back-to-back *Game of Thrones* – time to turn this day around.

The waiter who normally serves me isn't here, and an earnest young guy shows me to a table with a view into the kitchen. I dump the flowers on the chair opposite and sit back to watch the chefs pull the golden sourdoughs from the wood-fired oven: very therapeutic.

'Can I order right away, please?' I ask, as the waiter heads off to fetch a menu.

'I'll be two minutes.'

I take my phone out – 10.55 a.m. Still five minutes to order, I'm home and dry. I've been dreaming about this sandwich since yesterday morning. Ah, a message on Tinder! Probably Russell, telling me why it's my fault he shagged another girl . . .

'Yes, could I please have the bacon sandwich and a black coffee?' I say, grabbing the waiter.

He looks awkwardly over my shoulder. 'I don't think we've got any left, let me just check.'

He heads back to the kitchen and comes back a moment later. 'I'm so sorry, we just sold the last one to the table behind you.'

I turn around and see some guy, head down over a laptop, typing. Typical, some City boy writing emails to Merrill Lynch has just nicked my sandwich. Not happy about that.

'Is there no way they can make me half of one or something?'

The waiter looks confused.

'I'm happy to pay for the whole thing, but I really do need that sandwich.'

He comes back again from the kitchen, shaking his head. 'Sorry, there's actually no bacon left. We could give you the sandwich without the bacon?'

'Do you mean two pieces of bread?'

'Erm, let me just go and double-check that for you . . . '

'No, don't worry,' I say, taking the menu back from his hand. 'I'll find something else.'

I glance over it. That's so annoying! At 11 a.m. they switch to the elevenses menu: Eccles cake, Brownie, or Seed Cake and Madeira.

'Do you have anything savoury at all?'

'The lunch menu starts at twelve . . . The brownie's excellent?'

'Any chance I could order something from the main menu early?'

He shakes his head.

'Fine, seed cake and Madeira it is!' Seed cake is surely the opposite

44

of cake. Still, if it comes with a glass of wine I'll give it my best shot.

He looks relieved and heads back to the kitchen, only to return two minutes later with my bacon sandwich, which he carries straight past me to the guy behind. I turn round again to check whether the God of Bacon Sandwiches is currently in the E1 area and performing miracles. Nope – the laptop guy thanks the waiter, catches my glare, gives an apologetic smile and reaches for the ketchup.

I mouth the word 'enjoy' at him and turn back to check my messages. Oh nice! Russell asking if I'm still going to the cinema, if not could he possibly have the booking reference, rather than letting it go to waste. Yes, Russell, it's F1U2CK-OFF.

What the hell, I might as well see who else is on Tinder and interested in messing me around and lying to me for a few weeks . . .

- Dave, 36, photo of you with your arm around three glamour models in Hooters T-shirts. Next!
- Stephen, 35, photo of you on your wedding day, kissing your lovely wife. Next!
- Danimal, 33, camera in one hand, willy in the other. Next!
- Rick, 38, multiple facial tattoos. Next!
- Mike, 36, three photos: a Lamborghini, a motorbike and John Terry.

Why don't these guys understand that advertising themselves with photos of fast cars, footballers and strippers might impress other guys but it doesn't impress women?

I am so done with Internet dating. Done with Internet dating, done with all dating, done with men, done with this seed cake. Sod it, if I'm going to have sweet, I'm going in for the custard doughnut.

'Excuse me,' I say to the waiter, who's looking slightly scared of me. 'Do you still do the doughnuts here, or is it just at Maltby Street?'

'We do. Custard or jam?'

'Custard.' Definitely the custard. The St John Custard Doughnut. I did a half-page review of this doughnut when these guys opened their Maltby Street branch two years ago. It's the first time we'd ever dedicated that many column inches to a single pastry. (The subs spent a pedantic hour arguing over whether a doughnut is a cake, a pastry or a dessert. I say let them eat cake/pastry/dessert, our readers know what a flipping doughnut is! Though nowadays with your cronuts and your duffins, all the rules have changed.) Anyway, I felt it deserved an entire page, but Sandra wasn't having any of it – even after I brought in a dozen for everyone to try. Actually, that might have been the problem – a gesture like that earns far too many brownie points.

That's more like it! The waiter comes over with the doughnut and a relieved smile. He heads off and I pick up the doughnut, count to ten and take a deep breath. Russell has actually done me a favour. He has revealed himself to be an idiot after only three and a half weeks, it took Tom nine years. Russell has freed me up to find someone much better. In the mean time, I am an independent, attractive woman who has my health, friends, two great jobs and can afford to buy herself the best custard doughnut in London. Good, fine, processed.

I sink my teeth into the doughnut and nearly retch with despair.

'Sorry to be a pain,' I say, summoning the waiter again, and showing him the inside of the doughnut. 'But . . . .'

'I'm *really* sorry, I must have got confused,' he says, blushing.

'No, that's fine – but would you mind bringing me the custard one instead?'

'Let me just go and check.'

'What do you need to check?'

'Hold on.'

I am used to managing disappointment in my life. I am actually slightly more disappointed that this doughnut has jam in the middle than I am about Russell. But it's fixable.

I see the waiter with his head bent low in the kitchen talking to the sous-chef who looks over at me and shrugs. The waiter catches my glance, stares at the floor, then finally heads back to my table.

'I'm so sorry about this, but we literally just ran out.'

'You ran out?'

'Well, the . . . the thing is, the guy behind you ordered one, then I put your order in, I picked up the jam one, and then a customer bought the last two custard ones over the counter . . . '

'Hold on, hold on, back up . . . That guy behind me ordered custard or jam?'

'Erm . . . yeah, custard, he ordered custard . . . '

'So you didn't switch our doughnuts?'

'No.'

'He just ordered the same as me?'

'Right, exactly,' says the waiter, his hands clenching into small, nervous fists.

'OK. Next question – have you served him his doughnut yet?'

'Well no, because he ordered a coffee and I was going to serve the two together.'

'Fine! That's fine, you can just give me his doughnut then.'

'Erm, not really . . . '

'But why? What difference? Either he misses out or I miss out – I vote he misses out. He did get my bacon sandwich.'

'Yeah, no, I guess that is one way of looking at it . . . the thing is, he knows the guys here . . . he's in here all the time . . . I'm sorry . . . I can't . . . '

'OK, don't worry. Sorry. I'm not trying to give you a hard time. I'll just have a word with him myself.'

I take a deep breath, put on a smile and turn my chair round to face him.

He looks up. He looks like someone I know. He looks . . . really nice.

'Hello,' he says, and smiles. A dimple, on the right.

'Hi. Listen, I know this may sound insane, but here's the thing. I really need that custard doughnut that's en route to you. I just, I just really do need it. And the thing is, you did eat that last bacon sandwich earlier, and I'd been looking forward to it since yesterday. In fact I pretty much ran here to get it . . . '

He tilts his head to one side. 'Carry on. I'm listening.'

'Well, then the poor waiter got all confused, he gave *me* the wrong doughnut, jam, even though I'd ordered custard – just one of those

47

things, I know, not normally the end of the world. But still, regardless of all of that, I would *really* appreciate it if you'd let me buy that doughnut off you, because I actually do genuinely need it.'

'Why do you need it so badly?'

'Gosh, well, it's a long story but you wouldn't believe the morning I've had, but . . . '

'Try me?'

'No, honestly, I'd rather not, but let's just say it was not the best. OK, here's an idea. How about I pay for the doughnut, obviously, and I'll pay for your coffee as well?'

He raises his eyebrows at me.

'OK, and I'll pay for your bacon sandwich too? That's a good deal, isn't it?'

'But what about if I genuinely do need this doughnut very badly, too?'

'Why do you need it so badly?'

'Honestly?' he says, fixing me with the brightest blue eyes I've ever seen. 'I've had one of the worst weeks of my life.'

'Oh. I'm sorry to hear that.'

'That's OK,' he smiles gently. 'No one died. And it wasn't your fault.'

'Then . . . OK then. Well, how about if you just sell me half of that doughnut then?'

He smiles. A smile that could light up a life.

'A tenner,' he says.

'A fiver.'

He holds out his hand to shake on the deal.

'I'm Adam.'

'I'm Laura.'

'You get to choose which half,' he says, slicing the doughnut confidently in two.

'Impressive knife skills!'

'Been training since I was knee-high . . . '

'Which of us owns the custard on that knife?' I say.

'You want the knife as well?'

'Not if you're going to charge me extra for it.' He must be a City Boy.

'Remind me never to divorce you. The knife is yours,' he says grinning.

He's done a perfect bisection (maybe he's actually a surgeon?) – and I consider the halves on the plate, each spilling out heavy vanilla-flecked custard. How on earth am I going to sit opposite such a fine-looking man and eat such a messy, all-consuming thing without looking like a wildebeest?

He gazes at his half with a look akin to a man admiring his firstborn, then attacks it with gusto and has finished before I've even started. By the looks of it, he's one of those furiously annoying people who can eat whatever they want and never put on any weight – he has broad shoulders, a strong, lean upper body.

'If you're just going to sit there holding it and staring into space, you might as well give it back to me,' he says.

'No, I'm just trying to work out where I can find that fiver I owe you at such short notice.'

'Writing cheques your mouth can't afford . . . '

'I'm good for it, honest!' I say, as I gingerly take a bite from one side and watch as a large dollop of custard falls to the table.

'Don't look so sad. You can eat off the tables in here, they're very clean.'

'You won't judge me?' I dip the tip of my finger into the custard.

'I'm not going to get on Twitter and tell the world you go round licking tables. Your secret's safe with me.'

'I appreciate that, Adam. I'm a very private person, I'm like the J. D. Salinger of table-licking . . . '

'J. D. Salinger . . . *Catcher in the Rye*, right?'

'Yes!'

'That's the only GCSE book I ever liked. OK then, Smarty Pants, what does the J. D. stand for?'

'No idea, Jack Daniels? John Doe? Same as whatever it stands for in JD Sports?'

'Shame, I was going to invite you to join my pub quiz team . . . ' he says, crossing his arms and leaning back in his chair with a look of contentment. 'I do like this place. They make some of the best bread in London.'

'The waiter said you're a regular.'

'I always thought their bacon sandwich was my little secret.'

'I thought it was *mine*.' I look over my shoulder at the chefs at work. 'I love it here. The kitchen always looks so relaxed – none of that testosterone bullshit.'

'What testosterone bullshit?'

'You know, kitchens where you've got a bunch of heavily tattooed macho-men shouting and screaming at each other. Chefs are the new rock stars? Don't make me laugh! You've just flipped the perfect omelette? Come back to me when you've actually done something useful like saved a life. Half of those reprobates would be in jail if they weren't in a kitchen.'

'Would you like to see the tattoo I had done when they let me out of jail and I became an omelette chef?' He moves to pull up the sleeve of his jumper.

'Go on then.' I guarantee if he's got a tattoo of anything it'll be a Merrill Lynch logo.

'I'll spare you – I don't think I know you quite well enough yet.' He smiles the most outrageously contagious smile, which I can't help but mirror.

'We'll save that for next time,' I say as I blush. I think I've been blushing ever since I sat at his table.

We have been sitting and talking for two and a half hours over a bottle of white wine when his phone rings. He looks at the name on the screen and his smile suddenly falters. 'Two minutes,' he says, as he takes the call outside. Don't go outside! What if you change your mind and never come back?

I take my mirror from my handbag, put on some more lip balm and check that none of the seed cake is stuck in my teeth. Adam is outside, deep in conversation. I hope it's not with a girlfriend. I'm sure he's been flirting with me – though since the tattoo conversation, all we've talked about are random subjects – the smell of book-shops, the evolving nature of facial hair in East London, favourite pop video from the eighties: me – 'Sledgehammer'; him – 'Addicted To Love'.

His laptop's on the table and I sorely want to open it, to see what the document he was working on so intently was – it looked like a spreadsheet. I still haven't asked what he does for a living but I'd bet a tenner he's a banker. His navy jumper and jeans are classic, but they look expensive. His thick brown hair is slightly messy, but not in a poncey *I work in digital media* kind of way. Until he actually says 'I am a banker' I can live in a little bubble of fantasy where he's a doctor or a human rights lawyer or some other heroic profession.

He walks back in looking weary.

'Is everything OK?'

'It will be.'

'Was that your angry wife on the phone?'– Might as well put it out there.

He laughs. 'No wife, angry or otherwise.'

'Do you have to be somewhere?'

He looks at me, thinks about it, and shakes his head. 'How about another bottle of wine?'

I check my watch – it's just gone 2 p.m. 'This might sound weird . . . but . . . no, it doesn't matter, actually, it's a silly idea . . .'

'Go on.'

'Well, I have two cinema tickets that are going to waste, three fifteen, at the Barbican . . . dumb idea, you've probably got plans . . .'

'I haven't been to the cinema in years.'

'You don't like films?'

'I love films! I just never have time, with work. How come you've got two tickets? Do you just hang around nice restaurants, waiting to pounce on people's doughnuts, then kidnap them with the promise of a movie?'

'The minute I've got you in the darkened cinema, my crack team of organ thieves will have your liver in an ice bucket.'

'Not sure my liver's worth stealing,' he says, draining the last of the wine. 'I'll take my chances. How long's the walk, twenty minutes?'

'Twenty-five?'

'That gives us just under an hour. Can we do another bottle in fifty minutes, do you think?'

We're walking, well, wobbling, into Chinatown from the pub we went to after the cinema. I'm still clutching the roses, though I wonder, if I ditched them now, would Adam try to hold my hand?

This day is turning out so much better than I could have planned. Half a custard doughnut is better than no custard doughnut. Half a custard doughnut shared with an extremely cute, funny man is much, much better than a whole custard doughnut eaten alone. Half a custard doughnut, and then wine, and a walk, and a film, and another bottle of Rioja, and now a stroll into Soho as the sky turns to night . . . This might just be the perfect Sunday.

'Ridley Scott will never do anything that touches *Blade Runner*,' says Adam as we cross the road and he moves to walk on the pavement side.

'*Thelma and Louise* is *much* better than *Blade Runner*.'

'Ivan, one of the guys I work for, is trying to make a film. He keeps flying to LA, telling us he spotted Arnie in Malibu and Clooney down at Whole Foods . . . '

'What's the story?'

'He's hoping for Scorsese or Coppola to direct but he'll be lucky to get some talented kid out of film school.'

'No, I mean what's the film about?'

'Oh – it's his life story: Russian makes his first five million in a dodgy gangster deal, then goes on to run incredibly successful global business, buys mansion in Holland Park, marries trophy wife, applies for planning permission for a double basement extension . . . '

'Rags to riches, hold the rags . . . And this guy's your boss?'

'One of three, yeah.'

God, I absolutely wish this guy did not work in the City. He must be a hedge funder or some other blood-sucking Master of the Universe vampire type.

'Please – let's not talk work,' he says. 'I've got at least twelve hours before I have to go back in, and I'm having such a good time right now.'

Me too.

'Those roses are starting to look the worse for wear,' he says, taking them from me. 'They don't smell of anything, do they?'

I shrug. 'I'm more of a tulip girl myself.'

'Why don't we give them to whoever at that bus stop looks most in need?'

Of course, how sweet. 'You do it? I'm quite shy about talking to strangers.'

'Apparently not when there's a doughnut involved . . . '

'How about that woman in the grey coat?'

He walks over and the woman looks up warily. He starts explaining, points to me, then she nods, shrugs and takes them. After he's headed back I see her smile the sort of shy smile that can't help itself. It's the same smile that's on his face.

'Why did you buy them, though, if you don't like them?' he says.

'I didn't . . . '

'I knew there had to be something wrong with you . . . doughnut thief, organ thief, flower thief, is there no end to your bad behaviour?'

'Someone bought them for me.'

'Oh.' He's about to say something, then stops himself. His face looks exactly the way mine would if he'd just turned around and said he had a girlfriend. Slightly crushed, slightly confused, trying to work out what to say next.

If I wanted to be mysterious or try to make him jealous, I could tell him about Russell in a way that made me look more desirable. 'Some guy I'm seeing . . . nothing serious of course . . . though clearly he thinks I'm flower-worthy . . . ' But I'm not mysterious, and I would hate someone to try to make me jealous in that way. And besides, why wouldn't I tell him the truth? I'm not a liar.

'I had a date this morning . . . '

'First date?'

'Fourth.'

'Going somewhere.'

'No. Not really. I mean, not now.'

'What happened?'

'Basically he went out last night and shagged another girl.'

'How do you know that?'

'Because I asked.'

'And that's not OK because . . . '

'Because I didn't sign up to be in the harem of a bloke who works in IT!'

'Fair play. I was just checking he knew you wanted something exclusive.'

'Absolutely. I made it clear at the start, because of my . . . well, just because.'

'Some people think it's OK to see other people at the start of a relationship.'

'Four dates in? Are you one of those people?'

'Not at all. But then why would he tell you?'

'Because I had a hunch, I suppose. And because he knew he wouldn't get away with lying to me. He probably thought if he told the truth, I might be cool with it.'

'So the moral of that story is he should have kept his big mouth shut . . . '

'The thing is, I would have put up with his baggage, in theory . . . '

'What baggage?'

'A nightmare ex, and a kid. Actually I thought the fact he'd been married and had a child was a good thing – proof he wasn't a commitment-phobe . . . '

'So the kid and the ex didn't put you off?'

'No. I can handle baggage if I think someone's worth it.'

'Major baggage or just hand luggage?'

'Who hasn't got baggage? I have baggage, I'm sure you have too, but I cannot be dealing with a liar.'

'But he didn't lie.'

'He withheld information.'

'So now would be a good time to unload all my baggage, right here in the street outside Sainsbury's?'

'Yeah, go on then. What have you got? Raging alcoholic? Clearly you are – though I can hardly throw stones in that direction . . .

History of philandering? Drug habit? Secret love child? Porn addict? Psycho ex-wife? Your parents were first cousins? You shot a man in Reno . . . ?'

He opens his mouth to say something, then stops and shakes his head. After another thirty seconds, during which he actually appears to be doing some sort of calculation, he says, 'My father is a pathological philanderer, my sister had the drug habit, well, marijuana only; I did recently discover I've fathered a love child with a crazy waitress, but she won't return my calls. My father had an affair with a cousin – but they're second cousins, barely counts; plus with the volume of women he shagged it was only a matter of time before he called upon family. With all that going on, understandably I have no time left for a porn habit and I can safely say I've never been to Reno.'

'Me neither,' I say, relieved that his frown has turned into a joke, I was worried for a moment there I'd actually offended him. 'Adam – I don't even know where Reno is! Is it in Texas?'

'Nevada, I think.'

'While we're at it, full disclosure, I once stole a Kit Kat from our local newsagent after my sister dared me to. And I'm rather too fond of sniffing marker pens.'

'What colour?'

'Depends what's in the stationery cupboard, mostly the red ones.'

'They're the least addictive. Stay away from blue – they're lethal.'

'OK,' I say, rubbing my hands together. 'Well, that's all taken care of then. So I guess we're fine?'

'I guess we're fine.'

'Adam, these dumplings are amazing. Normally the veg are chopped so small you can't taste them, but the way they've cut these, it's like you can taste the texture.'

He stares at me as if I've said something strange. I guess it does sound strange, talking about the taste of a texture.

'I'm glad you like them,' he says, as he dips another fat little white parcel in soy and ginger dressing, and holds it out to me on his chopsticks.

'In the bowl, please.' When Tom and I first started dating he went all *9 1/2 Weeks* on me and tried to feed me a dim sum that was too big for my mouth – a fact I didn't realise until he'd stuck it in my gob and it got wedged there. It was too big to chew and there was no way I could spit it out; in the end I had to shoo him from the table with hand gestures before I choked to death. Not running the risk of death by violent dumpling at this point in such a perfect day.

'You know quite a bit about food, don't you?' he says. 'That thing you said about the vegetable's texture. That's an interesting detail to notice.'

'Oh. Well my dad is a good cook.' That's true. 'And I did a night course a few years ago.' Also true. Now that's plenty of truth! 'How do you know about this place, then?'

'One of the commis from work brought me here.'

'Commies? Do they not mind you calling them that?'

'Why would they mind?'

'They're Russian, isn't it kind of rude?'

'Dave's a Scouser and Marco's Italian?'

Oh. Weird. Maybe he calls them Commies because they don't earn millions like the rest of the capitalists in his office . . . does he call himself a Cappy? That's so *Wolf of Wall Street*. Please don't let him be that obnoxious. 'Do the Commies make the tea or something?'

'They make anything I ask them to – but I don't have time for tea nowadays . . .'

'Ooh, get you, Gordon Gekko, *I'm so busy making money, I don't have time for tea . . .*'

He laughs and looks confused. 'What do you think I do for a living?'

'Well . . . finance. Don't you?'

'Ah, Miss Marple. Very good. And how did you know that?'

'Er,' I feel myself flush, as if I'm on the verge of revealing too much. 'Well, you look quite clean-cut.'

'You make a watertight case!'

'Not just that! You were maybe doing some spreadsheets in St John?'

'I was doing my weekly numbers. What else?'

'Your boss is a Russian billionaire?'

'Only a wee multi-millionaire.'

'You seem a bit stressed about work. And you call the guys who run around in your office Commies, which is your way of saying they're not rich like you hedge fund guys.'

'Genius!' he says, tipping his head back and laughing. 'You're a genius, Laura.'

'Thank you!'

'But you're wrong.'

'Oh. Well why *do* you call them Commies then?'

'I call them commis because they are commis. Commis – it's a chef, a basic chef, bottom of the kitchen pecking order, slightly higher than the dish wipes.'

'Oh! *Commis* commis, I thought you meant Commies with an *e*.'

'Remind me to hold up cards with subtitles in future,' he says, nodding sagely. 'If you were hoping I was rich, you're out of luck – I've barely enough to buy you dinner.'

'Secretly I'm a bit relieved. Besides, we'll go halves.'

'No, I insist,' he says, signalling for the bill.

'So hang on, you're a chef?'

'I did say I've been practising knife skills since I was little, did you think I was a serial killer?'

'You're actually a chef?'

'A head chef, indeed.'

'Ah. You know earlier when you were going to show me your tattoo . . . ' I say, pointing to his right arm.

He pulls the sleeve of his jumper up slowly: his forearm is muscular, his hand strong yet elegant, like a sculptor's, with two tiny knife scars on the forefinger. The skin of his arms is unblemished aside from two small freckles on the inside of his forearm that I have a strange urge to reach out and stroke. There is no busty mermaid, no Sanskrit peace prayer, no Millwall tattoo in sight.

'Scared of needles,' he says. 'I'm afraid I'm a big wuss.'

'And just to double-check, *have* you ever been to prison?'

'I have never been to prison.'

'But you just sat there in St John and let me say those moronic things.'

'I thought it was funny! Besides, you were describing half of the guys I work with, what was it . . . *macho . . . testosterone show-offs . . .* '

'So hang on – can you get me a discount at Nando's or what?'

'I wish I worked at Nando's! I work at a very expensive new restaurant run by a trio of megalomaniacs who care more about tap fittings than where their meat and veg come from.'

I feel the blood fall straight from my face into my stomach, then down to my toes.

Ridiculous. Paranoia. There are at least a dozen places in London that fit that description.

'And it's three Russians who own it?' Three Russians, three Russians, three Russians . . .

'A Russian, a Dutch guy and an American . . . '

'In Mayfair?' though I know already it is not.

'Back in the Square Mile.'

No. No, no, no . . .

' . . . it's got the worst name of any restaurant I've ever worked in – LuxEris. Are you OK, Laura?'

I swallow the acid that's just shot up the back of my throat. 'That last dumpling . . . ' I stand and rush to the bathroom. Perhaps there's a small window I can climb out of, or even get wedged in, like a dim sum in my mouth. Anything to get me out of this mess.

Worst Sunday ever.

There is no way I can tell him. That would be insane, I've only just met him and I'll probably never see him again.

But if I ever do want to see him again – and I do, I really do – then I should go back out there, tell him the truth, because maybe he'll see the funny side of it. Maybe in years to come it'll be a hilarious anecdote, 'How I met your mother,' ha di ha ha . . .

There I go again, getting carried away! From the first time I wrote *Laura Loton* on my Form II maths book, after Jamie Loton copied my homework, I'm fifteen steps ahead of myself, thinking and hoping something will come of nothing. And this *is* nothing, a meaningless, drunken Sunday, some random guy who cheered me up in the after-math of the loser known as Russell. That's all.

So no, I'm not going to tell him, why would I? What? Just because I felt more comfortable with him after five minutes than I did with Russell after four dates? Because I feel like I've known him far longer than an afternoon? Because I have the strongest sense he is going to be significant to me? I have been *semi-drunk* since *before midday*; there is a reason people don't normally drink gin and tonics at 10.30 a.m., and *this is that reason*.

The weirdest thing is, I don't recognise him from the open kitchen. You have to have a good memory in my job and I am pretty sure the chef on the pass last Thursday was blond underneath his backwards baseball cap – he reminded me of evil King Joffrey in *Game of Thrones*. I would have remembered a face as handsome as Adam's.

Maybe he's lying? But why would he lie? This is crazy . . . I wish I hadn't drunk so much, I can't think straight.

OK, take a breath, go back out there. It's fine, it's none of his business. Say nothing, you owe him nothing. Pay for the dinner, though, definitely don't let him pick up the tab.

I splash my face with cold water and head back out. He's standing by the table looking towards the toilet anxiously. He puts his arm out to touch my back but I freeze.

'Are you OK? Were you just sick in there?'

'I felt a bit nauseous, that's all,' I say, reaching for my wallet. 'Please, let me pay for dinner.'

'Paid already. Are you sure you're OK? You look a bit pale.'

'Too much to drink. Sorry. Listen, I'm going to head off . . . '

'Can I take your number at least?'

' . . . I'm not . . . I don't think . . . '

'Is this because I'm not a banker?' he says, incredulously.

'No, of course not.'

'Did I say something wrong?'

How can I not give him my number? Look at him, those big blue eyes looking at me like he's actually disappointed. I grab a paper napkin from the table and scribble down my number before I change my mind. It's not like he's actually going to call, given the number of times I've embarrassed myself in the last ten hours. He's just asking to be polite.

He moves to give me a kiss on the cheek goodbye but my body stiffens, as if he's about to hit me.

'Are you sure you're OK? Let me give you money for a cab at least, I don't think you should get on the tube if you're feeling sick.'

'No! Thanks, but I'm fine.' I'm fine. This is fine. Nothing is going to come of this because he's not going to call.

He's too handsome, too nice, we get on too well and if history has taught me anything it's that I am one of those women whom it does not work out for. I'm not being a fatalist or melodramatic – it's just that some women (whether they're lovely or complete bitches) end up with a beautiful house and a good husband and excellent tableware – and some don't: I'm one of the ones who don't. One of the ones to whom people say, 'I don't understand why it hasn't worked out for you.' And 'I'm sure the right guy will turn up when you least expect it.' And 'But you seem fine being single, anyway.'

And I am fine being single, anyway. So when he doesn't call, this will be fine.

This will all be fine.

6

'That's cheered me right up!' says Roger, thumping his fist on his desk and laughing.

'What do you mean? It's a nightmare.'

'Nonsense! It must be destiny. Have you read your horoscope this morning?'

'Don't be ridiculous.' Though of course I have. Well, that's a lie – I couldn't wait until this morning, I read it as soon as I got home last night. Shelley von Strunckel is *never wrong*!

The events triggered by Thursday's alliance between your ruler, the Sun, and Venus, should convince you, despite reservations, to go along with developments. You won't regret it.

'So when are you meeting him?'

'He's suggested breakfast this week but I'm going to say no.'

'You told me he was *funny and handsome and charming and really got you* . . . and you couldn't look at me when you said any of those things.'

I pull the neck of my jumper up over my chin in the hope it might prevent me saying anything more incriminating.

'So what exactly is the problem?'

'Roger, are you winding me up?'

'Parker, I have had the pleasure of your professional company for four years and two months, over the course of which you have mentioned a few suitors, none noteworthy as far as I recall. Your face has never lit up the way it did just now.'

'Yeah, fine, so I like him. And that's the problem, this review is going to screw him over.'

'It's not like he owns the restaurant – chefs move around all the time. You know what Elbert Hubbard would say?'

'Here we go . . . '

'"The greatest mistake you can make in life is to be continually afraid you will make one . . . "'

'I'm not *afraid*! I just don't want to get into a Fergus-style situation. I have boundaries.'

'What has this got to do with Fergus?'

'There are parallels . . . '

'If anything you're doing the opposite.'

'I suppose . . . ' I say, pulling at the bottom of my jumper and noticing a new set of moth holes, like a staple wound.

'Besides, you didn't sleep with him already did you?'

'Roger! We went for a movie and then into Chinatown. We haven't even kissed.'

'Exactly! Fergus would have gone in for a quickie round the back of the Wong Kei.'

'Fine, well I'm not quite Fergus. But what if I end up seeing this guy properly?'

'Don't you think this conversation is a little premature?'

'Shall we have it after I've had three rounds of boiled eggs and soldiers?'

'You don't need to confess all on the first date, there is something to be said for the gradual reveal.'

'I think he might be rather short . . . like, five foot nine.'

Roger coughs loudly.

'I never think of *you* as short Roger, I mean, you have presence!'

'Given this chap's cooking, I'd be more worried about his lack of talent than height.'

'Exactly! Which brings me back to the problem: my review, his food – it's a clear conflict of interest.'

'For goodness sake, it's breakfast. Why do women worry so much about everything?

'Because men don't worry enough about anything?'

'Meet him.'

'I don't think it's a great idea . . . '

'That's an order.'

'Fine. But I'm only going because I feel bad he paid for dinner. One breakfast, cancel my debt.'

I get up to leave, then have one final thought. 'Roger, do you remember what the head chef on Thursday looked like? He was standing at the pass, shouting. Wearing a cap?'

'I was a little distracted by the hostesses' golden knickers . . . '

'You don't remember if he had dark brown hair or bleached blond hair?'

'Now I think about it, he did have one eyelash missing.'

'You don't remember him at all? You know what? It's probably nothing.'

Kiki is the best sub-editor in this building. She's all of five foot one, looks like a fierce Russian doll and has a razor-sharp brain and tongue. Roger loves her, Azeem has a major crush on her and Sandra's scared of her. (Sandra thinks tattoos are a sign of a personality disorder and Kiki has a dozen.)

Kiki drinks even more coffee than I do so I pop to the kitchen before heading to her desk on the second floor.

'Can I interest you in a cup of new harvest Colombian?' I say. 'Toffee notes, very smooth.'

'How're you feeling?' she says, giving me a broad, gap-toothed smile. 'Azeem delivered me a half-eaten pecan brownie on Friday and blamed it on you. Said the stress of Cake Run made him do it.'

'I was still recovering from Thursday . . . '

'When do I get to see your piece?'

'Next week, but in the meantime . . . ' As well as being brilliant at crafting sentences, Kiki's a dab hand at general subterfuge, and rooting out information: 'Could you call this woman at Gilded PR and find out a bit about the head chef? Not Jonn Zavragin, the next one down.'

As she picks up her phone I take my mobile to the corridor to listen to Adam's message again. Fifth time over and it's still making my heart flutter slightly.

'. . . Laura? Assuming this is actually you – then hello, this is Adam – the not-banker guy whose doughnut you commandeered . . . half-commandeered. I'm sorry the restaurant tried to poison you last night, I take full responsibility. To make up for it I was wondering: are you free for breakfast on Thursday? My shifts are a nightmare but I could do seven thirty a.m. till eight thirty a.m. And also you still owe me for that doughnut . . . So yes, ring me back before I call in the bailiffs. And even if you can't find the money, say yes anyway.'

God, I feel bad about the dim sum. And I absolutely will pay for the doughnut; I'll buy him breakfast, give him the fiver, make some sort of amends, and be done with it. Yes, that's exactly what I'll do.

Kiki's written half a page of notes already: 'Head chef's name is Adam Bayley. He's just been poached from The Little Green House, before that he was at Ducasse, then in San Sebastian and Tokyo, and before that at Jonn's in Chicago.'

'Did you not get his inside leg measurement, Kiki?'

'I wouldn't say no. Presumably he's the fit one, not the one who looks like Meatloaf?'

On her screen is a photo of Adam with Zavragin. The shot looks ten years old, and in it Jonn is presenting Adam with a diploma. Adam must have been mid twenties – his hair cut short, making him look even younger. He has those eyes that are a combination of utter sweetness and naughtiness.

'He looks like one of those sensitive ones who'd be proper filthy when you got down to it,' she says. Thinking back to the way he consumed that doughnut yesterday, she's probably right: healthy appetite.

'Hang on, did you say The Greenhouse, in Mayfair?'

She checks her notes. 'Little Green House, in Bray, senior sous.'

That'll be why I don't know his name. But two years ago I had an outstanding bacon millefeuille there, and a fall-off-the-bone lamb dish with cumin. He probably cooked it.

Well, it's a start. At least he's telling the truth about his job, though it would be better if he had been lying. But even so, I think the blond chef was running the show last Thursday. Maybe Adam had the night off? But that would never happen in an opening month. Maybe he was in another part of the restaurant? Perhaps they have a prep kitchen . . . ? Weird, though.

I text him back: Breakfast good, my treat. Where suits?

He replies instantly: If you're OK to come to the Square Mile do you fancy The Haute? Great views, and then I'll have more time with you.

I *love* The Haute. I gave them 18 stars when they opened. That's how you should do a restaurant in a skyscraper – at the top of the building, not in the basement.

But 7.30 a.m., east, up at 6 a.m. – do I like him that much? With all the potential stress involved if he starts talking about work and I have to pretend to know nothing about anything? It would just be so much easier to walk away from this situation right now, much smarter not to get involved.

See you at 7.30 a.m. Laura.

7

'Can I have some more toast, please?' I say to Sophie, who is standing in her kitchen, hands deep in a giant mixing bowl, fingers smothered in sticky cherry marzipan.

'Help yourself,' she says, poking her elbow towards the toaster. 'Could you pass the icing sugar first?'

I leap off the stool and grab the pack. 'Do you want a slice?'

'I'm having dinner with my sister-in-law in an hour,' she says, rubbing flour off her watch face with her cheek. 'Shit. In forty-five minutes, in fact.'

'Where are you going?'

'Urgh, Shelliii's a nightmare, no way I'm doing raw food, so we've settled on a Japanese place near her hotel.'

'When is she flying back?'

'Sunday, but she's got a casting with some director here on Saturday, so I've said I'll look after Elektra rather than leave her with a random babysitter for the seventh day in a row.'

'Why didn't they just leave her with your brother or your mum in California?'

'Er, because Shelliii thinks Elektra is an accessory, not a small human – and a beautiful three year old makes Shelliii look even more lithe for forty than her Chloé jeans do.'

'She's very . . . driven, your sister-in-law, isn't she?'

'Do you mean she's a selfish bitch?'

'Well, no . . . '

'This is the woman who had an early Caesarean so she could guarantee Elektra was a Leo!'

'What's the icing for?'

'This?' she says, holding her hands up like a sugar-coated Lady Macbeth. 'Actually, can you give my nose a quick scratch?'

I gently tickle the side of her nostril and she laughs. 'This,' she says, nodding back down at the bowl, 'is prototype Battenberg, going horribly pear-shaped. It was meant to be cherry and white chocolate squares . . . '

'OMG! Can I say OMG?'

'It might have been OMG but I think I scaled up wrong. Yesterday the marzipan was too crumbly and now I've overdone the corn syrup. Try,' she says, pointing her elbow at a spoon on the counter.

I scrape a sludge of cerise paste out of the bowl and give it a brief smell before I taste it. 'It's a bit sweet for me, Soph.'

She shakes her head in irritation. 'I thought so – but customers do seem to prefer sweeter. Fine, I'd better start getting ready.' She tips her head towards the taps for me to turn on.

'Do you want me to wash up while you change?'

'No, thanks, I've got to fix it when I get home Anyway, you didn't even get round to telling me when you're seeing the chef again?'

'Breakfast, Thursday!' I say, feeling a little thrill of delight at the thought.

'Now *that* is OMG!' she says, clapping her hands together, gently prising them apart and licking her index finger, then wrinkling her nose. 'Too sweet.'

'And you really think Roger's right about me not saying anything?'

She gives it a final thought. 'Yeah. I mean it's such early days. It feels like a big deal right now because you've only just written the review – but it'll seem less of a big deal next week.'

'Maybe . . . '

'Seriously, if I'd told Will when I first started seeing him half of the awful things going on inside my brain, he'd have run for the hills.'

'Like what?'

'Well – like the fact I wasn't over James at that point, at all. I still thought about him every day. And I used to feel guilty – like I should tell Will everything because that's what you're *supposed* to do in relationships – but I'm so glad I didn't because it wouldn't have given us a chance to get off the ground in the first place.'

'Yeah,' I say, kissing her goodbye. 'You're probably right.'

8

To: Laura
From: Sandra
Subject: Punctuality

It's after 10.00 a.m. and you are not at your desk; not sure where you are, Laura?? Need to see you ASAP.

Five of us sit on the first floor: Roger has his own office, my desk is right outside, and Sandra, Azeem and Jonesy, our commercial director, sit in the open-plan area in front of me. Whenever anyone wants to speak to anyone else they get up and walk the four seconds to their colleague's desk – because, you know, you could throw a rubber and not fail to hit each other's heads. You could throw a rubber pretty hard. Azeem occasionally corresponds via email, but only when the room is deathly silent and he's trying to make me laugh. (Sandra's head shot from her LinkedIn profile, Photoshopped on to various Fraggles' bodies.)

Sandra's the only one who tries to communicate exclusively via email. Partly it's because she doesn't like face-to-face interaction with anyone lower down the food chain; partly it's because she likes a full paper trail of everything she's done, but mostly it's because she likes a full paper trail of everything anyone else has failed to do.

Not sure where you are, Laura?? Is that true, Sandra?? It's 10.03 a.m. She saw me arrive at 9.50 a.m., smile, say hello and walk into Roger's office for a catch-up. Then she saw me head for the kitchen, where she'll have heard me boil the kettle (*Guinness Book of Records:* world's noisiest kettle.) Perhaps I was in there for three minutes instead of two because I have Adam on my mind – but it was three, tops. I swear she's keeping a file of every time I've spent more than three minutes in the toilet. One day I'll bribe IT to break into Sandra's neo-Stasi folders, delete them all and replace her *GOOD, BETTER, BEST* screensaver with a photo of a cheery Guatemalan coffee farmer.

She's looking at me now, so I head to her desk armed with my notepad and a fake smile.

'You wanted to see me, Sandra?'

She starts typing, then looks up as if surprised to see me standing there. 'You're back.'

I smile so hard, if the skin on my face was a balloon, right now it would pop.

'What's this I hear about you changing the flat plan for April's issue?'

'Roger's signed it off.'

'Yes?' she says, staring up at me with a frown. 'And?'

'Sorry, are you asking me a question?'

'No, I am not. I'm telling you that I oversee all flat plan changes,' she says. 'Unless someone's changed my job description overnight.' She smiles thinly.

'Right. OK, Sandra.'

'And Roger's told Dean to increase The Dish from a page to a DPS?'

Clearly you know that or you wouldn't be asking me . . .

'Firstly, that change should have been briefed directly to me,' she says.

'Roger told me he'd take care of it.'

'And secondly if you take up the whole DPS, I have to move that fractional ad.'

'OK . . . '

'And there's a hugely sensitive leader on Damian Bechdel in April requiring everyone's full focus, the last thing we need to worry about this month is the fluffy stuff . . . '

Would she call Henry's film reviews *fluffy stuff* to his face?

'Must you hog all that space?'

My knee-jerk reaction would be to say I'm not cutting a word: Roger's approved it, Roger loves it, Roger's my boss – and if she has a problem, speak to him. But one of my New Year's resolutions is not to rise to provocation: count to ten before answering back. It's not working out too well with Jess, but she's been my sister a while. Sandra is a different beast.

'Have you read the piece, Sandra?'

'Is there a reason I need to?'

Only interest. Or politeness. Or so you know what you're talking about . . . Take a breath . . .

'It's a list of ninety-nine problems with the restaurant, because they were playing the Jay-Z song, "99 Problems", while we were in the queue for two hours, so I wrote the ninety-nine problems with the restaurant. For example, instead of a "bitch" being a problem I said the kitchen's a problem . . . I just thought as an idea it had a certain . . . symmetry . . . '

'*A symmetry?*' she says, crossing her arms tightly and turning to an imaginary twin Sandra next to her with a face that says, *Get her with her* symmetry! *Who does she think she is? Jumped-up yet over-qualified secretary! Only got that job because her* mother *used to work with Roger. Shall we destroy her, invisible twin-Sandra? Yeah, come on, let's! We haven't tasted blood for hours!*

'You do realise,' she says, breathing out forcefully like she's taking a lung-capacity test, 'that you are fundamentally writing about beans on toast, not reporting on Bosnia?'

Nice alliteration Sandra! But the Bosnian conflict ended in the mid nineties, so if you are going to be a cow, try to be a more contemporary one.

Count to ten . . .

And another thing! Did you know, Jonathan Gold of the *LA Times* won a Pulitzer Prize for his restaurant column? A Pulitzer! – only the most prestigious prize in American writing! *Fluffy stuff* . . .

Count to twenty . . .

'Sandra, there were so many things wrong, I wanted to demonstrate the scale. But how about once legal and the subs have had a look, I'll see if I can shorten it?'

She sighs. 'And what's the central image on this spread?'

Why does she have to be like this? It's not my fault Fergus Kaye was 'let go of' . . . It's entirely Fergus's fault. If anything Roger kept him on well past his sell-by date. It's not like I asked Roger to give me the gig; I told him to find a proper journalist with a food background; he told me he had faith in my voice. I said I'd never even heard of an amuse-gueule till I read Fergus's column; Roger said buy a copy of *Larousse*. I asked whether a coffee palate was really transferable and then he told me to shut up and stop being a wimp. He took a massive chance on me and I try not to disappoint him. There's no point trying not to disappoint Sandra; her gall bladder secretes serotonin instead of bile.

'The central spread, Sandra . . . Hmm . . . It's either a photo of a deconstructed eel dish in brown butter . . . Or a photo of a gold-plated toilet with large breasts, my memory fails me . . . Hang on a minute . . . it's the gold toilet with breasts!'

'A toilet with breasts, that's the tone you want for your piece?'

'Yep.' *As you know*, because Roger will have briefed you on photography in your editorial catch-up. 'That's exactly the tone I want.' I smile as convincingly as a Miss World runner-up.

'Let me know about that word count,' she says, and resumes typing so ferociously I'm surprised her keyboard doesn't snap.

I'm really going to have to practise this counting to ten thing.

To: Laura
From: Azeem
Subject: URGENT BUSINESS

WTF did you do to piss The Laminator off this early in the morning, borrow her stapler?

To: Azeem
From: Laura
Subject: re: URGENT BUSINESS

Don't pretend you weren't eavesdropping, and don't make me bitch about her on email, I'm scared I'll accidentally send it to her . . . She's looking at me RIGHT NOW, am sure she knows I'm typing about her.

To: Laura
From: Azeem
Subject: Picture attached

Meanwhile, check out this Troll doll!! Look familiar? The hair is the exact same shade of pink, do you think it's actually a photo of Sandra when she was a baby?

To: Azeem
From: Laura
Subject: re: Picture attached

A striking likeness – but for one obvious thing: this Troll doll is clearly smiling. Now stop it! I have important things on my To Do list!

Not strictly true. Still, it's publication week so I busy myself looking through March's issue. The leader is an in-depth feature on the Glaswegian Mafia. There's another feature on gay marriage. Our European correspondent has written a comedic analysis on which country spoils its cats the most, and then there's travel and reviews: film, arts, books and food.

While the other writers have headshots at the top of their columns, my byline has a picture of a knife being sharpened. (When I won Best Newcomer at the FWA three years ago and Roger went on stage to pick up the award, I admit I was a bit gutted – Dad would have loved a photo for the mantelpiece. Sandra had drunkenly leant across the table and whispered: 'Hard to blow your own trumpet when there's a silencer in it . . . ' It's the same sentiment Jess has but Sandra means the opposite. Sandra's delighted I don't get credit in my real name but my ego is girl-sized, not Fergus-sized; I can think of little worse than being in the papers myself.)

March's issue only went on sale yesterday but the Twitterverse will have picked up on something already. Ah yes, no surprises, straight to the kittens . . .

> @minkowki: Brilliant article on spoilt Euro cats in #TheVoice
> – reminds me of Cat Cafés
> @MissKittyBotbot: Tokyo Cat Cafés #furryamazeballs!
> @Goatlover: Check out Tokyo Owl Cafés – #Harrypotter

Tokyo Cat Cafés, let's have a look what that's about . . . Oh my goodness, how extremely Japanese. Ah, but look at this adorable fluffy cat hiding from another cat, in a paper bag! This café's website has headshots of all the cats *waiting to meet you*! Look at little Birt! He looks like he's just been wearing a bowler hat! I send a link to Dad and Jess: even she'll find it funny. Maybe I should suggest to Fabrizio he introduce some guest cats for customers to stroke; might give him a stroke . . .

I flick briefly to my own column. There's my review of a New Mexican restaurant located in an old ironmonger's shop – Kiki came up with the headline 'Albuquirky'. Also my review of Trovese in Kensington, ferociously over-priced (£23 for Penne Arrabbiata?) And there's my piece on Pop-Ups: I've questioned whether we're seeing novelty over substance: last summer a pop-up Mac 'n' Cheese place on the rooftop of a luxury clothing store on Bond Street received gushing coverage in the press but the pasta had been as soft and grey as autumn/winter's cashmere.

That's the thing about food in London: it's become super-fashionable: posh burgers, trendy chickens, exposed filament lighting and Mayfair basements posing as Brooklyn bodegas. Some restaurants seem to have forgotten a simple fact: eating out should start with good food.

No doubt someone will get the hump over my piece – Lord knows there are more important things in this world to get annoyed about. But guaranteed, once an opinion is printed, people kick off. And nowadays they do it online, globally, in a heartbeat. It's only ever words, twenty-six letters, just in different orders. Words.

9

I'd forgotten how nervous I feel when I go on a date with a man I actually fancy. Last night I couldn't sleep and when I wake at 5 a.m. there's a tense throbbing in my stomach. Why on earth did I agree to a 7.30 a.m. date? I have dots for eyes at this time in the morning. At least when I met Adam on Sunday, I had a gin-and-tonic-meets-fury rosy glow to my cheeks – but today I look like a ghost. A dead ghost. Well OK then – a ghost.

Outfit . . . This blue and white polka dot dress is lovely! Short sleeves though . . . I open the curtains to peek outside. The sky is still black and it's that changeable time of year – one day icy, the next almost springlike so you never know where you stand. What the hell – I'm sweating with nerves anyway, I'll be fine after a coffee.

By the time I change Tubes at Baker Street, I'm in mild-panic mode, a loop of worst-case scenarios in my head. Sunday was so much fun, Adam and I didn't stop nattering all day but was that only because we were pissed? What if I immediately blab about my review? What if it's just horribly stilted and awkward? My mouth is so dry I can barely swallow.

At Liverpool Street station I rush to the coffee cart for a double espresso, then head outside to Hope Square, trying to calm down as the mass of commuters floods past me into the city, a life force, all desk-bound to jobs like my sister's: jobs that make no sense on paper, but make this city pulse and grow, then sometimes shrivel, only to surge back again.

Seven twenty-three a.m., best get a move on. The day has turned out bright but the wind is bitter and I pull my coat tighter as I head along New Street, quickening my pace. When I reach The Peak I turn my gaze up, and up, and up. It's just an hour of toast and a chat; it's not a big deal. Even so, my heart beats faster as I step into the glass lift, press the 66th and shoot north at five metres per second, my stomach heading south as we go.

I have no breath, I have no breath, I have no breath left to lose, but my lungs fill with sheer delight as the lift pulls me up through the sky and the city spreads out below. First sight is the church of St Botolph's, its old bricks and stones bordered by freshly cut grass; next to it the rectangular surprise of a basketball court. A moment later, barely visible through trees, the fattened brackets of Finsbury Circus give way to a Monopoly of streets and houses and stations. As we rise higher, a scattered patchwork of secret gardens and roof terraces unfurls, rainbow parasols halfway to the clouds, while on ground level dense thickets of park emerge, and to the left the still, black ribbon of the Thames. Far out on the horizon the bouncing arc of Wembley swoops a greeting to the whole of the west, you can see for miles and miles and miles.

At the top, the temptation to press the down button is too great, so I do, feeling my stomach flip all over again as I plummet back to the bottom, my ears popping halfway. They could charge for this, I'd pay ten times over.

Time to man up. Time to woman up. Get out of the lift, you idiot! I scan the dining room full of pinstripes and power suits, looking for Adam. The recession is clearly over, in this postcode at least, if they can charge £11.50 for toast and jam and still have a full house at 7.34 a.m. on a Thursday morning.

There he is, in the corner booth by the window. From this angle he's in three-quarter profile. His nose is strong, with a tiny bump on the bridge, and it makes his mouth underneath look almost vulnerable were it not for his strong jaw, which today is covered in dark stubble. I don't believe in anything at first sight – well, lust, perhaps. And this is second sight, but still, there is some very basic, hardwired connection between my eyes, my brain, and this man's face.

Adam turns, notices me, and his face relaxes into a smile. Those pale blue eyes under almost black brows . . . that dimple . . . He must know how good-looking he is, but there's none of that cock-sure arrogance you normally find with the pretty boys.

He stands to greet me; he smells clean and cool, like cold stone and limes. I try not to sniff him too obviously. I sit in the booth and he slides in close to me, our legs resting lightly together.

'Sorry I made you get out of bed early, my days are crazy – I didn't finish calling suppliers till two a.m., then my adrenalin was so shot I couldn't sleep.' He rubs his face with his hands until his cheeks colour. I resist the urge to smooth down a tuft of his thick, dark hair that's sticking up.

'How *do* your hours work, anyway?' Straight in there – where was he last Thursday?

'I'm doing AFDs at the moment – All Dayers – so eight forty-five a.m. through till one a.m., with the occasional split shift – thirty minutes off at tea.'

'Exhausting! You must have had a day off since you started?'

He counts on his fingers. 'Two weeks, four days and I've worked every sitting.'

'Not one shift off?'

'We barely have toilet breaks. My boss Jonn would go mad if I wasn't overseeing, and I don't trust the team. Max, my sous, is the worst: last week I discovered a job lot of silver gelatin he'd hidden in the store cupboard which should've been bronze – if you made a panna cotta with that you could play cricket with it. '

78 . . . Cauliflower panna cotta – as hard as a squash ball, less tasty.

'At least Sundays we're closed,' he says, giving me a quizzical look – then realisation dawns. 'Oh! It'll get easier after the first month. I should have more of a personal life then.'

He might have been in the far corner of that kitchen . . . For the whole time I was there, though? Still, if I probe any further he'd be within his rights to ask for a lawyer.

He hands me the menu. 'What do you fancy?'

You. And everything on this menu, but mostly the sausage, eggs and potato scones, with a side order of sourdough. I can't look that greedy in front of him. 'Yoghurt, granola and pink grapefruit?'

'Fibber!' he says, laughing. 'Honestly, what do you want?'

'Sausage, eggs and potato scones with extra sourdough.'

'My Granny Ailsa used to make the best tattie scones. She used to have to hide them so me and my sister wouldn't scoff the lot.'

'My grandma used to do that too!'

'With tattie scones?' he says, in surprise.

'Similar – potato latkes.'

'My gran used to stand with her spaniel Laddy at her heels, watching us search the kitchen. She'd pretend to be cross when we found her stash, but if I turned and caught her eye she'd have a secret smile on her face.'

'Oh, it wasn't cutesy hide and seek round Grandma Esther's. She once walloped Jess when she caught her with a mouthful and my sister had the audacity to go back for more!'

'My sister was crazy too,' he says, laughing as he snaps the menu shut. 'Right, two sausage, egg and scones – we'll see if they're as good as Gran's.'

'Oh. Is that wise?'

He raises his eyebrows. 'Do you think grandmas in the afterlife are hovering over us, primed to defend their potato legacies?'

'I wouldn't risk it. Ghosts can become quite uppity, you've seen *Poltergeist*.'

'That's very thoughtful of you,' he says, a smile twitching at the corner of his mouth.

'I mean, if I ordered them, you could always try some of mine?'

'Or I could just order them too? But by the way you're shaking your head, I'm guessing you're one of those weirdos who freaks out if two people order the same thing.' He raises his eyebrows at me indulgently. 'What would you like me to have?'

'I don't mind . . . '

'Full English with black pudding?'

'They have an annual black pudding throwing contest near where I used to live, I reckon I'd have won if I'd ever entered.'

'It's only the idea that's off-putting. You'd like it if you didn't know what was in it. '

'But I do know – once you know something you can't un-know it.'

'Eggs Benedict? No? Why don't you just tell me what I want,' he checks his watch. 'And then we might still have twenty minutes left to talk to each other.'

'Double stuffed French toast with mascarpone, berries and a side of bourbon glazed bacon?'

'A heart attack on a plate,' he says with delight. 'And ghost friendly.'

A familiar looking waiter approaches and smiles at me in recognition and I automatically smile back.

'Laura, this is Olly, an old mate.'

'Nice to see you again,' he says to me. 'How's it all going, Ads? I'm hearing insane shit.'

'Don't ask . . . I'm doing hundred-hour weeks, the menu's too big, the Robata can't get up enough heat. They spent all that cash on toilets, then bought the grill second hand – cheapskates! Any pot-washing jobs here?'

Olly laughs. 'Do you guys fancy a little glass of bubbly, on the house?'

'I'd better not, but Laura enjoys a tipple first thing in the morning, don't you, dear?'

I shake my head in embarrassment as Olly heads to the kitchen.

'So how do you know Olly?' says Adam.

Rather than say, quite innocently, *He recognises me because I have eaten here before*, my brain freezes. 'I don't know him.'

'He said "nice to see you again"?'

'He's your mate – he must have been talking to you.'

Adam shrugs.

'I guess I just have one of those faces,' I say. 'You know, I look quite generic.'

'Generic?'

'You know, a common face . . . '

'I know what generic means but why would you say that about yourself?'

'Because it's true. My features aren't distinctive.' I cover my eyes with my hands. 'Tell me, Adam, what colour are my eyes . . . '

'They're grey-green, Laura. When the light shines directly in them they're more green, and that dress is making them look almost blue.'

I feel colour spread up my cheeks.

'You know who you remind me of?' he says.

Please don't say Shaun Ryder.

'Cate Blanchett.'

I snort with laughter.

'You do, though,' he says. Oh dear, I think I love this man.

'Ah well, that must be who Olly thought I was, she'll have been in yesterday for a fry-up!'

'You've got a very kind, open face. Quite *malleable* . . . is that the word?'

'I think that means good under a hammer. But anyhow, please be quiet because you're making me blush.' And while I don't want to be one of those couples who snogs in restaurants, least of all at 7.39 a.m., I really want you to kiss me RIGHT NOW!

He smiles a naughty little smile, as though he can tell exactly what I'm thinking. 'By the way, Laura, you should order what you want, it doesn't matter what anyone else is having.'

'It's not what you're meant to do though, is it?'

He looks at me, perplexed.

'Not in my family,' I say. 'Mum and Dad used to take us out on our birthdays and Jess always used to think the grass was greener, so I'd have to give her half of mine anyway – it made sense to order different things. And God forbid I wanted the same as her . . . '

'So your menu phobia can be put down to sibling rivalry?'

'Yes, Sigmund Freud.' I roll my eyes. 'So you've got a crazy sister too?'

'Vicky? She's not crazy anymore, but she was wild when we were kids, always out getting stoned, whereas I was at home, helping Mum in the kitchen, my father in the background muttering I'd turn into a poof. But if I didn't go and find Mum there, I'd never see her so I was knocking round her knees from the age of five.'

'She was a chef?'

'She studied textiles, at Goldsmiths – some of her prints are actually in the V&A.'

'She must have been great with colour,' I say, noticing the blue shirt he's wearing not only brings out his eyes, but has beautiful detailing: sage cross-stitches on delicate cream buttons.

'But she jacked in everything when she met my father. She'd spend days cooking for his client dinner parties.'

'She gave up her career for him?'

'She sacrificed her potential, which is worse,' he says, his brow creasing.

'Did she ever feel bitter?'

'Not the type. Plus, she loved the kitchen, she had Elizabeth David on her bedside table.'

'My mum was a terrible cook,' I say, smiling at the memory of the salmon en croute, so slippery it could have swum back to sea. 'But my dad makes a fine chicken pot pie.'

He raises his brows in delight. 'Pastry's sort of my thing. Granny Ailsa again – her shortcrust was so flaky it was like filo. I learnt so much watching her and Mum,' he says, trying to keep from giggling. 'Mrs Collins, home ec on a Tuesday, didn't appreciate my expertise . . .'

'What did you do?'

'Just asked if she knew her crème pat from her crème Anglaise.'

'Crème pat's thicker, isn't it?'

'Exactly, even you know that. She had *Larousse* on her shelf, she should've read it.'

My well-thumbed copy lives on my bookshelf – my triceps were almost Anistonian after a month of reading it in bed.

'So did you go to catering college?' I say.

'Cooking wasn't the sort of *proper* job the men in my family did. I studied engineering. Why do you look so surprised?'

'Engineering's pretty academic . . . ' And most chefs I've encountered left school with not much hope of work outside a kitchen. And if you're good-looking and funny *and* clever, then what exactly is wrong with you? Do you have a drug problem?

'Laura, do you think all chefs are a bunch of unthinking savages?'

'No! I know running a kitchen is hard, it's just you don't hear of many chefs who are . . . brainiacs.'

'I never said I graduated.'

'Did you get into drugs then?'

'Never my thing. You can spot a chef on coke in a heartbeat –

their seasoning goes way off – their food tastes of salt before anything.'

That sounds exactly like the food coming out of his kitchen last Thursday.

'I'm sure Max is still caning it,' he says, his eyes narrowing.

'Where is our food?' I say, partly to change the subject, and partly because it's 8.02 a.m. and I feel like I'm on *Challenge Anneka* – I've now got only twenty-eight minutes left to make Adam like me.

'Morning shifts are tough on all the team. Anyway, where was I . . . Max . . . '

'Engineering!'

'Yeah, it was going fine, then in my second year I was reading about a group of engineers testing an early steam engine – one day they left it under a wooden shelter and went off to a nearby inn for roast goose. The engine caught fire and burnt to the ground, but all I could think about was that goose. I could practically taste it, smell it. And the following week I told my parents I was dropping out and training to become a chef.'

'Over a goose?'

'My father threatened to disown me, he thought it was proof I was gay.'

'Does he *still* think you're gay?'

'Er . . . not recently, no,' he says, looking thrown. 'But anyway, Mum was worse – she thought I should finish my degree and I didn't want to disappoint her, but you know sometimes you have a feeling?' He touches his chest. 'When something feels utterly right?' He looks at me with slow consideration, in a way that makes my heart beat a little faster. 'I've had that feeling a handful of times in my life and I've never been wrong. And if that bleach-haired prat Max sharpens up his act I should have my first star this year.'

'That's what it's all about? Michelin stars?'

He looks surprised. 'You make it sound like stars don't matter.'

'I guess it's your profile . . . '

'I don't care about critics – what's that quote? "A critic points out how the strong man stumbles" . . . '

Pretty cocky for someone responsible for last week's horror show. 'So other people aren't allowed to have an opinion on your food?'

'There are loads of people I respect in this business, all of them are chefs. I care what they think and I care what my customers think,' he says, his face lighting up as Olly approaches. 'Ah – breakfast is served!'

The scones look amazing – five golden discs of potato, speckled with crusty bits where the mix has browned in the pan. Adam cuts precisely through the French toast, halves the bacon and rearranges the slices perfectly on top. He divides the berries equally, spooning the mascarpone neatly on the side. His handiwork's a lot better than it was last Thursday.

'So . . . Michelin stars?' I say.

'I want a star so I can get financial backing. I'm done working for other people. I just want a place that's mine. That's what I've been working towards my whole career,' he says, smiling softly. 'That's what it's about, what you do with your own name.'

It's just as well I haven't used his name in my piece then, I think, resting my cutlery as I ponder whether Roger's advice might have been wrong.

'Anyway,' he says, shyly, 'I've been droning on about my work, I don't even know what you do? Let me guess. So: polka dot dress, very pretty dress,' he says, taking a longer appreciative look. 'You don't start work till . . . ?'

'Ten a.m.'

'Lucky you! So media or creative?'

'Have you been googling me, Adam?'

'Do people actually do that?'

Do people actually *not* do that?

'I don't even know your surname, Laura, so no, I haven't been stalking you!'

'Parker.'

'Bayley.'

We shake hands again. His is warm and strong; it holds on to mine far longer than mere politeness.

'Out of interest,' he says, glancing at my plate. 'How are those scones?'

'Amazing! The texture's so soft and yielding in the middle, then that chewy, crispy coating . . . '

'And what precisely do I have to do to you to get a bite?' he says, grinning.

I clumsily scrape the last one onto his plate. He transfers the perfect French toast and examines the scone. He pokes it with his fork, then brings it to his eye as if he's working forensics before gently tearing it apart to inspect the texture, finally popping it in his mouth.

'Verdict?'

He chews thoughtfully, then a smile spreads across his face. 'Laura – did you take maths GCSE?'

'I got a B. Why?'

'Then I'm surprised you're not familiar with the concept of fractions.'

'We never said we'd go halves!'

'It was sort of unspoken.'

'Well, if it was *sort of unspoken* it didn't happen.'

'Ah, so that's how your mind works. A master of manipulation, evasion and half-truths. You're not a lawyer are you?'

'I'm a secretary.'

'Cool.' He's the only guy I've told what I do for a living who hasn't immediately said, 'I can't believe you're only a secretary,' or some other dumb thing that suggests being a secretary is not a proper job.

'Who do you work for then?' He's also the only guy who's actually bothered to ask where I work, once I've told him I'm a secretary.

'A man called Roger Harris.'

'What does he do?'

'He edits *The Voice*?'

'*The Voice* is great! It's so free of bullshit, and it's got The Dish, hasn't it?'

'This view!' I say, putting my fork down and fixing my eyes to the far distance. 'Is that the Olympic Stadium?'

'So do you know the guy who does it?'

'Does what?'

'The Dish. He always nails a place so perfectly.'

'You like him?'

'Love him.'

'But you just said you didn't care what critics write?' I say, picking up my fork again.

'He's different. He doesn't write about himself, there's no ego. He sticks to the point: you get a knife-sharp view of what he ate, the ambience, the staff. You're right there at the table with him.'

'This bacon is amazing, isn't it?'

'Nowadays everyone's a critic – but your guy is properly insightful – and funny. And he's never vicious for the sake of a cheap laugh.'

'The bourbon glaze on the bacon . . . I love bourbon almost as much as I love bacon.'

'Yeah, me too. So what's he like to work for, this Roger?'

Thank God, safer ground! 'There's a line in an old Barbara Stanwyck film – she says all she wants is a man "to fight off the blizzards and the floods". And that's how I think of Roger. He's charming but sincere. Brave. And ballsy. A total hero.'

'Nothing like my bosses,' he says, cutting into the sourdough, then adding a bite of sausage, some egg and a snippet of scone to the fork. 'They're absolute . . . '

'You do what I do,' I say. 'You try to get an equal bit of everything into each mouthful.'

'A nightmare with roast dinners.'

'The peas always fall off at the last moment.'

'Doesn't everyone do that?'

'My flatmate doesn't, she never "cross contaminates".'

'That's the stupidest thing I ever heard,' he says.

'She tried to throw away my toaster when I moved in – she's scared of bread . . . '

'I thought being scared of clowns was weird.'

'Clowns are terrifying; scared of buttons is the weirdest.'

'You've obviously never been alone in a dark alley with a sewing kit.'

'She was slightly chubby as a teenager so now she won't allow bread in the flat. No bread, no *bread-enablers* . . . '

He shakes his head in confusion. 'Lunatic!'

'Oh she's fine, really – she's out loads. And her dog's adorable, when she's not pooing in the kitchen. The antidepressants disagree with her.'

'The dog's on Prozac?'

'You would be too, if you were forced to wear a leopard print onesie in public.'

'She sounds crackers . . . ooh, can I say crackers or do they count as bread? Sorry, terrible joke . . . ' he says, his cheeks turning pink.

'Honestly, I quite like Amber, we're just different. My room literally was her walk-in shoe cupboard, but then my salary's pretty compact too – and it means I can afford to have a job I love that doesn't pay six figures.'

'Most people are stuck in jobs they don't like because of their mortgage,' he says, wistfully.

'I used to have a mortgage,' I say. 'Up in Manchester . . . And a husband . . . ' There it is.

'Oh right.' He nods. Hurrah, hurrah! A gold star for you Adam! Unfazed I'm a secretary, interested in where I work and not bothered by the fact I have a failed marriage.

'You're not from Manchester though?'

'Muswell Hill, near Ally Pally – over the other side,' I say, looking down on to the curve of the Thames.

'Let's go see,' he says, standing and heading to the bar. I check my watch with a twinge of sadness, 8.28 a.m. 'I should pay.'

'Don't worry, Olly knows we're not doing a runner.'

'I'll see you there.' I need a make-up re-touch. In the ladies' the face in the mirror frowns back at me. Why do people moan about bad hair days? What about bad face days? This Boots Instant Radiance balm may help, if only psychologically. I do a quick primp and head back out.

Adam's standing looking down at the view. 'Prettier close up than from a distance,' he says turning and smiling.

'Me? You're joking,' I say, caught off guard by the compliment

– well, half compliment. Bloody hell, though, that Boots cream is totally as good as Clarins!

'I meant the Gherkin,' he says, laughing. 'You're pretty either way.'

I turn to the window so he can't see me beaming.

'This building is about two hundred and thirty metres,' he says, then points to The Needle. 'That one's mine; it's two hundred metres but only because they stuck a spire on top for extra height, so they could be seventh tallest.'

'Urgh, some egomaniac property guy cares enough to compete to be seventh? It's pathetic. Skyscrapers – just boys and their willies at the end of the day.'

He laughs. 'Maybe I should get them to rename it The Dick – the place is full of them.' He sighs and turns to me. 'What's your office like?'

'It's lovely, it's an old Victorian warehouse. We have half the building, and a TV company has the top floors. Every so often you'll smile at someone in reception you vaguely recognise; it's only once you get to your desk you realise they were actually the knob-head from last season's *The Apprentice*.'

'Come ride the lift and show me,' he says, a twinkle in his eye.

'You'll never see it.'

'Come anyway, they're so much fun.'

We race to the lifts like a pair of fourteen year olds bunking double physics, and step in, standing side by side, arms touching. I press the ground floor and down we fall, oohing and aahing at the speed and the view and the sheer sensation of it all. We ride down and up and down again seven times before he looks at his watch and panics.

'Laura, I'm so sorry, I have to be at The Needle in . . . minus ten minutes.'

'Of course,' I say, though my heart continues to descend even as the lift slows to a halt. We walk together out to the street and I feel an overwhelming desire to follow him all the way to work – I want to keep talking to him, I need more than one hour . . .

We say a brief goodbye before he dashes twenty metres down the road and unlocks his bike. He looks over his shoulder and I give a little wave, but instead of returning it he checks his watch, then looks back in my direction. For a moment he hesitates. And then he turns his bike around and quickly pedals on the wrong side of the road back towards me, coming to a stop beside me as I feel my heart rise again, up and up and up.

'What's wrong?' I say, as he leans forward, one foot resting on the pavement.

'I can't believe I was in such a rush, I forgot,' he says, looking sheepish. 'I'm an idiot.'

'Adam – the bill's on me.'

'I took care of that already.'

'Oh, you shouldn't have . . . '

He shrugs unapologetically. His eyes lock on mine and I have to force myself to breathe out.

'Well . . . then . . . Why did you come back? What did you forget?'

'I forgot to do this,' he says.

And he pulls me gently towards him.

And kisses me.

10

'Parker, what are you up to?'

Sitting at my desk, replaying that kiss. That was a good kiss, a properly good kiss.

'Roger – I'm sitting at my desk, changing your Eurostar tickets, and if you took ten whole steps from your desk, you'd see that for yourself. What is the point of wearing a pedometer if you're not going to move?'

'It has a jolly nice little digital clock on it.'

'How many steps have you done this week?'

'No idea . . . '

'Let me log in for you . . . '

'Don't bother . . . '

'You told me to keep on top of it . . . six thousand, three hundred and four! You're about four thousand short already.'

'Six thousand, three hundred and four? Sounds rather a lot to me.'

'Roger – I'm going to stop ordering cabs to take you to lunch . . . '

'Well, you'll have to do the steps for me today, I'm afraid.'

'What's wrong?' I walk into his office and nearly fall flat on my face over a golf bag. I haul it off the floor and drag it to a sliver of space in the corner.

'So? How was it?' he says. 'Nice dress by the way, very *South Pacific*.'

'The date? Oh,' I say, flopping down in the chair opposite him. 'It was a bad idea.'

'Was he different to how you remembered him? Did he look like the Elephant Man?'

'Worse – a bit like Paul Newman, those beautiful pale blue eyes but a slightly less perfect nose.'

'I can see why you're so upset. Oh come on, Laura – stop this nonsense, you're being neurotic. You have my blessing.'

Maybe Roger's right and I'm worrying about nothing . . . I was just doing my job . . . still, I fear it may all end in tears.

'Is that March's issue?' I say, noticing a copy of the magazine in front of him.

'Checking the type on the classifieds – I woke in the middle of the night with palpitations about the overlap – '

'They're fine, I already checked. Have you taken your meds today?'

He waves his hand at a stack of papers on his desk. 'I took whatever was in Tuesday's slot.'

'But it's Thursday!' I say, scrabbling under the pile to find his pill box. Monday to Thursday's compartments are now empty, the rest of the week's days still have a little pink statin and a red and white anti-hypertensive, nestling side by side. 'Roger, I do not appreciate you winding me up about things like that.'

'And I do not appreciate you treating me like a child, I am capable of taking my medication. Anyway – as I was saying, just checking they hadn't ballsed up again but panic over.'

'Do you want me to keep Print Tender on the agenda for tomorrow?'

He scratches behind his ear. 'Two cock-ups in nine months . . . Sandra will want to hang them out to dry. Still, I'm a firm believer in learning from one's mistakes, aren't you?'

I cross it off the list.

He flicks to my column and nods approvingly.

'Have you thought any more about Second Helpings?' I say.

'Show me something next month, this month's too busy; and have you decided about the *New York Times*?'

I was hoping he wouldn't ask.

'I'll hold them off for now,' he says, 'but I think you're being paranoid. Oh, and one more thing?'

'Yes, Roger?'

'Could I trouble you for a cup of March's finest? What's on the menu this month?'

'Are you taking the piss again?'

'Absolutely not! You know I love that stuff.'

'OK then . . . March's blend is a mix of Brazilian and Bolivian, a rich, sweet base, with ten per cent Mexican which gives it an earthiness, and a smidge of Ethiopian for a fruity note.'

'And what are the farmers' names?'

'Roger . . . '

'And will it taste exactly the same as last month's?'

'Roger!'

'I'm only joking, I think it's terrific. Three sugars and cream please and don't try slipping me sweetener.'

When I left Bean To Cup, Doug, my old boss, bought me an AeroPress coffee maker – £20, a brilliant piece of kit – and every month for that first year he sent me down a kilo of freshly roasted beans. He knew I was struggling and he didn't want me to be without good coffee. I didn't have the heart to tell him I'd lucked upon Fabrizio's so I brought Doug's blends in for the team here – there were only twelve of us back then. And I brought in the AeroPress. And because the AeroPress looks a bit like a bong I did a five-minute all-staff meeting on how to use it. And then I figured I might as well do a mini-cupping session with tasting notes – to give the team an overview of flavour profiles.

Everyone was slightly awkward at first, because the noise you make when you're tasting properly is a weird slurpy, sucking noise as the air hits the back of your throat. But Roger embraced it, and soon everyone else was getting into it, saying they could taste smokiness, and red fruits and of course Azeem – ever the joker – swore he could . . . why, he could actually taste coffee! Roger said anyone who could taste 'butterscotch and green bananas' in this brown liquid must have more taste buds than a catfish. (I googled catfish – quite disgusting, one site called them 'swimming tongues'.) We had such a laugh that day so Roger decided to allocate a budget for Doug's monthly blend. It wasn't like I was getting commission – I just wanted the guys to have better quality coffee. Little treats can make a disproportionate difference to one's happiness – a fact I was beginning to appreciate.

Everyone seemed very enthusiastic. Everyone except for one

individual who didn't understand what all the fuss was about and didn't think there was anything special about it and doesn't it make a mess and what's wrong with Gold Blend? I tried explaining freeze drying is about as delicious as any other hugely chemical, industrial process but she wasn't having any of it. She still sighs every time she walks into the kitchen and finds me using the AeroPress. Maybe that's why I feel quite so motivated to make five cups a day . . .

As the water's boiling my mind drifts back to earlier with Adam. When we were riding up and down in that lift, in the beginning I still felt the nerves you feel when you're in a small enclosed space for the first time with someone you have a crush on: that acute awareness of where your bodies are in relation to each other at all times. But the self-consciousness quickly faded as we gazed out of the window. Pretty soon I felt like a kid on the best private fairground ride ever. And that first time St Paul's came into view on our left, Adam said it looked like it was rising up from the past, and the ridiculous thing is I hadn't even noticed St Paul's when I'd ridden up on my own, I'd been so nervous. But suddenly, halfway up our ascent there it was and it was spectacular; hidden one moment, resplendent the next. And each time we rode up, even though I knew it was coming, its beauty took me by surprise.

Tom wouldn't have ridden up and down in that lift with me seven times. He wouldn't have done it twice, he'd have said it was dumb and boring and childish. And Russell would have tried to pull my skirt up to show the City my knickers. But with Adam, every up and down was its own little adventure.

This time next month I'll be standing here making coffee with this same kettle, this same coffee maker. This time next month I'm pretty sure Adam will be out of the picture but if by some miracle he is still around on publication day he won't be in the mood for riding up and down in any lifts with me. This time next month, the only thing that's certain is that things will not feel as exciting and as hopeful as they feel today.

So I should not allow my mind to linger on a memory of skylines and laughter and kissing in the street, because such moments in life – moments of pure joy and undiluted happiness – are fleeting.

II

'First things first,' says Roger, walking into our conference meeting on Friday morning with his files wedged under one armpit, and carrying two large brown paper bags with grease marks seeping round the bottom. 'I've got six bacon, and six sausage and egg, don't look at me like that, Laura, grapes are not sustenance for grown men.'

'Nor women,' says Kiki, taking the platter of fruit I've artfully arranged, sliding the grapes, apples and bananas off and replacing them with a pyramid of white, salty rolls. The ad boys descend like they've been on hunger strike, Heather, our lawyer, holds back for twenty seconds, and Azeem tries, and fails, to negotiate with Jonesy to swap his bacon roll for sausage.

'Right, last month's issue, cracking job, well done,' says Roger, plonking his files on the table and rolling up his sleeves. 'Mick, what are copy sales looking like?'

'Looking at hitting a hundred and twenty-one thousand, three up on the month, with returns on target.'

'Distribution?'

'PrintPro were late into depot, but they gave us fair warning and we made up the time in transit.'

'Hang on just one minute,' says Sandra, bringing the agenda closer to her nose. 'I don't see Print Tender on here, Laura, why isn't it on here?'

'I told her not to,' says Roger, skimming down the list. 'Right, Jonesy – ad revenues, what are the scores on the doors?'

'But after February's issue I thought—'

'PrintPro messed up, they won't do it again. Jonesy, numbers?'

Jonesy's face scrunches up in an attempt to look thoughtful. Jonesy is the perfect foil to Roger – he's lazy, has no ethics or morals and is entirely untroubled by doing the right thing. However, he lets his clients win at golf without looking like he's throwing his game, and remembers all their kids' names – hence he makes the perfect Commercial Director. 'Yep,' he says, tipping back in his chair and passing a hand over his shaved head, 'Storming month – March closed on eighty-seven k.'

'Hmm. And if I recall Feb closed on ninety-two k?'

Jonesy is not stupid, yet he still falls for Roger's chaotic act, thus continually underestimating Roger's ability to sniff out the truth whenever there is bullshit in the air.

Roger pauses – then flicks to a small slip of paper in the back of his files. 'Well Jonesy, it's reassuring to know that even though our sales are down, your expenses are up . . . '

Jonesy returns his chair to the floor with a bump.

'Six hundred and twenty pounds on lunch?' says Roger, holding the receipt up to the light as though checking for a watermark.

'That was a Fletchers campaign – it was meant to land in March but they pulled it last minute 'cos the product's fucked – some new range of high protein meals . . . '

Roger takes a closer look at the receipt. 'Looks like quite a high-protein meal you enjoyed yourselves! What have we got here . . . foie gras, rib-eye steak, Dover sole . . . '

Jonesy extends his arm across the table in an attempt to grab it. 'Client was there – Devron at Fletchers is a big eater . . . '

'Big drinker too, by the looks of it – three bottles of the ninety-seven Pauillac? A fine vintage, jolly good . . . What time did you leave then? Let's see . . . '

'Rodge! There was loads to discuss with next month's campaigns—'

'Six fifty-eight p.m. – that sounds like lunch *and* dinner,' says Roger, raising his eyebrows. 'So in that case how *is* April looking?'

Jonesy hastily opens his file and flicks to the upcoming issue's plans. 'So far we've got consecutive back pages booked by Audi, a double-page spread for BA's Easter campaign pencilled in and the supermarkets are going large on brand ads.'

'Well turn that pencil into a booking pronto – and how about this month you spend less time down The Ivy and more time selling those pages, Jonesy. Come on!'

Jonesy clears his throat and resettles himself on his chair as his two underlings try to keep from exchanging glances.

'By the way,' says Roger, turning to the table. 'Did anyone see Dolly Parton on TV the other day? Wonderful woman! Maybe we should do an interview with her? Or perhaps we could send someone to Dollywood – I might go myself, I've never been to Tennessee.' He scratches a note out on his pad. 'Right then, Voice of Youth, what are our friends online up to?'

'The cats have gone large, obviously,' says Azeem. '#spoiltkitty is trending at nine on Twitter.'

Roger waves his hand dismissively. 'No one with a real job pays attention to any of *that* crap.'

'You have a real job, don't you?' I say, remembering the time I heard Roger making peculiar rasping noises in his office. Terrified he was having a heart attack I rushed in, only to find him red in the face and guffawing at Buzzfeed – eleven pictures of cats that look like Rupert Murdoch.

'I meant, is anything more substantial getting traffic?' says Roger. 'Ed Miller's opinion piece?'

'Getting a slagging on the blogs but half those trolls clearly haven't read it,' says Azeem.

'You know what Elbert Hubbard would say?'

'He's been dead a century,' says Azeem. 'I wouldn't have thought he'd have too much to say about Twitter.'

'"To avoid criticism, do nothing, say nothing, be nothing" – a lesson for us all,' says Roger. 'Right, April's issue, editorial – Sandra, give us the rundown?'

Sandra smooths the invisible wrinkles on her laminated agenda. 'Extremely important issue, looks like we'll finally be in a position to run the Bechdel piece as the leader.'

Jonesy lets out a low whistle.

'The focus will be on Damian Bechdel – not his brother,' says Sandra, turning to Heather. 'Focusing largely on his financial affairs, with a spotlight on the discrepancies within his African charity project.'

'Still waiting on two key witnesses who are nervous about going on record – if neither comes through, we either hold another month or go purely on the UK business and property empire,' says Heather. 'But it would be stronger if we can include the charity angle – several household names are donors.'

'You finally going to nail him?' says Jonesy. 'I saw him on telly the other night – sanctimonious little rat.'

'What's the dirt?' says Kiki. 'I heard the second wife was Latvia's highest paid escort before she met him, and now she's reinvented herself as a cross between Mother Teresa and Angelina Jolie – never misses a photo op in a shanty town, always dressed in nude Louboutins.'

Sandra turns a withering gaze towards Kiki. 'Katrina, perhaps you'd like to apply for a job at the *Sun* if that's where your areas of interest lie?'

'Oh come on, Sandra,' says Kiki. 'Don't pretend you don't love a bit of gossip as much as the rest of us. Besides, I'm not taking anyone seriously who tells me to donate to charity while they're wearing six-hundred-pound shoes!'

Sandra lets out a deep sigh. 'Obviously this piece will be confidential until we go to press, the entire issue will be embargoed and I do not want anyone discussing this or any other editorial outside of these four walls.'

Kiki's eyes meet mine.

'We'll be focusing primarily on Bechdel's business dealings,' says Heather. 'His chief backer when he set up the hedge fund was Serge Kuranikov.'

'Never ask about the first million,' says Roger.

'Bechdel himself is under investigation by the SEC for that fund, which is now in administration, so the start of the piece investigates the money trail. There's plenty of meat there. We are looking at his annual charity gala, partly because of the drug allegations and partly because those guest lists make for rather interesting bedtime reading . . .'

'And the brother?' says Jonesy, nervously.

'Oh, it's definitely a family affair.' says Roger. 'The brother's ad agency has done the campaigns for the charity since day one – but the account director has shown us the billing sheets – they're charging double the rate card.'

'For a *charity* project?' says Jonesy.

'Exactly – you'd expect that to be done at cost – so the brother's creaming money off the whole thing too.'

'So what's our backup for the cover story if the Bechdel doesn't happen in April?' says Kiki. 'And does this mean we're going to have a nightmare end of month, subbing it all at the last minute?'

'The other big feature,' says Sandra, 'will be on turkey.'

'The country or the Twizzler?' says Jonesy, his face twisting with concern.

'It's an eight-page exposé of SunFarms Poultry – horrific animal welfare story, covers toe-clipping, cannibalism, violation of density per square foot allocations in shed birds—'

'Bollocks,' says Jonesy, shaking his head in disbelief. 'How many of the supermarkets are involved?'

'SunFarms don't supply into the big four, but they're part of Fletchers' supply chain so we will be naming Fletchers, and giving their CEO a right to reply,' says Heather.

'And I'm supposed to keep 'em sweet about the fact their ad for Easter Sunday roast turkey will appear on page fifteen while we're accusing them of torturing the poor buggers on page nine?'

'Tell them to run a lamb ad instead,' says Azeem. 'Or better yet, a nut roast.'

'Can't we at least hold it till May?' says Jonesy.

Roger ignores him and turns to me with a sly smile. 'Laura, you're a one-woman encyclopaedia of Things You Wish You Never Knew About Turkeys. Why don't you tell us all your charming Christmas tale?'

'Not now, Rog, not appropriate.' I shake my head violently.

'Bring a little cheer to the room.'

'I told you that story off the record!' Last Christmas, Amber, her animal activist step-brother Rafe and I had ended up stuck in London due to heavy snow. Sophie, bless her, had hosted us at the last minute. All had been surprisingly festive until Rafe had drunk too much fashionable gin and performed a nothing-left-to-the-imagination demonstration of a male turkey being wanked off: truly the mother-of-all-appetite-suppressants. Sophie has only recently started speaking to Amber again and only now in terse sentences.

'Apparently, the male turkeys have been bred to have such over-sized breasts—' says Roger.

'Stop it, Roger.'

' – they can't mate naturally or they'd break the females' backs, so the farmers end up having to turn them upside down and manu-ally . . .'

'Roger!' I say, catching the appalled expression on Sandra's face.

'Oh Parker, you're such a killjoy. Fine, we'll save it for the pub. Right,' he says, checking his watch, 'What time's my cab, Laura?'

'Eleven thirty a.m., table's at noon.'

'AOB, team?'

'One more thing,' I say. 'Last month's charity pub quiz – I'm still missing your ticket money . . . Jonesy and . . . ' I scan my list. 'Just Jonesy.'

'What charity was it for again?' he says.

'The charity of What Bleeding Difference,' says Roger.

'I don't think we should have to pay, the *Daily Metro* had their iPhones under the table, googling every bloody answer.'

'Just shut up and pay the woman, Jonesy, or you'll have your own nut roast to worry about.'

Jonesy puffs out his cheeks indignantly, then laughs, in spite of himself.

To: Laura, Azeem
From: Kiki
Subject: URGENT

When was the last time you think Sandra got laid?

To: Laura, Kiki
From: Azeem
Subject: re: URGENT

Valentine's Day, 1843.

To: Laura, Azeem
From: Kiki
Subject: Or perhaps . . .

More recently . . . !
   In case you'd managed to erase the horror – thought you
might like another view of this charming photo of Sandra and
Fergus on the dance floor after the pub quiz . . .

To: Laura, Kiki
From: Azeem
Subject: Help!

I need new retinas . . .

To: Kiki, Azeem
From: Laura
Subject: Enough!

Not having this conversation with you guys on email. And
Kiki – delete that from your phone, for God's sake.

To: Laura, Azeem
From: Kiki
Subject: More gossip!

Meanwhile, Damian Bechdel once propositioned my friend Lexie in Soho House. She said he got his cock out and was so drunk he couldn't get it back in his trousers. Apparently the wife was sitting next to him the whole time, so high she didn't blink!

To: Laura, Kiki
From: Azeem
Subject: I AM HUNGRY!

Isn't it cake o'clock yet, Laura?

To: Azeem, Kiki
From: Laura
Subject: Practice makes perfect . . .

Azeem – In light of your epic fail last week I think you should do it again.

To: Azeem, Laura
From: Kiki
Subject: Mine's a triple chocolate brownie

Yeah, go on Az – do it for me. No getting high on your own supply this time though –I know your bite marks!

To: Laura
From: Azeem
Subject: PRIVATE

Oh God – I love her.

To: Kiki
From: Laura
Subject: £600 shoes

Do you think Mrs Bechdel's a bad person just because of her shoes? You're not averse to a nice shoe yourself, young lady.

To: Laura
From: Kiki
Subject: NSFW

I don't think she's bad – I just don't want to be preached to by an ex-hooker who's using a starving Asian child as a prop. Meanwhile here's a link to a photo of Lady Bechdel from her modelling days c.1991. She's wearing shoes but not a lot else! Don't click on it when anyone's standing behind you, it's fully rancid.

To: Kiki
From: Laura
Subject: urgh

Don't ever send me stuff like that again. How do I delete my cookies on this computer without having to ask Azeem?

To: Roger
From: Laura
Subject: WORKLOAD

Hope lunch is good – make sure you order the brown sugar tart, it's worthy of the hype.

Also, is there anything *at all* that needs doing this afternoon? Have re-formatted the holiday chart, written up notes from earlier and done all your T&Es . . . Am officially at a loose end.

To: Laura
From: Roger
Subject: Re: WORKLOAD

Enjoy the peace while it lasts, Parker.

I won't be coming back from lunch – don't stay past 5 p.m.

To: Dad
From: Laura
Subject: Candy Crush

Stuck on level 262, send help immediately!

To: Laura
From: Dad
Subject: Re: Candy Crush

On level 401 darling, 262's ancient history. Striped candy's the key.

To: Jess
From: Laura
Subject: Saturday

What time does your Eurostar get in again? 3 p.m. or 3.30 p.m.? I'll meet you outside the main M&S in St Pancras.

To: Laura
From: Jess
Subject: Do you ever do any work????

I've re-attached the word document with my agenda for Sunday. I did already send this to you – do you not archive your emails? Have you bought my biscuits yet?

To: Jess
From: Laura
Subject: You are SO annoying

It would have been quicker just to type: 3.15 p.m. But thanks.
    By the way I've attached an agenda detailing when I'll be eating your biscuits between now and tomorrow.

To: Laura
From: Adam Bayley
Subject: Round 2

Afternoon. Just wanted to send you this photo of a stickman I made out of streaky bacon. He was delicious.
    Yesterday was the best breakfast I've ever had. Can we do it again next Tuesday, same time?

To: Adam
From: Laura
Subject: re: Round 2

Tuesday? Sure. But this time my treat x

To: Sophie
From: Laura
Subject: CHEF UPDATE

OK, so he's asked me for breakfast again . . .
    Don't think the greasy spoon I go to with Kiki for beans, fried slice and a builder's arse crack will impress him. The Wolseley's too posh/I won't get a table. Big Fat American-style breakfast, waffles, pancakes, etc? Would Will eat a steak at 7.30 a.m.? Or Café Aviv – chefs like all that shakshuka stuff, don't they?

To: Laura
From: Sophie
Subject: Breakfast, again?!

Go to Justin's Bakery – only a psychopath doesn't like a freshly baked croissant.

To: Sophie
From: Laura
Subject: They don't open till 8 a.m.

I thought breakfast was the new bloody dinner? Wish it was dinner . . . As Lumley says, 'Why wake up Annie Appetite before you need to?' The minute I start eating, my body remembers how magnificent food is and wants to keep at it all day.

It's like chocolate or sex – if you go without for long enough you forget why people make such a fuss. But put a toe back in the water . . . *Soph, how is he ever going to make a move on me at 7.30 a.m. in a public place?*

To: Laura
From: Sophie
Subject: Eureka idea!

Get Fabrizio to start selling my cakes – then you can meet Adam in the back room. Nice and cosy . . .

To: Adam
From: Laura
Subject: Missing strawberries

Here's a photo of the strawberry tart my colleague Azeem just bought me. Tell me, would any self-respecting pastry chef let a tart leave the kitchen with three strawberries missing?

On Tuesday, how about Bobby's near Goodge Street? It's new-wave Australian – avocado on toast, breakfast burritos, etc. My old boss, Doug, knows them so their coffee will be good and apparently their pastries are amazing.

To: Laura
From: Adam
Subject: Perfect

BTW – I was thinking about you ordering the food yesterday and it was making me laugh.

To: Adam
From: Laura
Subject: Gobby?

Did you think I was being bossy?

To: Laura
From: Adam
Subject: Not gobby

Not at all! It was refreshing – I'm not used to girls being so
forthright.

To: Adam
From: Laura
Subject: Forthright = polite word for bossy, no?

Next time I promise I'll keep my mouth shut.

To: Laura
From: Adam
Subject: Keep your mouth open!

It's one of your best attributes!
   I meant, Laura – you say what you feel, there's no bullshit
with you – which is a rare quality.
   The fact you're entirely yourself around me makes me feel
I can be entirely myself around you. It's great.

See you Tuesday (I shan't say Next . . .)
   Can't wait.
   x

12

As I watch my sister stride through St Pancras I still can't quite believe that this super-groomed, Parisian-thin brunette is the same Jess who'd bounce around our front room in a too-tight turquoise Pineapple leotard, making me do backup vocals for 'Love In The First Degree'. (It didn't occur to my five-year-old self that Bananarama had three members and if Jess insisted on being Siobhan Fahey I could be one of the other two, but no: Backing Vocalist, *Stand behind Siobhan AT ALL TIMES*!)

But look at Jess now: she's turned into the sort of woman who has a *uniform* instead of clothes. Her weekend uniform never consists of jeans or holey sweaters; rather, a combination of fail-safe *capsule pieces* – today a cashmere jacket over black trousers, Tod's loafers and a *so expensive it has no branding* bag, hooked in the crook of her arm.

'We're going to Pied à Tech,' she says, kissing me hello, then marching for the taxi rank.

'Oh Jess, I'm in no fit state . . . '

'All the more reason.'

'But I wanted to take you to this cute little tea shop . . . '

'My treat, I choose. Besides, I have to get to Diptyque before five p.m. for Nita's engagement present. Chartered surveyor. Met him on *The Times* website,' she says, arching a perfectly shaped brow.

'Why don't you buy Nita something more interesting than a candle?' I say, ignoring the dating remark. 'How about ScandiDesign for something a bit different?'

Her nostrils flare. It's not like Jess doesn't have imagination. She used to have plenty when she was making up stories to get herself out of trouble, or me into it. It's just with her infinite responsibilities (Office Role Model for Other Women, kids, Charles, Dad) – she has no time for creativity. You can't go wrong with a pair of black trousers, nor a Diptyque candle and Jess lives in a universe where being right is entirely about not being wrong – where the definition of wrong is different.

We get into a taxi and she tells the cabbie to go to Marylebone, avoiding the Euston Road.

'That's the straightest way there, love.'

'Also the most densely trafficked road in Europe,' she says, in a tone neither aggressive nor exactly conciliatory. 'Cut through via UCL, take Mortimer Street, drop us at the top of Devonshire.'

'If you say so,' he says, shaking his head in disagreement. 'It'll cost you more . . . '

She rolls her eyes, then flashes me a mischievous smile. 'So! What's the latest?'

Jess could mean work, love, or general – no doubt we'll cover all three – she's not one to dwell on a topic once she's told me exactly what I should think about it.

'Work's great, I've brought you copies of the new issue. My Pop-Up article's been retweeted over a thousand times since Tuesday.'

'Presumably you're keeping a record of these stats?'

'And Roger's been contacted by the *New York Times*, they're doing a feature on food critics around the world and they've chosen me as one . . . '

Her face lights up. 'Why didn't you mention this before? No!' she calls out to the driver, 'I meant the second right at UCL . . . '

'I'm not sure whether to do it.'

'It would be phenomenal exposure.'

'Exactly – it's asking for trouble. They'll shoot me in darkened silhouette, but you can still work out a person's body type, hairstyle. And I'd say something innocuous, like "I used to work in coffee" and next thing I know I'll be on the cover of *Heat,* papped with Bitchy Resting Face. I'm not doing it, Jess, it's a slippery slope.'

'Did I miss something or have you been shagging David Beckham?'

'Look: I eat the food, I write about the food. I trust what's going in to my mouth – not what might come out of it. If I'm exposed this gig is over.'

'Dad will agree – you're insane to turn it down.' She folds her arms tightly across her chest. 'And what exactly are your medium to longer term plans?'

'What do you mean?'

'Your plans for returning to a career.'

'Last time I looked I had a career – and a half.'

'I've been running the numbers: the London coffee scene is in triple-digit growth.'

'One minute you're saying splay myself across the *New York Times*, next you're saying go back to my old job?'

'Do both, you'd be in a stronger position financially.'

I shake my head violently. 'I love my job, and my boss. How many people can say that?'

'Or set something up in Paris!'

'One indentured slave in the family not enough for you?'

'Excuse me, driver! Here's fine,' she says. He pulls over sharply at the entrance to a private mews.

I practise my counting skills, then drag Jess's case over the cobbles as she charges ahead.

'I've booked us fifteen minutes Power-Relax, then Speed Threading.'

'Jess, do you think one day I might see you without it being turned into a multi-tasking extravaganza?' Last time, she dragged me to Smythson to order personalised envelopes, then for her haircut, then tea with three colleagues, where all talk was of Distressed Bonds.

'You're so over-sensitive,' she says, reaching a perfect petal-pink manicured fingertip out to the discreet buzzer of a five-storey Georgian townhouse.

Pied à Tech is so exclusive you can only book treatments if you work at Vogue House or can afford not to work at all. Behind the darkened windows are a series of faux-medical white chambers where women in dark glasses sit, chewing the insides of their cheeks (low-carb) – waiting for beauty to be bestowed in cash-rich/time-poor sessions.

My sister is the type to clean her apartment before her cleaner arrives – and the same principles apply to her body: she's utterly moisturised and plucked before she even crosses the jasmine-infused threshold. Me? Less so.

'I can't believe you didn't warn me,' I say, tangling with a pair of paper pants in the changing room. 'I've got a bikini line like a Greek sailor.'

'They wax half of Europe's minor royals in this place, they've seen it all, now hurry up! We're late for Serenity.'

We've been lying face down for five minutes, our heads poking through holes in massage tables, listening to a medley of traditional Thai lute music. From the vague pummelling noises I can hear, Jess's masseur seems competent but I've ended up with a damp squib of a newbie. Her fingers slide greasily over my back like slugs. Tension is bunching up in my neck; I'm desperate to ask her to give it some welly but the minute I do I fear the silence will be broken, Jess will remember I'm here – and start telling me how to live my life again.

I can't bear it any longer and clear my throat in preparation, but sure enough:

'Laura – how many people read your column?'

'Jess – this is meant to be relaxing,' I say, as my masseur gestures for me to flip on to my back. Oh please, not the full-frontal rub-down! I don't care what Jess says – I'm sure no Spanish contessa turns up here with shin stubble.

Jess props herself up on one elbow. 'How many readers?' she hisses.

I open my eyes and stare up at the reflective white tiles, then close them again.

'Quarter of a million in print, a million online in the UK, another two million globally.'

'That's phenomenal!' She reaches over to squeeze my little finger. My hands are now so oily her fingers slide off mine. 'You have an established platform, a clear voice, now monetise it! Leverage yourself, become a brand!' she whispers. When Jess starts talking like I'm a fabric conditioner it makes me want to Velcro my ears shut, or better yet – her mouth.

'Jess, can we talk about this in ten minutes?'

Her tut bounces loudly off the walls.

Bad idea to delay part two of The Jess Lecture! We're now lying in reclining chairs with two Indian ladies behind our heads, armed with what looks like dental floss, about to attack our eyebrows. I am officially trapped.

'Charles and I think you've paid your dues, you should be pushing Roger for new opps in editorial.'

'If I had a pound for every time you use the word should—'

'You should be earning a salary commensurate with your abilities.'

'Have you had threading before? It's no more painful than a wax,' says the beautician, rolling a thread of cotton over my eyebrow, then flicking it and ripping out half my excess eyebrow hairs from the root.

'Urgh, holy shit! Please don't do that again,' I say, struggling to sit up in the chair.

She brings her face close to mine. 'I have to do the other side or you'll be unbalanced.'

'If you rip the other eyebrow out of my face I'll be unbalanced.'

'Bloody hell,' says Jess, 'Over-sensitive eyebrows, who knew?'

'Will you shut up!' I say, sitting up in the chair.

'You shut up yourself. You know Mum and Dad didn't put you through university so you could become an expert photocopier. You can't seriously tell me you're going to be a secretary for the next thirty years?'

'Haven't quite finalised the thirty-year plan, but I'm certainly doing these two jobs for as long as I'm happy,' I say, gently prodding what's left of my brow.

'I *said* – keep the writing job if you go back into coffee!' she says, lying back down again.

I don't even get as far as counting to one: 'Jess! You are not my boss and you're not my mum.'

'Find something more substantial for the ninety per cent of your time you're not writing. It's been over four years, it's enough now. You've proved your point.'

'Four years ago I was not *proving a point*. I was trying to survive.'

Jess sits back up again and fixes me with a look I expect she uses a lot at work. 'Either you're in denial, or you won't admit it to me, but you hide in that PA job just as much as you do in the critic job; it's a comfort zone – you're too scared to leave.'

'Can I have a mirror please?' I say to the woman who's hovering nervously behind me. 'Jess – look at my eyelid! I've had enough,' I swing my legs down from the chair. '*Please* can we get a coffee?'

'I'm only giving you a hard time because I know you're capable of more,' says Jess, her voice softening temporarily as we take a seat in the top-floor café. 'And I know you get bored or you wouldn't be emailing us all those *Funny Things Cats Do* on the Internet . . . '

'*Cats In Tights* is what the Internet was invented for. And porn. Hopefully never the twain . . . '

'Stop being facetious, you know I'm right.'

Unfortunately my sister has a point. 'Honestly? There are times when I feel a little unchallenged. But I have a huge brain stretch with the writing, it's a dream job. It balances out. And being Roger's secretary is better than most PA jobs . . . '

'I know you're loyal to Roger but he's not in a position to repay the favour. How many years before he even retires? Your loyalty should be to you!'

'Two Americanos, please!' I say, catching the waitress's eye.

'We don't serve caffeine,' she says, as if I've just asked her to score me some crack.

Jess waits until the waitress has moved off, then reaches under the table and brings out a pistachio-coloured cake box.

'You remembered!' Sophie introduced me to Jean Clement's mille-feuilles a few years ago – she claims they can cure migraines. Medicinal properties aside, they do have eighteen layers of almost-burnt super-buttery flaky pastry, a heavy praline cream and a delicate vanilla sugar glaze. The first time I ate one I tried to eat the little JC disc on top even after I realised it was card, not sugar.

'And I have your stuff.' I reach into my bag to retrieve the Parmesan biscuits. 'And some posh gingerbread for the girls.' The biscuits have scarves and hats of blue and white stripy icing, and cute wonky smiles that look as though the gingerbread men have just done something naughty.

'You might notice your millefeuille's smaller than usual . . . ' says Jess, a smile on her face not unlike those of the gingerbread men.

'You ate some of my cake?' I grab the box from her hand. 'Outrageous!'

'You're always telling me to eat more cake.'

'Clearly I didn't mean mine!'

'How's your landlady?'

Landlady makes me think of an old woman in rollers and a floral housecoat – not a size zero blonde, who would wear a housecoat, but only if Carine Roitfield ordained it. 'Amber's started piloxing! Half pilates, half boxing . . . '

Jess sighs again. 'When are you going to find somewhere else to live?'

'Same day Sheryl Sandberg offers me a job as her second in command.'

'So, you intend to keep squatting in a spare room indefinitely?'

'Jess, do you think a random person's old shoe cupboard is my dream home?'

'And *that's* why you need a better-paying job!' she says, poking a victorious finger in my direction.

'And *that*'s the compromise I live with so I can do a job I enjoy. Change the subject.'

'What are you doing about finding a decent man?'

'Not that subject.'

'Come on, Laura. You're looking good – apart from your right eyebrow. But trust me, the collagen in your face will degenerate rapidly over the next five years. Find another partner now or before you know it you'll be forty and single.'

'Which is obviously the worst fate that could strike a twenty-first-century woman.'

'Oh, *I'm sorry*. Don't you want a healthy relationship? A family? Is that all so terribly bourgeois and distasteful to you? Your problem is you're too picky.'

Jess met Charles during Freshers' week. She has never experienced self-doubt about her attractiveness and has no idea what it's like being single in London right now: the illusion of limitless choices, everyone thinking they can do better than the person sitting opposite them in a pub, auditioning like they're on dating *X Factor*, no one giving anyone more than seven seconds to impress. I'm tempted to flick her through my Tinder Greatest Hits to show her the landscape I live in: would I show her the photo of the guy who's made a love heart out of hand guns? The pole dancing married man who says he misses the thrill of new conquests?

'Treat dating like a job. If you have a disappointment get straight back up again.'

'Actually, I did meet someone, ten minutes after I binned the last one,' I say, immediately regretting my inability to keep my mouth shut.

'So you are seeing someone!'

'We had breakfast on Thursday.'

'As in *Nice Girls Don't Stay for Breakfast*?'

'No, I don't mean a sleepover.'

'Who is he?'

'He's lovely,' I say, unable to keep from smiling. 'Bright. Funny, easy to talk to.'

'What does he do?'

'That's the slight problem . . . '

'You can't date a man who's unemployed.'

'He probably earns twice what I do. He's a chef.'

'Desperately anti-social hours.'

'That's not it either. He works at that place with the toilets.'

She allows herself a small gulp of laughter. 'So what? You haven't told him about your review?'

'No . . . '

'Well don't. You're always banging on about your anonymity like you're Deep Throat – why confide in a man you've just met? It's none of his business.'

'It's entirely his business.'

'What good could it possibly do you?'

'It's not about what good it could do *me*. I feel bad hiding something from someone I care about.'

'Oh, *this* conversation again!' she says, shaking her head in frustration. 'Laura, I don't know why you can't accept after all this time – we did what we thought was best in the circumstances.'

'Oh for God's sake Jess – this is not about Mum.'

She fixes me with a stare.

'It was not,' I say softly.

'Because it sounded like you were having a dig . . . '

'Well I wasn't. But actually now you mention it – the point is, you and Dad should have told me, you should have given me a choice.'

'You're not thinking of doing something stupid like pulling the review for his sake?'

'Absolutely not!'

'He served a terrible meal; your job is to hold the restaurant to account. What are you pulling that face for?'

'I'm not convinced he cooked it . . . '

'Well, go back and eat there again.'

'That's not how we work – plus it'll make me look flaky and unprofessional.'

'Then stop worrying!'

I'm about to say: but if Adam suffers because of my review, and he wasn't even cooking – that's not fair, but I can already hear Jess loud and clear: *Who on earth told you life was fair?*

'Anyway,' she says, taking her phone from her bag. 'You don't want a man who works nights. In fact! I'm going to set you up with JPM.'

'What's that?'

'*That* is James Paul-Martin. He's a total dish, looks like Federer, incredibly dynamic, newly divorced . . . '

'Oh right, the divorceés anonymous thing.'

'His ex was some dreadful South African gym bunny.' She leans forward and lowers her voice. 'Cheated on him with her Pilates instructor. I'll tell him to take you for dinner.'

'JPM's a bank, isn't it? Look, don't,' I say, trying to grab her phone. 'I really like this chef.'

'It never hurts to keep your options open, Thursday? Worst-case scenario, it's a free dinner.'

There is no such thing.

After Jess has left, I walk home to unwind from the onslaught. It's almost mild, and I meander the backstreets of Marylebone, head down, wishing I'd brought shades, or at least an eye patch.

I do not want to go on a date with another one of her banker friends. I would like to go on a proper date with Adam – and I don't want to have to wait a month until he gets a night off. It sounds so foolish – a week ago he was a stranger – but I've been thinking about him constantly since we met. Maybe it was the random greatness of last Sunday combined with that perfect breakfast on Thursday, the lift, the kiss, the kiss . . .

The truth is, I've tried to tamp down the hope that's trying to rear its head but I'm so excited about seeing him on Tuesday I can hardly wait. I fear I might have jinxed it by even mentioning him to Jess. I want to go to bed early tonight so I can wake up and it will be Sunday and then it's only two more sleeps till we meet. That's how children think about Christmas: that's because children still believe in Santa Claus.

And the truth is also this: I hate feeling this way, because it feels like I have someone – if only in my head. And if I have someone, then I also have someone to lose.

13

Monday is one of those days where I'm starving from the moment I wake up. By 11 a.m. I've demolished a lonely porridge pot, a banana, a packet of salted cashews and seven of Azeem's Munchies, so it's a relief when Heather summons me up to her office.

In my limited experience, I always thought a corporate lawyer's job was easy. All you had to do was cover your arse and say no to everything in varying shades of paternal concern: *Oooh, sorry but there's a risk involved; That's just too big a risk; Oh no – we cannot afford to be exposed to such unknown levels of risk* . . .

But Heather has a far ballsier perspective. She never says 'Cut this sentence out'; rather 'How can we keep it in?' She'll recraft your copy so it skates just the right side of the line, allowing you to say exactly what you intended, without the danger of someone suing, and putting our independent, not hugely well-funded magazine out of business.

'Laura!' she says, placing a copy of my review on her desk. 'Can I send a copy to my husband? He works with a bunch of Vulture Capitalists, and they're always trying to out-do each other with the most ostentatious restaurants; I'd better warn him off!'

'I can safely say it's the worst three hundred and eighty-seven pound meal I've ever eaten. So what do you think, how much needs revising?'

'Sit!' She pats the chair next to her. 'There are some specifics and then the general tone.'

'Sounds ominous . . . '

'Let's see:

> *1. Making diners queue in the rain for two hours when they could queue inside is inconsiderate. Making them queue to a single Jay-Z track is way past inconsiderate – it's a torture treatment devised by Kevin the Teenager.*

'2. Next time Kevin's rifling through his iTunes ask him to pick a song that doesn't refer to women as bitches – us bitches get uppity so easily.

'3. If there is a 'No reservations' policy, how come the table of six wearing Deutsche Bank fleeces walked straight to the front of the queue?

'4. And the couple who pulled up in an apple-green Ferrari . . .

'5. And the B-lister from I'm A Celebrity plus entourage . . .'

'That's all fine. Ah yes, points six and seven . . .

'6. With an eight million pound budget, I'm surprised you dress your hostesses head to toe in American Girlz batty riders.

'7. Did I say head to toe? I meant head to mid-butt cheek, like a gaggle of low-budget twerkers.

'Tell me,' Heather says, her fountain pen poised. 'What are batty riders – anything to do with Nora?'

'Definitely not. A batty is a bottom and batty riders are very, very short shorts that reveal most of one's . . . batty. So they're sort of like Spanx but with the opposite intention.'

'And how do you know these ones were from American Girlz?'

'I was trying to convey the fact the outfits looked quasi-porn starrish.'

'But did you actually see inside their batty riders?'

'I practically saw inside their batties . . . '

'Oh great Scott. All this talk of feminism,' she says. 'Sometimes I think it's a figment of the media's imagination. OK, so you're using American Girlz as shorthand for trashy – but you can't substantiate it so think of another way of communicating it. And perhaps consider changing batty riders to something old folk like me can understand? Next: the fact they tried to charge you for the cloakroom, are you certain it wasn't a suggested gratuity?'

'I handed my coat over, the girl said, "Five pounds." I thought she was joking. She wasn't, so I kept my coat.'

'And they refused to serve free tap water?'

'They added twenty-four pounds to the bill for a litre and a half of filtered tap water – we'd made it clear we wouldn't pay for it; Roger nearly had fisticuffs with the waiter.'

'Fine. The broad beans frozen, the strawberries not seasonal . . . ah yes, now this coffee thing: I feel embarrassed even asking, given all the lovely coffee you provide, but are you positive about this?

'89. Spare me your three-page coffee list. I know a little about coffee, and what you served me was Posh Instant, not in any way related to the single origin, El Salvador bean you charged £9 for.'

'One hundred per cent,' I say. 'The complexity of flavour profiles in real coffee is incomparable to granules or pods. Think of fresh coffee versus instant as the difference between watching *Gravity* at an Imax, versus watching it in black and white with no sound, on an iPod mini.'

'Because you're potentially accusing the restaurateurs of fraud . . . '

I shrug. 'They're lying to their customers and stealing from them. The fact their customers don't seem to know or care is beside the point.'

'OK. But if you're wrong, it's defamatory.'

'I'm not wrong.'

'Then keep it. Then your end comments – change "This is the worst restaurant in the Northern Hemisphere . . ." to "Is this the worst" . . . again, moves it from defamation. And then the last paragraphs are quite inflammatory, verging on ridicule.

'Jonn Zavragin – I've seen you on YouTube playing guitar. I'm sure if you asked AC/DC nicely they might find you a job better suited to your mid-life crisis . . . '

'You think I should tone it down?'

'It worries me slightly,' she says, tapping her pen distractedly on her desk. 'This is the most brutal tone you've taken; it reminds me of a review Fergus wrote years ago where he called Matthieu Garrigue the worst chef in London.'

'What happened?'

'Garrigue's lawyers kicked up an epic stink, said it was defamatory, claimed it had put customers off and that Fergus was a charlatan. Garrigue claimed he'd served Anjou squab instead of guinea fowl and Fergus had been too drunk to notice.'

That sounds like Fergus. One time I went for dinner with Roger and Fergus and the waiter accidentally gave Fergus my halibut, not his sea bass. It was only once the plates were cleared and I asked how he'd enjoyed my fish that he realised. He's never forgiven me, though Roger laughed so hard he practically needed the Heimlich.'

'Did Garrigue try to sue?'

'They sent a solicitor's letter but we argued Honest Comment and Vulgar Abuse.'

'Vulgar Abuse?'

'If you say something insulting but don't mean it *literally* – and that's clear to a reader – for example, "I'd rather cut out my own tongue than eat Garrigue's langue de chat" – you can get away with it. Anyway, Garrigue's PR firm leaked the whole thing to the papers. After that tiff you couldn't get a reservation for love or money. Sometimes you have to wonder if these spats aren't manufactured in the first place.'

'Would you rather I changed the end?'

She pauses. 'If Roger's happy? We've got this big exposé on Damian Bechdel, and the turkey piece, and if anything's going to kick off, it'll be those. So yes, it's fine. It's better than fine – you should give yourself a pat on the back.'

My subconscious must have taken Jess's warnings to heart because I find myself in my kitchen later, staring at a selection of collagen-rich ingredients on the counter. My phone rings. Panic! I'm so entirely over-invested in tomorrow's date, I bet it's Adam calling to cancel – but it's Sophie, telling me she's just missed her train. 'The next one's not till eight fourteen p.m., and they're going to make me buy a new sodding ticket. Can we eat at ten p.m.?'

'Could we do tomorrow instead?'

'Will the coast still be clear?' Sophie is currently avoiding my flat, given her and Amber's current beef/turkey.

'She's away all week, Gestalt-Ashtanga. Try saying that when you're drunk, definitely don't try doing it.'

The mackerel and asparagus go back in the fridge. Instead I look on the Leftovers website (it's genius) to see what to make with some old boiled potatoes, sour cream and bacon, and find a south-western jalapeño hash that's spicy, smoky and utterly delicious. Besides, a good night's sleep will make me look just as young as an oily fish. It's a shame Sophie's not around though, I could do with some distraction from thinking about Adam.

I could make a start on Second Helpings. It's an idea I pitched after I brought Roger a takeaway from Arrigato, off Gray's Inn Road. From outside it resembles a massage parlour and if you realised it served hand rolls, not hand jobs, you'd be even less inclined to enter, but it's one of the best sushi bars in London. I want to scream from the rooftops: look past the dingy walls and the green neon because THE FISH IS EXTRAORDINARY AND YOU CAN STUFF YOUR FACE FOR LESS THAN A TENNER! But it's the sort of restaurant that will never get reviewed – not just because Kelly Brook would never be papped falling out of its doors, but because it's been there a decade. There are over 10,000 restaurants in London and the only ones we review are the shiny, the sexy, the new. Surely it's far more interesting to read about places customers have stayed loyal to? I pour a glass of wine, start writing notes and the next time I look at my watch it's 10.30 p.m.

In the aftermath of my divorce, I decided food was the only reliable pleasure in this world – food and great American TV. Men can hurt you, friends can hurt you, butter cannot hurt you (your arteries might disagree). And so I literally do pinch myself (and I never use *literally* unless I mean it) on nights like tonight, when time flies and I remember how lucky I am to have a job that doesn't feel like work.

As I climb into bed, I can't work out whether I'm more excited about this idea or my date. I have so much adrenalin buzzing round me, I feel like I've drunk four double espressos.

Only eight and a half hours to go!

14

It's 3.23 a.m. All is silent outside my bedroom window, but inside my head it's party time! One negative thought bumping into the next and inviting more to join them for piña coladas.

The start of a relationship is such a fragile thing . . .

Stop thinking and go back to sleep.

Fragile like that coral shell on Aunty Ruth's mantelpiece all those years ago . . . It was an accident, I'd barely touched its delicate surface yet suddenly I felt it lose its shape under my fingers . . .

Meditation! Focus on your breathing!

I'm great at breaking things on date three . . . There've been half a dozen men since Tom, to whom I've said something damaging on the third date and things have fallen apart before they've started:
  Barrister Steven: I'd mentioned my divorce. He'd scrutinised me over his roast pork belly: 'Divorced? Already? Must be something seriously wrong with you.' I should have told him I was divorced earlier, but it hadn't come up.

I try adjusting my pillows, curling the top one into a ball, then two minutes later, fling it to the floor.

Joe from Guardian Soulmates, who told me to redirect my monthly donations away from Breakthrough Breast Cancer and towards the human rights charity he worked for. Apparently calling a guy a hectoring dick on a third date is a deal breaker . . .

If you turn the lights on now, you'll be admitting defeat.

Marc 'with a c', who said a woman over thirty who refused to give head on date three was over-estimating her market value, a 'seller in a buyer's market'.

Maybe the problem – now I think about it – was what those guys said to me, rather than my death-knell responses. Maybe I shouldn't have allowed them second dates, let alone thirds . . .

Still, I'm convinced I'm going to say or do something today that will make Adam realise I'm deeply uncool and far too keen. Even though we're only meeting for an hour again, I know I'm capable of doing considerable damage in such a short time.

Sod it: I turn on my bedside light and root under the bed till I find the equivalent of a horse tranquilliser: *Advanced Food Chemistry*. I've read so many books since I started my column but never made it past page 47 of this bad boy. And sure enough, next thing I know my alarm's going off at 6.00 a.m. and I've been using a diagram of an Extended Protein Peptide Chain for a pillow.

Right – not risking my outfit being the deal breaker; I pull out my ASOS red jersey dress with the low neck. Clearly too sexy for a 7.30 a.m. date but I love this dress and now it matches the veins in my eyes perfectly.

Bobby's is lovely – a bright airy space, with a wide selection of freshly baked pastries piled high on platters on the counter, flower pots of fresh mint on every stripped wooden table, and a mix and match of crockery.

Adam's sitting inside, head down over the paper, reading intently and when I say hi, he's caught unawares and looks up almost guiltily.

'What's Tuesday like for Capricorns?' I say, tipping my head to see what he's so interested in.

He closes the paper quickly and stuffs it by his side. 'It says, "Don't be swayed by what a Gemini orders. Tread your own path but why not order the praline brioche?"'

'You know what?' I say, taking a seat. 'I *was* thinking the praline, or perhaps the chocolate and raspberry croissant.'

'Actually I could do with ordering both – did I mention I'm doing a new pastry project? One minute . . . '

His phone is ringing and he reaches into his jeans pocket, looks at the caller ID then frowns. 'Sorry, I have to take this . . . ' He strides outside before answering and stands by the window, talking animatedly.

I order coffees and pick up his *Daily Metro* to see what he was reading. Not the horoscopes, I'm sure: . . . 'Energy firms hiking prices in spite of massive profits' . . . 'Fathers 4 Justice campaigning for improved fathers' rights' . . .

Oh, I see: *that's* what he was reading, Fergus Kaye's review of his restaurant. Little fibber, pretending he doesn't care what critics write.

10/10: 'Perfectly executed small plates . . . a simple tomato salad a master class in flavour . . . Cobb salad, festooned with elephantine chunks of avocado . . . ragwort sorbet made me want to scale The Needle and herald its glory . . . The most exquisite interiors since Claridges' Art Deco bar . . .'

You know nothing, Fergus Kaye.

68. It takes an immense talent to mess up a tomato salad.
69. The avocado was missing from my London Cobb salad. I double-checked, put my glasses on, used my Torch app: nada.
70. Also missing: the flavour, the texture.
71. Are you quite sure ragwort is edible? Last time I checked it was used to kill horses.

And 'Exquisite interiors'? Only if your idea of exquisite is Versace meets Liberace at a Bunga Bunga party. Fergus is obviously still shagging Petronella, LuxEris's PR girl – of course he's gushing. If Marina in the *Guardian* had given them top marks I might consider re-reviewing . . .

It's now 7.46 a.m. and Adam's still in heated conversation outside.

I bet he'll have to rush off on the dot of 8.30 a.m. Our time together is so limited, I can't help but calculate he's been on the phone for twenty per cent of our date. Might as well catch up on the gossip:

Recipe for Disaster
Celebrity chef Declan O'Brian today announced he is separating from his wife of 14 years. Rumours of an alleged affair had been circulating on Twitter, including one photo showing a sex act taking place in a walk-in fridge.

Humble Pie
O'Brian had previously begged forgiveness from his wife after admitting to fathering a love child with his PR manager. O'Brian blamed his behaviour on work. 'People have no idea of the extreme pressures of the professional kitchen, it's beyond anything imaginable . . . '

Those bomb disposal guys in Iraq might have something to say about that, Declan!

'Sorry . . .' says Adam, slipping back into his seat, looking perturbed. He takes a sip of his coffee before realising it's turned cold.

'Have you seen this?'

'No thanks,' he says, glancing at the pap shot of a defiant-looking O'Brian. 'I did part of my apprenticeship with him. The man's an octopus, thinks his staff are a perk of the job. He used to say "Pick a waitress, any waitress. It's not about if, it's about where and when . . ."'

'Where being the fridge, when being all of the time! Why *do* they call them love children when they're invariably conceived in a broom cupboard?' I say. 'Not a whole lotta love in that set-up.'

He glances again at his phone.

'You must have been out with a few front-of-house girls?'

'It's not something I'd go out of my way to do again in a hurry,' he says, briskly.

'By the way, Adam, were you not going to mention it?'

His face suddenly falls.

'Aren't you proud of yourself?'

His voice sounds almost panicked. 'Are you being sarcastic?'

'What?'

He pauses. 'What are you talking about?'

'The boy done good?'

'Laura, how did you . . .'

'You don't have to pretend you don't care what's written about you, I'd be happy. You don't look happy?' In fact he looks almost sick. 'You must be pleased with a review like that? I mean Fergus is a dick, but still . . .'

He shakes his head, as if rousing himself from a bad dream. 'Well . . . I . . . yeah, if it gets Ivan and Erek off my back . . .'

'Are you OK? You look stressed?'

'Yep . . . Sorry . . .' I can feel the vibrations from his leg tapping against the table.

'Adam, is something wrong?'

'Back in two secs . . .' He grabs his phone and heads outside again but this time moves away from the window. He's gone another ten minutes and I'm just debating whether to call him, text him, leave the café or order the pastries, when he rushes back in looking panicked.

'I'm sorry, Laura . . .'

'It's fine, we've still got almost half an hour—'

'I'm going.'

'You're what?' I stand abruptly as the paper falls to the floor. This is a new low for date three, even by my standards. 'You won't even stay for a quick coffee?' I wish the words falling out of my mouth didn't sound quite so desperate. I wish the dress I'm practically falling out of didn't look quite so desperate.

He shakes his head but moves closer and for a moment I think he might kiss me again. Instead, he takes a deep breath and fixes me with an expression that reminds me of Tom in the months before I found out about the affair.

There is guilt in this expression and something withheld. In Adam's case this look seems tinged with sorrow, seems to say: *I can't give you what you want.* The look I used to see in Tom's eyes had a different note: guilt without remorse: *I'm taking what I want; just not from you.*

'Laura, things are . . . I promise it won't always be like this.'

'What won't always be like what?'

'You and me.'

So we're *you* and *me* in his head too . . . And yet *he* can't spare *me* ten minutes for a coffee . . .

'Why do you have to rush off?'

He freezes. Now's the time to *let him speak*.

'Is it a work crisis, Adam?'

'Can you do tea later? I've got a split shift, I can bike over at four p.m.?'

Answering a question with a question: that is a definite sign, not a good one. Ignore it at your peril.

'I can't do tea today,' I say, my voice hardening.

'Breakfast then? Thursday?'

I shake my head.

'Shit. I have to go,' he says, looking pained. 'I'll make it up to you, I promise. It's such a bad time . . . but things in my life will be a lot clearer in a few weeks.'

'Whatever,' I say, and he's out the door and on his bike before my shoulders have even finished shrugging.

It's fine: the sun is almost warm, I can stroll to work through the tree-lined squares of Fitzrovia. The daffs are out, the crocuses too – buds wide open like newborn chicks, drinking sunshine. And I'll have time for a proper catch-up with Fabrizio. It's not Adam's fault there now seem more hours in the day than there were before I met him.

It's really fine: Adam doesn't owe me a thing. I'm an idiot for having invested so much mental energy in his direction, but I can't blame him for my daydreams. Do I need to be told, at my age, that Santa doesn't exist?

And it's fine because I reckon Adam has some issues. I'm sure he was having a row with that caller just now. And he's always moaning about his job and it's never good to be with someone who's unhappy in their work, it just isn't . . .

I knew it would fall to pieces sooner or later: better sooner – less of a disappointment, right? A short little slap in the face from reality never did anyone any harm.

The start of a relationship is fragile because it's made of pure hope: easier to crush than a shell.

'I don't understand why you're so upset,' says Sophie, pouring me another glass of wine as I clear our dinner plates.

'It's not like we were properly dating. I know it sounds ridiculous but I felt connected to him. I know about his family, his career, the name of his dead grandma's dead dog – but I guess all that is meaningless, just data, purely what a person chooses to tell you about themselves.'

'Laura, I understand why you like him. I don't understand why you think it's suddenly over?'

'If it had been the other way round, I'd at least have stayed for a coffee. Maybe it *was* something I said, I was rude about Declan O'Brien, and I teased Adam about his review . . . '

'Surely he's not that thin-skinned?'

'He said something weird, like "there are things in my life that will clear up soon . . ."'

'He's talking about his work,' she says, reaching under the table for the cake box she's brought over – Battenberg 2, Chocolate Boogaloo.

'Do we need forks?'

'A knife wouldn't hurt.' She follows me into the kitchen. 'What's Zoolamber got stashed in here anyway?' She opens a cupboard and starts inspecting the contents. 'What's she doing with a king-size bottle of Xylitol?'

'If Paltrow eats it, so does Amber.'

'*Egg white crisps*? They sound like the opposite of everything a crisp should stand for, and what on earth is Astaxanthin?'

'A son of Zeus . . . Do you want a cup of tea? You could sample Amber's Golden Rot and Knobgrass? Golden Rod and Knotgrass. Contains birch leaves and horsetail?'

She steers me back through to the wine. 'Don't look so worried. Adam sounds lovely. And that phone call will be nothing to do with you.'

'Maybe he met another girl before he met me, and that's who he was with on Sunday? I *thought* it was weird he didn't ask to see me on his day off . . . '

'Then he would have cancelled before the date,' she says, shaking her head. 'So he came back to tell you he couldn't stay? Or he sent a text?'

'He came back, flustered, looking shifty.'

'At least he came back.'

'Soph, only you can see the glass half full in being stood up mid-date. He offered to pop over for tea but I said no and I haven't heard from him since.'

'He'll be in touch, it's just a teething problem. You shouldn't have been so sharp with him about tea,' she says, finally opening the cake box.

'You've fixed your marzipan!'

She cuts through the icing to reveal a patchwork of cherry and chocolate squares. 'Dark chocolate, makes it less sweet but the frangipane balances it out. I'm going to try again on Thursday with milk chocolate. Laura: I understand why you're holding back; after James I thought I'd never trust anyone again.'

'It's more complicated than that . . . '

'Give him the benefit of the doubt.'

'I don't understand why you don't think his behaviour is weird?'

'But he's done nothing wrong.'

'Well, I'm obviously not explaining myself properly.'

Because if I was, I'm pretty sure she'd agree something's not quite right. But if I try to put it into words, I admit it does sound a little paranoid.

15

Roger's having a meeting in his office on Wednesday morning and while I'm making drinks my phone rings. For a moment I dare to hope it might be Adam but it's Kiki, calling from upstairs, with a message to come and see her.

'Are those new?' I say, spying a pair of hot pink suede boots in the jumble under her desk, toes pointing inwards like they're dancing to the Bee Gees.

'Forty pounds down from two hundred and eighty in Selfridges' sale, the joys of having size two feet,' she says, taking her red biro from behind her ear and making a note on the page in front of her. 'Maximum respect, Laura, you've ripped these guys a new one.'

'Thanks,' I say half-heartedly.

'I've got a few tweaks, so sit. OK, first up this needs revising:

> '2. *Next time Kevin's rifling through his iTunes, ask him to pick a song that doesn't refer to women as bitches – us bitches get uppity so easily.*

'You think Kevin The Teenager's too dated a reference?' I say.

'Not the problem. You're revealing you're a woman.'

'How did I not notice that? OK, put the full stop after the first bitches.

'Yeah, but having an issue with the word *bitches* in a Jay-Z track makes you sound like a politically correct pseudo-feminist – I'd rethink it. Right, point twenty-four:

> '*Describing your Earl Grey Long Island iced tea as Rohypnol in a glass is funny if you think rape is funny. Less so if you don't.*

'You don't need that second sentence,' she says.

I look at the page – she's right, as always.

'Then this whole section about water:

> '*25. Can your Water Waiter really not take an order for Diet Coke? The Water Waiter oughtta . . .*
> '*26. Let's spend a minute with the Water Waiter (if only his name was Walter, but no: Stefan.) Stefan described your fourteen waters' provenances. Tahiti, Cumbria, the Dolomites . . . I'm quite loyal to Thames Water but Stefan explained that 'House water'– triple filtered in-house – was the closest thing if I was 'on a budget'.*

'Down to here:

> '*33. Still on that water: £8 for a small bottle of in-house tap water? Next time: put your hand in my pocket and steal directly – much quicker.*

'Halve it – and that colon is superfluous.' She scribbles it out, then tips her head as she reconsiders. 'Actually, keep it. Then these:

> '*41. Rock salmon is not salmon from Rock in Cornwall.*
> '*42. It is also not 'Rock and roll' salmon – nice try, waiter number three.*
> '*43. It's OK to not know the answer – but don't lie!*

'Amalgamate to one – and finally:

> '*92. Semi-open kitchen – great to see the chefs at work. Less great when you have a kitchen run by a head chef who seems unable to control his team or even his frying pan.*

'It's quite vague,' she says, turning to me with a questioning look.

'Kiki, they were all over the place, you could feel the chaos in the air.'

'So put something more specific?'

'At one point there was a mini fire – the saucier must have let some cream run on to the solid top. I actually started feeling sorry for the station cooks, they panicked . . . '

'Put the fire in?'

'You know what? Don't. I need to keep word count down, and lose the word "head" from "head chef".' It's the least I can do.

'So it's worse than that Chelsea burger place?'

'Same owners! The Russian one wanted Kanye to play at his one year old's birthday.'

Kiki mimes a fake vomit on her desk so convincingly it makes me feel sick just watching.

'You should have heard the girl on the table next to us, moaning about how her dog wouldn't fit in her Hermès bag,' I say.

'Have you seen this?' Kiki types 'handbag – dog – California' into Google, then clicks on a photo of a labradoodle strutting down Hollywood Boulevard on its hind legs, carrying a handbag on its front paw. 'I can't believe the sub didn't go for a WAG joke in that headline,' she says in disgust. 'Amateur! And check out these poodles doing the conga!'

'Gotta love the Internet.'

With Kiki's revisions, the review will go down a few hundred words, though not enough to placate Sandra. I tinker with it till the end of the day, my heart growing heavy. Part of me thought Sophie was right and Adam would be in touch. She was probably right about me refusing to meet him for tea, it will have come across as harsh; still, I had my reasons. Though I can't work out now if it was instinct or pure paranoia – post-Tom I get the two confused.

I take my phone out to double-check Adam hasn't texted. No, nothing. I feel the disappointment afresh, a dull flip in my chest. Maybe I should text him to say I could do tea after all?

No. I shouldn't have had breakfast with him in the first place: this serves me right. My phone weighs heavily in my hand, my thumb hovering over his name. Surely it wouldn't hurt to say hi? My thumb taps insistently on the phone like a heart beat. I put my phone back in my bag, then take it straight out again, hold my breath and press delete, and delete his messages and his emails.

All gone.

And I feel so disappointed in him, or in the situation, or perhaps in myself, that when I find an email later from JPM asking me for a drink tomorrow at the most over-priced, pretentious bar in London, I say yes please, that would be lovely.

16

'Good shoes,' says Azeem, as he spies me putting the finishing touches to my outfit: dangly earrings and a pair of purple suede heels: minimal effort, no point trying to compete with the Beckham-clad Botox-faces at Marabou. 'Hot date?'

'Lukewarm, at best, Az.'

'Luke Warm's a lucky guy.'

'Not remotely funny, even by your standards.'

'Meow.'

'Sorry. I'm in a grump. Where are you off to, anyway?'

'Blues Kitchen with the ad boys. Come for a swift one?'

'I'm waiting for a call back from Stationery World . . . '

'Living the dream, Laura.'

I'm really pissed off with Jess. Ever since our row I can't help but notice the boring parts of my job now feel even more tedious. I'm in no rush to meet JPM – far from it, I only said yes out of despair. Still, Az is right; there's more fun to be had on a Thursday night than waiting for a call about missing lever arch files. I'm clearly irritable about Adam; it'll pass.

The phone rings a moment later. That'll be the files. 'Roger Harris's office, Laura speaking.'

'Laura speaking, it's Azeem speaking. I'm downstairs.'

'Don't tell me: Bradley's back.'

Azeem once called in hushed tones to tell me Bradley Cooper was in reception. He must have been in to see the TV guys upstairs! I raced down, only to find it was Jimbo, our 18-stone bike courier, wearing baggy meggings and a sweaty Mötorhead Live at the NEC T-shirt.

'No Bradley – but there's a package on front desk with your name on it.'

'Roger's tickets for his seminar next week, they said they'd bike them over.'

'I don't think so. Not unless they've warmed them up and stuck them in a cake box.'

Bless her! Well, that's a chocolate lining to a grey day. I'm tempted to eat Sophie's cakes while they're oven-fresh but I strongly suspect I'll need a healthy dose of sugar and fat to cheer me up in about two hours' time.

I'm going to kill Jess.

Technically you could call JPM handsome; his face is well structured, his hairline good for a forty-three year old. But there's nothing attractive about him once we start talking, or rather he does.

And I would have left by now, I would, but I am conducting an experiment to see how long it will take him to ask me a single question, even if that question is 'Laura, what do you think of me?' I may well see in my 40th birthday sitting on this Philippe Starck Perspex Ghost chair, if the piles don't kill me first.

So far he's covered his career: highest earning trader at Paribanque, retired at thirty, now investing in emerging markets. Also covered: the stunning refurb of his Fulham pad: glass staircase from kitchen to ground floor, floating glass staircase to the roof terrace, retractable glass roof. Lots of glass . . . even a flatscreen TV in the shower. (Sounds like a fire hazard to me.) Also, his cars: his Mercedes SLK, and the VW Touareg – he needs space for his golf clubs and actually it's the same body frame, doors, et cetera as the Porsche Cayenne. It's practically the same as the Porsche. (If only his T-shirt said *My other car is a Porsche* I might warm to him. But no; it says Hollister.)

He's currently talking about his ex. He can't bring himself to say her name, but refers to her only as The Ex. I am so tempted to ask whether the bloke she was shagging had a flatscreen TV in his shower too, but Jess would never forgive me.

'I was married less than a year and my ex walks away with two point three?' he says. 'How is that fair?'

I nod.

'You're divorced too, right?' Oh, if only that counted as a real question I could leave, but it's rhetorical so it doesn't count. 'I hope you didn't fleece your ex like The Ex fleeced me.'

'We were together nine years, married for two – but I didn't take a penny.'

'Are you serious?' Aha! A question! Now I can go!

'I used to earn the same as Tom. Besides, the day money actually helps mend a broken heart . . . ' I shrug.

'Your sister didn't mention you were a hippy.' He looks unimpressed. 'And now you're a journalist?'

'What?' I put my mojito down a little too forcefully.

'Your sister said you write for a newspaper?'

'Did she indeed?' I pick the straw out of my glass, my thumb pressed over the top, then release the cocktail, drop by drop, back on to the crushed ice. 'Well, I'm a secretary.'

'I thought you were a writery type?'

'Yes: I write emails and letters.'

'That's temporary, presumably?'

'No.'

'But I'm sure your sister said you do something with food?' All of a sudden it's Twenty Questions – I'm so killing Jess, twice.

'I just like to eat.'

'Oh. Do you want some food?'

'No, I'm fine, thanks. I should be getting on.' I pantomime look at my watch: I can't believe we've been here less than an hour.

'I consider myself a bit of a foodie. This place does great small bites, nothing too heavy.' He glances at the menu, snaps it shut and beckons the waitress over.

I reach forward to look: pretentious, over-priced fusion food, designed for customers with made-up eating disorders.

'We'll have four mackerel kimchee rolls and an eel ponzu ceviche but does that have soy? No soy,' he says to the waitress.

'Are you allergic to soy sauce?' I say.

'It has wheat in it.'

'Are you coeliac?'

'Wheat is bad for you.'

'Could we have the avocado salad too, please?' I say to the waitress. JPM's gaze moves from her cleavage to my thighs then swiftly back as he realises I've clocked him.

'And do your noodles have wheat in them? They do? Terrific, egg fried noodles with crispy duck.' I smile warmly at her. 'And extra sweet chilli sauce, please.'

'Don't worry, I'll pay for them,' I say, catching his look of disapproval.

'Did you know avocados are full of fat? And one bite of duck has three hundred per cent more grams of fat per hundred grams than skinless turkey breast meat.'

'Oh, please tell me more about skinless turkey breast meat?' It is possibly my greatest achievement as an adult female that I manage to say this sentence without it sounding sarcastic.

'Really?'

'Absolutely! I'm super interested. Like, is that nutritional analysis based on the breast being . . . boiled in water or fried in a non-stick pan?'

'Griddle pan, I think. I suppose you could poach it.'

'I shall try that!' Next time I give a flying rat's tit what you think about my weight.

'Do you not . . . are you not . . . ?'

'Not what, JPM?'

'Oh, nothing,' he says, then blows out the air in his cheeks. 'Do you ski?'

'Ski? No.'

'I just did my Advanced Off-Piste All Terrain in Verbier. I did Tough Mudder last year.'

I shrug my total lack of interest.

'Have you not heard of it?

'Hmm, I did read a piece about the modern male mid-life crises. Men nowadays either have an affair, buy a menoporsche or do the fitness thing.'

'Did you just say *men-o-porsche*?'

'Yes, it's an expression. Have you not heard of it?'

He shudders. 'There's nothing wrong with keeping fit.'

'And there's nothing wrong with the fat in an avocado – it's the good fat, there is such a thing.' Though obviously never to be found on a woman, as far as JPM is concerned.

He opens his mouth, his jaw juts out as if he's about to say something rather unpleasant and then he decides better of it. I have a vision of Jess's eyes darkening. A vision of her ranting about how RUDE and UNGRATEFUL I am on email tomorrow, and the day after . . .

'So, JPM. You're a foodie; do you cook much?'

'My ex used to do the cooking, clean and lean stuff. No point cooking for one, I usually grab a bento box after the gym and I eat out a lot with clients.'

'Where do you like to go?'

'There's so much going on in London, a lot of very cool places. I like Chiltern Firehouse, La Petite Maison in Mayfair, they've got one in Dubai too, I always pre-order the Label Rouge chicken with foie gras.'

'What's Dubai like?' I always imagine it would be soulless and money-obsessed.

'The weather's great, the shopping – they've got exactly the same places we've got here.'

'So you sit on a plane for eight hours and end up in a sun-scorched version of Knightsbridge.' But with a few less women's rights.

'Exactly! Terrific place for a holiday, you feel right at home. You should go.'

Yeah I *should* go – home. Right now, to Maida Vale.

It's nearly 11 p.m. by the time I extricate myself. For some reason, while JPM is able to ski a black run backwards, blindfolded, while giving Victoria's Secret models multiple orgasms just by thinking about them, he is unable to detect disinterest. That is *so* the key to success: be utterly thick-skinned, impervious to other people's opinions of you. What's that quote by Chanel? 'I don't care what you think about me, I don't think about you at all.'

I'm sure JPM's a perfectly nice guy. Scrap that: I'm sure he's not. But either way he's about as far from my type as I am from his.

When he asked me who my role models were, and I told him my mother, Tina Fey and Dorothy Parker, he said 'No men?' – then gave me a look that screamed: LESBIAN!

And when I asked, in a moment of drunken generosity, if he'd like to share a cake and mentioned I happened to have some Battenberg in my bag, he looked at me as if I'd asked him to lick a still warm badger I'd gnawed to death.

His loss, I can have it all to myself while I enjoy the final night of an Amber-free flat. I fling my coat on the sofa, off come my heels and I leave them *on the living-room carpet*. I grab my toaster from the bedroom to join us: I'm having a pity party, guest list: me. I fetch the cake box and lift the lid, ripping it roughly past its sellotape closure. Is it the milk chocolate version she mentioned on Tuesday or a revised dark chocolate? Quite heavy box, she's probably made both.

Oh. Or neither.

Inside the box are nine miniature pastries sitting on purple tissue paper. Three praline pecan brioches, three raspberry and chocolate croissants, and three savoury pinwheels – caramelised onion with bacon and rosemary.

And sticking out from under the tissue paper: a note.

From Adam.

He must think I'm playing it super cool, when the truth is if I hadn't deleted his details I'd have contacted him immediately and offered to lay myself down at his feet.

I attempt to eat one of each pastry, slowly, but three are gone in nine bites: the first a light as air, not-too-sweet brioche topped with a sticky salty toffee sauce, crowned with caramelised pecans. Remind me – how do French women not get fat?

The dark chocolate and raspberry croissant is the same flavour I was eyeing up on Tuesday, but Adam's taken the concept and run with it. Dark and white chocolate chips have semi-melted against the raspberries to make the whole thing jewel-like. I don't know how he's achieved this texture, either; it's rich and buttery without a hint of greasiness, layer upon layer of delicate pastry with a dark intense, oozing rope of chocolate at the bottom.

But my favourite is the savoury one – it's the best thing I've eaten since . . . since 3 June last year, when I ate a pulled pork bun at Pitt Cue, which moved me almost to tears.

The pastries alone would have done the trick but then there's the note:

Laura,

When you google 'ways to apologise to a girl + endearing breakfast-related quotes', you get nothing, nothing I tell you! I'll have to say it myself: breakfast is not the same without you, Laura Parker. My life is a world of pain right now, but bear with me?

PS Are you around on Sunday?

OK, so I *was* reading too much into Tuesday. Sophie was right: all is fine, all is fully back on track.

17

He texts me the following morning as I'm sitting at my desk, buzzing with the return of hope.

Did you get the pastries? What do you think?

Delicious – hope you don't mind, I gave one to Sophie, and Fabrizio.

Sure – I meant, what do you think about Sunday? Are you OK to come to mine?

At last! A breakthrough! Get to see his flat, get to snuggle up on a sofa with a bottle of wine. More importantly, get to the bottom of it once and for all . . .

Adam, can I ask you a favour for Sunday?

As long as it doesn't involve Morris dancing or watching Moulin Rouge.

On Sunday, please will you cook for me?

Sandra is standing with her back to me in Roger's office as I hover awkwardly behind her.

'The less heads in the room the better,' she says to Roger. 'We need a closed session with Heather.'

Roger tries to catch my eye, but she blocks him like a goal defence. He looks exhausted today, and slightly yellow. He had an editors' dinner last night at the House of Commons – he must have been hitting the Scotch hard. 'What are we covering again?' he says.

'The housekeeper's testimony, and the transcripts from the receptionist at The Latimer, confirming Bechdel's stay; so the seck-sual allegations,' she says, her voice as repulsed as if she's having to clear up Damian Bechdel's wet Y-fronts from a bathroom floor. 'And the contents of the Play Room in the Cotswolds house.'

Roger raises a brow. 'The Play Room!'

'I cannot stress how sensitive this material is,' she says, clearing her throat. 'And we need to discuss SunFarms: the source at the abattoir, and the evidence of cannibalisation in shed birds.'

He looks up at me with a wry smile. 'Sex, drugs and turkey-eating turkeys! You're missing out on all the fun this morning!'

I raise my hands to say it's his call. 'I don't mind, but who's going to take minutes?'

'Don't worry about that,' says Sandra, sharply. 'Did you shorten your piece yet?'

'A bit. It's in the studio, waiting to be laid out.'

'Well, if you haven't enough to do, get us lunch.'

'Roger?'

'Hmm?'

'Are you OK?' I say.

'Just need to call Gemma . . .' he says, rubbing his left shoulder. 'What's the time difference in Bangkok, eight hours?'

'Low fat cheese salad for me,' says Sandra. 'Roger . . . ?'

'Oh, just a sandwich.'

'Filling preference?' I say.

'Anything but turkey.'

'Kiki – do you fancy coming down Whitecross Market for lunch?'

'Give me ten, I'm just editing Henry's review of the new Sorrentino.'

Ten minutes – more than enough time to check out Barnaby Ballen's latest witterings. After three years of writing The Dish I've come to know the other critics' palates well. It's reassuring when a critic I love agrees with me; but nothing gives me greater pleasure than when Barnaby disagrees, because Barnaby should be stuffed in a KFC Variety Bucket and force-fed popcorn chicken until he explodes. He literally uses the word 'literally' in every review: never accurately.

This week he's reviewing Milktavern, a place I ate at last month. The waiters were eager but the food was sub-average: hard potato dauphinois and a crème brûlée like tinned Ambrosia with cocoa stirred through – barely acceptable on a desert island.

Milktavern is delicious, delightful and udderly delectable.

If I made jokes about udders, Roger would fire me on the spot; and don't get me started on that alliteration . . . Oh, and wait for it!

I was literally in heaven when I ate the chocolate crème brûlée.

No, Barnaby, you were not in heaven, you were in Clapham, I can assure you they are not the same place, and if your dad weren't also your boss you'd be in Borstal.

My phone rings – Kiki. 'Sod it, I'm outside already, having a fag.'

We walk up Clerkenwell Road, drawn by the smoky smell of chorizo. The market here is amazing – proper street food, not the overpriced crap passing itself off as that at LuxEris. Within a twenty-metre stretch, you can find lunch from fifteen different countries, all for around a fiver.

'I'm tempted to get Sandra an Ethiopian curry,' I say, as we pass a stall selling a pungent, bubbling stew alongside puckered flatbreads. (Sandra believes any food with garlic in is not to be trusted. She also believes homosexuality is a choice.) 'Do you fancy a curry, Kiki?'

'Not as much as I fancy duck confit on brioche with melted cheese and caramelised onion chutney, served by a Michael Fassbender lookalike,' she says, peering towards the end of the row of colourful stalls.

'He's at King's Cross on a Friday, how about Le Bowski?' I say, checking my watch.

Le Bowski is a grey-haired French hippy – could be 45 and a heavy weed-smoker, could be 70 and a yoga fanatic; either way, the man takes SIX minutes to make a single sandwich – but what a sandwich! He sources the best ciabatta in London (from Bread Ahead) – slices it in half, then drizzles its insides with fruity olive oil. Then he lays down the freshest salad as a bed for Italian tomatoes, seasons them with Maldon and leaves them to get fruity. I think maybe Le Bowski *is* permanently stoned because he seems unaware of the price of avocados; he puts a whole one in each sandwich, and then three-inch wide ribbons of cheese, decorated with fresh herbs. And on top of all that, you get a cabaret. Today he's playing Stevie Wonder, and dancing like my dad at a wedding.

'You're looking chuffed!' says Kiki, as we stand, salivating at the work in progress. 'Did you get some last night?'

'No . . . but I do have a hot date on Sunday!'

'Tinder guy?'

'What, Russell? He's long gone,' I say, silently cheering as the man in front checks his watch, shakes his head and abandons the queue.

'I don't blame you,' says Kiki. 'I wouldn't date a man with a kid either.'

'That had nothing to do with it.' I'm surprised she thinks it would.

'Way too much baggage. All those boring play dates and having to weave bracelets?'

'I like kids. I quite like weaving bracelets.'

'I might get up the duff when I'm like forty, but step-mum to some other woman's kids? No way.'

'In some respects I think it's reassuring – it shows a man doesn't want to pursue an entirely selfish existence. Better than some eternal playboy . . . '

'Having a kid doesn't make you unselfish,' she says, sharply. 'The shagging bit's not hard.'

I turn to Kiki – so confident in her youth. 'When you're heading to the wrong side of your thirties you kind of expect you'll meet someone with a bit of history.' And I'm *a seller in a buyer's market*.

She shrugs. 'Look who I've matched with!' she says, taking her phone and tapping a photo of a shirtless guy who looks like an Abercrombie model. 'He's a fireman, or says he is!'

It's impossible to keep up with Kiki's love life. She has a massive churn rate due to her intolerance for *flaws*. She applies her subbing skills to any incoming male communications and woe betide the man who uses excessive CAPS or an exclamation mark where it might, perhaps, be unwarranted. She once dumped a cute, quite funny doctor because he finished a text with ;-)

Perhaps when you're beautiful, petite and twenty-eight you can afford to be so cavalier. Still, I feel like shaking her and saying: if you can find a man who doesn't secretly hate himself or hate women, and smells reasonably fragrant, hold on for dear life.

To: Laura
From: Sandra
Subject: URGENT

Can you write up the minutes from earlier by 3 p.m.? If there's anything you can't understand – don't guess – ask.

Yes, actually, two things! One – if it was so top secret I wasn't even allowed in the room, why am I suddenly allowed to write the notes up? And two, when are you less of an officious cow? Bank Holidays? Leap Years?

Still, even she can't rain on my parade today.

To: Sandra
From: Laura
Subject: re: URGENT

My pleasure. Would you like a Nescafé? Am just about to make myself a drink.

To: Kiki
From: Laura
Subject: help . . .

Are you at your desk? I can't decipher Sandra's handwriting and don't want to give her the satisfaction of thinking I'm a moron.

To: Laura
From: Kiki
Subject: re: help . . .

In post-cheese sarnie carb coma.
   Sandra's handwriting always gives me a migraine, but come to my desk and I shall assist – plus I have a new photo of fireman and his pole!

To: Azeem, Laura
From: Kiki
Subject: Third time lucky

Laura actually has some real work to do this afternoon, for once – so looks like you're on cake run again. I believe in you, Azeem – I know you can do this!

To: Dad
From: Laura
Subject: Skype

I'm with Sophie tomorrow morning, so call me anytime after 3 p.m.? Hope the ballet goes well – give the girls a kiss from me.

To: Laura
From: Sophie
Subject: The nuts!

Tell Adam his praline brioche is as good as anything I've had from Jean Clement – and could you possibly find out where he's sourcing his pecans from? They're impossible to make work commercially.

PS See, paranoid android? I told you there was nothing at all to worry about.

To: Sophie
From: Laura
Subject: Nut job

I thought you said finding a nut in a brownie was like finding a tooth in one?

To: Laura
From: Sophie
Subject: Blondies have more fun . . .

Nuts have no place in brownies, blondies are a different ball game: maple pecan, pistachio white chocolate, etc. . . .

To: Laura
From: Adam
Subject: Celebrity cheapskate

Check out this picture of who was in at lunchtime. He left a 4% tip. I'm sure he's on the *Sunday Times* Rich List, and the right end at that.

BTW, any preference on what you want me to cook on Sunday? My signature dish is a 72-hour braised short rib, but we've only got 37 hours between now and then, most of which I'll be spending kicking Max's arse.

To: Adam
From: Laura
Subject: Easily pleased

You're the chef, I'll leave it in your hands . . .

PS – Sophie loved your pastry – and asked if you know a good pecan supplier?

To: Laura
From: Adam
Subject: re: Easily pleased

Beans on toast it is, then.

PS Ping me her email and I'll hook her up with our guy.

To: Adam, Sophie
From: Laura
Subject: Pecans

Just hooking you two up so you can talk nuts . . .

To: Sophie
From: Laura
Subject: Quickie

Do you think I should get a wax or is that tempting fate?

To: Laura
From: Sophie
Subject: Tempting fate – and wear your worst pants

Just had a phone call about catering a huge party for you will NEVER guess who! Tell you more when I see you.

Adam is a total sweetheart! He sent me his supplier's details and is going to get me a trade discount – I wasn't expecting that.

To: Laura
From: Sandra
Subject: Accuracy

There are two ways of spelling discrete: discreet and discrete – and they mean entirely different things. Could you revise page six, paragraph four of your notes accordingly.

18

Dad calls me on Skype on Saturday, just as I'm taking a saucepan out of the cupboard and working out which pasta shape to boil.

He appears on my computer screen, sitting in his living room, bookshelves in colourful disarray behind him.

'I've got a video of the Munchkins for you,' he says, his face as excited as a child's.

'Can I watch it after supper?'

'Watch it with me now – it'll only take five minutes. I've just emailed you the video file.'

I put the saucepan down, take a seat and drag the file out of my inbox and on to a separate window on my computer, so I can see the video – and Dad – at the same time.

'Is it working?' he says. 'Turn it up so I can hear which bit you're watching.'

I press play and the school assembly hall appears. Dad's camera pans round to show an audience of around sixty parents and grandparents, iPhone cameras at the ready – all chattering and looking expectantly at the stage at the back.

'I arrived early to get a decent seat and would you believe? The Doucettes beat me to it – they must have camped overnight. Your sister arrived a minute before kick off, as per usual . . . '

In the video, you can hear Jess in the background hissing to Dad: 'My meeting ran late and I couldn't find a cab. Urgh, bloody Patrice Doucette and his stupid oversized SLR, the man's insufferable.'

Twenty little ballerinas, dressed in pale-blue tutus file on to the stage to form four uneven lines. Rose is standing in first position on the front row, shoulders back, neck long, chin high, her eyes focused on the teacher. Milly, her skinny calves dotted with bruises, and a plaster on one knee, stands at one end of the back row, her gaze already distracted by a collage of dinosaurs made of felt, stuck to the wall.

'Wow, good hair, Dad. What's that called?'

'Rose? That's a waterfall plait with a high bun – it took me hours studying YouTube to get the hang of it.'

'And Milly . . . what happened there?'

'Oh dear . . . she wanted it to look like the younger Princess from *Frozen* but she wouldn't stop fiddling with it. Ooh, here we go!'

Hush descends in the audience as a pianist starts playing and the ballerinas start the dance, moving round the hall in a scattered circle, half-elegant, half chaotic.

'Wow, Rose is getting good,' I say, as my niece pretends to pick daisies and places them in an imaginary pannier, her tutu gently rising and falling as she bobs gracefully to the floor.

'She's been in character all week. If anyone's going to be a prima in this family besides Jess . . . '

'And what is Milly up to?'

'It looks like an arabesque, though if I'm not mistaken it's supposed to be a demi-plié.'

Milly's face is a mix of confusion and panic as she looks towards her sister – two minutes her elder – to check how the move should be done.

'*Jeté derrière*,' cries the teacher, and Rose springs up and down, smoothly, like water in a fountain, the tip of her tongue poking out in concentration.

' . . . and there's Milly's doing La Danse du Pogo Stick, as it is known by our Gallic cousins . . . ' says Dad, his face crinkling in delight.

Milly's efforts descend into a blur of tulle, pink cheeks and giggling while her sister pirouettes past, confusion now on her face.

'Rose asked me the other day if Milly was adopted,' says Dad.

'You did point out the obvious, didn't you?' I say, as the music ends and the dancers come to a stop – their faces a mixture of relief, satisfaction and pride.

'I'm pretty sure she was joking but you never know with Rose.'

Milly starts waving to Dad, then rushes to give him a hug. Jess takes the camera from Dad's hands to film Milly as she settles, temporarily, on his lap.

'Say hello to your aunty,' says Jess, and Milly's beaming smile fills the screen as she waves at the lens.

'Look at this, Law-law!' she says, wobbling one of her bottom teeth violently for the camera.

I press pause on the video. 'Has that fallen out yet?'

'Last night! She hasn't yet worked out what she'll spend the Tooth Fairy's money on but I guarantee it will be purple. Press play again – you must watch the curtain call, Rose does a perfect Princess Kate.'

Back on the video, Milly's small fingers move towards the screen as she fiddles briefly with Jess's hair. Then she clambers off Dad's lap and bounds back to take her place next to her sister. Dad's gaze stays on the dancers taking their umpteenth bows as the air fills with delighted applause. When he turns back to camera, I notice he is smiling gently, but his eyes are watering.

And it's hard to know whether the tears are simply brought on by his love for these perfect little imperfect creatures, swirling and curtseying and giving one final twirl for the crowd. Or whether they're because Dad is thinking – as am I – of the one person who's missing from the audience.

19

On Sunday I find myself outside a small Victorian terraced house around the back of Angel in a quiet road full of Volvos. I double-check I've got the right address, then climb the front stairs and ring the doorbell to Flat 23a.

No answer, but there's a light on downstairs and I can hear music. I ring again. Still no response. I've been burnt like this before: a third date who invited me round, then wasn't there himself! I check my watch – midday, on the dot. I call Adam's phone and he picks up on the second ring, blues playing loudly in the background. 'Sorry, stereo was on, I'll be right up.'

He opens the door with a broad smile. He's wearing a grey T-shirt and jeans and he's obviously been cooking as there's a tiny smudge of flour on his cheek.

'Thanks again for being so cool about today,' he says, leaning in to kiss me briefly on the lips.

I wasn't aware I had much choice! Just as well I didn't bother getting a wax, 12 p.m. till 1 p.m. and then he has 'stuff to take care of'? Still, at least it wasn't a blow out.

'We could have re-arranged,' I say – but I only say it because I'm standing with both feet already in his hall.

'Sorry again about Tuesday,' he says, taking my coat, 'I don't know where this week has gone.'

My week has lasted a month; the three minutes spent watching JPM chew like a rabid hound on his mackerel sashimi felt like an entire day.

'And besides, I didn't want to cancel – I want to borrow your mouth,' he says, grinning.

'Any time. Is that Welsh Rarebit I can smell?'

'Come see!' He turns on his heel and heads down the stairs.

'Adam, whoever cuts your hair has missed a bit.'

'Where?'

'Just here, at the back,' I say, reaching out to touch the nape of his neck. His skin is warm and soft. He rests his hand briefly on top of mine to find the spot.

'Do you want to straighten it out for me?'

'Me? Now?'

'I'm not precious, I can't see the back anyway.'

I follow him into his bathroom. He roots around in his medicine cupboard until he finds scissors, then sits on the edge of the bath and looks at me expectantly.

I move closer and end up standing sideways on to him, half his body touching mine. He must be able to feel my heartbeat quicken against the back of his shoulder through his thin cotton T-shirt. There is silence in the room, but for our breathing, and all I can think about is how great he smells, how I want him to pull me closer, how much I want him to borrow my mouth. The angle would be awkward for kissing, and I'd have to mind these scissors, but our bodies could be entwined in less than two seconds . . .

I try to concentrate, taking a lock of his hair. It's so thick and soft and shiny I find myself rubbing it slowly between my thumb and forefinger.

'Are you sure you don't mind me doing this, Adam?'

He tips his head back and looks at me through dark lashes. 'I like you doing that.'

Almost imperceptibly he shifts his left arm, which is hanging down by his side. He moves it very slowly, and only a matter of centimetres, until his little finger ends up making contact with my leg, gently grazing the front of my knee. It is the tiniest of moves but it stops my breath.

He doesn't acknowledge it, I don't either, but its presence there makes my insides flip over. He shows no signs of moving his finger away but nor any signs of moving it further north. Heavy silence spreads through the room like an aerosol. The skin on Adam's neck is so smooth, I have a powerful urge to lean over and kiss it. My body leans closer into his and I have to force myself to stand up straight and take a breath.

'Sorry, Adam, I meant you don't mind me cutting your hair with nail scissors?'

He looks up at me again with those pale blue eyes. 'I trust you, Laura.' I hold his gaze as the remaining air in the room seems to vanish down the plughole. 'But you might want to hurry up, if you don't want lunch to burn . . .' He turns his head to face forward and down again to offer up a better angle for the scissors.

I snip carefully through the strands between my fingers, then brush the stray hairs gently into the bath, blowing delicately to rid his skin of the remaining dark flecks. 'Do you want me to do that mirror thing behind your head?'

'You're all right,' he says, standing back up and rotating his broad shoulders in a circle. 'That kitchen's going to kill me.' He reaches one arm behind him to massage his shoulder and his T-shirt rides up at the side exposing a firm, flat stomach. I catch sight of myself in the mirror. The lust blazing in my eyes reminds me of a teenage boy at an end-of-term summer disco. I force myself out of the bathroom before I go all out and grope him.

'Wow, major kitchen envy,' I say, as we enter a bright open-plan kitchen, flooded with light from a glass wall at the back. Stainless steel and copper pans sit on open shelves alongside kilner jars filled with colourful beans and pulses. 'So, what's on the menu then, Chef?'

'Please don't call me Chef, it reminds me of work.'

'All right then, Grumpy, what are you making?'

Laid out on the central island are various metal bowls of ingredients: chopped tomatoes, green chillis, grated Emmental, crispy fried lardons, smaller bowls of coloured salts.

'You're getting baked beans,' he says, taking a cast-iron pot from the oven.

I laugh, and dodge out of his way as he carries the pot to the hob.

'Oh, I'm serious. Home-made beans and an omelette – given how dismissive you were about the skill it takes to perfect one!'

'I know it's not *that* easy but it's not exactly open-heart surgery.'

'Backtracking already? Well, either way,' he says, sweeping his arm out in front of the array of ingredients, 'May I present you with the Laura Parker Omelette Bar.'

I clap my hands in delight. 'You have no idea how much I love an omelette bar, it's the thing I get most excited about if I ever stay in a posh hotel.'

'Thank goodness.' He dabs his forehead with the back of his hand. 'I thought you might be disappointed I wasn't making anything fancier – but I'm more into simple stuff.'

'"Simplicity is the ultimate sophistication . . ."' I say, remembering the quote I'd used for the noodle bar review we've now dumped for April.

'That's very true; you're so smart.'

'Oh, it's not my line! Leonardo da Vinci said it.'

'Well, he's very smart, then. And seriously, if you do like simple food, stay well away from my gaff . . . '

'Actually I was thinking I might come and eat there quite soon . . . '

'Really? It's totally overpriced. But if you do – don't order the eels. That dish is proof Jonn has finally lost it. He wanted something quintessentially English but to him that's some weird hybrid of *Downton* and *Mary Poppins*. He can't just let ingredients speak for themselves, he has to give everything a *punk twist*. For example – savoury puddings are big in New York . . . '

> 88. *I don't care if savoury desserts are trendy in The Big Apple; your Apple and Veal Crumble with tarragon custard made me want to cut out my own tongue.'*

'. . . . And Jonn basically lets puns, rather than intelligent flavour combinations, dictate his menu, so he came up with Eels Flottante . . . '

A flashback comes to me, of sitting on my bathroom floor with one of those eels trying to slither its way back into my mouth.

'. . . I have begged Jonn to take that dish off the menu, it's the most horrible force fit of ingredients that should never be in the same room as each other . . . '

"'A mail order bride of a dish, a marriage that isn't fooling *anyone* . . .'" I say.

He stops in his tracks. 'That's a perfect way of describing it!'

One that will now have to be cut from my review . . .

'Laura, you do have a way with words, don't you?'

'Adam, do you mind if we talk about something else?'

'You don't like eels?'

'It's not the eels.'

Tell him.

He pauses, looks a little crestfallen. 'You don't like it when I talk about work, do you?'

'Don't I?' Now who's the one answering a question with a question?

'If I talk about the restaurant you often change the subject. I guess it's boring for you.' Now he thinks I'm uninterested and rude.

I really could just tell him, right now. Explain everything, it would all make sense, it's not *that* big a deal, as Roger always says, it's tomorrow's fish and chip paper. Maybe Adam would appreciate the fact I've tried to avoid him talking about his work?

Or maybe he'd think I was a bitch for not telling him sooner.

'It's not that, Adam. It's just . . . people are so defined by their work; there's more to a person than their job.'

Cop out! Go on: slip it in, make it casual!! Or better yet, ask him: *where the hell were you on 27 February, between 9.05 p.m. and 12.14 a.m. even though you've already told me you haven't had a shift off? Why am I asking? Oh, no reason, just making chit chat . . .*

Leave it, it'll ruin today. And besides, if his cooking's better – re-review: the problem disappears.

'But being a chef's not a normal job,' he says. 'Your life *is* your work. It's in your head and your heart.'

Awesome – I'll be stabbing him in two body parts then – three if you include his back. Unless . . .

'Adam, I'm sorry if I made you feel bad. You were saying, about Jonn's ethos.'

'You sure?' The relief in his voice is palpable.

'I like talking about food. Not eels maybe.'

156

'OK then . . . Well, Jonn wanted a savoury twist on Bread and Butter Pudding – I suggested a version with a brioche loaf, bacon jam and a topping of three cheeses.'

'You had me at bacon jam.'

'But Jonn wanted to shoehorn afternoon tea into the dish so he layered in Darjeeling-smoked cucumber foam – '

I laugh. 'Like anyone ever sits down to eat, thinking, "Wow, I am *seriously* craving a plate of foam today."'

'Jonn's dish doesn't even make sense conceptually. He used to have the best palate and now he's just a gimmicky, bloated, coke-raddled sell-out.'

'That restaurant is so not you, Adam.'

'I didn't realise it would be quite so bad – I'm improving the menu and bringing the team up to scratch, but it's the attitude I find depressing – style over substance. Get my star and get out!' he says, rolling his eyes skywards. 'Anyhow, the whole savoury pudding disaster got me thinking about savoury Viennoiserie. Viennoiserie are usually sweet breakfast pastries – croissants, pains au chocolat – normally made using lamination, where you wrap layers of dough around butter.'

I nod my interest, though I know a bit about Viennoiserie, all about cold butter, cold fingers.

'I'd like your opinion on the pastries in the oven, they're part of a project I'm doing for myself – but first things first,' he says, checking his watch. 'Hold on, bread!' He bends to take a paper bag from the shelf and as he stands, winces in pain, his hands moving to his lower back.

'Are you OK?' I say, moving closer, stopping just short of rubbing it for him.

'My back's ruined, and my knees. Occupational hazard, nothing a little Voltarol won't fix. I should get some physio but I haven't got a spare moment.'

'You should make some more time for yourself.' And for me! Though I can't work out how he's ever going to do that. 'Take a holiday?'

He laughs and hands me the bread. 'Even just a day away would be better than nothing. Would you mind slicing that, please?'

'Will you throw something at my head if I don't slice it straight?'

'I'll have you clean the deep-fat fryer,' he says, grinning.

I give the bread a squeeze. 'This is St John sourdough isn't it?'

'You really know your food.'

'Crime scene – bacon sandwich . . . '

'Ah, yes, interest on that doughnut fiver's accumulating,' he says, as he grabs an omelette pan and places it on the hob. 'Slice it about one point five centimetres thick?'

'Yes, Grumpy.'

'Why Grumpy?'

'You said not to call you Chef.'

'Oh, I'm not grumpy anymore,' he says, looking directly at me. 'I'm happy. For the first time since I last saw you.'

Did he just say that? I pause, and look up from the chopping board.

He's gazing at me with the sweetest expression. He does look incredibly happy and for a second I forget we're not married, not even a couple and I automatically do this silly thing I used to do with Tom: point my finger at my eye, my heart and then at him – before realising with horror what I've just done.

In panic I instinctively turn and walk to the fridge. After ten seconds of standing frozen, staring at the door, I open it – pretend to look for something – and instead stare at the light at the back for two full minutes, as the smell of bread toasting scents the air.

How utterly mortifying. It wasn't even about Adam. It was just – for a moment there – I thought I was back in domestic bliss. Tom and I ended up using that gesture as shorthand for a hundred things: *I'm happy* or *Thanks for taking the bin out* or *Your turn to do the dishes*. It came to mean so many things – and I feel a desperate need to explain this fact to Adam: *of course I didn't mean 'I love you', Adam! I merely wanted to communicate that I'm looking forward to my omelette and beans.*

Perhaps he didn't actually see me do it? Maybe he was reaching for the eggs as I pointed to my eye? Behind me I hear the sound of one egg being cracked, now two . . . Yep, I might have got away with it. And then again, I might not.

'What do you want in your omelette, Sous?'

'Er . . . yeah, eggs,' I say, wishing I could climb into this fridge and freeze off this burning shame.

'Anything else? You looking for something?' His voice registers nothing either way. I hear the butter start to sizzle in the pan.

'Bacon?' I say, finally turning round. Adam's deep in concentration, pouring the eggs into the pan and looks up at me with a questioning look.

'You OK?'

'Just looking at . . . at that picture on your fridge. Where was that taken?'

'Two secs.' He grips the pan, nudges the edge of the omelette with the spatula and deftly folds the eggs into a perfect roll, which he slides on to a plate on which sits the buttered toast. Swiftly he moves to the hob and carefully spoons a swirl of luscious beans in a curve, hugging the side of the toast, then dips his fingers in a bowl of salt flakes and lets them fall in a delicate cascade. He carefully picks a few strands of micro-cress from another bowl, places them on the omelette, then gets a squeezy bottle of dark green oil and traces a delicate scratch over the dish. His whole body is focused yet relaxed. It moves instinctively – as though his muscles are so familiar with every tiny movement they could perform independently of his brain. I can't help but stare at the flex in his forearms as he works, then down to his fingers – strong, nimble.

'Omelette and beans, Madame,' he says, looking down modestly at his work of art, then pulling up a barstool next to me.

66. Sophocles said The First Taste is With Your Eyes: worth passing on to whoever plated up tuna ceviche with deranged brown smears zigzagging over the plate, like Jackson Pollock's toilet exploded.

'Adam, is it ever so hectic at your place you don't have time to make things look as pretty as this?'

I look at him closely though what am I expecting to see? The word *guilty* to flash on his forehead in neon? A hastily written confession, admitting he was in the cold store room shagging a waitress on a bag of Puy lentils?

Not a flicker. 'The whole point of a well-run kitchen is consistency. You should have enough time, otherwise someone's not doing their job properly. You're not allergic to baked beans are you, Laura?' he says, looking suddenly worried.

'Love them,' I say, dipping my fork in and taking a mouthful, then another, then a third. 'Oh my goodness . . .'

'It's just a few quality ingredients.'

'But how are you getting such a deep base flavour?'

'Oh, the *soffritto* – I cook it for, like, four hours . . .'

'Four *hours*? And is that green drizzle chive?'

'Smoked chive oil – it just lifts it.'

'And there's something else smoky as well as bacon – is it bourbon?'

'I'm going to have to get up pretty early to get anything past you! Are you sure you're not a secret Michelin inspector?'

'That photo?' I say, craning my head back to the fridge.

'That's my favourite restaurant in the world, in fact it's named after you, Da Laura.'

'How nice of them! Is it in Italy?'

'Yup, the next town along is Portofino, which is wall-to-wall douche bags wearing Hermès – but San Fruttuoso is tiny – three houses and an abbey, and Da Laura's this shack on a pebble beach, rickety wooden steps, paper tablecloths, ten seats. They serve the thinnest home-made lasagne sheets, covered in incredible fresh pesto. It's so simple and so low key – I'd love to take you there because I'm not doing it any justice in words. I know it sounds cheesy but they cook from the heart.'

'Can we go there please?'

'Would you want to go there with me?' he says, pulling back to look at me.

'Absolutely!' You're not sure if I like *you*? Perhaps you did not actually see me just now, miming 'I love you'.

'I'd better show you those pastries before you go,' he says, abruptly getting up and clearing the plates away.

'I'm going *now*, am I?' A lump of unease lodges in my gullet like gristle.

'It's five to one,' he says, checking his watch.

'What are you up to again?' I try to make my voice sound breezy but it has to work its way round the lump in my throat and ends up sounding like a strangled accusation.

He pauses as he bends over the oven, then slides the tray on to the counter. 'Got some stuff to sort out with my mum. Right, so here we've got three savoury Viennoiseries – a Parmesan and bacon brioche; a Welsh rarebit and wild mushroom double-layered crois-sant and a caramelised leek, shallot and Gruyère spiral. So listen,' he says, hurriedly placing the pastries in a box, then straightening them up carefully, as though the thought of closing the lid on them when they're not in perfect rows would pain him. 'I'm putting three of each in – they're actually not at their best piping hot anyway, and then when I see you on Thursday you can tell me what you think?'

'Thursday?'

'I thought I'd pop over in my split shift, around teatime?'

'We're doing tea now, are we?'

'Do you not want to?'

'No, I do. I just . . . it would be nice to see you for more than an hour snatched here and there.'

'Er . . . next Sunday night? Let me see if I can move things around . . . ' he says. 'Laura, I feel so rude shoving you out of my house but . . . '

'No, it's fine. It's like a proper restaurant with a very fast turn-around.' Though seriously? It is the opposite of fine!

On his doorstep I feel the lump still sticking in my throat. If I don't get it out now I'll choke on it.

'What time?' I say.

'What time what?'

'Tea. On Thursday?'

'Oh, four p.m. Sorry, Laura, I'm a bit distracted . . . '

Yeah, I can see that. And I can go home and waste my time angsting about why that might be. Or . . .

'Adam, can I ask you a question?' Though why even ask? If he's anything like Tom, he'll just lie.

'Shoot.'

'Are you seeing someone at the moment?'

'What? A shrink?'

Why would you be seeing a shrink? 'I meant another woman.'

He laughs. 'My goodness, no, definitely not.' He looks me straight in the eye when he says it. I know what a lie looks like: this isn't one.

'Are you seeing a shrink then?'

'No – I just didn't know what you meant by *seeing someone*. Listen, I know we never seem to . . . I want to spend time with you, I know it's odd right now but things will clear up soon.'

'I just have this weird feeling . . . '

He pauses. 'Look: there's some on-going stuff but I promise you, I'm not seeing another woman.' He puts his hands on my shoulder. 'Can you bear with me? In a couple of weeks I'll be in a better place all round.'

He smiles and I smile. We stand on his doorstep, his hands still resting on my shoulders. He moves them down my arms, then pulls me towards him and kisses me tenderly. His mouth is so perfect I could kiss him for hours. My body leans in to his but after a minute he pulls away, looking sheepish.

'Adam, you are quite sure it's your mum coming round now, not your one o'clock girlfriend?'

He looks over my shoulder and breaks into an awkward smile. 'If you don't believe me, you can see for yourself.'

Behind me, an attractive brunette in her early sixties stands at the bottom of the stairs, carrying two heavy cloth bags. She looks surprised, then glances at Adam, nods, and smiles.

'You must be Laura!'

20

This place would be perfect for Second Helpings, I think, as I sit waiting for Will and Sophie at Darband, a tiny Persian den off Edgware Road. It won't win any awards for decor – the walls covered in yellow plaster, the floor in peeling lino – but it's one of my favourite restaurants ever. Yes, the food is brilliant – but it's the owners that make it special. They are generous and hospitable and make every guest feel equally welcome.

I stumbled across it walking back from town one day. I smelled chargrilled meat and when I crossed the road for a closer look, I saw a chef in the window, working a gigantic disc of dough, spinning and slapping it between his palms like a meditation. Ten minutes later, I was sitting inside, mourning all the meals I'd already missed here. That bread! Light, crispy, buttery bread that anyone with eyes, a mouth or a pulse would demolish. (It would give Amber a panic attack.) And their rice! Mountains of lightly buttered basmati, each grain separate and fluffy, delicate and comforting – people don't get excited enough about rice!

'Laura, I'm so sorry, we lost track of time,' says Sophie, as she bustles in, arm in arm with Will. These two are a great couple to hang out with – they never make you feel left out or grossed out. On the rare occasions Mark visits Amber at the flat, they're either licking each other's faces or bickering; Amber once claimed they're the Liz Taylor and Richard Burton of West London. Sometimes I admire Amber for being able to look through rose/frankly black tulip-tinted spectacles to see Mark as Richard Burton, when the facts might suggest otherwise: a paunchy forty year old who farts all the time and blames it on poor Annalex.

'We brought some plonk,' says Will putting down two bottles of red.

'Thought you might need a drink after your hot date . . . what?

No action?' Sophie sits down heavily, my disappointment weighing as much on her as me.

'Should I pop to the offie for a third?' says Will.

'Don't worry, Will, it wasn't *bad*, just odd.'

'What happened?' she says. 'Hang on, can we order first?' Sophie cannot concentrate in a restaurant until she knows food is on its way.

'The usual?' I say.

'The usual?' She turns to Will, though it is a rhetorical question.

Will nods, fills our glasses and raises his for a mini cheers. 'And extra bread.'

While we're waiting for our food I tell them what happened – how flirty Adam was, but yet made no attempt at a real move.

'He almost groped you in the bathroom?' says Sophie.

'It wasn't a groping! More a casual rub – like he didn't realise he was doing it.'

'Didn't realise he was doing it!' says Will, looking at me like I'm from a different species.

'It wasn't a *move* kind of move, Will. It's weird – it feels like he's holding back . . . '

'Has it occurred to you,' says Will, leaning back in his chair as the waiter descends with a basket of breads so large they're draping over all sides. 'This guy might actually be honourable?'

My hand freezes inches from the warm flatbread. *Honourable*? He might as well be speaking Farsi for all the sense he's making. I have never dated a man of honour. If a guy on Tinder is not texting me about a threesome before we've even met for a coffee I now assume he's asexual.

'Don't look so dumbstruck,' says Will.

'Will? Have you ever tried dating men in London?' I say, ripping a piece of bread and popping it into my mouth.

'Not recently . . . '

'Don't. I have: online, offline, friends of Jess . . . I can safely say the concept of honour is not one I've encountered in the last four long years.'

'Soph, tell her to stop being a cynic. Perhaps this guy wants to get to know you first? Perhaps he doesn't know if you're interested in him?' he says, looking shyly at Sophie.

'This one took forever to make a move,' she says.

'*This one* was being a gentleman,' says Will, taking her hand.

'You two worked together, it's different – you have to wait until the Christmas party to jump colleagues. Why do you think Adam isn't asking to see me after he finishes his shift?'

'You'd find a two a.m. booty call more romantic?' says Sophie.

'I'd find it more normal!'

'Just give him a chance, it's only been two weeks,' says Will, moving the plates aside so the waiter can set down the metal platter of chargrilled chicken and lamb. 'I'm popping to the loo, if you're still talking about this when I return I'm going into the back room to watch football.'

'It's probably a good thing you're not getting a chance to shag him yet,' says Sophie. 'You might get lost in the hot sex cloud, all that oxytencin.'

'The spot cream?'

'Oxycontin, oxytocin, floods your brain, clouds your judgement.'

'Maybe you're right. Oh my God, and I finally ate his food!' I whisper, though Will is nowhere within earshot.

'And?'

'Ridiculous. Literally the best thing I've eaten this year, better than the crab ravioli at Galvin, better than that beautiful prawn dish we had at Moro . . . '

'He pulled out all the stops for you!'

'Soph, it was beans on toast and an omelette. But he'd sweated the background veg in the beans for *four hours* – most people would do that for twenty minutes. That's a genius idea, but you'd only do it if you were a perfectionist. And his plating, this oil he put on top – the colour of it was like an emerald – his ideas, the execution . . . flawless.'

'So you're going back?' says Sophie, refilling our glasses to the brim and in the process creating three red circles on the paper tablecloth.

'I have to. I just hope Roger won't freak . . . '

'Why?'

'Well . . . in theory he might be OK, some American newspapers send their critics back multiple times – but they have bigger budgets – and I'm talking about a restaurant that charges sixteen pounds for eight quadruple cooked chips . . . '

'Ouch.'

'But it's more that. I made such a fuss about having boundaries between personal relationships and work . . . '

'But if you slate the food and every other critic praises it, won't that be weird?'

'Exactly – it's my credibility on the line too.'

'What are you whispering about?' says Will, sitting back down, eyebrows shooting north as he sees we've devoured all of the lamb and half the chicken.

'There's loads of green pepper left,' says Sophie.

'Yeah, I came here for the green pepper,' he says, laughing.

'I didn't even tell you – *I met the mother,*' I say. 'I was saying goodbye and she turned up . . . '

'And?'

'Lovely – one of those women who instantly makes you feel comfortable.' My ex mother-in-law used to blanch if I didn't move my soup spoon to the outer edge of the bowl while eating her consommé. 'And she knew about me!'

'He's told her about you,' says Sophie, clasping her hands to her chest and looking at Will. 'Told the mother, already! So did you have a cup of tea?'

'Well, no. It was kind of weird. She said she'd love to meet me properly, but said they had family matters to talk about, and gave me a look that was kind of . . . I don't know . . . '

'Enough with the paranoia. Meanwhile, guess who's put in an order for their "Fortieth" with me?'

'Give me a clue.'

'Dolly-bird celebrity chef, face of Fletchers' Fat Bird range . . . '

'If Celina Summer is forty, I'm still doing my GCSEs – do GCSEs even exist anymore?'

'I'm not sure if I should take the job,' she says, frowning.

'Tell her to stop being an idiot,' says Will.

'It's not the fact she's insufferably smug and pretends to eat like a normal woman but doesn't. It's two things – firstly, she wants New Ideas – which she's blatantly going to steal . . . '

'Fletchers rip off your ideas every six months anyway,' says Will. 'All they have to do is look on your website – *sincerest form of flattery* and all that.'

'I'm a one-woman business and they're a giant supermarket, so I don't see it that way – but it's not just that. It's three hundred guests, August Bank Holiday – plus goody bags, it's full on.'

'And that's why she's offering you a healthy chunk of change,' says Will. 'And you'll get new clients.'

'I can't do it on my own, though.'

'We'll help you,' I say.

'But I'll need full-time help the whole month before. It's massive on top of the day job.'

'Say yes now, worry about it later,' says Will.

'You would say that,' she says, laughing. 'You're a man.'

After dinner the three of us walk home together, stuffed with carbs, humming with red wine. How wonderful to eat like a king, then lie down next to someone you love, I think, as I kiss them goodbye outside our front doors.

How un-wonderful to rattle round your landlady's bathroom with mulberry-stained lips, knocking over tubes of overpriced serums, playing over the embarrassments of your afternoon – all three of them.

God, that 'I love you' mime was awkward.

And Adam's mum turning up when we were snogging on the doorstep was not ideal either, as first impressions go – but she seemed cool about it.

But I am most tormented by the shame of grilling him about another woman. It was utterly insecure. I should have hidden that side of myself better – there's nothing more unattractive than neediness.

I drag a warm, wet flannel across my face, wipe it clean.

He is not Tom.

Not all men are liars.

The only way I'll stay sane is if I trust him.

21

'Good weekend, Roger?' I say, as we're heading to the boardroom on Monday morning.

'I finally managed to FaceTime Gemma at midnight,' he says, wearily. 'She's found herself a job on this tiny island they're staying on – some sort of a beach bar . . . '

'Oh Roger, it's only for a few months. At least she's actually working.' Rather than scrounging off you, like she normally does. 'Listen – can I have a quick word with you after Conference?'

'If we make it out alive.'

Heather and Sandra are already in the room, heads close in conversation, and Azeem and Jonesy turn up a minute after Roger and I do. Before I've even finished pouring the coffee, Jonesy's chomping at the bit. 'So where are we at with the cover, on or off?'

'I thought I'd been extremely clear about the fact this issue will be embargoed till day of sale if Bechdel's on the cover?' says Sandra, frost in her voice. 'Bechdel is represented by Manderbys. If Manderbys get wind of it they'll slap an injunction on us before it's out the door. Obviously we'll need to be watertight on leaks, it'll be going into the chain at the last minute – no internal copies.'

'Yeah I know all that, Sandra, I'm not a novice – what I'm asking is – are we running the Bechdel or not?'

'We've been through the revised draft on Friday,' says Heather.

'There are half a dozen allegations that still need going over with a fine-tooth comb,' says Roger, his hand inadvertently forming a fist, which taps his mouth.

'We're not yet in a position to call it either way,' says Sandra, straightening up in her chair. 'Currently the risk of litigation is too high. The possible resource in cash and time that a libel case from the Bechdel camp would demand is prohibitive. The last time he took a paper to court it was a five-year battle. He lost, but we cannot afford to enter those sort of battles.'

'If we can't get the former account director at the charity to talk on record, we can't touch the charity stuff,' says Heather.

'Why won't she talk?' says Jonesy.

'Her boyfriend still works for Bechdel, she's scared it'll come back on him.'

'She's probably right,' says Roger, shaking his head in disgust. 'What else have we got?' He picks up a piece of paper from his file and I hand him his glasses as he scans down the list. 'Right – charity fraud, still relying on an un-named source,' he says. 'The proclivities –Heather, no way the ex-wife will be persuaded to talk?'

'Sitting by the pool in Monaco with eighteen million reasons to stay loyal.'

'But we could still get the lifestyle angle from the London or Oxfordshire staff?'

'Hearing back from the chauffeur's lawyer at three p.m.,' says Heather. 'If we get the chauffeur, we get the housekeeper – then we get the Berkeley Square townhouse. We've got all the transcripts, it's just not on the record yet.'

'We've got the hotel on record, so we've got the escorts, and at least four household names.' Roger throws the list back down on his desk. 'Right – we start with the money, that's watertight. The property portfolio, the trading anomalies and the tax avoidance. You put that lot together, that's front-page news in itself, and more than anyone's got on him before. We've got witness corroboration and the ex-employee testimonial. Work on the basis that's all we're getting and let me see how that looks in layout,' he says.

Roger, Sandra, Heather and Jonesy spend the next twenty minutes having a heated debate about whether they should do a sidebar on Bechdel's younger brother. He's MD of one of the biggest ad agencies in London – and allegedly has two ex-members of staff on permanent paid leave, nursing toddlers who look remarkably like him, poor things. His wife is in the shadow cabinet, and is vehemently pro tax breaks for *traditional families*.

'I don't give a monkey's where he puts his todger,' says Roger, 'it's about the wife's hypocrisy in lambasting single mothers, when her husband's affairs aren't clean.'

'The wife possibly doesn't know?' I say.

'The wife always knows – at some level,' says Sandra.

'If you attack the brother you've got twenty blue chip clients at his agency who'll pull their bleeding campaigns from the mag for the rest of the year,' says Jonesy.

'So shall we just run editorials that praise the scions of our most corrupt media dynasties? Perhaps we should print a hagiography of Stalin while we're at it?' says Roger.

'What the fuck's a hagiography?' says Jonesy.

'A book about Sandra,' Azeem whispers to me.

'Roger,' I say, checking my watch. 'You've got a twelve thirty with Sandra and the auditors – they're probably waiting in reception. Do you want me to go and babysit them for twenty minutes?'

'No, it's fine,' he says. 'Team – let's take a view tomorrow. If we get the housekeeper and the chauffeur, we drop the sidebar on the brother, if not, Jonesy, you'd better polish your shoes because you'll be pounding those streets, hustling. Laura, go fetch them – and grab me a cup of sweet coffee on the way back up, I need some caffeine.'

'You look exhausted,' I say, quietly.

He waves me away. 'Time difference, Thailand. Stop fussing.'

It's peculiar, it's 2.15 p.m. and Roger should be out of the auditors' meeting he was just in with Sandra and Jonesy, but there's no sign of him, even though The Laminator's back at her desk crunching on Ryvita, and I saw Jonesy leave for a lunch a while ago.

I do a thorough check of the building, try Roger's mobile twice, then pop round the corner to The Eagle where he sometimes disappears for a pint after a confab with Jonesy – but he's nowhere. Eventually I'm forced to ask Sandra if she knows his whereabouts.

'Last time I looked at your job spec you were in charge of his diary,' she says, scraping a smidgen more fish paste over her cracker.

'Sandra he's meant to be in his office, and he's got a two-thirty with the Press Association. You were just with him earlier?'

She shrugs.

'Did he say where he was off to after the meeting?' Perhaps he went to buy a sandwich, though it's hardly like Roger to do the practical things like feed himself. He might have popped out for some fresh air.

An hour later he texts me:

Can you shift today's appts to tmrw please?

You're at a seminar all day tomorrow. Where are you, anyway?

Shift the appts to Wednesday then, ta. Fancied a round of golf.

Which is sort of a strange message.

Because not only has it started to rain. But when I go back into his office to double-check, I see his golf bag, standing in the corner in its usual resting place.

22

Roger is at an all day Governance seminar on Tuesday but he phones at noon.

'Manning the fort, Parker?' he says, cheerily.

'It's so quiet – Heather and Azeem are up in planning, Jonesy's out to lunch.'

'Hold the front page . . . Any messages?'

'Elizabeth rang about Gemma's allowance, and the Head of the BRC wants to move your lunch to next week, if you're happy, I'll change the booking?'

'Uh-huh.'

'And . . . Dr Fabelman's secretary rang. You left your umbrella in their waiting room . . . '

There's a pause. 'You wanted to ask me something yesterday? We never got round to it.'

'Oh – it can wait, I'd rather ask you in person. Though actually – would you mind if I took a couple of hours off this afternoon? There's something I'd like to do.'

About nine months after I started writing The Dish, shortly after I won my first award, I received an anonymous note in the post: it wasn't a love letter. It said I was totally unqualified and was doing a shit job: 'Stuffing your gob for a living isn't hard.' Of course they were right: my job isn't hard – being a nurse or a soldier is hard. Being a food critic is not *entirely* easy though.

The palate part's fine: I eat a lot, I think about food and read about it a lot.

The being secretive part I've always found tough – particularly these last three weeks.

The memory part can be tricky. I don't take notes or photos. It draws attention, but it's more than that. Call me a grouch but I think interrupting your meal to adjust your Bratwurst for Instagram, like some culinary Terry Richardson, is rude to your fellow diners, plus it puts a filter between you and the experience. (It reminds me of when Dad and I went to see the 'Mona Lisa' and all I saw was a swarm of iPhones.) So I don't drink on the job – sure, it enhances your enjoyment, but it clouds your brain; try remembering which five micro leaves were in your starter when you're halfway past pudding and two bottles of red.

But the hardest part? It's also the most fun part: bread. Trying to describe bread in a new way every time is not a piece of cake. And I always eat the bread because if you can't get your bread right, you probably can't get your ballotine or your en cocotte right. You have to think pretty hard how to describe the texture of the inside of a roll for the 150th time.

So after I've cleared it with Roger, I divert my phone and hop on the Tube to Edgware Road.

'Back again?' says our waiter from Sunday, as I walk into Darband after the lunchtime rush. Two old men sit silently smoking shisha pipes by the window, their strawberry smoke mingling, not unpleasantly, with the smell of chargrilled meat.

'I've come to ask you a small favour.'

'You want the recipe for the bread?' He shakes his head. 'Family secret.'

'I wondered if I could watch you making it?'

He looks at me like I'm some sort of gluten pervert, then shrugs.

'Nima – show the lady the bread!' he shouts to the cook standing in a grease-stained apron in the small open kitchen.

The chef takes a springy dough ball from a selection resting under a tea towel, dips one side in poppy seeds, then rolls it on the floured counter till it's barely a millimetre thick. He grabs an oversized flattened pincushion from under the counter and delicately drapes the tissue-thin dough over it, then turns to the clay oven, an Ali Baba style pot with a circular opening at the top, a fiery furnace below. With one hand he takes the dough-draped cushion and thwaps it hard against the inside wall, so the dough sticks to the pot like a cartoon character who's just run into a wall. He whips away the cushion and the bread stays happily stuck to the side of the baking hot clay for thirty seconds, at which point he plucks it out and brushes it with melted butter.

He gestures for me to sit while he slides the giant circle on to a plate, prepares a small side dish of yoghurt, another of radishes, and pours me a fresh mint lemonade.

The waiter watches from the corner with quiet satisfaction as I tuck in.

'So what *is* in it?' I say.

He laughs. 'Flour, water, poppy seed and nafas.'

'Is that a spice? Like sumac?'

'Nafas? We put it in all our food, but you don't buy it, you create it. The word means breath . . . but more than that, it is a quality, like love or soul. You can taste it, can't you?'

I finish the last bite and take a fiver from my wallet.

He shakes his head. 'It's on the house.'

'I insist.'

'And I insist,' he says sternly. 'Today you are my guest – tomorrow I may be yours.'

Now *that's* what I call good service.

Back in the office it's still a ghost town, so I set to work thinking about how best to describe the bread. Its surface is cratered and dimpled like the moon, but coloured in shades of cream and brown, and pockets of charcoal. Its texture is three different things simultaneously, chew and crunch and soft, like a great southern Italian pizza, but without that small millimetre of slightly wet dough you get at the front of your teeth when you bite into it.

Sandra reappears from upstairs at 5.30 p.m., and gives me a suspicious look. For the next two hours she sits, twitching and occasionally looking over her monitor to see if I'm making any attempt to move. It will physically pain her to go home before me – she would rather sleep in her chair. She wins – at 7.45 p.m. I realise I'm hungry again. I email the document to myself so I can carry on at home.

I've finished Darband, and am halfway through writing up the old Thai café near Wormwood Scrubs prison with the amazing papaya salad!

As I shut down my computer and say goodbye, a flicker of relief passes over her face.

23

There's been a constant stream of visitors to Roger's office all day – but at 5 p.m., I seize the opportunity of a gap in his schedule, arm myself with two cups of tea and find myself hovering on the threshold of his doorway.

'Parker, am I supposed to be somewhere?' He looks up wearily.

'Have you got a minute?' I say, biting the inside of my cheek as I notice the wall behind him. April's page layouts are up and my two pages have now been typeset and pinned in pride of place behind Roger's head. The photo of the toilet has been dropped in and the designer has pulled out a quote in bold next to it: '*GREED, PRETENSION, VULGARITY.*' It's not exactly ambiguous.

'Looking good, isn't it?' he says, proudly. 'And for a headline Kiki's suggested "Bog Standard" or "Nightmare on Eel Street", though how about "Flash In The Pan"?'

'Very good,' I say, taking a deep breath. 'Roger: I wanted to ask your advice.'

'Ooh, I like giving advice. A bit like an insult, more fun outbound than in.' He holds his palm out for me to take a seat.

'OK. So the thing is, the night we went to LuxEris, I'm almost positive Adam wasn't on the pass, and I think his sous-chef mucked up the entire meal.'

'OK.'

'Adam cooked for me at the weekend and I'm convinced he's hugely talented, is a perfectionist to the point of being anally retentive, and that the night we ate there was an anomaly.'

Roger says nothing, but turns to look at the layout behind him.

'And I'm aware I have a personal relationship with him,' I say, blushing. 'And I'm even more aware heaven and earth have been moved to give me extra space which I'll need to fill.'

'Keep talking.'

'And I'll pay for it myself, but I think the food deserves a second chance. Not the toilet, not the pricing, just the food, because it's his reputation on the line, but it's also mine.' Please, please, please . . .

Roger closes his eyes briefly, then opens them and smiles gently. 'The thing about advice is, no one ever actually listens to it, do they?'

'I'm asking because your opinion matters to me more than anything. If you think I'm doing a Fergus . . . thinking with my penis . . . '

'If you do have a penis, perhaps you'd like to write about it for May's issue?'

'If you think I'm letting my feelings cloud my judgement, please say, because I don't want to do a Fergus. But I think this scenario is different. And if the food is terrible second time around I'll say it is, Roger, I won't fudge it.'

'Laura – I worked with your mother for a decade, I've worked with you for nearly half – you're cut from the same cloth.'

'And we can also run the noodle bar copy which is done, and fill the space with one of these?' I say, handing him my work. 'The Persian's the strongest.'

He gives the pages a glance. 'Laura, I'm sure these are good. Regardless: my advice is to sleep on it. What you've written,' he points behind him, 'is the most original copy you've done – it's powerful, it's sharp and it has impact. I can see you're worked up about this, but I would take a moment to consider what you're throwing away here.'

'OK . . . and I'll come back to you tomorrow?'

'Make it Friday, tomorrow's wall-to-wall turkeys.'

I do the calculations: I don't want to revisit on a busy Friday or Saturday. They're shut Sunday, so Monday.

'If I do go back—'

'Don't ask me to come with you,' he says, half-smiling.

'Please?'

He buries his head in his hands. 'I must have done something truly terrible in a former life.'

'Thank you, Roger,' I say, getting up to leave. 'Oh – by the way, how was your seminar?'

He brings his hand to his throat and pretends to choke himself.

'As good as that?' I say. 'And golf, on Monday?'

His smile remains on his face but I can see it's being held up.

He nods, and I nod back. His nod seems to say: *some secrets are secrets for a good reason.*

'Hey babe, you're home,' says Amber as I walk in and find her lying on her yoga mat wearing a pink vest and a silver thong. Annalex, also in a pink vest which says 'Downward Dog', sits by her feet, occasionally licking one of Amber's tangerine-painted toenails.

'How was your day?' I say, kneeling to pet Annalex. She looks at me plaintively from under furry grey brows, as though she's scared that one day Amber will humiliate her further by dressing her in a matching dog-thong.

'Exhaustifying.' Amber rolls on to her stomach and stretches out her arms like Superman. 'I had a meeting at Berners Tavern for like two whole hours. Then I had to pop to my atelier, then I saw my therapist,' she says, her perfect mouth forming a pout.

'And?' I stay standing. If I dare sit Amber will have me trapped for the evening.

'She thinks the whole argument was because Mark can't express his hurt child.'

'I thought Mark had a hissy fit because you broke his juicer?'

'She says I need to visualise everything I want Mark to say – and then it will happen.'

'Is that so?' I say, nodding in wonder at how Amber's therapist manages to squeeze Amber like an orange for £150 an hour in pursuit of Amber's Higher Purpose. I wonder if her methods work for the Grand National?

'Everything happens for a reason,' says Amber sagely, as if this is the first time she's used this phrase, rather than the first time she's used it tonight. She rolls herself up from the mat in one elegant curl, scoops Annalex under one toned arm and heads for the bathroom.

The only time Amber and I ever had an actual argument was when we were watching footage of a typhoon a few years back. The reporter had done the dummies' guide to what causes cyclones and then the footage had switched to heart-breaking images of crying orphans. The death toll was in the thousands and Amber had piously said, 'Everything happens for a reason.'

'What possible reason would that be?'

'It's too early to tell.'

'Amber, you just heard them say it happened because of atmospheric pressure in the North Sea. That's the *reason*.'

'*Everything happens for a reason* means it'll turn out for the best.'

'It is often used in that way, but it's not what those words literally mean.'

'Laura, it *will* have a Higher Purpose.'

I'd pointed at the woman on the screen standing in wreckage, tears streaming down her face. 'Tell *her* about your Higher Purpose.'

'*Everything happens for a reason* means make the best of the situation.'

'It doesn't. What those words literally mean is: causes make things happen: you drop a glass and break it because your hand is slippery, not because God wants you to have better glassware.'

'No, babe, er, no.'

'OK, take us: the *reason* I live with you is *because* my old flatmate sold her flat.'

'That's so simplistic: a Higher Purpose is at work. People enter your life for a reason, a season, a lifetime . . . '

Seriously? Mum died, Tom ran off with whore-face and I abandoned my career so I could end up in your shoe cupboard hiding a toaster in my wardrobe? Please don't tell me *that* is part of a cosmic master plan.

'Babe, I guess some people are just more spiritual than others.'

You can't stay irritated with people for long though; certainly not the ones you have to live with, so now, anytime Amber says 'everything happens for a reason', I just let those words wash over me like one of her Moroccan Rose Oil mist sprays that hovers in the bathroom air long after she's finished spritzing.

When I get into bed later, I think about the reason Adam's path crossed mine . . .

Is he the one?

Is the universe finally compensating me for a decade of heartache?

Is life showing me that good things can happen to good(ish) people, and that I am actually one of those girls who it *does* work out for?

No. Adam's path crossed mine because I was trying to lay my hands on a custard doughnut. Mind you, if that's not a Higher Purpose I don't know what is.

24

'*Bellissima!*' says Fabrizio, as he kisses me hello and circles his finger in the air for me to do a twirl. 'You have a quiet afternoon?'

'Yeah, I'm meeting a friend here.'

'Man friend?' he says, sniffing the air.

'The one who made that pastry I gave you.'

His eyes widen. 'My God, I forgot, I was so angry last Friday, three customers busting my balls about wait time – if you want shit coffee, visit the Albanian!' (Fabrizio is at war with a café round the corner that sells muddy brown liquid and cinnamon-caramel chai lattes.) 'I wrap the pastry in tissue and leave it under the counter and I only find it again on Monday, when I think – pastry, three days old? Should go in the bin.' He shrugs.

'You threw it away?'

'No – but only because I always check, maybe the smell is OK – I smell, actually is OK so I eat.'

'And?'

'Eh, Madonna!' he says, patting his heart. 'Is like . . . ' His eyes narrow as he tries to pin down the thought. 'Is like the *most* beautiful crispy, light pastry, like . . . like *una sfogliatella pero' non dolce con, all'interno, una fantastica sorpresa . . .* '

'Slow down, Fab, you've gone into Italian.'

'*Allora*, OK, is . . . light, but not light like a feather, ah, in Italian there is a word but in English?' he says, pointing to the sky. 'The guy who made it: he's an Italian?'

I shake my head.

'Not Albanian?'

'You can ask him yourself,' I say, as Adam pulls up outside, parks his bike and enters the café.

'This place is great,' says Adam, 'I had no idea it was here – it's like a little secret.'

'Adam – this is Fabrizio – he just used the word Madonna to describe your pastries; he normally only uses that word when describing Monica Bellucci.'

'Is beautiful,' says Fabrizio, shaking his hand warmly. 'But you make me break my diet.' He pats his small paunch, currently ensconced in a bright green Joe T-shirt. Fabrizio wears a T-shirt that says Joe on it at least once a week, and then gets the hump when people don't realise Joe is slang for coffee and make the mistake of thinking Joe might actually be his name. 'What can I get you, filter or espresso?'

'What's good?' says Adam, looking at the specials on the black-board.

'Everything! I give you one Nyeri and a Yirgacheffe,' he says, as he measures out two sets of beans and pours them into the grinder.

'That's a labour of love,' says Adam, as he watches Fab trickle boiling water from his swan-necked kettle on to the filter paper. Fab takes an average of three minutes to pour a single coffee – unless he's taken exception to you (possibly about his T-shirt) in which case he'll rush it in two.

'I've brought you some new samples,' says Adam, taking his ruck-sack off and removing a plastic container. 'I've tweaked the recipe since Sunday, let me know what you think.'

I point to Fabrizio.

'Yes, of course!' he says, placing two on a napkin for him.

'Fab – if you want to steal a march on the Albanian, you should start selling these.'

Fab finally finishes his pour with a flourish and hands the cups to us proudly. 'On the house – is a fair exchange!' he says, whisking the napkin with the pastries off the counter and sinking his teeth into one.

I lead Adam through the curtain to the back room and he takes his jacket off and settles into a chair. 'What a perfect place to hide!' he says, stretching his arms over his head.

'What are you hiding from today?'

'Usual chaos, we're a man down, idiot chef de partie nearly severed his finger at lunch.'

'Not much blood at my place. Well, actually there's plenty but it's all turkeys'. Sandra pretty much physically blocked me from entering Roger's office earlier – I was only bringing them drinks; sometimes I'm tempted to jack it all in and come and work here.'

'You used to work in coffee, didn't you?' says Adam.

'For nearly ten years.'

'OK: I drink at least three cups a day.' He stops, takes a sip. 'This is delicious, but it seems like that whole world of posh coffee is all a bit Emperor's New Clothes.'

I smile. 'People often say that about things they don't understand.'

'May I?' He takes my cup from my hand and sips it. 'That tastes not dissimilar to the one I'm drinking.'

'Do *not* let Fabrizio hear you say that, your bromance will be dead in its tracks.'

'They *are* similar!'

'About as similar as chicken korma and fish fingers.'

'You can taste a dramatic difference?'

'Yours has blackberry and vanilla notes, mine's very floral; if you tasted them cold brewed, you'd easily tell them apart,' I say, as his eyes narrow in scepticism. 'Doug, my old boss can blind-taste a hundred cups and tell you how close to the equator the beans were grown, that season's rainfall, and how many minutes the roast was.'

He takes a sip of his, goes back for another of mine, tipping his head to one side as if really trying to taste the difference.

'Growing and processing the beans properly is one thing,' I say. 'But what you really need is a skilled barista to make it.'

'Baristas *totally* piss me off. They make you feel stupid if you don't speak their language.'

'That's why I loved Bean To Cup – it wasn't pretentious. We had friendly, passionate staff who wanted to give our customers the best possible start to their day – the perfect cup. And coffee's such a vast universe, it has more varietals than wine, thousands of flavours, and every time you do a roast and make a cup you have a chance to start afresh.'

'You make it sound romantic,' he says, smiling, then rapidly scrunching his face into a frown. 'We've got a ludicrous coffee menu, and the other day I found out we're charging a tenner for a cup that's listed as "rare micro-estate blah-blah-blah a Vietnamese weasel shat it out", but the bar guys forgot to re-order so they were passing off instant as the real thing. Good job our customers are so pissed by the end of a meal no one's noticed the difference. But I went mental – I mean, that's practically stealing, don't you think?'

'Yes, I do.'

'No wonder our gross profit's so high; Laura, you look like you're glazing over.'

'I'm listening!' And trying not to listen at the same time: physically rather challenging.

'Anyway, we've re-ordered now but that really bothered me. Sorry, rant over. So why did you leave?'

'I left Union Roasters because I loved the way Doug worked; Bean To Cup was all about traceability, integrity, Fairtrade – knowing the farmers have been given the fairest price. It just felt like a very honest way of doing business.'

'No, I meant why did you leave Doug's? You obviously love coffee.'

'Well . . . You know I was married? Basically my husband had an affair with a friend of mine . . . '

If Jess were sitting here now she'd wrestle me to the ground to stop me telling the truth about Tom: *Why would you ever tell anyone that someone's treated you badly? They'll assume you like that sort of thing and then they'll treat you badly too.* If that's all it takes to make someone be cruel, they're probably cruel in the first place.

'You don't have to talk about it,' he says. 'If it makes you feel uncomfortable.'

'No, it's fine. But I was desperate to escape Manchester. I couldn't afford to wait for a perfect job in coffee to come along, so I applied to Roger as a temporary move, because I liked his paper. I admired its ethos – truth, honesty – if that doesn't sound too wanky.'

'Nice to be able to afford to admire an ethos . . . '

'I didn't care about money. I felt bruised. I wanted to be somewhere people weren't lying. And I think it made me feel closer to Mum . . . '

'Your mum?'

'She used to work with Roger.'

'She was his secretary?'

'She was an investigative journalist. Corporate bullying, any instance where someone was abusing their power.'

'Didn't you ever want to become a journalist?'

'I'm nowhere near as smart as Mum was, nor as fearless.'

'I think you'd be a great writer, the way you describe food is so interesting.'

'Your mum was lovely.'

'Huh?'

'Your mum. On Sunday. I really liked her.'

'She liked you, too,' he says, looking thoughtful. He's about to say something, then stops himself.

'What?'

'It doesn't matter . . . '

'Go on.'

'Your ex-husband; was that why you asked me whether I was seeing another woman?'

'What?'

'It just felt a bit . . . like, when we were on the doorstep – you seemed to think I might be some sort of two-timing love rat. I wasn't sure why you'd formed that opinion of me.'

'Oh,' I say, feeling foolish all over again. 'Well, you're a little elusive. And I guess I do have a bit of an issue about trust.'

'That's fair enough,' he says. 'If someone cheats on you, it must be hard getting over that.'

'It wasn't just the Tom thing, it was the fact he cheated with a friend. And also it came not long after the whole Mum thing, where my entire family lied to me. Anyway . . . ' I say, waving the rest of the sentence away.

'What did your family lie to you about?'

'Er, well, my mum wasn't well, and they didn't tell me when they should have.'

'They kept it a secret?'

'Yes. Well – yes, it's such a long story . . . ' I shake my head.

'You don't have to if you don't want to – but I'd like to know if it's important to you.'

'Well . . . My mother had found another lump . . . ' I say, as I feel the familiar throb of pain flare up inside me. 'She found it two weeks before my wedding day but she refused to have the operation before.'

'Presumably she wouldn't have waited if the doctors had said not to?'

'They said it was urgent but not an "emergency" – so she delayed it until the week after the wedding.'

'That sounds like what a lot of parents would do, in the situation.'

'Yes, but her, my dad and my sister didn't tell me.'

'Right – but that sounds like they were being unselfish. They didn't want to ruin your big day.'

'Yes, I know that.'

'They were trying to protect you, out of love.'

'I know that too. But it should have been up to me to decide. I wasn't a child.'

'But you'll always be their child.'

I've been through all of this countless times before with Dad and Jess. 'But they didn't even tell me before I went on honeymoon, so there I was in Sicily, having the time of my life and she was having her operation and I didn't know.' I take a deep breath. 'And the operation itself went fine, she was recovering in Intensive Care, doing well apparently – breathing on her own, talking . . . ' I pause, as a terrible jag of memory pierces my brain. 'And at that point I knew nothing about it because all three of them were *still* thinking it was the "right" thing not to tell me. And then – the day before I came back, she crashed. She'd caught an infection which spiralled and by the time I'd landed they'd put her in an induced coma.' The memory of that missed phone call tries yet again to push above the surface and I struggle to keep it as far from me as I can.

Adam moves his chair closer to me and takes my hand. 'It's OK, you don't need to talk about it, I shouldn't have asked you to.'

'No, it's absolutely fine,' I say, biting my lip just hard enough for the pain to keep me on track. 'So yes – Dad met us at Gatwick, drove us to St Mary's, they said things were stable, and, you know, it's pretty common to have complications . . . And then we sat there and watched for a month and two days – as every part of her stopped working and started being run by machines and drugs, a huge plastic ventilator forced down her throat, a central line here,' I say, touching the side of my neck, remembering with horror how savage that looked. 'Six different tubes in and out, pumping her full of blood and drugs and fluids, a machine behind her bed doing the job her kidneys were meant to do for her . . . '

Adam shakes his head in sorrow.

'And I sat and watched her. I talked to her every day. I told her all about the honeymoon, how much fun we'd had – the beach we'd found, water so blue it seemed lit from the bottom of the ocean bed; the tiny trattoria that served wild red prawns; the dessert wine that tasted like liquid honey. We'd brought her and Dad back a bottle and I promised we'd drink it together as soon as she was home again.' I shake my head. 'And I stroked my mum's hair and I played her favourite music for her – and I watched the person I loved most in the world fade away.'

Adam looks down at the floor. 'If something like that was happening to my mum, I don't know what I'd do.'

'But that's the thing, Adam – you're helpless. There's nothing you can do . . . '

'Laura,' he says, gently squeezing my finger. 'I'm so sorry. That sounds grim.'

'The thing is, she'd had a good life,' I say. 'I know there are far greater tragedies than a fifty-two-year-old woman dying, surrounded by the people who loved her – I can accept that.'

I take a deep breath and struggle to compose myself as he hands me a paper napkin.

'But say what you like about my family doing the right thing, you will never convince me it's true – because the last conversation I had with Mum was a rushed phone call in a minicab on the way to Gatwick, when she was nagging me about buying more suncream at the airport.'

I stop short of saying the rest out loud.

But what I mean to say is that I never got around to telling her how very much I loved her. How sorry I was for all the times I was difficult, or mean, or short with her. I never told her how lucky I felt to have had her as my mum – to have been loved by her every day of my life. How much I'd bloody miss her, how I've thought about her every day since she's been gone. What I can't accept – and I've tried to and I do try – is that I never had a proper chance to say goodbye.

Sophie and I are in Selfridges' food hall after work. She's come to see what the competition are up to; I'm here because I need something comforting after this afternoon's little meltdown.

'I think I put a suitable downer on the date,' I say, as she picks up a packet of glittery cupcakes.

'Six pounds for four? They look like a deranged Barbie made them,' she says. 'Laura, you don't have to be "fun" all the time, you know. He's not going to judge you for having a wobble.'

'I should never have brought it up though. I feel stupid getting emotional about it now.'

Sophie puts down the cupcakes. 'Laura – it's your mum. I still get upset about my dad sometimes, and that was nearly thirty years ago.'

'And by the time I'd finished crying, I had proper panda eyes. Adam said he was going to ask Fabrizio to play some Alice Cooper so I'd feel less self-conscious.'

'Come on,' she says. 'Let's treat ourselves to a posh chicken, yellow legs or black legs or whatever – one that costs twice as much as you actually want to pay for a chicken.'

'The turkey stuff's putting me right off poultry. I could do a steak though. Hold on a minute . . . ' I say, reaching into my bag for my phone, then showing her the caller ID.

'Are you OK?' says Adam. 'Did you find some eye make-up remover?'

'Kiki had some in her drawer. Thanks for being so sweet earlier.'

'Don't mention it. Listen, I have a quick question for you.'

'And I have one for you – I'm about to buy a rib-eye – do I oil the meat or the pan?'

'The beef – and make sure you rest it properly at the end.'

'Thanks. What did you want to ask me?'

'I've been thinking about what you said – how we never get much time together. I wondered what you were up to Sunday week?'

'I'm free . . . '

'And could you take the Monday off work? I'll go insane if I don't have a break from that madhouse.'

'What did you have in mind?'

There's a pause at the end of the line. 'A surprise.'

'I hate surprises.'

'A nice surprise. Oh, and you'll need a passport.'

I hang up and slowly put my phone back in my bag.

'What did he say?'

'I might need to buy us a bottle of red to go with those steaks,' I say, feeling hope surge through me so powerfully, it scares me.

'What's wrong?'

'Oh, Sophie, help me. I think he might actually be one of the good ones.'

25

'I've brought you elevenses,' I say to Roger, handing him a plate with one of Adam's new pastries from yesterday.

'I take it you've made up your mind,' he says, taking a bite, then looking shocked. 'Haven't the EU got a law about using this much butter?' he says, jokingly clutching his chest. He polishes off the croissant in three quick bites, then picks the flaky crumbs from his desk with a licked finger. 'So – what's the plan?'

'Monday? Your diary's free. That'll give me three days to write it, get legal and subs on it. Do you think everything will be tied up on the Bechdel by then?'

'We're almost there, housekeeper's in, driver's in, we've got a final legal over the weekend.'

'Thank you for letting me do this. I know it's a pain . . . '

He holds his hand up. 'You have to follow your instinct – your mother always used to, even if it meant chopping and changing copy at the last minute, and that was a damn sight more painful back then.'

He gets up from his desk and stands, surveying the layout on the wall. He moves to take it down but I reach out to stop him.

'Let's just see what happens, Roger. It's not a done deal.'

He puts his arm around me and squeezes my shoulder. 'You're a good girl, Parker, remember that.'

Behind us I sense a presence lurking in the doorway. It would have to be her.

'Let's see what Monday brings.' He gives me a wink. 'Sandra, dear, what can I do for you?'

To: Kiki
From: Laura
Subject: Zzzzzz

I am so bloody bored! Are you having a fag anytime soon? If so I'll come and hang with you and you can fill me in on all your latest filthy fireman stories.

To: Laura
From: Kiki
Subject: re: Zzzzzz

We are stupidly busy with turkeys today – I knew this would happen if we ran late on the Bechdel. No time for fags! (Fireman has been fired. He says 'pacific' every time he means 'specific' – can't deal!)

To: Laura
From: Adam
Subject: Date night . . .

Hope the steak turned out well. How are you fixed on Sunday? Would be great to spend the evening together like normal people do. I haven't been out for so long, is there anywhere you'd like to go?

To: Adam
From: Laura
Subject: re: Date night

How about you make me that amazing pesto lasagne?

To: Dad
From: Laura
Subject: Round two . . .

So, I'm going back to LuxEris on Monday. Have been hanging out with the head chef, Adam – I'm pretty sure he wasn't cooking last time. May need to wear that fake 'tache – I don't want the water waiter to recognise us (not sure I can persuade Roger to wear a dreadlocks wig . . .)

To: Laura
From: Dad
Subject: re: Round two . . .

Your sister mentioned you'd met this fellow. Have you told him about your review?

To: Dad
From: Laura
Subject: ???

No! Roger and Jess said not to, and if the food's better, he'll never know.

To: Laura
From: Dad
Subject: re: ???

Well 'Roger and Jess' aren't always right. Perhaps you should tell him anyway – your mother always thought it was better to be transparent about things, makes life less complicated down the line.

To: Dad
From: Laura
Subject: re: ???

Are you serious?

To: Laura
From: Dad
Subject: re: ???

Oh Laura.

To: Jess
From: Laura
Subject: Cheers

Thanks for telling Dad about Adam. And now I have *Dad* lecturing *me* on keeping secrets?

To: Laura
From: Jess
Subject: re: Cheers

Am far too busy for this nonsense. Get a proper job, which doesn't give you countless hours to sit around getting pissed off about things that happened years ago. You don't have a monopoly on missing her you know.

To: Sophie
From: Laura
Subject: Grrrrr

What is it about my family that makes me go from zero to homicidal in five seconds flat?

Anyway, date night with Adam on Sunday – *note time of day*: NIGHT! Please come to Wolfie's tomorrow, please? I know you hate it but I hate it too . . .

To: Laura
From: Sophie
Subject: Crazy woman

Firstly, there's nothing wrong with your body.

Secondly, you're not going to get thin in one hour.

Thirdly – I HATE WOLFIE'S.

But OK, seeing as it's you. xx

To: Laura
From: Adam
Subject: Herb's the word

That pasta needs Ligurian basil and it's too early in the season but I've spoken to my veg supplier and he's sourcing some Italian greenhouse stuff – next best thing.

To: Adam
From: Laura
Subject: re: Herb's the word

Sounds amazing. How about we go to your local first?

Herb's the word – why does that sound familiar?

To: Laura
From: Adam
Subject: re: Herb's the word

The Duke of York is two minutes from mine, 7 p.m.? The lyric is Blackstreet, 'No Diggity' – we were playing it in the kitchen during clean down earlier, and I was dancing.

To: Adam
From: Laura
Subject: Your work schedule

BTW, are you working on Monday? Am thinking of popping in for early supper – but only if you're cooking! (And dancing.)

To: Laura
From: Adam
Subject: re: Your work schedule

I'm always working! Let me know – it's no reservations but they let VIPs book, and you're way more of an IP than the knob-head who was throwing his weight around on table 14 earlier. Barnaby Ballen – arsehole critic, bullying the staff and trying to ponce freebies. Still, I have to be nice – don't want a bad review or Ivan and Erek will go mental . . .

To: Adam
From: Laura
Subject: VIP/VUIP

No red carpet treatment for me, thanks.

To: Laura
From: Adam
Subject: V.VIP

Well, if you do come, don't forget – stay away from the eels.
See you Sunday x

Oh good Lord, I almost forgot to change that line about the mail-order bride . . . What if we do end up running the original review and I hadn't caught that in time? He'd know immediately it was me – does not bear thinking about.

I log into the system and delete the phrase. What to put instead . . . My mind's gone blank. *A mish-mash of a dish?* Not good, *mish* and *dish* make that weird internal rhyme. *Mish-mash mouthful of horror?* I sound like Barnaby Ballen. *A mouthful of horror?* Not the best – it'll have to do for now.

I re-save the copy, go back in to double-check I've spelled mouthful with one 'L', then close the document, feeling as much panic as if I hadn't remembered to change it at all.

26

'You never said it was Hotter Haunches!' says Sophie, looking unimpressed as she walks in to the lobby of Wolfie's Workout two minutes before our class is due to start.

'You wouldn't have come. Anyway, don't you want to look like Katja?' I point to the poster of Katja, tanned and oiled up in a bikini, looking over her shoulder seductively with a 10 kg dumb-bell in each hand. 'I bet Katja never has a lie-in on a Saturday morning.'

'And I bet Katja's never had chicken korma, cheese naan and two king-sized Cobras on a Friday night, and I am totally fine with not looking like Katja,' she says, tying her shoelace as the woman next to us performs an ostentatious toe-touch, her entire forearms flat on the floor. Sophie takes in her diamond earrings, perfect high ponytail and coordinated pink trainer/Lycra combo, then shakes her head. 'I swore I'd never do this masochistic bullshit again after the post-James bootcamp.'

'I still can't believe you let that douchebag torment you about your weight.'

'If I bumped into him now I'd pie him in the face – if that weren't a waste of good custard. This place is brutal,' she says, staring at the poster of Wolfgang Wolf in full potty squat, top lip straining, teeth bared, with the words PAIN IS YOUR TEACHER! above his head.

'It's brutal but it's only twenty-eight minutes of your week – bosh – then you're done.'

The worst twenty-eight minutes of your week, to be fair: eight minutes of uphill sprinting, eight minutes of gruelling floor work, back on the treadmills till you nearly puke, then finally a stretch, and an excruciating group bonding exercise involving high fiving on all fours.

The rest of our class – a mix of alpha males and females and glamour models, hover at the entrance to Wolf Hall and rush through the doors as the previous class stagger out, their faces the colour of Veruca Salt, mid cardiac arrest – so sweat-drenched they look like they've been swimming. Sophie and I are the last to file in – the only ones not branded with Wolfie water bottles or discreet wolf head tattoos, the only ones with BMIs over twenty and unhealthy attitudes.

Eight-per-cent Body Fat Katja stands at the front, knees pumping as she shouts into her earpiece: 'Wolf Pack, let me hear you howl!'

Twenty men and women, who I'm sure live in four-storey West London houses, not padded cells, get down on all fours and bay at our leader.

'Strong Wolves, Lean Wolves, Beautiful Machines Wolves,' shrieks Katja. 'Time for some Huff and Puff!'

'Does she mean these treadmills are beautiful machines? Or that wolves are?' hisses Sophie, as we attempt to keep up with the sixty-year-old sinewy Iron Granny to our right, pounding uphill at 12 km per hour.

'Stop talking,' I say. 'Makes it harder if you still have an interest in breathing . . . '

'Run through the forest! Girls on nineteen and twenty, less chat, more speed! Now on the floor! WORK THOSE HAUNCHES!'

'These mats smell like my brother's bedroom when he was four-teen,' says Sophie, frowning, as we lie down, ankle weights strapped on, failing to replicate the leg lifts everyone else seems to be doing effortlessly.

'Their weights must be lighter than ours,' I say, feeling the front of my thighs burning. 'Oh, please no press-ups – this was meant to be lower body only!'

'No slacking in the corner! Wolves don't quit!' says Katja.

'Nor do they do tricep curls,' says Sophie. 'Bollocks, we've still got twelve minutes left, what's twelve minutes in seconds?'

'How many weeks to your wedding, Sonia? Two?! Then up to ten kilograms, my love! Now back to the forest trail! Notch it to the next level! Fourteen kilometres per hour, let me see you FLY!'

'The only thing flying will be last night's curry . . . ' says Sophie, turning a deep shade of scarlet.

'Pilates next time,' I say, gasping for oxygen. 'Why does – nobody's – mascara – even – smudge?'

'Ladies chatting at the back, stop acting like Wolverines!'

'Is a wolverine – a real – animal?' says Sophie. 'I thought – it was just – Hugh Jackman.'

'No,' I gasp, 'it's also – a fat – hairy – little – weasel.'

'Oh!' she says. 'Like my old boss, Devron,' then chokes on her laughter, as the man next to her makes a feral sex grunt, and has to pull the treadmill's emergency cord.

'Great work, Wolves!' says Katja, as we finally haul our trembling bodies towards the exit. 'And remember, "Red Meat is Your Friend, Sugar is Your Enemy"! And don't forget to buy an Isotonic Wolf Juice, available in reception now, in four refreshing fruit flavours!'

'Urgh, never again,' says Sophie, wiping the sweat from her forehead with a towel. 'Quick shower, then lunch? What do you fancy?'

'What would a wolf eat?'

'Not Katja, she's far too bony.'

'Ooh, did I tell you Adam's making me this amazing pasta tomorrow?'

'Finally – a proper date, at night, with booze!'

'Adam's all het up because he can't source the right Ligurian basil. Little does he know, I'll be so drunk by the time he lays the table, I'll be lucky if I can tell pesto from Bolognese.'

27

Everything is going according to plan! (The plan being: get Adam and myself so steamingly drunk a fumble is inevitable.) We've been in the pub half an hour. I've bought a bottle of white and have been refilling our glasses like an over-zealous sommelier. I'm tipsy, not full-blown pissed – that can wait till dinner – but having starved myself all day in a last-minute attempt at a flat stomach, I've just sent Adam to buy snacks to soak up a bit of booze.

He's standing at the bar, waiting to be served, and I can't help but stare. He's wearing a checked shirt, jeans and brown leather boots, and even though this is standard issue round here, Adam seems to look smarter than other guys. He's so at ease with himself, relaxed, and stylish without coming across as prissy. I really wonder what he looks like without his clothes on though . . . Broad shoulders, strong legs from all the cycling . . .

'Crisps, cashews and wasabi peas,' he says, laying three bowls of snacks on the table, and putting his arm round me as he settles back down.

'I love wasabi peas,' I say, nestling closer to him. 'Sophie calls them Russian roulette for the nose.'

'Like Revels – you never know which one's going to be the wrong 'un.'

'The coffee one?' I say.

'Clearly.'

'Agreed – they're an insult to any coffee lover,' I say, crunching down on a pea with delight. So much in common, he even hates the same Revels as me!

He takes a couple of peas and casually tosses them in the air, then catches them in his mouth.

'If I tried that I'd have an eye out,' I say.

'It's easy, just focus on it as it lands,' he says, throwing another up into the air, then expertly catching it again. 'Try.'

He throws the pea ten centimetres above my head and laughs as it lands on my nose, then bounces on to the floor.

'Told you I'm useless,' I say, laughing.

'Come here,' he pulls me closer and gently licks the wasabi powder off my nose.

'I cannot believe you just licked my nose in the pub.' I cannot believe I quite liked it. 'Meanwhile, attacking me with a savoury snack – would that be ABH or SBH or what?'

'Oh God,' he says, 'I had the biggest row with Max last night. The little shit had ordered some beef from a mate of his, without checking with me – I bet he's getting a hefty brown envelope in the back door.'

'What, like a backhander?' I say, taking another large sip of wine.

'Yup,' he says, taking a strand of my hair between his fingers and twirling it. 'And they'd charged us for Wagyu but this beef was as tough as goat, I had to make mini burgers with it, no way I could charge a premium for that crap,' he says, grabbing a handful of cashews.

'What did you say to Max?'

'I read him the riot act. The little bugger tried to claim he knew nothing about it! He's an idiot, did he think I wouldn't find out? His signature's on the paper work! Nothing worse than a liar,' he says, shaking his head in disgust.

'Tell me about it,' I say, taking another three peas from the bowl and crunching down hard.

'Oh, yeah, I guess you know a bit about that?' he says.

'Me? A liar?'

'No! I mean your ex. Did you go mental when you found out about the affair?'

'I didn't actually. It was too much of a shock. I got angrier two weeks later when his mother came round; then I lost it.'

'What happened?'

'Oh God,' I say, taking another huge swig of wine. 'He'd moved in with Tess the previous weekend and he sent his bloody mum to pick up some of his stuff.'

'Total coward,' he says, his eyes narrowing.

'And I was having a bit of a moment, feeling sorry for myself . . . '

'Every right to,' says Adam, indignation in his voice, as he takes another handful of peas. 'Oooh, I just got a spicy one.' He waves his hand in front of his face as if fanning a flame.

'The heat goes right up the back of your nose!' I say, taking three more. 'They're so addictive, stop me or I'll have no room left for pasta.'

'Eleven left, then back to mine,' he says, grinning.

'Anyway, at one point I started crying – not like full-on crying, but still. And you know what she said? "No tears, Laura. We don't cry in this family."'

'I'd have punched her.'

'Yeah, well, unfortunately *we don't punch in my family*! But I don't think I've ever hated anyone as much as I hated her at that moment. And I said: "Thank God I am not your family anymore," and told her to fuck off out of my house. And this is a woman who has a funny turn if you use the word "toilet" instead of lavatory.'

'Hell yeah,' he says, leaning back from me so he can give me a proper high five. 'You must be well glad to be rid of her.'

I grab a few more peas. 'Seriously! If that's not a silver lining!' I say, biting down hard on one of the peas and feeling a sudden, stabbing pain in my gum. 'Argh!' I say, my hand rising to my jaw in reflex. 'That pea just bit back!'

'What happened?' He places his palm gently on my cheek.

'Ow, I'm not sure. I think the outside of that pea is stuck in my gum,' I say, awkwardly.

'Show me.'

'Hang on.' I poke my tongue to the back corner of my mouth and try to dislodge it.

'Let me have a look.'

'No, this is embarrassing enough as it is . . . ' I poke my tongue back harder and waggle it furiously but the wedge isn't moving. 'Maybe more wine will help loosen it?'

'These peas should come with a health warning.'

I nod, but am silent as my tongue pushes harder against the snack's edge. Not budging an inch. It's viciously sharp and spiky and poking straight down into my now tender flesh. This corner of my mouth has been nothing but trouble since I had root-canal work ten years ago at that shonky dentist in Salford.

I keep forcing my tongue against it but it makes no headway, it's caught right in the margin between tooth and gum. I must look like such an idiot.

'Adam, could you just turn your head, this calls for some drastic action.'

'Time for something stiffer . . . I'll get us some bourbon,' he says, heading to the bar.

Right. Fingers in mouth. Least Audrey Hepburn-like manoeuvre ever. My forefinger reaches back into the depths and I feel the sharp, smooth tip of the shell and grab on to it between thumb and fore-finger, then give it the gentlest of pulls.

Nope. My fingers grapple with it and I'm forced to pull harder – still nothing. It's wedged so tightly, it's totally stuck! I should probably do this in front of a mirror but Adam's just paying, I don't want to make an even bigger deal of it.

I pull once, twice and yank a third time and finally it is released! Aaah. Result! I hold the shard up in front of me. It's big! A centi-metre wide and half a centimetre high, pale cream in colour, almost an off white. Actually shouldn't it be a little . . . greener? I bring it closer to my eye to inspect it: sharp, thin off-white disc of pea. Sharp, thin, off-white disc of pea?? Sharp thin off-white disc OF TOOTH, not pea, TOOTH!

I put my hand over my mouth as I try not to vomit. My tongue darts back to where the tooth was and feels, instead, gum, half a tooth, and the tangy, iodine taste of blood.

'What's wrong?' says Adam, putting the drinks down and staring at me.

I shake my head in alarm, my hand still covering my mouth, and rush to the loo. That is the absolute most disgusting thing in the entire world . . . *Oh yeah, hey, supremely gorgeous chef who I desperately fancy, I am so drunk and such a tramp – I've just drunkenly pulled out half my own tooth while angrily ranting about my ex mother-in-law! Now do you fancy a quickie?*

In the safety of the loo I inspect the damage. Good grief, I look like Skeletor if Skeletor'd had a deranged Salford butcher for a dentist. It's the second molar from the back, which, up until ten minutes ago, was a shell of a tooth with a silver filling. Now what's left is half a tooth, cracked down the middle lengthways, so that if I run my tongue against it from the inside it's intact, but from the outside is a metal filling, then bone, blood and gum. My legs start to wobble at the sight.

I sit on the toilet and ponder my options. My dentist works well-paid, lazy hours and certainly doesn't work Sunday nights . . . Maybe I could call a friend and get them to pick me up from the toilet and whisk me to a hospital? Maybe I should just go medieval, pull the other half of the tooth out and be done with it? Great idea, Viz Top Tip, why not pull out all my own teeth while I'm at it – save on future dental bills? Then I won't have to pay to eat at LuxEris again because I won't be able to chew, and maybe Adam will fancy me even more without teeth and Amber's right and *this is all happening for a reason.*

Calm down. Go out there and tell him you have to go. On the way home call Sophie – she might know an emergency dentist. Go on! And stop sticking your tongue in the bloody gap!

I head back to Adam, who's sitting, looking anxiously at his phone.

'You're not going to believe this . . . ' I say, slurring out of the left hand side of my mouth. 'But I've broken a tooth.'

'I think we can safely blame your ex mother-in-law for that, don't you? Are you in pain?'

'A little?' I say, gingerly.

'Those damned peas! Let me see,' he says, tilting his head to the side in an attempt to look inside my mouth. I keep my lips firmly sealed.

'Laura, show me.'

'Uh-uh, it's gross.'

'Just show me!'

I gently pull down the side of my cheek and he peers at the mouth carnage in a way that's almost impressed.

'Wow, you did some damage didn't you? Let me see if the Eastman does emergency walk-in . . . ' he says, taking out his phone.

'But what about dinner?'

'Let's see what the dentist says first.'

'It's fine. I'll go on my own, there's no need . . . '

'Don't be ridiculous!' he says. 'Hmm. No, they don't do walk-in . . . there must be somewhere . . . '

'I don't need you to come with me,' I say, putting my hand out to stop him. 'I'm fine on my own. It's gross and I feel a little embarrassed if I'm honest.'

'What sort of a person would abandon you at a time like this?'

Tom? Useless at the sight of blood; if I nicked my finger slicing onions on the mandolin he'd swoon like a Victorian maiden.

'You've got an early start, Adam. Please – I'm fine.'

'Hold on . . . There's one just off Oxford Street, claims it's twenty-four hours . . . '

He dials the number and starts explaining the problem.

I grab his sleeve. 'Don't tell them how it happened!'

'It's not like I'm taking you to A&E with a hamster stuck up your arse . . . ' he whispers. 'Or is that why you took so long in the bathroom?'

'Tell them I've still got the other half, can they glue it back on? Would that be cheaper?'

'OK . . . Yup . . . half an hour,' he says into the phone. 'Oh, and how much will that be? Oh. Oh. All right then . . . see you soon.'

'What did they say?'

'The good news is they can see you in half an hour.'

'The bad?'

'It might cost a few bob. They said they can't quote without seeing it, but sounds like they'll need to fit a temporary crown and you'll have to go back for a permanent.'

'A crown? Oh no, Dad had one last year and it cost seven hundred euros . . . '

'Don't worry about the money. I know your salary's . . . If you need to borrow some cash, I can put it on my credit card.'

'No! That's extremely generous, but no. Besides,' I say, smiling weakly, 'I still haven't paid you back for that doughnut, I don't have a very good credit rating . . . '

'You won't be eating any more doughnuts unless they're through a straw if you don't get that sorted.' He stands behind me and puts his hands on my shoulder and gently manoeuvres me out of the pub. 'Don't make me push you all the way there.'

'But the lasagna! You got the basil in specially . . . I could eat on the left?'

'If the dentist says you can eat tomorrow, I'll drop some in to you at work.'

'I'm coming to the restaurant tomorrow night.'

'I don't think so,' he says, pointing at my jaw.

BOLLOCKS. Tuesday then. It'll be fine by Tuesday.

Out in the street he hails a taxi and we head towards town. 'Adam, I need a cashpoint . . . '

'In the nicest possible way I think you should stop talking, it can't be good for your mouth.'

We drive past King's Cross, both staring out the window. My hangover's kicking in prematurely and I start worrying about the cost of the crown and Tuesday's meal, but most of all I'm worrying that Adam will wake up tomorrow with a single thought: Thank goodness I never got round to shagging *that* mess – she's a nightmare, drinks too much and then will do anything for attention – pulled her own tooth out to try and impress me!

'Are you OK?' he says, as he notices both my hands now cradling my jaw.

I nod and attempt a smile, though the taste of blood is making me feel sick.

He shuffles closer and puts his arm around me. 'You don't have to be brave,' he says, as we pull up outside a shopfront that is half dentist, half mobile phone shop. 'I'm going to hold your hand whether you like it or not.'

And he does. He takes my hand and places it in the comfort of his, while a dentist with fingers like knives fills my mouth with grey putty and pushes down on the root of a nerve making me gag with pain. Adam holds my hand as I'm sitting up in the chair, rinsing with green mouthwash. And even though he lets go when we walk back into reception and I take my wallet out to pay £180 for the last half hour's delights, he takes it back as soon as I've finished putting my PIN number in and pocketed my credit card. He holds my hand all the way back to my flat in the cab and kisses me gently on the knuckle of my forefinger as he says goodbye and makes me promise to call if anything goes wrong in the night.

And as I'm standing on my street, waving to him as he drives off, I think: I had forgotten how nice it is for someone to hold your hand when you really need them to. When you're having a hard time. I had forgotten that you don't have to try to cope with everything on your own all the time.

Please don't turn out to be one of the bad ones, Adam Bayley, don't let me down because I'm not sure my heart could take it.

28

'Parker, why do you sound like you've got a mouthful of cotton wool?' says Roger, looking at me suspiciously. 'You haven't gone and got yourself one of those adult braces have you?'

'I had a fight last night with a small green vegetable – and lost,' I say, removing a feather boa from the chair and wrapping it around Lumley's neck. 'Why have you got this?'

'Azeem obviously thought my office wasn't sufficiently messy.'

'Roger – I have a favour to ask, well two . . . ' I say, looking down at my hands as if the answer to all my problems lies at my finger-tips. 'Could we move our dinner to Tuesday so I'll be able to chew? And can I please have Friday off to go to the dentist?'

'Friday, yes – Tuesday, no – I'll be here till late doing final sign-off. Why don't you take a friend?'

'I'd rather wait for you. I could write Wednesday night, file Thursday? Legal and subs will be free by then?' It's so up to the wire as to be beyond the wire, but it is, technically, do-able.

'You do want to punish me.'

I laugh, and stand to go: 'You all set for conference? Starting in five?'

'Be up in a tick,' he says, rubbing his shoulder distractedly. 'Just have to make a quick call.'

'Right – we're finally signed off with legal as of ten forty-three a.m. this morning, so let's make this brief,' says Roger. 'I want this laid out by end of play – subs, studio, all hands on deck. First things first – pagination – the final Bechdel is running at eleven thousand words, so we'll need two more editorial pages on current plan, bumping by four in total. Dean – put a call in to PrintPro asap, check they've got paper stock.'

'The run will be bigger too . . . ' says Sandra.

'And Jonesy, I'm sorry to break it to you, but we're going to have to surgically remove your thumb from your arse.'

Jonesy tips his head back in protest. 'Can't you trim it to one extra page of editorial and drop the crossword and some of the classifieds? You can't expect me to get two full pages of ads this close to deadline.'

'And who's going to apologise to seventeen thousand angry subscribers whose commute we've ruined? I didn't think so. Two full pages – get Fletchers. Promise them Wimbledon centre court – well, you can promise them women's semis.'

'Number of copies . . . ' says Sandra, tapping her pen irritably on the table.

'Yep,' says Roger. 'Print run – this'll be our biggest issue since the hacking scandal, we'll need to box out to retailers – I'd say . . . forty per cent?' he says, glancing briefly at Sandra.

'Twenty per cent or returns will be huge.'

'I'm not risking running short on a story this size – forty per cent. OK – Bechdel on the cover, I need to work out the headline with subs. Right,' he says checking his watch. 'Next, turkeys: copy's legalled and subbed, just need to sign off the main image – Sandra, the spreads?'

Sandra silently moves to the centre of the room and lays out four different images on the table, each more distressing than the last.

'These were taken by the whistle-blower who's our main source. He took them on a phone he sneaked in but it's repro quality. So we've got the hatchery shot here,' she says, pointing to a photo of a huge metal contraption with a rotating blade. 'This shows the macerator where the live chicks are thrown when they're "surplussed",' she says. 'Then this shows the reduced living space of the female birds on the breeding farm. Then the shed birds – you can see the general state of distress.'

'Fucking hell,' says Jonesy, turning to the side as if to vomit. 'Good job you're not doing this in December's issue.'

'And this fourth one is the abattoir – showing breaches of care in waiting time for the gassing.'

'This one,' says Roger, pointing at the picture of the shed birds, their skins torn and their wounds infected. 'Horrific. Says everything you need to say in one image.'

'You can't run that in colour,' says Jonesy, shaking his head. 'Too much blood, retailers will kick up a shit storm, you'll get delisted.'

'We cannot afford to fall foul of the majors again, Roger,' says Sandra.

Jonesy looks at her with surprise, then he snickers. 'Good one, Sandra.'

'Good *what*? Oh, right, yes, "foul", I see. The point is, Roger, there's no point having a huge exclusive like the Bechdel if your readers can't buy the magazine. We could change the shot to black and white?'

'Play the game, Roger,' says Jonesy.

Roger's face creases in annoyance. 'Bring back the good old days when newsagents sold newspapers – and you could print the truth, without worrying about pissing off your chief client at a supermarket . . . Fine, run it mono,' he says, throwing up his hands in resignation.

'What are we going to trail on Twitter?' says Azeem. 'Can we seed the Bechdel on social media?'

'Are you not listening?' says Sandra.

'A picture of my derriere, for what it's worth,' says Roger.

'Yeah – not sure three B-list celebs retweeting our tweets translates to a single punter walking into a bloody newsagent,' says Jonesy, shaking his head.

'Guys – I can show you the data?' says Azeem.

'I don't care about the data, tweet the goddamn turkeys. Choose the most powerful image from the spread.'

Sandra shakes her head again. 'Same problem as the retailers. We need something less gory.'

'Picture of a turkey escalope?' says Jonesy.

'No emotional engagement,' says Roger.

'How about the poults, the newborn chicks?' I say, thinking back to Sophie's Christmas lunch and the photos of little yellow balls of fluff that Rafe had shown us on his phone, just as Sophie took the cooked bird out of the oven. 'Chicks are far more photogenic than grown-up turkeys, and the Internet goes mad for a fluffy baby animal?'

Sandra's eyes narrow.

'Yep, that'll work,' says Roger.

Azeem scribbles it down on a Post-it note, which will invariably end up on the sole of his shoe.

'Do you want me to help source some shots?' I say. 'You'll be snowed under.'

'Lifesaver, Laura, cheers.'

'Rodge?' says Kiki. 'The final Bechdel piece is covering the Feeding Africa charity he runs?'

'Have you had a thought?'

'If you wanted to kill two birds with one stone, how about your cover line is just "STUFFED" – and then you do two subheads, "Damian Bechdel and the Missing Charity Money", plus "Behind the Scenes at SunFarms"? '

'Put "DOUBLE STUFFED"!' says Jonesy, smirking. 'You'll sell shitloads.'

'You could even trail The Dish under that?' says Azeem. 'London's Worst New Restaurant . . . ?'

'Yeah – "The Evisceration Issue"!' says Kiki. 'Corrupt philanthropists, turkeys and chefs . . . '

'You cannot trail a food review on the cover,' says Sandra, indignantly.

Roger gives me a reassuring look. 'It's too tabloid, all of it. We focus on Bechdel – and keep it simple: "TRUTH AND LIES IN THE BECHDEL FAMILY".'

29

To: Laura
From: Sandra
Subject: Inappropriate behaviour

Roger is too diplomatic to say anything but may I remind you your role in conference is to take minutes, not input on picture sign-off on feature editorial – this is not magazine by committee. Thoroughly inappropriate behaviour yesterday – deeply unhelpful and sets a bad precedent.

To: Kiki
From: Laura
Subject: !

Just got an email from Sandra – subject header 'Inappropriate behaviour'. I thought she'd discovered those photos you showed me of her licking Fergus's neck at the pub quiz. Delete them, and delete them from your bin and your iCloud – the iCloud is not safe!

To: Laura
From: Roger
Subject: URGENT

Fuck! The housekeeper's bottled it – call emergency meeting in one hour with core team, in the mean time find Heather – she's not answering her phone!

To: Roger
From: Laura
Subject: re: URGENT

She's in the loo. She says calm down – she'll be with you in five.

To: Laura
From: Roger

Call off the emergency meeting! Heather's put in a call to the housekeeper's lawyer, we're back on. Jesus Christ, I'm getting too old for this game.

To: Laura
From: Adam
Subject: Shane MacGowan

Are you sure you didn't fake the whole tooth thing just so you could get out of eating at LuxEris? Maybe go nil by mouth till Sunday? I want you to fully enjoy your shredded wheat at the Skegness Travelodge xx

To: Adam
From: Laura
Subject: On the mend

I'm still coming on Wednesday – if you're cooking?

To: Laura
From: Adam
Subject: Masochist

I'd wait a couple of weeks if I were you. I'll be introducing new dishes to the menu.

To: Laura
From: Dad
Subject: Hello!

Did you go back to the restaurant last night?

To: Dad
From: Laura
Subject: re: Hello!

No – I broke my tooth, feels like I've been punched in the face by Tyson. I'm eating there again tomorrow. Does £450 for a crown seem extortionate to you? And that's the cheap one, not even the ceramic!

Such a manic day – putting v. exciting scoop to bed – am running round keeping everyone fed and watered/coffee-d. Roger's normally calm under pressure but he's super-stressed today.

To: Laura
From: Dad
Subject: re: Hello!

Don't scrimp on your teeth – they're yours for life.

Your mother used to love the adrenalin of a proper exclusive.

She'd have been glad you're getting to experience that environment.

To: Roger
From: Laura
Subject: Quick one

I don't want to interrupt – you seem pretty ensconced – but shout if you need anything? Will bring in afternoon tea (and maybe carrot cake?) in an hour.

To: Azeem
From: Laura
Subject: I want to adopt him!

I've spent the last hour sourcing pics of baby turkeys. If you don't think this is the cutest thing you've ever seen then you are probably a serial killer.

To: Roger
From: Laura
Subject: Sorry to interrupt . . .

It's coming up to 7.30 p.m. Was going to get you guys pizzas and beers. Yell if that's not OK?

To: Roger
From: Laura
Subject: Me again . . .

I don't want to bother you but it's 9.50 p.m. – I'm thinking of heading home.

To: Laura
From: Roger
Subject: re: Me again . . .

Thought you'd have left ages ago! Just finalising with legal.

To: Roger
From: Laura
Subject: re: Me again . . .

So is it all clear? Is it safe to publish?

To: Laura
From: Roger
Subject: re: Me again . . .

Safe? No. But some levels of risk you just have to live with.

30

Roger arrives late on Wednesday and spends an hour with the door shut before summoning me. When he does, his glasses are already on, which is never a good sign.

'Is everything OK, Roger? You must be relieved yesterday's over.'

He nods. 'Long day. I've got some bad news, I'm afraid.'

I feel a lurch in my stomach. Please don't say you've found a lump. 'Are you OK?'

'Me? It's not me, it's your piece. I'm going to have to go back on my word, I'm afraid.'

He's changed his mind. Goodbye Adam. *Adios*, holiday. 'No re-review?' I say, trying desperately to strip the disappointment from my voice.

'I mean, I can't come with you tonight,' he says, looking confused. 'I'm sorry – it's short notice but perhaps you can still find a friend?'

'Oh Roger, I was worried for a minute. I'll go alone if necessary.'

'OK. Sorry . . . I . . . I'm taking Thursday and Friday off, having a little rest. Nothing in the diary that can't be moved is there?'

'I'll take care of it. So, if it is a rewrite, do I email you the revised copy tomorrow?'

'You know what you're doing, run it past a sub and legal, and run the Persian and the noodle.'

I'm just about to leave his office when I turn back again. 'Roger – are you sure you're OK?'

'Just feeling my age.'

'Make sure you get some proper rest at the weekend.'

He shoos me out of the office with a smile.

'Soph, it's me. I need you to come to dinner tonight at Adam's restaurant.'

'Soph, me again, it's five thirty p.m. – I can't go on my own, I'll look like a stalker.'

'Kiki – are you in the pub with Azeem? Or some dodgy Tinder bloke? Either way, call me asap, it's six thirty p.m.'

Ah, finally! Oh, no.

'Hey, babe, where have you put my avocado slicer, I can't find it anywhere?'

'Amber – meet me at Bank station in an hour, I'm taking you for dinner.'

Just as I'm about to leave the office, Sophie calls.

'Manic day, I decided to do the Celina Summer fortieth – and spent the whole day with her agent. I have so entirely made the wrong decision, but anyway, do you still want me as your dinner date?'

'Amber's on her way there . . . '

'Oh . . . '

'Come!'

'I can't handle your flatmate in an enclosed space.'

'Please?'

'Can't you get rid of her?'

'No – but I need you for moral support.'

'Oh bollocks . . . OK, but I'm not sitting next to her.'

Kissinger would have a hard time playing peacemaker between those two.

'I didn't have an arse that tiny when I was five,' whispers Sophie, as the three of us follow the hot-panted hostess through the restaurant.

'She was probably born a boy,' I whisper back. 'Try not to stare.'

'Why did she look at us as like we smell of fish sauce?'

'Ignore the attitude – it's all part of their *brand*.'

'Ladies, your table,' says the hostess, spreading her arms like she's introducing the Academy Awards. We've been led to a premium corner seat with a fantastic view of the bustling room. 'Enjoy your meal,' she says to Amber – who's the only one of us who looks like she belongs here.

'Just popping to the little girls' room, babes,' says Amber, dashing off the minute we've sat down.

'Powdering her nose, is she?' says Sophie.

'She gave all that up after the last deep colonic.'

'So which one is he?' she whispers as she meerkats towards the kitchen.

'Three-quarter sleeve whites, standing at the pass.'

'Talking to the waitress? You never said he was so good-looking!'

'Stop staring! Look over there, isn't that what's her face?'

'She's even thinner than she looks on telly! Do you think we're the only ones in here with our original faces and bodies?' she says, surveying the room of stretched, snipped and sculpted skin. 'You do know Zoolamber's nose isn't real? Sinus problems my arse, I reckon her first nose worked fine till she shoved half Colombia up it.'

'Sshhh! She's on her way back, and her ears work fine.'

'I hate this crowd,' says Sophie. 'All these over-fumfed Shane Warne-y types. And their girlfriends are all two decades younger. I bet my ex will walk in any minute. Seriously, where are all these people in the daytime? You never see them in Sainsbury's. It's like *Made in Chelsea* meets *TOWIE* meets *When Plastic Surgery Goes Wrong*!'

'This place is stunning, babe, toilets are gorge!' says Amber, sitting back down and surveying the room. 'Funny smell, though.'

'Caviar air freshener . . . ' I say, my shoulders giving an involuntary wriggle at the memory.

'What?' snorts Sophie. 'Were they all out of the smell of gold?'

'OMG, it's Aimee from Pilates!' Amber rushes over to a table of four: two chunky men, chatting across a lump of bleeding beef on a wooden board, two distinctly un-chunky women, sitting straight-backed by their sides, holding forks as though they're alien tools.

'Is she going to be working the room like this all night?' says Sophie.

'The more she works the room, the less you have to talk to her.'

'Aimee's so inspiring,' says Amber, returning only to whip out her iPhone for a series of selfies.

'Look at the menu,' I say, thrusting it towards her.

'There's nothing on here for less than thirty pounds,' says Sophie, in disgust.

'Chips are only sixteen pounds . . . ' I say, raising an eyebrow at her.

'A side of kale's only fifteen,' says Amber. 'Anyway, Laura said—'

'It's on me, yes, absolutely, go for it.' I mean please don't actually go for it, obviously.

'But it says you have to order five or six dishes per person!' says Sophie. 'And what on earth is a deconstructed Freekeh Pisco Srirachra Lollipop?'

'Tomato salad for me,' says Amber, 'but do you think they'll do it without the dressing?'

'You want a twenty-three-pound tomato salad with no dressing?' says Sophie.

'It's fine,' I hold out my hand in an effort to tone down her outrage. 'But let's get the dressing on the side?'

'Sure, babes. And I'll get the black cod, if they can do it without the black bit.'

'Fifty-six pounds! Amber, choose something else. You can't let Laura pay fifty-six pounds for a piece of fish!'

'But there's nothing else I can eat on this menu,' she says, pouting.

'Why is that?' says Sophie. 'Does your naturopath say you're allergic to anything that isn't horrendously overpriced?'

'Honestly, girls, it's fine! Let's order some drinks?'

After ten minutes of sticking my hand in the air I finally manage to catch the eye of one of only three serving staff visible, who insists on bringing us the water menu, but not the booze menu.

'Tahiti water!' says Amber. 'Yum! Shall we get a big bottle?'

'At fourteen pounds? We'll get tap water,' says Sophie.

'They don't serve it . . . ' I say.

'The smoked jalapeño umeboshi martini sounds good,' says Amber. 'Do you think jalapeños are alkaline?'

'Laura, is it OK if I have booze? Sorry, but it's sort of a psychological necessity. Let's see . . . "Goat's curd gin and fennel pollen tonic". What? They charge for *ice cubes*? Are they going to charge for the glass too?'

'The ice cubes are flavoured,' I say. 'They also charge extra depending on what salt you want with your food: Himalayan pink, Volcanic grey . . . And don't get me started on the pepper menu.'

We order our drinks and manage to persuade the water waiter to send over the wine waiter, though the food waiter is nowhere in sight. We sit for twenty minutes, me trying to keep a low profile, Amber basking in her natural habitat of reflective surfaces, and Sophie trying to sip her wine as slowly as she can. She keeps picking up the glass and forcing herself to put it down, only to pick it up again and take a tiny sip.

By the time the food waiter comes over everyone's glass is empty. Luckily he refuses to take an order for another round, which buys me at least ten minutes without drinks. I order as many of Adam's dishes as I can afford and some of the dishes I tried last time so I can make a fair comparison, and avoid anything with a major chew. Amber butts in to check the pH of her tomatoes and asks the waiter to double-check with the chef. He heads over to the pass, chats to Adam and I see Adam's mouth twitch briefly, unaware of who the comment has come from before he looks up, sees our table and grins a huge welcome. I beam back at him and mouth the word 'Amber' and he laughs and shakes his head.

'You've only ordered twelve dishes,' says the waiter, returning and looking at his order pad as if it's a cheque we've forgotten to sign.

'Twelve's plenty,' says Sophie, fixing him with a stare.

'The chef's special is exquisite,' he says to Amber and me. 'Eels in a *beurre noisette* with micro lovage.'

'Has it got butter in it?' says Amber.

Sophie picks up her wine glass, forgetting it's empty, and places it down again with a thud.

'We'll be fine with that lot,' I say.

'The dishes will be served when they are ready,' says the waiter, and turns on his heel before we can ask him again to send over the booze waiter.

'What does that mean, "when they're ready"?' says Sophie. 'He made it sound like they're doing us a favour.'

'It means they bring out what they want, when they want,' I say, feeling my heart sink. Nothing's better so far – the service, the hot pants, the attitude . . . Am I wasting my time, and a whole lot of money, for Groundhog Day?

We spend the next twenty minutes making strained conversation. We have limited common ground, other than the block of flats we live in. Discussing the colour of the communal radiators and whether Mr Macauliffe down the end of our corridor is visited by a string of rent boys or merely handsome Brazilian cleaners only gets us so far. As the chat has dried up, I take the opportunity to study Adam in action, to try to get to the bottom of what's going on in that kitchen.

At the moment he's standing at the pass with Max. Together they're working through the orders: Adam will pick up the order as it comes through, call it out to the team, then rapidly but smoothly shuffle the tickets along like a Vegas croupier, all the while checking the progress of the tickets already in front of him. At the same time Adam's entirely aware of what his team are up to behind him. One moment he notices the salamander overhead grill has three pans below it the chef has forgotten and he walks over and quietly removes them before they burn. The next he's back at the pass, tweezering nasturtium petals and slivers of candied clementine on to a golden crème brûlée. As soon as dessert resembles a mini work of art, almost as if he has a sixth sense, he turns to the meat station and sees the saucier is falling behind so he walks over, prods two steaks with his finger and whips them off the heat and with a huge knife cuts the sirloins into thick slices – all done in less than thirty seconds. He flits between precision and brute strength without a single mis-step.

While this is happening a waitress tries to take a dish Adam hasn't checked and he catches the plate in time and re-arranges six polenta chips into a geometric stack, rather than a pile that looks like it's been dropped from a great height by a disgruntled dinner lady. The waitress giggles and twirls a strand of her hair as she waits. He smiles at her politely; I wonder if he'd flirt back if I wasn't looking in his direction. As soon as she's taken the dish, he's back, fully focused on checking and re-checking the status of the tickets again.

The whole process is mesmerising. He's like a conductor with his back to his orchestra who still manages to create perfect rhythm and harmony. I have seen many good chefs at work but I've never seen one manage a kitchen so calmly. The pressure of such a big operation doesn't faze him at all; he is fully in control.

'Earth to Laura!' says Amber, giggling. 'Hello? You were just staring into the distance like a zombie, babe.'

'Sorry. Just thinking.' Just thinking: there is an entirely different energy in that kitchen to a month ago. And I have a strong suspicion the food will be entirely different too, and sure enough, when it arrives, it's incomparable.

Firstly, everything looks beautiful. But more importantly, everything tastes phenomenal. The Cobb salad is more luscious avocado than lettuce. The tomato salad dressing makes me think of an idealised summer afternoon in the Tuscan hills. Balance and texture and seasoning and temperature across every dish are perfect. By the end of the meal, Amber is swiping the dressing out of the mason jar with her finger.

'I wasn't expecting it to be that good!' says Sophie, placing her gold lamé napkin down. 'Shame about the decor and the staff and the prices.'

Oh, the prices. When the bill arrives I have to use the light on my phone to check it. They've only charged us half price for the food. I point this out to the waiter but he says Chef has insisted.

'Thanks, but I can't let him do that,' I say, though looking at this bill I jolly well can.

He heads back to the pass to chat to Adam. Adam looks over at me, shakes his head violently, then raise his hands in the air as if to say 'What are you doing?'.

The waiter returns. 'We can't override it on the system now and Chef insists.'

Sophie looks over my shoulder at the bill and flinches. 'Jesus, Laura, that's a weekend in Paris!'

'More like New York,' I say.

'Let me give you some money.' She grabs her handbag for her wallet, while Amber makes another dash for the toilet.

'I insist,' I say, handing the waiter my card. 'I do feel slightly sick,' I say to Sophie under my breath.

'Do you think they've poisoned you again?'

The bill. Still, it was the right thing to do – the truth is worth the price.

'What did you think of it all, Soph?'

'Me? Great food, vile place. More importantly what are you going to write?'

Good question.

31

A thousand words; 1,000 words to encapsulate the crazy, paradoxical experience of the restaurant I ate in tonight. It is not the same restaurant as last time but, bar the food, it's still obnoxious.

I start with the food:

The menu has jumped on the bandwagon of every trend going – and is driving on the wrong side of the road at that. Nonetheless, Adam Bayley does a transformative job. Everything works and works harder than it should, dishes that make no sense on paper make entire sense in the mouth.

There's no way I'm letting them off the hook for rude staff, greedy pricing, the contempt in which they hold their customers. I try my hardest not to use the first-hand knowledge I've picked up from Adam about the restaurant's margins, their crazy ethos, all the short cuts and tricks. It's hard though – like black pudding, once you know what's going on inside, you can't un-know it.

I've been typing like Angela Lansbury at the start of *Murder, She Wrote* and by six a.m. I've done 800 words but I'm stuck on the coffee. I ordered the same cup earlier, and even though it had been prepared by a ham-fisted coffee-hater who'd brewed it so long it had turned bitter, at least it was the El Salvador it claimed it was; it would be disproportionate to hang a man for it. I take the view that what happened a month ago with the instant coffee was a mistake – a deliberate one – but one that's since been rectified.

By nine a.m. I've showered, had a quick re-edit, and emailed Roger a copy. En route to work I have to go via the offie, which doesn't open until ten a.m., so I am eleven minutes late – normally not the end of the world, but normally Sandra's not running the show.

She'll probably have seen the email I sent Roger already – that could explain the toxic fury that's radiating off her like a Ready Brek glow. Either way, I'm lying low until I've spoken to legal and a sub and can at least present her with fully approved copy so all she has to do is press play on the copy swap.

I've been doing the job long enough to feel confident there's nothing libellous in the new review but to be sure, I pop up to ask Heather. Then I pay Kiki a visit – she owes me several favours for all the times she's dragged me down The Betsey on benders sold to me as *one quick drink* – so I call them all in, and give her the bottle of Jägermeister I bought earlier – in exchange for a speedy sub job during her lunch break. By 2.45 p.m. Kiki's tweaked and polished everything and Heather's cleared it for take-off: if only every day flew by this quickly.

Now for the tricky bit. Getting Sandra to physically authorise the swap. I have to play it down slightly – if she gets wind of the Adam part she'll have me for breakfast. She'll be difficult, I'm sure, but the bottom line is, Roger's OK'd it.

There's never a good time to disturb Sandra but particularly not when she's eating a Fletchers cheese and salad cream sandwich. Maybe I'll give her another five minutes, she might have treated herself to some Quavers? Ah, no, the antiseptic wash has come out and is being vigorously rubbed over her hands.

'Sandra, have you got a minute?'

'It'll have to wait,' she says, her eyes fixed on her screen. 'We're on deadline.'

'That's why I need to speak to you.'

'Not today.'

'Sandra, it's urgent.'

'As urgent as the Bechdel leader?'

'No, but—'

'So it will have to wait.'

'Sandra, I need to make a copy switch on my column, but it's all ready to go. And Roger's approved it.'

Her body stiffens. 'You filed that almost four weeks ago.'

'Yes – but there was an issue.'

226

'With your *symmetry*?'

'Some factual errors on my part which I didn't feel comfortable putting my name to.'

'Not actually your name.'

'Errors which I've now changed. The photo stays the same, it's just a copy swap, it'll take ten minutes. I can speak to studio myself?'

'When did this happen?'

'Roger and I were talking about it last week, but I only wrote the review last night.'

'Well, he hasn't mentioned it to me, and . . . ' she says, clicking on her production file spreadsheet, 'it's going down the line . . . tomorrow morning, so I'm afraid not.'

'Sandra – I made a mistake, OK? And I'm trying to put it right.'

'I'm not sure where the confusion is, but the day before we go to print is too late to change a layout.'

'It can be done, we've done it before.'

'On an actual news story, not on a lifestyle piece. And there's no time for legal or subbing. Has Roger even seen the new review? He can't have.'

'I've shown it to Heather.'

'You went directly to Heather without showing Roger?'

'And it's been subbed – Roger said I should.'

'Have you got that in writing?'

'He said it in his office last night – I wouldn't make it up.'

She shakes her head in disbelief. 'It's taken you four weeks to realise you made a few *factual errors*? There must be more to it than that . . . '

'Sandra, as you say, it's only a lifestyle piece.'

'There you go. As if we haven't got enough going on with the Bechdel piece. If it's not business critical, I'm afraid I can't indulge you.'

Change tack, pronto!

'Sandra, I'm sorry I'm being a nuisance. I'd really appreciate it if you could authorise the switch on the system. I know it's not that straightforward . . . ' But it's not that bloody difficult either.

'*And* we moved that fractional ad to accommodate you.'

'Look – if you don't believe me, I can email Roger and ask him to confirm.'

'Roger is having a much-needed break – I wouldn't *dream* of disturbing him over something this trivial.'

'And nor would I! I just meant if you wanted further proof.'

'Fine.'

'OK then. So it's saved as "New Review" with today's date on, same photo. Thank you. Sandra, I know it's not ideal . . . '

Well, I wasn't expecting a love-in.

'You know someone with Fergus's experience would never have done this,' she says, as I'm walking away.

I stop and pause. I've only just managed to persuade her to do it, there's no point in antagonising her further, but I'm so desperate to argue back and say: Thank goodness I am not Fergus, because someone with Fergus's experience would just write favourable reviews based on his personal relationships. But of course I stop myself, because this could be construed as precisely what I am doing. If someone didn't have their facts straight. If someone was trying to cause trouble.

32

The dentist has just tipped me backwards and told me to open wide when I have a horrible thought. What if Sandra didn't actually mean yes when she said *fine?* Or what if in the rush of yesterday afternoon she forgot to action the change? I'm out all day, so I'll have to nag her from a distance – probably a blessing.

As soon as the dentist's finished, I race to my phone to email her. It'll put her back up enormously but I cc Roger in too – even though I know she'd never do the favour for me, she'll do it for him.

My phone beeps. Sandra, already? No, it's a message from Adam, telling me to meet him at Victoria coach station at 4.30 a.m. on Sunday with passport and carry-on luggage.

Should I pack a bikini?

If he says yes I'm not going.

No – same sort of weather as here. Bring tooth glue if you're planning more party tricks.

Oooh, where can it be? If the weather's the same as here, perhaps the passport thing is a decoy and we're staying in England, maybe going to the New Forest?

Right – I need a bikini wax, I need to paint my toenails, exfoliate, decant toiletries . . . But I'm going to just give Sandra a quick call now because I cannot bear to wait all afternoon for a response, it's making me nervous.

Her landline rings out, as does her mobile – I should have blocked my number to see if she's avoiding me. That's probably paranoid, even for me. I leave a message asking her to call me back urgently, then call once again, just in case she's back at her desk. No.

OK, bikini wax – it's been a while. When I shagged Russell, I hadn't been planning to; he was still hovering in the grey area of 'good on paper/maybe I'm being too fussy'. On that third date he'd ambushed me, deliberately dithered about, missed the last train home, then asked if he could crash on my sofa. I was not so far out of the game I didn't sense a ruse. Besides, there was no way he'd be allowed to crash on Amber's pristine white sofa, but I figured I should just get on with the sex. As a consequence, my bikini line was not match fit but I didn't care – frankly Russell was lucky to be getting any action.

But with Adam it's a different story. If he doesn't make a move, a serious move, not a finger on the knee move – then I am done. I'll hold up my side of the bargain – no self-mutilation getting in the way of a snog, and I shall turn up as prepped as a woman can be.

Amber's had all her body hair lasered off but she used to use a waxer who can remove a hair before it's even decided to be a follicle. She laughs down the phone and tells me her earliest appointment is September. Fine, I head to Selfridges and get a walk-in. Halfway through, warm golden wax stuck to my inner thigh, I panic again and try calling Sandra but there's no reception – so the minute I'm back in the main part of the store I try again, no reply. Then I realise I've missed a trick. I call Kiki and hold my breath as I hear her fingers on the keyboard checking what's on the system.

'It's all fine, doll, I can see it in front of me, two versions, the second one?'

'Thank you.' Thank you. I'm so relieved I treat myself to a Portuguese custard tart from the food hall. Then just to dot my 'i's and cross my 't's, I call Sandra once more, and this time she picks up.

'I've had two missed calls on my mobile from you, Laura.' Yes, that's correct! And a voice message and an email – and I wouldn't have had to stalk you if you'd replied in the first place.

'I just wanted to double-check everything was OK.'

'You are seriously testing my patience. It's all put to bed, done.'

Now I feel foolish for triple-checking. Of course Sandra would do it, once I brought Roger into the loop. Still, better to annoy Sandra and get confirmation than leave it vague.

'Thank you, Sandra. I do appreciate it. And sorry again to nag.'

Maybe I'll bring her back some Toffifee from Duty Free if we do get on a plane.

The minute I hang up I realise I have another problem. I've forgotten to change that Leonardo Da Vinci quote in the noodle bar review, the one I quoted at Adam.

Oh, that is not cool: not cool at all.

OK, risk assessment: what are the chances Adam will read the LuxEris review? A certainty. He secretly does read his reviews and even though I'm unstinting in my praise of the food, I'm lacerating about everything else, so his bosses will probably have a tantrum about it.

What are the chances of him then reading the review of a noodle bar printed on the same page? Very high – he loves Japanese food.

What are the chances of him remembering I said the Da Vinci quote? High too. We talked about it, although he might have forgotten, he was quite distracted that Sunday.

What are the chances of him putting two and two together and realising I only remembered the quote because I'd put it in an article, which I in fact wrote? So-so . . .

And what are the chances of me calling Sandra back and asking her to remove the quote and substitute it for another? Less than zero.

The truth will out. The truth may out. Some levels of risk you just have to live with.

33

On Saturday night I'm so excited, I can't sleep, then so nervous about missing the coach, I wake at two a.m. I double-check my hand luggage – best underwear, snacks for the journey and my optimum nightwear – the short silk and lace slip from M&S that looks a little like La Perla, or might do in the dark.

Adam's sitting on a bench at the station, waiting. He looks knackered and tips his head back as if it's the only way he can keep his eyelids open. He stands, leans his body against mine and pretends to fall asleep on my shoulder. Full body contact in public: excellent start.

'I had to do Monday's rotas at two thirty a.m.,' he says. 'I was still packing when the cab picked me up, I'll be lucky if there's even a toothbrush in my bag.'

'Where are we going? I've got enough chocolate raisins to get us halfway to Skeggie but after that we'll have to start foraging.'

He looks suddenly panicked. 'Laura, please tell me you brought your passport?'

'Yeah, of course. I just figured it might have been a white lie to put me off the scent.'

'Gosh, you really do have trust issues, don't you? I can hereby confirm, we are not going to Skegness,' he says, taking my hand. 'Right – coach A6, keep those chocolate raisins on standby.'

If he hadn't fallen asleep the minute we boarded the coach I suspect I'd have told Adam about the review on the way to Stansted. This week has been so crazy and I'm so tired from Wednesday's all-night writing session, my defences are down; for the first time since I met him I feel guilt free, better than that, *I feel proud*: I've done the right thing by Adam, by the paper and by myself – at significant financial cost. I've retained my journalistic integrity and my reward is I get to go on holiday with this gorgeous man! *I* have made life fair.

'You're in a remarkably good mood,' he says, as I bounce back from WH Smiths, carrying the Sunday papers, *Grazia* and a box of Toffifee.

'Just happy to be spending proper time with you.'

'Me too,' he says, smiling, then stopping to look at me as if for the first time.

'What?' I say, searching his eyes for an answer. Those eyes, such a beautiful baby blue.

He pauses, tilts his head to one side. 'Just thinking how lovely you look today.' His gaze flicks to my mouth and he leans in and kisses me. Under fluorescent lighting, standing in the departures lounge with stag parties en route to Latvia wolf-whistling and screaming toddlers barging in to us, we kiss and keep kissing until a loud speaker announces the last call for flight 2950 to Amsterdam, and Adam finally pulls away.

'We're going to miss our plane,' he says, grabbing my hand and heading to security.

'Amsterdam? I love Amsterdam!'

'It's not Amsterdam,' he says, handing both boarding cards to the guard.

'Are you keeping it a secret till we're back home? You're good, I'd have blabbed by now.'

'You're on a need-to-know basis, Da Laura.'

'Oh my God, are we going to the pesto place?'

'That was mean of me, no – it isn't open till Easter. Maybe we can go later in the year, if you're still talking to me after you've put up with a night of my snoring?'

'Have you not booked us in separate rooms? Next you'll be expecting me to show you my ankles.'

'At least show me one,' he says.

I grab his bicep with both hands and give it a little squeeze. 'I am so over-excited right now, Adam Bayley. I just needed to say that to you.' I feel like I might pop with happiness.

He still won't tell me where we're off to and we sit happily airside, holding hands as I study the departures board: Ljubljana? Aarhus? Ostrava? I don't know where half these places are.

'Adam, does it begin with a vowel?'

'Stop trying to guess. You'll know soon enough,' he says, rubbing his thumb gently against my cheek. 'You look tired.'

'All those early breakfasts.'

He smiles apologetically. 'It must be a nightmare trying to have a relationship with a chef – such crazy hours.'

'So this is definitely a relationship?'

He looks perplexed. 'Do you often snog random men in airports?'

'It's just . . . I guess we're a bit of a slow starter . . . physically.'

'When have I even had a chance? Besides, I thought you were a classy lady.'

I shake my head.

'Laura – the first time I met you, you refused to give me your number. And when I had to leave that morning you seemed massively unimpressed; I thought you didn't want to see me again . . . '

I'm about to ask *who* were *you arguing with on the phone, anyway?* but stop myself – totally unnecessary.

'Laura, I didn't know if you liked me or not. I was trying to be respectful.'

'Well, please be a little less respectful in future. So this *relationship* malarkey . . . what does it involve? There's putting up with snoring, what other demands do you have?'

'Let's see . . . OK, number one, always being on my side.'

'I can do that.'

'Number two, never ask me to go clothes shopping with you.'

'What else?'

'You've probably realised I'm pretty obsessed with my work, so not taking that personally.'

'I like my job too.'

'And you have to be honest about my food. I know I can be a little over-sensitive but I want to get better. I want a star.'

Do it! Do it now! This is your window, and not one you have to jump out of! He's as good as said: I want a girlfriend who's a critic.

'Hold that thought . . . ' I unzip my handbag. There's so much crap in here today, passport, cash, lip balm, where is my phone . . . ?

'Shit, that's us!' he says, staring at the screen. 'In red – last call, Gate Fourteen, Perugia.'

He grabs my hand, I grab my bags, and we race, panicked, through the airport; past Pret, down the escalator, along a mammoth corridor just squeezing through the closing doors of the shuttle train, up another escalator, all the way to the back of the terminal, the furthest possible gate, have a barney with the man at the gate about my luggage, cram my magazine into my coat pocket, newspapers under my arm, chocolate into the bag, board the plane, last ones on, sitting nowhere near each other, me in the middle – him at the back by the loo.

I wedge myself between a couple who thought they'd scored three seats between two and who immediately re-establish elbow supremacy of the armrests. As I wriggle to get comfortable I feel my phone knock against my thigh – it was in my jacket pocket all along. If I can download the attachment now I'll show Adam once we're airborne. Even if he's a bit annoyed at first, he won't be *that* annoyed on a plane.

The man next to me tuts loudly as I scroll through my inbox. Where is it, when did Kiki send me her edited version? Two forty-five p.m. on Thursday. Aha! Here it is: right, download.

From nowhere a stewardess looms and tells me to please switch off my phone, her tone suggesting the exact opposite of please.

'I've just got to find this document quickly . . . one minute? No? OK . . . ' I say, pressing the off button. 'The engine isn't even on yet . . . '

'Thank you,' she says, with such venom I'm surprised her teeth don't melt.

That would have been an ideal opportunity to show Adam: 'a head chef totally on top of his game, a future star in the making'. How could he not be pleased with that? 'Vulgar decor, even more vulgar pricing, an attitude problem worse than Lindsay Lohan's.' Well, he might not be delighted with that bit, but it's fair – and it's not like he'd disagree. I could download it when we get there I suppose, but the moment will have passed.

He can read it in situ in black and white on Tuesday morning.

It's only forty-eight hours now. It'll be a nice welcome home present, soften the blow of returning to work.

'So, what shall we do first?' says Adam, buckling up in our hire car so cheap and plasticky it feels like we're inside a kid's toy. 'Mum's given me a long list.'

'What's on it?'

'Assisi: huge church, very important frescoes, all about St Francis . . .'

'Famous for preaching to the birds?'

'Then there's Todi: ancient Etruscan town, legend has it four thousand years ago an eagle dropped a tablecloth on it, home to one of Italy's finest Renaissance churches?'

'What else?'

'Montefalco – '

'Falcons?'

'Bird bingo! Picture perfect Umbrian hilltop town with fifteenth-century frescoes?'

'Church, frescoes, church, more old frescoes. Hmmm. You know what I think we should do?'

He checks his watch – 11.00 a.m. – and nods.

We've driven past so many stunning pink-stoned trattorias perched on hills overlooking the magnificent countryside that when Adam pulls off the winding road and into a dingy lodge that looks like a rundown version of Crossroads motel I suggest he might have misread the map.

'Mum said the food's amazing,' he says, walking into the fusty reception and greeting the old lady behind the desk in fluent Italian. She leads us into a deserted, yellow-walled space that feels like a train station waiting room and is dominated by a 50-inch flatscreen TV booming out the rolling news.

'Is it definitely the right restaurant?' I ask, looking out of the window at a small swimming pool covered by a tatty tarpaulin weighed down with brown leaves and dirty water.

'It's not exactly LuxEris, but I reckon that's a good thing, don't you?' He glances at the wine list. 'Four euros a carafe!' His face lights up. 'See? You can't even get a glass of water for that at mine,' he says, taking my hand in his and resting them on the table.

'So how long has your mum had her house?'

'She bought it about ten years ago,' he says. 'But I haven't made it out here once – just been working and working. Here, try one of these.' He holds out a basket filled with rectangular orange slices of what look like cake, scattered with yellow nuggets. 'Easter bread – it's a local specialty.'

I take a bite, then another. 'Yum – it's like a Cheesy Wotsit in bread form!'

'Right – let's get down to business. What are you having?'

My eyes flick over the handwritten scrap of a menu. 'I know it's sacrilegious but I'm going to have pasta followed by pasta.'

'Good, because I'm having truffles followed by truffles. Why are you pulling a face?'

'Fergus, our old critic, used to foam at the mouth at the mere whiff of a truffle but I've never understood what all the fuss is about.'

'Try mine, you'll see.'

'OK, I finally get it,' I say. 'But they don't taste this delicious back home.'

'That's because they grow them ten minutes from here. I'm kind of jealous of yours,' he says, poking his fork into my second bowl of pasta. 'Squash and ginger fettuccine!'

'Mellow and crazy but great, right? Like Bill Murray in a bowl.'

'The Bill Murray of pastas? I think *you* might be the crazy one.'

'The drunk one,' I say, pouring the last of the carafe into my glass.

'The Italians do know what they're doing,' he says, going back in for another bite.

'Can you open an Italian restaurant in London please, preferably round the corner from my flat? And make sure there's a dessert trolley?'

'I'd love to. I can probably afford the trolley, but then there's lease premiums, licences, kit, fit-out, salaries . . . Fancy lending me quarter of a million?'

'I wish . . .' I say, leaning my cheek against his bicep. 'But couldn't you do it cheaper? People are doing great stuff – less traditional – on smaller budgets nowadays. There's this really cute café in Hackney they converted from an old public toilet. That can't have cost quarter of a million.'

'Laura – I'm not a snob. I wouldn't want my place to be silver service, far from it – but I draw the line at urinals in the dining room.'

'You should start with a food truck or a stall – nobody else is doing anything like your savoury pastries. Then you wouldn't need mega-bucks and you could set it up much faster too.'

'The thing I don't like about being head chef is that so much of it is rotas, schedules, paperwork – it's taking me away from what I love most: the cooking itself.'

'Have you heard of Kitchenstarter? Sophie got some funding from them last year – they're brilliant at supporting new creative businesses. You could use that cash to start something small with the pastries, but create a brand identity that feels fresh, have a website. You should look into it, you really should,' I say, catching myself as I realise I'm starting to sound like Jess.

'Here's the plan! How about we jack in our jobs and drive around town on a bike serving London's best breakfasts. You could be coffee guru, I'll do the pastries,' he says, smiling.

'Getting up at five a.m. every day? Sounds way too much like hard work. Besides, I like my job.'

'We could have a fifty-inch telly on the handlebars, just like mamma used to . . . ?'

'Generator-powered by my pedalling, no doubt. And what will we call this magnificent new mobile dining concept?'

'Tandem and Cash?'

I let out a low groan. 'Adam, if you *ever* have a go at me for making a bad pun – ever again – just remember this moment. You and me, sitting here – me, massively unimpressed; you, trying not to giggle at your own joke.'

'Laura, I will remember this moment my whole life . . . not least because on the TV behind you there's a busty blonde on a game show, currently stripping down to her kecks.'

I turn to check the screen – the news is still playing. 'Why Adam Bayley, for a minute there I almost believed you were telling me the truth.'

He leans over to kiss me and our lips meet in well-fed contentment.

'What time is it, anyway?' he says, sitting back up again as the bill arrives. He holds it out, victoriously. 'Less than thirty euros, including tip! You'd pay triple that in London.'

'It's two fifteen p.m. Fresco o'clock?'

'I have a much better idea,' he says, grinning.

A shag?

'Ice cream.'

'This is the best day I've had since I can remember,' says Adam, as we stop at a traffic light and he leans over the handbrake to kiss me.

'Is that because of the hazelnut gelato or because I've spared you a tour of important medieval churches? We'll have to do them tomorrow if not today – it's sort of obligatory, when in Rome and all that. Green light!'

'It's the best day because I've never met a girl who can flit seamlessly between singing Whitesnake, the Backstreet Boys and the theme tune from *Bugsy Malone* without knowing the words to any of them.'

'Well, I've never met a boy who could drive a hairpin bend while doing jazz hands. Not that I'm encouraging your behaviour. Besides, I'm pretty sure "Fog on the Tiber" is not the correct lyric either.'

'And nor is "Here Comes the Red Snapper"! Being with you is like hanging out with a deranged jukebox,' he says. 'A very pretty deranged jukebox.'

'How come *you* know all the lyrics to *Backstreet*?'

He shrugs. 'I make no apologies. Have I told you I'm a massive Brian Harvey fan?'

'Er, Brian Harvey is *not* a Backstreet Boy.'

'Er, like, I know that. I'm just saying I'm a fan.' He laughs. 'Ever since he ran himself over after eating too many jacket potatoes.'

'Whitesnake. Why do you think they went for white? Not very scary for a snake, is it? Blacksnake – scary, Greysnake – good, gothic. White? Might as well be Lilacsnake.'

'What did you want to be when you were five, Laura?'

'Hairdresser or air stewardess. You?'

'Astronaut. What's your favourite cheese?'

'All cheese.'

'Silly answer.'

'Silly question,' I say. 'What's the meanest thing anyone's ever said to you?'

'Other than that I'm crap at map reading?'

'You said I sound like a cat being garrotted when I sing Kate Bush!'

'I meant it as a compliment! Some of my favourite blues singers sound like they're undergoing bodily harm. OK, let me think. Urgh, OK . . . When I was thirteen Darren Burns said, "You're kind of cool, but you look really ugly when you laugh . . ."'

'Ouch! What a horrible thing to say! I bet he was jealous because the girls fancied you.'

'I used to practise different laughs in front of the mirror,' he says, shaking his head in shame. 'Have you ever tried laughing with your mouth shut?'

'Oh, you look handsome when you laugh, Adam Bayley, you really do.'

'Well you make me laugh, Laura Parker – and not only when you sing.'

'Church . . . hill . . . green field . . . yellow field . . . church . . . rolling hill . . . are you sure this is the right way?'

'She said it's in the middle of nowhere.'

'Well, we're there all right. Maybe give her a ring just to check?'

He laughs. 'And what landmark should I tell her?'

'Trees, church spires and a lot more trees?'

'Hold on, this might be it.'

At a small blue sign for Monte Verdure we take a left, then bump along a gravel road which snakes slowly up a hill for five miles, then take a smaller red clay track, even bumpier and steeper, until finally we hit a grey, rocky track that leads to a wrought-iron gate at the top of a huge hill. We park the car in the shade of an umbrella pine and carry our bags up the final stretch of path till we reach a collection of ancient buildings that make up the dwelling.

'This whole thing was a medieval borgo,' says Adam, standing with his hands on his hips, surveying the view. 'A stopping point en route for pilgrims to Assisi, sort of like a travel lodge.'

'A bit nicer than a Travelodge,' I say. 'It's more like a fortress!'

The huge, grey stone exteriors are draped in lavender-blossomed wisteria, with narrow lookout windows dotted throughout. They form the best part of a square, surrounding a central courtyard garden, wild with sage and rosemary and a fig tree not yet in fruit. We take a tour round the outside of the buildings before Adam stops in front of a heavy studded double door set in one of the walls and raises his eyebrows in delight.

'Check this out!' he says, pushing his shoulder against the door. 'We've even got our own on-site chapel – we can tick churches off the list after all!'

We step inside the tiny chapel – sixteen chairs on each side, high vaulted ceilings, ancient wooden beams. It's so simple; so quiet. Adam takes my hand and together we walk down the aisle towards the altar and stand silently breathing in the air. We kiss under cool stone arches and Adam runs his hands through my hair and pulls me closer. We kiss and kiss, then stop – aware this kiss is turning into a distinctly non-churchy kind of kiss.

'Let's dump our bags and work out a plan,' he says, taking my hand and leading me out of the chapel and back across the courtyard to one of the houses set in the stone on the south-facing side. It has hanging terracotta window boxes by the door filled with tiny white flowers that smell of honey. He turns the key in the lock and I follow him through. On our left is a tiny kitchen, two electric hobs and a miniature fridge; in front of us the main living area – a small but cosy room with a brick-tiled floor and a fireplace against one wall, a sofa and an armchair filling the remaining space.

'It's pretty basic – there's a bedroom and a bathroom upstairs,' he says.

'It's lovely!' I move closer to him and put my arms around his waist. 'Adam, I'm sorry but I have a terrible confession to make . . . '

'Go on?'

'I'm having a total double-pasta and ice-cream crash. I know I'm a granny but if I don't have a tactical nap now, I'll be zonked by six p.m.'

'I'm struggling to keep my eyes open too. One hour's sleep on the coach and a kip on the plane . . . Probably wasn't the smartest idea of mine to come all this way just for one night, was it?'

'I'm so glad we did.'

'If I get us blankets, do you reckon it's warm enough to doze in the garden?'

'There's a garden?'

'Oh yes – she chose this place for the view.'

Through the living area and out the back door is a huge grassy lawn covered in giant clover, dandelions and daisies, the tips of their petals scarlet as if quick-dipped in beetroot juice. We must be at the top of the highest hill in the area – you can see for miles and miles and miles – every shade of green from chartreuse to moss to midnight, greens like yellows, greens like blues. The grass under our feet is so vivid, it's practically luminous – it almost hurts your eyes. Its colour makes the mass of scattered olive trees immediately below us look grey in comparison. Beyond the olive groves, a vast landscape spreads out – gently sloping hills covered in darker patches of woods and forest, fields of crops and scattered vineyards curving all the way to distant mountains.

Adam sets up two deckchairs facing the horizon and grabs two picnic blankets. We kick off our shoes and hold hands under the blanket. The gentlest of clouds hang overhead, as static as if they're painted on the sky. Wood smoke scents the air and the only noise is the echo of a dog's bark and the sound of birds, of which there are many – at least six distinct bird songs in ear shot – one like a hinge, one like a buzzing bee. We must doze off listening to them because the next time I open my eyes it's 7.10 p.m., the sun beginning its descent behind us, the sky turning rapidly from blue.

Adam opens his eyes a moment later and smiles at me. 'You know one thing that would make this moment even better?'

The man's a genius. We sit with a bottle of local red, watching the vast ever-changing sky like it's a movie.

'Everything good, Laura?'

I nod. I nod because I don't want to lie. Or rather I nod because I don't want to tell the truth, which is this: I feel scared because I feel so happy. I feel the extreme happiness in my bones, which I've felt only rarely as an adult: delight, excitement, contentment, almost radiating through my body.

The last time I felt this good was on honeymoon. Tom could only spare five days so we'd poured the money into posh Sicily, and while I'd baulked at the price per night, by the time I lay poolside in the baking heat, I'd managed to un-baulk. For five days we'd drifted along in a state of bliss, cosseted from the real world by an army of starched mind readers whose sole happiness depended on administering to our vital sensory pleasures.

You're a fraction too hot right now – open your eyes and you'll see I've just placed a glass of iced water with cucumber and mint next to your lounger, and a fridge-cold flannel. Ooh, and now it's six fifteen p.m. and you're tired, a little dehydrated, your body's craving giant green olives and a salty little deep-fried snack that will go perfectly with the fresh peach Bellini you didn't even realise you wanted until you sat up – and yes, the pinky-orange hues do complement this sunset nicely, don't they?

I remember walking back to our room on the final evening, across a lawn cast with tiny pools of light, the throb of crickets surrounding us like a low fast pulse, and thinking: life is great, life is amazing, aren't we lucky? I remember getting on the plane, cheeks burning from those last twenty minutes of sunshine grabbed at the airport. I remember landing smoothly and then the shock of Dad's face at the airport – the terrible fear in his eyes he was trying so hard to hide. I remember that first sight of Mum, eyes shut, face wrinkle-free, looking entirely at peace – but for the tube down her throat – and I wish I could forget everything after that.

Thirty-three days of staring at a monitor: four coloured lines: red, yellow, green, blue; thirty-three days of increasing blackness. Days of thinking, *I understand what the blue line means now: oxygen saturation in the blood. That links to the metal clip on her finger, that number says ninety-two at this precise moment and ninety-two is much improved from eighty-four. And the green line, that's heart rate. That's not looking so good right this second but it was good this time yesterday. And that tube straight into her neck, that's noradrenalin, and we* love *noradrenalin because it stabilises her. And because I understand these numbers on the screen, am doing my homework, am starting to make sense of this impenetrable world of medicine, now you, God, will make her better. That's the deal, isn't it?* But that wasn't the deal.

So I don't trust this level of happiness at all, which is a shame.

But then I feel Adam's hand in mine. I look up at this immense, shifting sky of blues and pinks and oranges and I think: this world is full of possibilities. Sometimes things do work out. Why shouldn't I be one of the lucky ones? If I don't believe I can be happy then of course I won't be happy. Feeling scared won't protect me from life. I just have to take a chance . . . And by the time I've run through half-a-dozen mantras, I can't help but laugh because I'm beginning to sound like one of Amber's self-help fridge magnets.

'What are you thinking about, Laura?' he says, gently squeezing my fingers.

'How random life is. How quickly things change. How you never, ever know what's around the corner.'

He lets out a small, rueful laugh, opens his mouth as if to say something, then shakes his head again.

'What is it, Adam?'

'There's a poem Mum put up, after my father left. I can't remember the words, but it's by Rumi, and it's something about greeting all things – good and bad – with the same attitude. Because what looks like bad news sometimes turns out to be good – and vice versa. Does that make any sense?'

I think back to Tom. How at the time it felt like my future was being torn from me, but now it feels like I dodged a bullet. I could have had kids with him – he'd still have been a liar and a cheat.

'You're not going to say everything happens for a reason, are you, Adam?'

'No . . . just that you don't know what things are, sometimes, till you're further down the line.'

'What made you think of that poem?'

He pauses, as if he's about to say something else, then shakes his head. 'I guess . . . being in Mum's house. This view, this peace – seeing how she turned her life around.'

But there's more to it than that.

'You couldn't drive to the shops even if they were open on a Sunday night,' I say, holding up the empty bottle of red wine.

'Grab another,' he says, pointing to a small wooden rack nestled in the corner of the living room. 'I totally should have planned this whole trip better. I wanted to make you something with local ingredients. Not even a packet of pasta in the cupboard. Mum just buys everything fresh when she's here . . . Hold on a minute – beans! One measly Tetra Pak of cannellini beans. All I'm ever going to make for you, Laura Parker, is beans,' he says, laughing.

While Adam is cooking, I pop upstairs for a shower. It feels mildly ridiculous to change into a little black dress if there's just the two of us in the living room. Instead I put on my sexy underwear, a lower cut top and my jeans, and head back down to the kitchen when I hear Adam calling my name.

'You look pretty,' he says, kissing me. 'Minty breath.'

'Dinner smells amazing!'

Laid out on the counter are two bowls, each filled with a perfect pile of creamy beans, flecked with little red dots of chilli and topped with tiny blue rosemary flowers.

'It's just beans, olive oil, chilli and rosemary,' he says, leading the way again to the garden. 'But actually the raw materials are pretty good quality.'

Back on the deckchairs we sit and eat, looking out at the distant yellow and white lights shimmering over the endless horizon. Lavender still perfumes the air, and the night sky is crisp and clear. We gaze at the silver sliver of moon, and the constellations sprinkled across the vast black canvas, in wonder.

'Are you sure the food was OK?' he says, finally taking my bowl from my lap and placing it down on the grass, inside his.

'I'd take that over dinner at Nobu any day – that was one of the best things I've ever eaten.'

'You say the sweetest things, Laura.' He sighs contentedly and takes my hand again. 'Oh dear! Your poor fingers feel like they're getting a little cold.'

'They are! They're freezing!'

'Then maybe we should go inside.'

We move to the sofa and start kissing and before long I end up sitting on his lap, facing him. All I can think about is sex. I'm pretty sure the sex will be good – the kissing has been amazing – but as Adam's hands reach down my lower back and gently pull me towards him, I find myself so turned on I actually feel almost sick with desire. As he pulls off his T-shirt and my top, I find myself having to lean back and take a deep breath to compose myself.

'You OK?' he says, stopping to look at me, and tracing his finger down the middle of my body.

I put my hand down to touch his firm, flat stomach. 'Good, yeah, I'm good. Keep going . . . ' I say, as he gently strokes my nipples with the tips of his fingers. 'That feels *so good* . . .'

Within minutes, he is down to his boxer shorts and I am in my knickers and I can feel him through my knickers, hard between my legs. I kiss his neck and I feel him push towards me, then suddenly stop.

'Are *you* OK, Adam?'

He blows out in frustration and looks at me with an embarrassed expression.

'What's wrong, Adam?' He hasn't lost his erection, I can feel it between the tops of my thighs.

'I haven't got any condoms,' he says, looking pained. 'I packed in such a rush. I'm sorry.'

'Mmm . . . ' I say, kissing behind his ear. 'That's OK, we can do it anyway, I'm on the pill.'

He takes his hands away from where they are, currently cupping my bottom, and puts them down by his side.

'What's wrong? You haven't got any lurgies have you?' I say.

'It's not that,' he says, looking away awkwardly.

'Well, I'm fine too . . . ' I say, kissing his neck and then his shoulder. I feel him straining against me, and I push myself harder against him. 'Just do it . . . please, that feels so good, oh God I want you . . . ' I move to kiss his lips but he jerks his head to one side, recoiling, as if I'd just belched.

That does not feel good at all.

He pushes me gently but firmly off his lap and stands. 'I'm sorry Laura . . . I can't . . .'

'Adam, I haven't got anything, I even have the text from the clinic to prove it! Don't put your jeans back on, Adam, what are you doing? Adam? Where are you going? Adam?'

Is this the most humiliated I've ever felt, I wonder, as I sit on the side of the bed, fully clothed again, picking at my thumbnail? What has been worse than this? Food poisoning on the train from Delhi to Mumbai? Different sort of bad. Am I more mortified than humiliated? Mortified's worse, isn't it? Mortified's probably the one.

Three twenty-five a.m. He's been gone for nearly three hours. Has he gone back to the airport to catch the first flight home? The car's still here. Now what am I meant to do? Drink, clearly.

I walk back down to the kitchen and pour myself a large glass of wine and take it out to the garden. I strain my ears for any sound of taxis: nothing but silence and my internal soundtrack of shame. After half an hour of imagining I can hear cars approaching, I pour another glass of wine, head back upstairs and lie down on the bed, fully clothed.

* * *

I wake to the sound of the front door gently closing. I hold my breath and hear footsteps treading softly up the stairs. I do hope it's not a serial killer because that would just make a perfect end to my perfect night.

'Hello?'

The door opens and Adam's head pops round the side of it, looking thoroughly apologetic. 'I didn't think you'd still be awake.'

I sit half up and rest on my elbows. 'What time is it anyway?' Outside it's still dark, but the birds have started to tweet. 'What happened, where did you go?'

He comes and lies down next to me on the bed and puts his arm out for me to rest on.

'It's OK, Adam, we don't have to have sex . . . I can be your friend, I think. If you don't fancy me? If you don't fancy girls?'

'Don't fancy you? Laura, you are so fucking sexy to me I just want to maul you.'

'Then what the fuck was all that about?'

'I just freaked out . . . I'm sorry.'

'About what? Where did you even go?'

'I went for a walk . . . to the nearest twenty-four hour chemist!' He shakes his head, as if laughing at his own ridiculousness. 'Forgive me?'

He moves in to kiss me again and our lips touch and it feels as though I've been waiting not just the last four hours for him but my whole adult life. He pulls my top up and I yank his T-shirt over his head and he moves on top of me and with his other hand unbuttons his jeans and kicks them awkwardly from round his ankles as neither of us is willing to stop kissing. And now he is on top of me in his boxers and my top is ruched halfway up my chest and most of our skin is touching and he feels warm and strong and solid on top of me and then I feel him, hard again, through his pants, pressing against my thigh and we are still kissing and he reaches over to his jeans on the floor and takes from the pocket the biggest box of condoms, rips it open, tears one of the foils and in less than twenty seconds he is inside me and I want this moment, this exact moment to last forever and yet we are now both so

248

breathless and turned on that we manage only seven minutes of urgent, life-depends-on-it shagging before he comes to rest on top of me, legs shaking slightly, his face buried in my neck.

And perhaps it was just two bodies taking what they wanted, what bodies are programmed to do. And yet lying here with Adam, the soles of my feet resting lightly on the tops of his, I find it almost impossible not to think that perhaps this sense of absolute rightness, this sense of belonging – that this might actually mean something.

We spend the next twelve hours in bed, we miss breakfast, we miss lunch. At one point I must doze off and when I wake, Adam opens his eyes too. We smile, we kiss – and then he slowly takes his finger and points it to his eye, to his heart and then to me.

On the plane home Adam dozes off and I find myself sitting with a dumb grin on my face, replaying my memories from earlier. Does everyone do this? I keep going back over certain bits, thinking maybe they'll lose their charge if I play them too many times, but the thoughts still make me lose my breath. The look in Adam's eyes when he was on top of me, that absolute lack of apology or shyness – it was the eye contact, not some lad-mag move, that was the greatest turn on of all. And that is how I now feel: turned on. Like the body I had yesterday is not the same body I have now. It is different – yes, currently a little spent, but it feels charged, revved up – reminded what it is capable of.

How long does it take to fall in love? One breakfast, one lunch, two dinners? A month? Does it creep up on you, or hit you in the face? Was it yesterday, when he was singing show tunes in the car like his life depended on it? I think I loved him a little from the doughnut.

Oh good lord, help me, I sound like a moony teenager. Sophie warned me this would happen – I'm lost in the hot sex cloud. It's not love. It's just hormones. Oxytocin. Nothing more. It's not love, just sex. My mind swings back and forth like a metronome. Everything/nothing/everything/nothing.

34

On the coach back into London I rest my head on Adam's shoulder as we drive along the darkened stretch of the M11, the occasional light twinkling in the distance. The coach is packed, but the stifling heat and the smell of other people's salami sandwiches does nothing to dent my happiness.

It's been so peaceful not having phones on for the last two days. We should turn them off more, I think, as I reach into my bag and take mine out. I'm tempted to keep it off till tomorrow morning, but just in case Dad or Roger have tried to get hold of me, I switch it on.

Nothing. Just a text from Amber asking if I can look after Annalex overnight; she's forgotten I'd be back late. And one from Sophie, and one from Kiki too – did I even tell her I was off work today?

Adam shifts his arm around me and kisses the top of my head. He's really not that short. In fact our heights are perfectly compatible. I sigh contentedly. I'm almost looking forward to work tomorrow – I hope Roger likes the revised piece. I'm going to take him back to LuxEris maybe next payday – to thank him.

My phone beeps. Kiki. Again? She's probably out pissed with Azeem – her Monday nights are as messy as anyone else's Fridays.

Laura, have you seen what Azeem's tweeting?!?

She must be looking at photos of baby turkeys, in the pub. Kiki in the pub, not the baby turkeys.

Hope he used the picture I found for him, I christened him Chick Norris!

WTF are you talking about?

She must be three Jägers down and too young to know who Chuck Norris is. I wonder if I can get the turkey's photo off Twitter and stick Chuck Norris's head on it.

'Adam? Do you know which App I can use to Photoshop from a Twitter photo?'

'Huh?' he says, lifting his head slowly – he must have been about to doze off.

'Don't worry.' I'll figure it out. Right, where are we . . . @TheDish_ Online . . . here we go . . .

Oh. My. God. That's not right. I sit bolt upright and click the link through to our main website.

Oh, that is not right at all. If this is an April Fool's it's a particularly unfunny one, and a day early at that.

Ha ha Kiki, very funny. Tell him to take it down NOW please? X

Ten seconds later my phone rings, Kiki. I press reject.

Stuck on coach, please tell Azeem it has to come down NOW.

Beside me, Adam yawns and sits up. My phone rings again. Kiki.

'I can't talk . . . ' I say, as quietly as possible.

'Dude.' She sounds extremely sober. 'Did you brief Azeem before you left?'

I reminded him about the turkey pics, did I forget to tell him about my own copy change?

'I just thought you might have switched back to the original version at the last minute,' she says. 'He's obviously picked the wrong one off the system.'

'Could you give him a call, ask him to switch it, and let me know? Thank you.'

'Everything OK?' says Adam.

'It's fine.' Absolutely not, hell no. Azeem is an idiot. He obviously didn't see the second file had been loaded. Sloppy, just sloppy. 'Are we still in Essex?'

'No idea. Are you sure you're OK?'

'Fine, thanks . . . have a nap.'

I'm an idiot too. I should have called him on Friday to warn him. Too busy literally painting my toenails.

'I'm starving,' says Adam, straightening up in his seat. 'Do you fancy grabbing a bite when we get in? There's an amazing Chinese near Victoria, should still be open.'

Hurry up Kiki, text me back . . .

'Checking your watch every minute won't get us there any faster,' he says. 'Do you have a hot date when you get home?'

'Huh? Oh, Amber's left a message about the dog . . . ' Kiki. Hurry. Up.

OK, think this through: Azeem's stuck the original review up but Adam won't see it. A few hundred readers might, but it can be replaced as soon as Azeem pulls the right one off the system.

Ah, finally! The man himself. 'Hiya!' I say, forcing the jollity into my voice.

'What's the problem?'

'Yeah . . . the thing is the old thing . . . there's a newer thing . . . just swap the things.'

'What?'

'Can't talk, I'm on a coach but there are two, just take the bottom one.'

'Your column?'

'Yup.'

'I matched the paper copy.'

'No, there are two,' I say, trying to keep my voice light. Azeem is such an idiot! 'One has three bits, one is a big long one . . . '

'One long review, yes.'

'There's a newer one.'

'The big one's running in the mag.'

'Was. Isn't.' What is wrong with him? 'It's fine, just switch them now, could you?'

'Let me go and check.'

For goodness' sake!

'Problem?' says Adam.

'Urgh . . . Amber . . . dog stuff . . . dog kit . . . you know, the dog has all these toys and stuff . . . Amber doesn't know how to use them and she's using the old . . . dog . . . thingy you know . . . what's that thing called? Anyway, the thing the dog uses.'

He laughs. 'I can't wait to meet Amber properly. What's the dog's name?'

'Annalex.' CALL ME BACK! 'Very cute eyebrows, tufty . . . Ah, here she is again!'

'Sorted?' I say.

'Yeah, I'm doing the right one.'

'Thank you!'

'One long list.'

How many more times??

'Laura: I've got April's issue in my hand. It's your ninety-nine problems . . . '

Oh.

Shit.

Better make that a hundred.

'I'm going to head home,' I say, as Adam and I stand in the coach station and I try not to vomit.

He puts his hands in the back of my jeans and pulls me towards him. 'Stay at mine?'

'I'm exhausted,' I say, opening my mouth to fake a yawn, which turns into a real one.

'We could just crash? I'll make you breakfast in bed?'

'That would be nice.' But the possibility of waking up tomorrow and you reading the review while I'm in your house less so. 'But I'll see you later in the week.' If I haven't gone in to hiding.

He pauses and his gaze shifts from mine. 'This week is impossible . . . '

Oh God, we're not back to this again? 'You're not blowing me out now you've had your wicked way with me are you?' Might be ideal timing though.

'No,' he says, biting the inside of his cheek. 'No, Laura. I had the most amazing time with you. Listen, I'll call you tomorrow, shall I?'

'Sure,' I say, confused by his sudden change of mood. 'Are you catching the Tube?'

'I think I'll get some fresh air while I still can. Big week . . . ' He pulls me towards him for one final kiss and I have no idea why but a thought goes through my head: this will be the last time you kiss him. I watch as he walks away and suddenly I feel like bursting into tears. The last thing I need is for Adam to go weird on me now – or go back to being weird.

I have to call Roger. Not that there's anything Roger or anyone else can do now, short of intercepting twenty-three lorries or buying

253

up every copy of the magazine before six a.m. tomorrow. Roger's phone is off, he must be in bed. Please let him be in tomorrow because I'm planning on hurling these Toffifees one at a time at Sandra's head and I need someone to restrain me. This must be her fault. Either that or the printers picked up the old file – but my money's on Sandra. How can she think she'd get away with this?

In bed I churn over when to tell Adam the truth. If he can't see me before Sunday, it'll have to wait till then – telling him over the phone feels cowardly. How on earth did Tom live with me for a year carrying his secret morning and night? It feels like a burning rock I can't wait to offload.

Even though I keep reminding myself I've *sort of* done nothing wrong, I feel guilty and slightly sick. The last time I felt this way was twenty years ago; Jess had bought a brand new sheepskin jacket and hung it on the back of a dining-room chair. I'd been sneakily trying some of her Clinique Dramatically Different moisturiser and had managed to spill pale yellow cream all down the back of the jacket. Me pointing out she shouldn't have left her moisturiser in the dining room, or her jacket on the back of a chair, didn't wash well (ditto the jacket.) Jess threatened to do something dramatically different to my face.

OK, so Adam will be annoyed and upset, but he'll get over it – they're only words. But all that money wasted, all that effort trying to do the right thing.

I'm so irritated, angry and anxious I take two pills and sedate myself into sleep: it isn't the end of the world.

But I'm going to have Sandra.

35

The birds wake me at 5.58 a.m. I lie in bed listening to them tweeting – they're really going for it this morning. After a while they fade, replaced by the sounds of life going about its business. I'm already on my second coffee when Roger calls at 8.00 a.m. 'Rather annoying turn of events, all things considered. You're not too upset, are you?' he says.

'Pretty unhappy, if I'm honest.'

'It'll be forgotten by Thursday.' Roger's voice is so mellifluous, he instantly makes me feel calmer. 'It's tomorrow's fish and chip paper – over-priced chip paper at that!'

'But Sandra—'

'Don't worry – the three of us will sit down first thing. I'll do the talking.'

'I suppose I could speak to the printers, they do make mistakes – but frankly this is what happens when things change post-deadline,' says Sandra, blinking innocently at Roger. 'Deadlines are deadlines for a reason. And such a fuss about a restaurant review. We've already had Damian Bechdel's lawyers on the phone, do you not think that's a little more pressing?'

I bite down so hard on my lip I'm scared my front tooth might break.

'Wait until Manderbys actually send a letter before we get our knickers in a twist,' Roger says impatiently. 'The issue here,' he gestures in my direction, 'is that Laura went to great lengths to make sure her piece was revised.'

'I didn't get that impression,' says Sandra shrugging. 'She wasn't at her desk till well after ten a.m. last Thursday, in fact didn't you visit the off licence on your way in?'

Roger said to let him do the talking but he didn't specify who should do the punching.

'All I want is for the revised version to go online,' I say. 'Azeem can have it up almost immediately. We can explain it was two visits, two very different experiences.'

'A ridiculous idea,' says Sandra. 'It makes us look sloppy, incompetent and indecisive.' (*Us* meaning *me*.) 'It draws attention to the mistake, and it will have a detrimental effect on our readers' opinion of our ability to deliver accurate reporting. This is a restaurant review, not Dewey and Truman.'

Roger scratches the back of his neck, then turns to me with an apologetic look. 'Laura, I appreciate your logic but I think it's a case of the proverbial stable door horse bolting.'

'But it might help mitigate—'

He shakes his head. 'We're just going to have to ride the storm on this one. There's no escaping the fact the paper copy is out there. I'm sorry,' he says, gesturing for me to go. 'Sandra – could you stay a moment?'

'What did the gaffer say?' says Azeem.

'No switch,' I say, heading back to my desk, a feeling of dread creeping over me.

In Roger's inbox is an email from Henry, our film critic:

Stonkingly brilliant issue (and not just my review, ha ha!). Glad Damian Bechdel got the kicking he deserves – and those nouveau riche restaurant guys. 'The experience leaves a worse taste in the mouth than your Smoked Shiitake Labneh Scarmoza Foam' – you tell 'em.

PS Labneh Scarmoza sounds like a Bond villain! Have retweeted the link.

I know I shouldn't but I send Henry an email from my own account:
Would you mind deleting the retweet . . . slight errors in current copy, sorry.

It's out there now, but Henry has 43,000 followers on Twitter, and I certainly don't need it out there to that degree.

From inside Roger's office comes the sound of voices raised.

Damn right. I hope Roger yellow cards Sandra for this. I move towards the door and hear Sandra's voice: '. . . *she lacks the dedication, the education* . . .' On second thoughts I'm not sure I want to eavesdrop this conversation.

If I didn't know for a fact Sandra's insides are made of metal and plastic, I'd swear her eyes were slightly watering when she finally emerged from Roger's office.

Must be hay fever; it's that time of year.

Adam texts me later that night saying he's been thinking about me all day, and asking what I feel like doing on Sunday. Buying up all the copies of *The Voice* and building a big bonfire?

Maybe country pub lunch and a walk? The bluebells will be out.

In bed I force myself to push my worries about the review to one side – they're spoiling the enjoyment of my sex memories. That thing with the condoms . . . I wonder if Adam might need to go to a clinic to get the all-clear? He'd never have enough time in his working day. When I went, after the Tom/Tess/Toss revelation, I spent *four hours* in a waiting room that was like an episode of *Skins* – I was the oldest person in there by a decade. There must be a clinic in Soho that's open on Sundays, perhaps I could suggest that as our date? Bluebells? Or a swab up your willy?

Shall we see what the weather's like on the day?

Though Adam did say he didn't have anything, didn't he? Was he suggesting *I* might have something; that I was *lying* when I said I didn't? That's doubly insulting, isn't it? Maybe that's not what he meant. I try to go back into the memory of that earlier part of the evening but all is dominated by a flashback of the intense humiliation of being shoved off his lap as I begged him for a shag.

No, I don't want to play back that part of the night at all. I think I'll just fast forward to the good bits.

36

In my inbox is an email from Sandra sent last night. She hasn't spoken to me since Roger gave her a bollocking yesterday but now she's sitting there, jaw grinding overtime as though limbering up for a proper fight. I can't believe I went home yesterday feeling marginally guilty that Roger almost made her cry, while she must have been at her desk crafting this beauty:

Three years ago, when Fergus Kaye moved on . . .

Moved on? Fired. You know it, I know it, we all know it . . .

I make no secret of the fact I shared with Roger my concerns about you – I did not think you would be an appropriate person to fill Fergus's shoes.

Fergus did not fill his own shoes! They were those long, pointy-toed brogues – far too rock and roll for a fifty-three year old whose role model is Jeremy Clarkson.

Your immaturity in yesterday's meeting speaks volumes of your lack of experience and professionalism. Above all, I take great exception to your snide implication I somehow deliberately misled the printers.

She thinks I can't prove it.

Regardless of the minutiae of who said what to whom on that Friday, you should never have put us in that situation in the first place. Any further and unnecessary resource directed towards this would be unwise.

That looks a little like a threat; and also like a neon sign pointing me to call the printers myself, to get to the bottom of it.

I write a note on my list, to follow it up when she's not sitting directly within earshot.

Roger's with Heather all morning, but calls me in at lunchtime. The back walls are free of layouts again and I try to remember that what's on newsstands today will be forgotten in a month.

'I wanted to check you're not still upset,' he says, smiling gently and offering me a seat.

'It's fine, Roger, I understand your position.' I just don't like it. 'Is there anything I can do to help on the Bechdel piece?'

'Heather and I were actually discussing turkeys!' he says, shaking his head. 'It always comes from the direction you're least expecting. SunFarms are claiming each of their turkeys has two centimetres squared more living space than the figure we cited. I doubt they've got a leg to stand on. Much like those poor birds. Still, Heather will hopefully tell the buggers to get stuffed . . . ' he says, looking up at me from under his brows to check whether I'm smiling.

'I'll buy you lunch if you stop making bad poultry jokes?'

He grins. 'Deal. So: how's May looking?'

'Tonight I'm off to a meatball place in a car park in Shoreditch, then the Clapton Smoke House on Friday and the Ludo Brunelli opening on Monday.'

'Good – business as usual. Meanwhile, I want your opinion,' he says, rummaging around till he finds a piece of paper tucked under the *FT*. 'Which of these shall I get framed for the wall?'

'More Elbert Hubbard . . . '

Be pleasant until 10 o'clock in the morning and the rest of the day will take care of itself.

'I like that one . . . '

It's pretty hard to be efficient without being obnoxious.

'That belongs above Sandra's desk . . . '

If pleasures are greatest in anticipation, just remember that this is also true of trouble.

I just hope that one's true.

Meatbalzac in Shoreditch is foul: chewy defrosted lobster meatballs drenched in acidic thousand island dressing on stale white rolls. I can't get out of there quickly enough, but there are severe delays on the Tube home. When I'm finally above ground again I see two missed calls from Adam. He normally wouldn't phone during service, let alone twice. He'd normally leave a message.

He calls a third time as I'm turning into my street. I very much feel like throwing my phone straight into the canal, but I clear my throat and pick up the call.

'Laura – can I see you later? Around midnight?' From the strain in his voice it's safe to say this isn't a booty call.

'It's a bit late; I don't want to wake the dog. Could we meet in the morning?'

He sighs loudly. 'You know what? The way I'm feeling now, that's probably better. But I've only got fifteen minutes. Eight fifteen a.m., there's a builder's caff just behind Bank Station. Meet me there.'

37

I've run through it a dozen times in my head; I've even composed a little tune to accompany it: "Twas me. I wrote it. I'm very, very sorry. I'm really very sorry in-deed. Ta da!' Not sure if I should do the jazz hands at the end?

Once it's said, it's done – it's out there. The relationship may be done too, but if Adam honestly doesn't care what critics say, then he should have a sense of perspective. It's only fluffy stuff, after all.

I'm going to walk into that builder's caff, lay it down on the table like a copy of the *Sun,* straight away, job done. He won't go as ballistic as a teenage Jess, he's not the type.

Adam's sitting with a plate of uneaten toast and Marmite, head down over a copy of the magazine. He looks up with a face full of stewed anger.

'Hey you,' I say, taking a seat opposite and giving him a small smile. 'Listen, before you say anything I need to tell you—'

'You must have known about this?' He's already so angry, a vein in his forehead has started to throb.

'I didn't know those exact words were going to run but yes, in fact—'

'You should have warned me.'

'Yes, I should have.' I nod, then pause. 'Although actually – what could you have done about it?' Stop sidetracking. Tell him. Otherwise this pit is going to get deeper, darker and full of snakes and not adorable, fluffy snakes.

'I could have braced myself for the impact,' he says, gripping the side of the table, then puffing out his rage. 'Sorry. I'm angry. I know it's not your fault, I'll be OK in a sec . . . '

'Don't apologise, I should have told you – and you say it's not my fault but actually—'

'You couldn't have stopped it.'

'Erm, yes. Here's the thing . . . '

'But seriously!' He instantly whips himself up into an even bigger peak of rage. 'How dare he? Who does he think he is? Sitting there, guzzling away like Mr Creosote, some fat pig . . . '

'Not that fat.'

'Stuffing his face with lard and statins, some bitter, lonely loser like Anton Ego in *Ratatouille*. . .'

'Anton Ego's really quite sweet once you get to know him,'

'Vicious! Sticking the knife in, just listen to this venom!

The whipped chicken-liver butter was like eating the output of a liposuction clinic . . . A bunch of try hard Noma-wannabees . . . Even Dot Cotton would gag at the level of smoke on the brisket . . . '

'I don't need you to read it out, I'm more than familiar with it because I—'

'You *know* that's not a fair description of my food,' he says, scowling down at the pages.

'Your food is so much better and that's why I went—'

'It's because he's a dwarf! Five foot seven? What sort of height is that for a man? He's a poisonous troll, a little–'

'Adam,' I say, holding my hand up to try to quiet him. 'Please stop talking for a minute, I need to tell you—'

'I'm no giant but this man *really* must have a short man complex to be so hateful, all he can do is tear apart someone else's work.' He runs his hands through his hair, then raises them in a plea in my direction. 'I bet he's never even set foot in a professional kitchen *in his life* and yet he has the nerve to pass judgement on me.'

'But . . . I thought he was the one critic you kind of liked?'

'He clearly knows fuck all about food. *And* he's a liar: these are *lies*! I would *never* send a plate out like that.'

'The points about the decor and the service aren't wrong though.'

'I can't believe you're defending this review!'

'But you've said it yourself, the prices are ridiculous, the menu's fussy and contrived. I think perhaps you're overreacting a tiny bit.'

'Laura, I swear, if I ever met him I'd have a hard time not punching him.'

'Well . . . erm . . . would you punch him if *he* turned out to be *she*?'

'Do me a favour, *look* at those sentences?' he says, stabbing his finger at the page.

'I don't need to, I know them by heart because I—'

'That obnoxious, self-confident, swaggering pompous conviction *he* knows better. *That* – I'm sorry to say – is a *male* trait.' I'm not sure whether he just complimented or insulted me.

'Well, hang on a minute. Why can't a woman's writing be . . . self-assured?' Ooh, but this ice is thin.

'I'm not here to have a debate about feminist sentence structures, Laura. I know he's a man because he's a dick.'

'Listen to me, Adam! I am telling you: *he* is not an *anything*—'

'I agree, he's a piece of shit but he's clearly a man, because no woman I've ever met, no matter how jaded and miserable her pathetic little life was, could be such a complete and utter self-satisfied toxic prick.' He tears the pages out, rips them in half, chucks them back on the table, then stands and puts his jacket on. 'I'm sorry, Laura, I don't mean to take this out on you. But this review is out of order, these are *not* accurate descriptions of my food and I'm not having it.'

And he's stomped off before I can try, once more, to get the truth out.

Well fine: it'll have to wait until Sunday.

He'll have calmed down by then.

38

'Double bacon sarnies all round!' says Roger, jubilantly piling three paper bags on to the boardroom table on Friday morning. 'Right, let's make this quick, I've got a meeting at the Frontline at . . . ?'

'Twelve thirty,' I say. 'Cab's booked for twelve.'

'Round the table, copy sales – Mick?'

'EPOS so far's huge, we'll be hitting a hundred and sixty-two thousand if it stays on track.'

'Any production issues?'

'Flawless run, PrintPro handled the embargo brilliantly, no leaks.'

If Sandra genuinely had nothing to do with the wrong review, she'd have pointed out that PrintPro picked the wrong copy off the system. But she's sitting there looking like margarine wouldn't melt in her mouth.

'Jonesy, sterling job, filling those two pages at the last minute, I presume you charged nowhere near rate card?'

'Rodge, it was so last minute, I had to make it worth their while. Anyway, you won't be getting much in the way of meat ads for the foreseeable future.'

'Did you see the SunFarms' spokesperson on *Newsnight*? What an absolute bell-end,' says Roger laughing. 'Worth publishing just to see him making such a buffoon of himself on camera.'

'We've had an exceptional response to the SunFarms piece in other media,' says Sandra. 'However, we've also had Fletchers' Head of PR on the phone yesterday, demanding we print a retraction of the density per square footage allegations.'

Roger waves the comment away. 'It'll blow over.'

'What about Bechdel?' says Kiki. 'Is he kicking off?'

'They were squawking on Tuesday but they've gone quiet,' says Heather. 'They know we can substantiate our facts.'

'Tends to shut the lawyers up,' says Roger. 'Azeem, go on, I can see you're dying to talk.'

'Guys – I know some of you are a little dubious about the value of social media, but I want to share with you some amazing stats. In the last three days, the Bechdel piece has had over sixty-three thousand retweets and the turkey piece has had forty-two thousand.'

'Do turkeys tweet?' says Jonesy.

'Not the ones at SunFarms,' says Kiki.

'They gobble, Jonesy,' says Roger. 'Have you never seen that marvellous Jennifer Lopez/Ben Affleck clip? And they gave that man an Oscar!'

'Guys, I haven't finished: the biggest surprise is The Dish. Since it went online at nine p.m. on Monday, it's had more traffic than the Bechdel and turkeys combined. That toilet photo's had almost as many retweets as the latest selfie of Kim Kardashian's arse.'

'I'm surprised their PR guys haven't been on the phone already with some hysteria-laced invective,' says Heather.

'Perhaps they realise life's too short,' says Roger.

'Azeem,' I say, trying to keep my voice calm. 'How do these trend curves tend to work? Presumably this will be the peak of the wave, three days in?'

'Depends if it snowballs over the weekend.'

'Tomorrow's fish and chip paper,' says Roger.

'Not just tomorrow's,' I say. 'It's the day after's, and the day after that.'

'You'll be fine,' says Kiki. 'The minute Miley Cyrus shows a nipple people will move on.'

When I get back to my desk, there's a missed call from Adam. Anxiety pulses through me as I head outside to call him back – I didn't want to tell him over the phone but I just can't bear keeping it a secret anymore.

His voice on the phone sounds tender, embarrassed. 'Laura – I'm so sorry about yesterday morning . . . It's been a truly terrible week.'

'Because of the review?'

'Not just that, but I'll tell you on Sunday, it's not one for the phone.'

'Are you ok?'

'Uh-huh,' he says, pausing. 'Are you?'

'Yes. Adam, listen, about yesterday I absolutely—'

'Laura, you were right: I overreacted. I've been feeling like a total arse.'

'Please, there's no need to apologise, in fact I need to tell you, and I should have mentioned it earlier – '

'The thing is, I've been thinking about it – and it makes no sense.'

'Er, what doesn't?'

'Your guy is normally bang on the money. But the avocado salad, the tuna ceviche . . . ' he says, confusion in his voice. 'I can swear an affidavit, a hundred per cent, I have never let a plate leave the pass like that.'

'Adam, listen to me—'

'Laura – there's something I need to get to the bottom of.'

He knows. I should've had the guts to tell him sooner. My mouth seems incapable of forming words. All I can hear is my heart beating in my chest.

'You know who wrote the review,' he says.

'Yes I do,' I say, then take a deep breath and in a voice so quiet I can barely hear it myself: 'I did. It was me.'

'So could you find out whether he came in on the last Thursday in February, at around nine p.m.?'

I almost drop the phone on the pavement. 'The what?'

'I have this terrible feeling he came in that night.'

I'm pretty sure my mouth is hanging wide open but I can't seem to move my jaw to close it.

'I wouldn't ask you to find out if it wasn't a big deal, Laura.'

'Hang on. Why are you asking me about the timings?'

'Because if that's when he came in, there are . . . repercussions for me at work.'

'But why?'

'Please – could you just do this one thing for me?'

'What difference does it make when we visited?'

266

'It just does.'

'You weren't there, were you?' I say, disbelief in my voice. 'You said you hadn't had a single shift off. Why did you lie?'

There's a pause on the other end of the line. 'I didn't lie. I was there at the start of the shift; I had to leave in the middle.'

'But what was so important you had to leave the pass for it?'

Silence.

'Adam? Are you still there.'

'Laura – I will tell you on Sunday, I don't want to have this conversation on the phone.'

'And neither do I.' I can feel my cheeks flush with indignation. 'You lied about your shift and you've been hiding something ever since I met you.'

His voice sounds guilty. Confused and surprised, but definitely guilty. 'Now who's the one overreacting, Laura?'

'What were you doing that night, Adam?'

'I'll tell you on Sunday, I need to explain properly—'

'Yeah. Yeah, you do,' I say, and I hang up with only one thought on my mind: I knew it: I knew it all along.

People react in different ways when they find out your husband's been cheating. Some pity you; awkward smiles, a little pat on the arm – as though adultery has transformed you into a partially deaf maiden aunt. Others (Tom's parents) behave like it's *your* fault. Wifely shortcomings must have driven him to it: pursuing a career path or some other deeply unfeminine behaviour. And then there's a third group, who treat you like you're stupid. More than one person asked me, 'Did you *really* have no idea?' Kind of a grim question to ask someone who's just been punched, metaphorically, in the face. It suggests *they'd* have known better. There *must* have been signs? Didn't he go to the gym more? Leave the room to take calls?

Here's the thing: I had an instinct. Very early on I felt . . . a twitch in the energy between us. How do you confront your husband with *a twitch in the energy between us*? It buzzed in my head, a tiny fly – impossible to catch, impossible to ignore. Over time, it moved to my stomach and made itself a home there. I tried to convince myself it was paranoia until it swelled to the point of discomfort, at which point I confronted Tom and he told me the same story: I was paranoid.

And when I finally had proof, clutched in my hand – he still denied it! I could have forgiven the cheating; possibly even with a 'friend'. But I couldn't forgive the tissue of lies it was all wrapped up in.

At first he claimed their texts were harmless flirtation, Tess had developed a crush – hardly his fault! Of course it was unrequited but he didn't want to embarrass her and meanwhile why was I snooping in his phone in the first place? The dinner they'd been spotted having? *Clearly* a work dinner, and he hadn't realised being married to me meant he was obliged to tell me where he was 24/7. Whoever told me they'd been kissing was a liar, and who was it anyway? Why wouldn't I tell him? Was I making it up?

Aaaah! The reason I was imagining this nonsense must be my hormones – were they out of whack? No? OK then, depression – I must still be grieving Mum. Tom even encouraged me to go on antidepressants; he went as far as booking me an appointment with the GP. I married a man callous enough to hide his affair behind the faded cloud of my mother's death. That really is something to get depressed about.

But then Tess rang and asked if she could pop by and it was she who ultimately had the balls to admit it. I think she only did it to force Tom to move in with her. And long may they live happily ever after – just not anywhere near me.

So I have learned the hard way: trust your instinct. Be vigilant. Even the smallest signs are still signs and there are always signs. A tingle in your arms, a throbbing in your head – these are your body's way of telling you to use your ears: listen more closely. Pay immense attention to the phrasing of sentences. Omission. Circumlocution. *I'm not sure what time I'll be back*, is worse than *I'll be back late*. It leaves the door open to not come back at all. It slams the door in your face.

There have been various signs with Adam – signs I chose to ignore. The phone calls, the weird behaviour at his house. But one in particular haunts me: that morning he ran out mid-date. Obviously running out mid-date wasn't a wonderful sign. The look he'd given me – loaded, guilty – was hardly encouraging. But that wasn't it either. It was the way he'd answered my question with a deviation. I asked a direct question, he sidetracked me, asked me for tea. It was a classic blocking move, I've done it myself plenty this last month. Russell did it too, answered a question with a question – and I waded in, elbows out like a pub brawl and got straight to the bottom of the problem.

With Adam I let it slide.

So I guess I've known from the start – Adam was too good to be true: he was hiding something.

I just didn't want him to be.

The waitress at the Clapton Smoke House is doing her best to give me great service; it's not her fault I've forgotten what I ordered. And it's not the chef's fault I can barely swallow the chipotle short ribs and spicy slaw in front of me. All I can do is stare down at the cabbage shreds on my plate as my mind festers.

Where do ambitious head chefs rush off to, mid-service on a Thursday night, when they're meant to be earning a Michelin star?

Someone they're scared of: a drug dealer/an angry woman.

Or someone they're in love with: a woman.

If Tom hadn't cheated I wouldn't necessarily think it was a woman, but he did, and so I do.

What did Adam mean when he said there were *repercussions* at work? Will Max get fired? Will Adam? The review may well be the first time that Adam's been made aware of how bad Max's food is. And I guess it wouldn't have mattered anyway, if it wasn't now popping up all over Twitter like the measles.

'Was everything OK? Can I get you dessert, coffee?' says the waitress, looking at the barely eaten food.

'Mmm? Er, no thanks, just the bill.' I'll have to come back and eat here again, too, I think, as she clears away the full plates.

Whatever Adam's hiding, one thing's for sure: there's no way I'm waiting till Sunday to find out.

* * *

Adam's sitting in a booth at Maxwells, nursing a bottle of beer. He looks like he hasn't slept for two days – the dark circles under his eyes are almost purple.

'This was the only place I could think of that's open late and doesn't play banging house music,' he says. 'The cocktails are good.'

'I don't want a drink,' I say, brushing the menu aside. 'Please, just tell me what's going on.'

He takes a deep breath and looks up to the ceiling, then his gaze meets mine – his eyes filled with sorrow. 'This is totally not how or where or when I wanted to have this conversation.'

'Tell me.'

'Please, Laura,' he says, shifting forward on his seat and taking my hand across the table.

'It's something major, isn't it?'

'Promise me you'll try to understand my side of the story,' he says, giving my fingers a gentle squeeze.

'Tell me.'

'Promise?'

'Adam, just tell me!' I feel like he's about to inflict a massive amount of pain on me – the sooner it starts, the sooner it finishes.

He buries his face in his hands, then looks up at me. 'OK,' he says, steeling himself. 'OK. Right. Last year when I was working in Bray I became quite friendly with one of the front-of-house girls, a waitress called Katie.'

And so it is: a woman.

He bites down on his lip, then hesitates.

'Adam . . . '

'A bunch of us used to go out after work to let off steam, she was a bit older, thirty-nine, very outgoing, always the first and last at the bar.'

Men: they are all the same.

'She'd found a lump a few years before and they'd caught it in time but she'd had some treatment and it'd messed up her chances of having kids. We hung out, we got drunk, I was a bit of a shoulder to cry on.'

I feel dread, creeping into my limbs. 'More than a shoulder—'

270

'Please, let me speak. One night she made a massive play for me and we ended up hooking up. We slept together maybe a dozen times over a fortnight.'

'I don't want the details . . . '

'It was never going to be anything more – for either of us. And I called it – she partied too much, she was all over the place. Anyway, a month later she quit, we didn't even swap emails.'

What was that thing his old boss said about chefs and waitresses? '"It's not a question of if, it's a question of where and when . . ."'

'Laura. Please. Then my grill chef bumped into her in Chiswick six months later.'

'So she's back on the scene . . . '

He takes a huge breath, like he's about to dive to the bottom of a deep pool. 'And she was quite obviously pregnant.'

I laugh, I can't help it – though it's the strangest noise I've ever made. 'Ah, wow, Adam – you have a baby! A baby you forgot to mention, that is a touch forgetful!'

'Laura,' he says, holding his hands out to calm me down. 'Hold on a minute: she told him it was her ex-boyfriend's.'

I turn around and beckon to the nearest waitress. 'Double vodka and tonic please?'

'Laura—'

'So what? She was shagging both of you at the same time? Has she given you an STD? Is that what the condom thing was about?'

'Laura – I told you I'm clean, I'm not a liar.'

I bite my tongue but my eyebrows shoot to my hairline. 'So why are you telling me about her?'

'Because . . . the timings were too close for comfort. And her behaviour, in retrospect –' His hand comes up and rubs over his mouth as if trying to erase a mark on a whiteboard.

I take the vodka and tonic from the waitress's hand before she's even laid it on the table.

'Like what?'

'Well, for a start I think she lied about being able to get pregnant.'

'Yes Adam – I suspect that is a reasonable deduction to make.'

'I mean, Laura – I'm not sure if she was lying about her illness – or whether she was hitting forty and decided to find the nearest sucker available . . . '

I take a large swig of my drink, then finish it off in one long, slow gulp.

'She seemed . . . very determined to . . . '

'Determined to what, Adam?'

'To seal the deal.' He shrugs, helplessly.

'What does that mean?'

'To have unprotected sex.'

The condoms. I recall with horror how I must have come across on Sunday night – similar desperation, different motivation. I turn to look out of the window: it's starting to rain.

When I turn back, Adam looks like he might cry. I don't want him to cry. I want him to tell me this is all a wind-up.

'She refused to speak to me before the baby was born, but about a month ago I got a call at work . . . '

I feel a small part of my heart break.

'She knows how unreasonable it is to call mid-service but she said if I wanted to speak it was now or never, so I biked over to West London in the pouring rain.'

'The Thursday night?'

'Your guy couldn't have shafted me harder.'

'And I met you on that Sunday,' I say. 'You said you'd had a bad week . . . '

'Timing is everything, hey?' He chances a half-smile, which I weakly mirror.

My brain is trying to put together all these pieces but it isn't working fast enough. 'So . . . what happened?'

'She finally admitted it might be mine, and then it took me another two weeks to persuade her to actually go through with a DNA test.'

'That day you ran off?'

He nods slowly.

'You've had the test?'

He nods again.

'When did you find out? Before we went away?' If he says yes I will never see him again.

'Two days ago.'

'How do you feel?'

He pauses and his eyes darken. 'If you're asking me would I impregnate her again tomorrow – clearly the answer's no. If you're asking do I regret having a son? No.'

'So now what?' My heart seems to be beating from the middle of my throat.

'I have no idea what Katie will agree to. Mum's started looking at the legal side of things, but it's not very hopeful.'

'And you don't think you could make a relationship work with this woman?'

He blows out angrily. 'Not sure a pathological liar is what I'm looking for in a partner . . .'

Women: we're not all the same, really we're not.

'Laura, I've been wanting to tell you from the start, I know how much honesty means to you, with your ex and everything.'

'But you kept it a secret anyway?'

'You probably won't remember, but the day we first met we were walking into Soho and you said I should tell you all my secrets and I thought . . . fuck it, just say it – and I did a dickhead thing and I said it – I did, but . . .'

'What?'

'I said, "I have a love-child," but you thought I was joking.'

'You cannot *seriously* have that as your defence.'

'You laughed and my instinct was to shut up because it did sound exactly like the sort of thing a girl like you would run a mile from. And I didn't want to lose you because I liked you already.'

I shake my head.

'Laura, from the minute I met you I knew you were a game changer and the more time I've spent with you, the more I know it. You make me happy. I have no idea if I'm going to have access to my kid – and if I'm not, then what possible good would it have done to tell you? If I never see him again it's a painful mess for me

273

and it doesn't affect you at all. I was going to tell you when it was resolved one way or the other.'

He tries to take my hand again but I move it to my lap.

'Please – say something, Laura.'

'Can I have the rest of your beer?'

'Are you going to pour it over my head?'

The bottle is warm from being gripped in his hand these last twenty minutes. I take a small sip and sit, my head nodding of its own accord until I'm finally ready to speak.

'You want to know what I think?' I think: brilliant. You've impregnated some random woman, and for the next eighteen years you're going to have aggro with her over your son, and as much as I want to take this opportunity to tell you how gutted I am that you kept this from me – I have no stomach for my own hypocrisy. If you're a liar and a coward, you can add that to "I hate coffee Revels" – just two more things we have in common. I don't have a leg to stand on, not a foot, not one toe.

'Laura, I know how bad it sounds if you only look at the headline . . . '

I do so hope he bears that in mind in the near future.

'Maybe it was a mistake not to have told you before now, but there was never a good time.'

Yup – hold on to that thought too.

'And I figured if you at least got to know me properly, you'd understand I'm not a player. And if you knew me then maybe you'd feel enough to give me a chance, because I feel something very strong for you, Laura. I know it's only been a month but I don't think I've ever felt this close to anyone—'

'Adam, stop!'

'Because I can imagine starting every day with you. I want us to build a future together, I want—'

'What's he called?'

'His name is Josh.'

'Josh,' I say, swallowing a huge lump of emotion I haven't even begun to process yet. 'That's a really sweet name,' I say, standing abruptly. 'I'm going to go home now.'

'Laura . . . '

'It's fine, I'm tired.' It is taking super human strength to try and be an adult about this, and if I stay any longer I'll start acting like a child. I can feel it – disappointment and hurt welling up in me – and I want to do it off-camera.

'Let me at least call you a cab, it's raining,' he says, moving to help me as I struggle with the sleeve of my jacket. I pull away from him instinctively, as if he's about to hit me.

'Laura, please! I don't want to lose you – we've only just found each other. People can make things work if they want to make things work.'

'It's just a shock, that's all . . . ' I say, shaking my head to try and dislodge the news from a point where it seems to be lodged, directly behind my eyeballs, making me dizzy.

And as I walk out in to the dark street a thought comes to me through the haze: you reap what you sow.

39

Saturday's the first truly warm day of the year and Regent's Park seems to be operating a couples-only policy. Teens with their hands up each other's tops lie snogging on the grass; thirty-something tired partners push double buggies towards The Garden Café. The old couple with the matching hats are back on the bench, this time in matching cardigans.

I'm actually in a threesome – one of whom has four legs and is wearing a Juicy velour onesie. Annalex, Sophie and I have been walking, mostly in a large circle, processing the news.

'You look like shit,' says Sophie.

'Yeah, well – I was up half the night, trying to get my head around it. One hideous thought after another came hurtling at me; it was like dodgeball. Firstly, I felt jealous of this woman—'

'That's kind of irrational.'

'I have an image of her and Adam going at it, hammer and tongs for a fortnight and then I have a flashback to him and me last weekend and it makes me feel sick.'

'Try not to think that thought.'

'Try not thinking of a pink elephant! And then I think how messed up all this is: I was with Tom nearly a decade and I never have to see his muppet face again; Adam spends two weeks shagging this girl and she'll be in his life forever.'

'Wouldn't it be worse if they'd been a proper couple? Imagine if they had an entire photo album of happy memories together; Adam didn't have an issue with the fact you're divorced.'

'Why should he? I'm not in love with Tom anymore.'

'Exactly,' she says, coming to a halt by a beautiful cherry tree, bubble-gum pink blossom stuck all over its branches. We sit underneath it on grass more white than green, a blanket of daisies. I lie back and stare at the sky as I run my fingers up through the flower stems. I know this is not the worst thing at all, I do know that.

'Soph, I had entirely reconciled myself to a man with kids; but a newborn love child never entered the equation.'

'I know it's not ideal. But maybe it's easier when a kid's so young? They won't be resentful of you like an older stepchild might be?'

'And then I have this horrible selfish thought: this little boy will be Adam's priority, he has to be. But I would like to be the centre of his attention, for a while at least. Adam barely has any time as it is. So now I'm jealous of a baby, how shameful is that?'

'He's not going to get anything like half the custody. Did you speak to him about what he's doing about access?'

'He doesn't know yet. He's texted and asked me to meet him for lunch tomorrow, he said he wants to talk it all through, about how we go forward from here. Part of me feels I should walk away right now, it's messy, it's complicated – it was clearly doomed from day one—'

'Bullshit!'

'But . . . if I think about the last four years, it's basically been a barren wasteland, temporarily lit up by flares of false hope. Adam wipes the floor with everyone since Tom – including Tom. But I have no idea how it would possibly work with this baby.' I prop myself up on my elbows; maybe my brain will be able to process all this if it's vertical.

'It's Adam's child, he's going to have to figure it out. But I reckon he could use some support.'

'It's far too early in our relationship to be thinking about any of this. A baby? I mean that's a full-on responsibility.'

'I doubt he'll ask you to be the wet nurse.'

'Soph – I don't know if I want to take this on. And this Katie woman . . .'

'Laura, just go along tomorrow with an open mind.'

'You know what's the worst part?' I say, picking a daisy, and running my thumb through the centre of its stalk, then threading another daisy through the slit, then another. 'The thing I'm most upset about is the thing I have least right to be. Even though I understand why he kept it a secret, it pisses me off so royally.'

'Come on, Laura! What was he meant to say? "I've fathered a love child with a lying cougar – and I may or may not ever set eyes on this child." You'd have run a mile from that.'

'I wouldn't. I'd have told him to sort himself out and come back to me when he knew what his situation was with the baby.'

'That's bollocks! You'd have judged him on the spot – as a womaniser, irresponsible and too complicated.'

'And he's none of those things, Soph. I think he's fundamentally a decent, honest person.' I say, tipping my head back to feel the sun on my face. 'Which brings me back to the bloody review. The minute I walk into his house I'll tell him. And the only possible silver lining to all this is that he's no longer in a position to take the moral high ground.'

'It's not that big a deal compared to his stuff anyway. He might even appreciate the irony of the situation.'

'You reckon?' I say, chucking my makeshift daisy chain back on the grass.

She nods convincingly.

'Annalex?' I turn to address the dog directly. 'Do you think Adam will have a sense of humour about all this?'

Annalex gazes back at me and appears to give the question formal consideration – then barks once.

'I speak fluent dog,' says Sophie, picking up my discarded daisy chain and chucking it at my head. 'And one bark means yes.'

40

On the Tube over to Adam's, Jess's voice plays in my head in black and white: *Adam's a fully-grown adult, contraception is both parties' responsibility. Why feel sorry for him?*

But when he opens his front door, pale, exhausted and with two days of stubble, all I want to do is hug him.

'I wasn't sure you'd turn up,' he says, looking at me with a small but hopeful smile. 'I thought you'd probably still be upset about Friday night.'

'It was all a bit of a shock,' I say, following him down to the kitchen. 'But listen – there's something else I need to talk to you about.'

'Do you want tea or shall I open a bottle of wine? We're having roast chicken.'

'Open the bottle,' I say. He pours two glasses, while I silently replay my speech in my head, and he comes to sit next to me.

I take a sip of wine, then another, then put my hand in my pocket to check the piece of paper is still there. 'Listen, Adam. One of the reasons I'm here today is because I understand why people keep certain things to themselves. The thing is . . . when I moved back to London, I took the first job I found . . . Adam, whose scarf is that?'

'Huh?'

'On your chair?' A beautiful print of purple peonies on a cream silk background.

'Oh, it's Mum's,' he says. 'Go on?'

'Your *mum's* here?'

'She just went to get some cream. You were saying?'

'Hang on, you didn't tell me your mum was having lunch with us?'

'She's not, she was just helping me with some paperwork earlier and then thought it was a crime I wasn't making you bread sauce,' he says, smiling softly. 'If you think I'm a perfectionist, wait till you see her in action. You were saying, you took the first job . . . '

'When did she go out?' There's a Waitrose by the Tube, a Tesco nearer – she's more Waitrose than Tesco, which gives me an extra five minutes to confess.

'Laura, don't look so panicked, Mum's cool. You were saying, you took the first job you found when you came down to London . . . '

'Er, OK . . . I took the first job I could find so I was Roger's PA full time – which was fine for a while because I was still feeling a little fragile and there was a lot of change in my life. But then after a year an opportunity came up at the magazine, and Roger – because of my coffee background and also because he thought the readers might respond well to a more down-to-earth point of view – well, Roger decided to let me have a go at writing The . . . Adam, has your mum got a key?'

'She took mine, why?'

We both look to the ceiling as a light footstep passes overhead and moves down the stairs.

'Adam, they only had single cream at Waitrose, so I'm afraid I had to go to the dreadful Tesc– Oh, is it one o'clock already?' she says, her face lighting up when she sees me. 'I didn't think I'd get to say hello.'

She comes over and kisses me, then holds me at arm's length and gives me a sympathetic look. 'Not the best week, all round?'

'Mum!' says Adam.

'I'm just saying! Anyway, carry on, I won't interrupt you two, I'll just make the bread sauce and head off.'

Adam flashes me an apologetic smile, and refills my wine glass. 'Sorry, Laura, go on.'

Behind us, his mother lines up the ingredients on the counter and stands, hands on hips, surveying the line-up.

'Mrs Bayley – ' I say.

'Anna, please.'

'Anna – thank you so much for letting me stay at your house in Italy. It was the loveliest place.'

'Oh, my pleasure, dear! I'm glad you enjoyed it.'

'We had such a good time,' I say, looking over at Adam, who flashes me a smile at the memory.

'Adam was quite cross with me that I don't stock that kitchen like a professional chef, but there's a fantastic little market in the nearest village on weekdays, and I tend to buy bits and pieces as I need them. He did take you to La Collina I hope?'

'The place with the truffles?'

'Isn't it wonderful? And so reasonable, not like the nonsense prices they charge at his new place. Adam said you're into food – have you ever made bread sauce?'

'Never, actually.'

'Mum, we're in the middle of discussing something!'

'Oh, hush – it'll only take ten minutes, I've already infused the milk, come over here,' she says, beckoning to me.

Adam shrugs in resignation. 'You'd better do what she says, she never takes no for an answer.'

'We can't open a third bottle,' says Anna, looking at me with a mischievous smile suggesting that's exactly what we can and will do.

'I'll get you a cab home, Mum, you might as well,' says Adam, looking at his watch.

'Go on then,' she says, flashing me a smile. 'It is rather good wine. And I'm having such a lovely time!'

As am I.

I've learnt how to make world-class bread sauce. I've been introduced to the basics of painting on silk; and I am rather drunkenly enamoured with Adam's mother.

After the first bottle of wine we bonded about marrying rubbish first husbands. 'Painful but instructive. Never let a man make you feel less than who you are. Now my daughter, Vicky – she got it right first time round. Slightly boring, dare I say it – but his heart's in the right place.'

After the second bottle, when Adam popped to the loo, she gave my arm a little squeeze and told me he seemed happier than she'd seen him in years, and that he deserved a chance. 'You know it's about the way you play the hand, not the hand itself.'

Halfway down the third bottle, she touches on the Katie situation. 'Always disappointing when a woman behaves quite so badly.' For a minute, she reminds me of Tom's mum who always made excuses for Her Golden-Balls Boy Who Could Do No Wrong.

But then she looks at Adam, and says, 'You may have been unlucky – but you're as much to blame as she is. Anyway – I shan't say "unlucky", that's a terrible word. Children can be exhausting, infuriating and frankly a pain in the arse – but they are without a doubt the greatest luck you can have in this world.'

As a final act of generosity, as she's leaving she invites me to her flat next Saturday, to share with me the secrets of Granny Ailsa's shortcrust pastry. We tipsily hug our goodbyes, and it's only as Adam and I are walking back downstairs that I remember my own secret, with dread. In the now-quiet kitchen, the good cheer still hangs in the air like the smell of roast potatoes, but I feel the imp of truth tugging impatiently at my hem.

'I'm so sorry about all that,' says Adam, as we stand together at the sink, him washing up as I slowly run a tea towel over the surface of the first plate. 'She wasn't meant to stay past the bread sauce – ' He pauses and turns to me with a hopeful look. 'Do you want to talk about Friday?'

'Before we do,' I say, putting the plate down, my arms tingling with fear as the words start to come. 'I . . . I need to tell you something. The other day, you asked when our critic came in.'

He looks taken aback. 'You found out already? I wasn't expecting you to—'

I feel almost sick with nerves, my hand trembles as I steady myself on the edge of the sink. 'It was February the twenty-seventh.'

'Just after nine p.m.?' His eyes scan my face for the answer, then crease in annoyance when I nod.

Deep breath, I feel my pulse quickening, here it goes. 'That's when we came in.'

He frowns, then smiles in confusion. 'You just said *we*?'

I nod again.

'You were *with* him?' He places the washing-up brush down on the side of the sink as I shake my head. 'Jesus, Laura – I was going to say . . .' he says, laughing at the thought, and reaching into the sink to pick up another plate.

'I wasn't with him,' I say, feeling cold dread shiver through my body. 'I . . . I *am* him.'

He frowns again, this time without a smile to chase it. 'What?'

My voice is heavy as I say it again: 'I wrote that review.'

His face crumples in confusion.

'I write that column . . .'

He shakes his head in slow disbelief as he lets the plate slide back into the murky water.

'. . . And before you go totally apeshit, I need you to read this.' I take from my pocket the copy of the second review. 'This was meant to run and Sandra told them to run the other copy, I'm sure of it. When I ate at your place the first time it was . . . bad . . . but then I had a hunch you hadn't been cooking, so I persuaded Roger to give it a second chance and I came back and wrote this.' I thrust it towards him. 'Please read it – because then you'll understand I was trying to do the right thing, I tried my best. It's all just very . . . unfortunate.'

He looks straight through me, like he doesn't recognise me, then stares down into the soapy water, his chin dropping to his chest.

'Adam,' I say, carefully balancing the review up on the shelf so it doesn't get wet, then gently resting my hand on his shoulder. 'We ran the wrong review. And I know it's critical but it wasn't *your* food, and these things always end up being tomorrow's fish and chip paper, I mean no one really pays attention to this stuff anyway – it'll all blow over by next week.'

His gaze stays fixed in the sink, though I can see his jaw has set firm. I have to say, he's reacting far more calmly than I'd anticipated.

'So . . . I'm really very sorry, Adam. And I did try to tell you.'

He turns to look at me, eyes wide. 'Did you?' he says, lightly.

'Yes.'

'When?'

'On Thursday.'

'Of this week?'

'Adam – when I first met you I didn't think we'd still be together one month later. And then I thought we'd be running a re-review you'd be pleased with,' I say, grabbing the review and unfolding the paper so he can start to read it.

'I'd be pleased?' His eyes skate over the first sentences. 'A bit shorter than the other one, isn't it?'

'I should have told you sooner, maybe, but people do make mistakes. As you know.'

He blows out a long, slow breath, then finally takes his hands from the sink and turns to me. 'You're right,' he says. 'It is . . . "unfortunate", Laura.'

'Isn't it?' Wow, he's being amazingly cool. 'I've been feeling so bad about it, Adam, I can't begin to tell you.'

He nods again, his eyes closing briefly.

'So . . . shall we finish the washing-up and then maybe go to the pub and we can talk about Katie?'

He moves his head back sharply, as if avoiding a fist. 'Katie? Now?'

'Oh. OK . . . well, maybe we can have tea or something tomorrow, or Tuesday if you're free?'

He looks down at the floor and shakes his head, then raises his face, finally, to look at me.

'Laura – these things don't always just *blow over*.'

His voice is shaky and I can see anger in his eyes, his pupils tiny dots.

And I can see what looks like overwhelming disappointment.

And there is hurt too, quite a fair bit of hurt.

If I'm honest, he doesn't really look like a man appreciating the irony of the situation.

41

To: Laura
From: Jess
Subject: Is there anybody out there?

You're very quiet this week. It's Wednesday and you haven't sent a single picture of a cat wearing jeans and shoes. Are you OK/are you working on the Laura Parker Brand Strategy?

To: Jess
From: Laura
Subject: Copy check

I am OK. Had a good tasting menu on Monday at Ludo Brunelli – what do you think for the last paragraph?

A box of delights to finish: mini chocolate doughnuts, paper-thin buttery shortbread, and tart apple jellies were served in an old-fashioned biscuit tin, gratis. A generous end to a lovely meal.

To: Laura
From: Jess
Subject: Buying you a dictionary for your next birthday – and a thesaurus!

Don't use the word 'gratis' – it sounds poncey. Or like you're trying to be a gangster. Either way: lose it.
  And what sort of a lightweight word is 'lovely'?

Not the first that springs to mind when describing you . . . She's right though. 'A lovely meal' is not a highly sophisticated way of describing dinner. But it's all I can do to put adjective in front of noun at the moment. Oh, and I've forgotten a verb in that final sentence . . .

To: Laura
From: Sophie
Subject: I have your earrings

And your hair clip. And one of your socks.
Dare I ask if he replied?

To: Sophie
From: Laura
Subject: V. bad hangover indeed

I shouldn't have texted him, but Wolfgang Wolf couldn't have held me back at that point in the Chardonnay. If he hasn't forgiven me, the least he could do is call to tell me I'm a bitch?
    (I hope he hasn't told his mum, I was hoping she'd adopt me.)

To: Laura
From: Sophie
Subject: Hmmm

He has no right to get this annoyed. He sounds like one of those people who re-ignites their anger from the embers of the anger-fag they're just putting out. He'll calm down sooner or later.

To: Laura, Dad
From: Jess
Subject: And another thing!

Why didn't you tell us #TheDish is trending on Twitter?

To: Laura, Jess
From: Dad
Subject: You are a Meme!

I finally know what a Meme is! Immensely proud of you.

To: Jess, Dad
From: Laura
Subject: re: You are a Meme!

DO NOT want to talk about THAT.

To: Laura
From: Kiki
Subject: Fame at last! Your review is going stellar!

Have you seen page 24 of the *Guardian* this morning? They've
done a piece showing how many weeks you could feed a family
of four for the same price as dinner for two at LuxEris – seven
weeks and six days apparently!

To: Laura
From: Azeem
Subject: URGENT

COME TO MY DESK.

This had better be some actual work.

'Azeem, if you show me one more singing toilet I'm sticking my head in a toilet,' I say, keeping my voice low. (The first toilet mash-up was on Monday: Jonn Zavragin's head, superimposed on to the lady-toilet, quickly followed by a photo of all three owners' heads, rotating like in *The Exorcist*. Some other wag with too much time on their hands then programmed the heads to rap my review, and in the last two days we've had Gordon Brown's head singing 'Flush Gordon', a purple toilet singing 'Tonight We're Going to Potty Like It's 1999'; and Roger's favourite – the toilet with a giant clock on a chain which raps to Public Enema.)

On the screen a basic 1980s computer animation appears, in the style of PacMan. When Azeem presses the space bar, a mini-stickman critic trundles into view and chomps his way through the word LuxEris, then enters a cavernous basement, where two mini-hostesses in gold knickers chase him round in a circle, trying to grab his cash.

'The aim is to get through the meal without getting fleeced,' says Azeem, navigating the critic to a pentagonal table, where he waits a full minute before a mini water waiter approaches. Azeem presses down furiously on the arrow keys as the waiter attempts to wrestle the wallet from his trousers – at which point the critic karate chops the waiter and runs for the exit only to be grabbed by the ankles by a giant Russian bouncer who tips him upside down and shakes his money out of him. The coins tumble to the ground as GAME OVER throbs, centre screen.

Azeem and Roger seem to think this is all great publicity – but that's because they're not nearly as paranoid as I am; and also because they're not responsible for it.

To: All Staff
From: Azeem
Subject: Record stats!

Latest retweets: Bechdel – 103,000. Turkeys – 87,000. The Dish
/Toilet – 201,000. Amazing numbers!

To: All Staff
From: Jonesy
Subject: Digital bollocks

Aren't we missing a trick? Can't we put Damian Bechdel's head
on a turkey, stick him on a toilet – and put Rihanna's tits on
him for good measure?

To: All Staff
From: Sandra
Subject: USE OF ALL STAFF EMAIL

If you are intent on sending non-work related emails during
work hours, please create a separate sub-group cluster in
Outlook.

To: Sophie
From: Laura
Subject: You're right

Adam *is* out of order ignoring my text! Am thinking about it
and am officially pissed off now . . . oh, hang on a minute . . .

To: Laura
From: Adam
Subject: Got your text

We need to talk. Can you come round tomorrow morning before work?

42

His hair's still wet from the shower but his face looks so pale and traumatised when he opens the front door, he looks like he's come up from near-drowning.

'I brought us some coffee from that little Piaggio van by the station,' I say, holding out a cup for him. He makes no move to take it – in fact he stares at it like it's an insult.

'Listen, Adam, I'm sorry again about everything. I hope you're not in trouble at work because of it?'

'Laura – I can't talk to you about work stuff anymore,' he says, folding his arms tightly.

'Oh, OK, well fine.' I hold out the coffee again but he ignores it.

'So I take it you didn't ask to see me because you've forgiven me?' I say, self-righteousness starting to override my disappointment.

'What am I supposed to be forgiving you for?' His voice is calm, though there's a spark in his eye that reminds me, scarily, of Sandra.

'For the fact I didn't tell you about my column earlier?'

He raises his eyebrows in mock surprise. 'The fact you wrote the most savage review about my food imaginable, all the while telling me how talented and great you thought I was?'

'Adam—'

'Or the fact you repeatedly sat there and talked about the reviewer like it was someone else? For all I know, you're not actually a secretary and you were lying about that!'

'Oh Adam!'

'Don't *Oh Adam* me! When I first met you, I thought you were the answer. This funny, feisty girl with an appetite for life, pretty and interesting and smart.'

I can't help but smile, but this only seems to infuriate him.

'But more than anything, I thought you were someone who had values you believed in.'

'I do.'

'"Fairtrade" this, "Truth and honesty" that . . . '

'Can you please take this cup from me? It's hot.'

'You are literally the opposite of the person I thought you were.'

'Not literally,' I say. 'You don't mean that *literally*.'

'No, it's true, Laura. As you know, I'm not a huge fan of liars, from my recent experiences with another pathological liar—'

'That is a *totally* different scenario—'

'But it's not even your lies,' he says, wrinkling his nose as if there's a bad smell. 'It's your hypocrisy!'

'You think *I'm* a hypocrite? You're having a go at me about keeping a secret, a professional secret I had bloody good reason to keep – when you kept *your baby* a secret?'

'It's hardly the same!'

'Correct – it's not the same *at all*, a baby is an actual person! A person has far greater repercussions on the future than my review of your stupid overpriced restaurant.'

'Wow. You thought *you* had immunity because *I* was the victim of an insane woman? You could get away with trying to destroy my reputation and lying to my face?'

'The victim, ah yes, poor you!'

'Laura . . . ' he says, his eyes darkening.

'Adam – I processed your bombshell like a mature adult, because that is what I am. But you? You've just festered all week and blown this stuff up out of all proportion in your head.'

'The only reason you processed it like *a mature adult*—'

'That doesn't sound like my voice, Adam.'

'—like *a mature adult* was because you knew you were hiding something ten times worse!'

'Oh right! You win the prize for your secret being less horrendous than mine? What do you want? A gold-star sticker? Or a little statue of a saint with his trousers down?'

'From the first time I met you it was clear,' he says. 'You even said it in St John – you hate chefs, we're all stupid—'

'I was joking! You laughed about it!'

'I didn't realise you were serious!'

'Of course I wasn't serious!'

'And speaking of jokes – is this supposed to be funny? "Your Poulet de Bresse chicken was half-decent but for a hundred and thirty pounds, it should come stuffed with a PlayStation, not garlic."'

'It's not supposed to be *funny* funny, it's more sharp than funny.'

'You couldn't even fit a PlayStation in a chicken, Laura.'

'Fine, next time I'll stick a Nintendo DS in it – *you are charging one hundred and thirty pounds for a goddamn chicken, I will say what I like.*'

'And you obviously have a major problem with men, because of your idiot ex-husband.'

'*What?*'

'Even when you talk about skyscrapers you say they're stupid because *men* built them.'

'Clearly I don't hate men, I like Azeem, Fabrizio, Roger—'

'Oh, Roger, yes! How could I forget wonderful Roger, Roger who can fight off blizzards and hurricanes! Roger gets the loyalty, and Adam? Adam gets "I'd rather cut out my tongue than eat his food".'

'You said yourself the menu is insane, you said it a hundred times.'

'Yeah, maybe I did, but I *didn't say it in print.*'

'But I've told you already – that version we printed was the wrong one, it was a mistake. Have you even read the right version, the one I left with you on Sunday?'

'I cannot imagine anything less relevant at this point.'

'Nice. I came in with a broken tooth and paid a fortune of my own money because I was being loyal to you.'

'Jesus, if this is your idea of loyalty . . . '

'I tried to do the right thing by you – I even gave your guys the benefit of the doubt about your vile rip-off coffee – and you won't even read it?'

'You're not seriously asking for my sympathy are you?' he says, shaking his head in disgust.

'Look, can you please take this cup and can we sit and talk about this like normal people?'

He takes the coffee from my hand, looks at it like it's a bleeding dagger, then hands it straight back. 'No, I'm not having this bloody coffee. In fact, of all the things you could bring into my home—'

'What now?'

'Single estate is it?'

'Yeah, what? Why are you looking at me like that, Adam?'

'Because I've only just realised that I was the one who actually *told* you we were serving instant coffee, and you went and put it in your review!'

I stare at him to see if he's joking but his eyes are full of fury and two deep creases have formed on his brow.

'Are you serious? Adam, you know what I used to do for a living, why would you even think that came from you?'

'Because we had that exact conversation at Fabrizio's. Or did you think I'd forget?'

'What?!'

'If Ivan and Erek found out I shared that with you they'd fire me.'

'Adam: you *are* an idiot! You are *literally* a moron. I wrote that review before I even met you. Is that what you actually think? That I would take stuff you told me and put it in the piece? Adam, what sort of a lying bitch do you think I am?'

'I think that's obvious – one that's standing in front of me holding two cups of coffee.'

He looks in frustration past my shoulder, as if all he wants to do is march out of his own front door but can't because he'll lock himself out of his flat.

'Adam – when you've calmed down and this has all blown over, I'd like to think we could talk about this like adults.'

'Laura – there is no woman I've ever met who is more full of shit than you. If you had ever cared for me you could not have done this.'

'Stop talking, Adam – I know you'll regret saying all of this.'

'That's the worst thing – I thought you *did* know me. I thought I knew you. I felt closer to you after one month than I've ever felt to anyone in my whole life, I thought I was in love with you, fucking hell – my mother's almost in love with you. And now I feel like the biggest idiot in the world.'

'That's because you *are* the biggest idiot in the world!' I say, feeling rage shake through my body all over again. 'How could you think I would use that coffee stuff against you? I am *appalled* you would think that of me.'

'Great. Moral high ground – it's all yours Laura, go for it. Hope the view's magnificent, you can take the lift up there on your own next time.'

'Fuck you Adam Bayley. Fuck. You. What, so you asked to see me today just so you could insult me?'

He laughs. 'No – I asked to see you today because, like you said, I *am* the biggest idiot in the world. Believe it or not, for some insane reason, I actually wanted to warn you.'

'Warn me? About what?'

He shakes his head in exhaustion. 'Believe me – it had nothing to do with me. But there's something in the post for you this morning, and you're not going to like it.'

43

Coombs & Forthmere
164 Brook Street
London W1

Roger Harris
Editor in Chief — The Voice
108 Clerkenwell Green
London EC1

10 April

Dear Mr Harris,

We act on behalf of our client, VanRek Holdings Ltd, in
respect of an article appearing on pages 77 and 78 of the April
issue of *The Voice*, under the headline *FLASH IN THE PAN*,
(by-line: Anon/The Dish.)

False allegations raised in points 16, 49-59 & 89 — suggesting
sharp practice, dishonesty, trading of poor quality goods and
a lack of moral integrity — give rise to serious harm to our
client's brand and reputation and are severely distressing. We
require you to take the following steps urgently:

a. Immediately withdraw the online version from your website
and prevent further distribution of the offensive content.

b. Publish in the May issue a full retraction and apology, in wording to be approved by VanRek, in a space size equivalent to the offending article.

c. Pay our client damages for injury to their reputation and for the hurt and humiliation caused, and indemnify our client in respect of all costs.

If point a) of the above is not addressed within 24 hours of receipt of this letter, we will apply, forthwith, for an Interim Injunction in the High Court.

Yours sincerely,

William Coombs

'So . . . a Beginners Guide to defamation . . . ' says Heather, placing a humongous volume of *Halsbury's Laws* down on Roger's desk. 'A person or a business is entitled, in English law, to their good name. Laura – you and Kiki took the word *head* out of the phrase *head chef*, didn't you?'

I cast my mind back a month. 'That makes a difference?'

'It means you're not associating the cooking with one identifiable individual. You're attacking a company – a company is not consider-ed to have feelings, so VanRek can't claim for aggravated damages, merely reputational injury.'

'Reputational injury?'

'You've exposed them to contempt, ridicule – made the average person think less of them by saying something false.'

'But everything I wrote in the review was true,' I say, feeling Sandra's eyes fix on me.

'Yes – but unlike in a criminal case, the burden of proof is reversed. The onus is on you – the defendant – to prove you're not lying.'

'Surely we just chuck Section Twelve of the Human Rights Act at them?' says Roger. 'Freedom of speech, freedom of expression?'

'The ECHR doesn't grant you licence to make things up.'

'But I'm not making things up,' I say.

'Which brings me to our defence. Your review is a mix of facts and opinions: fact – the toilets resemble naked women. Opinion – this makes them vulgar. We have two defences: Justification for facts: the facts are substantially true. And Honest Comment for opinions – would a fair-minded person agree with you?'

'It's not going to actually go to court, is it?' I say.

Roger shakes his head. 'They're doing this for column inches, guaranteed they'll leak it to the press – their business is built on publicity. They're far too savvy to waste money on a trial. Besides, we still have a free press in this country – otherwise we'd be in court every month.'

Heather holds her hand up. 'Actually, there is a worrying precedent: a restaurant in Sydney took the *Morning Herald* to court for a scathing review, back in 2003.'

'Ancient history,' says Roger.

'They spent eleven years in court . . . ' says Heather, as Sandra presses her fingers to her temples. 'Two jury trials, two appeals, then on to the High Court . . . '

'Bloody waste of time,' says Roger, his hand on the table flexing in and out of a fist.

'The judge found in favour of the restaurant . . . to the tune of six hundred thousand dollars.'

'Are you saying this could end up costing us money too?' says Sandra.

'What does she mean *too*?' I say to Roger, under my breath.

'Escalating turkey wars . . . '

'There's no way we're risking litigation on two fronts in one month,' says Sandra. 'It's utterly clear what needs to happen here. Take the piece down immediately, print a full retraction in May's issue, admit you got your facts wrong and your judgement was flawed.'

'Sandra – my readers trust me. If I say I'm unreliable, how could they ever trust me again?'

'Well, quite: why should they? You said – when you asked to change copy *the day before we went to print* – that the original copy was wrong.'

'Not wrong exactly . . . '

'Excuse me?' she says, turning to Roger, then back to me. 'Are the facts wrong or aren't they?'

'They're not wrong but—'

'So were you lying to me then or are you lying now?'

'Lay off her, Sandra, she's not in court yet!' says Heather.

'I don't think we should take it down,' says Roger.

'Six hundred thousand dollars? Eleven years in court?' says Sandra.

'If they're going to exploit this for publicity, so should we. Have you seen the latest toilet?' he says to me. 'Total Eclipse of the Fart.'

'That might be the problem,' says Heather. 'The longer it's up, the more traffic it gets, and the more they can argue the extent of reputational damage. It could mean an increased payout if we lose – that's why the damages were so high in Sydney – the paper kept the piece online. If we take it down today at least we look like we're cooperating.'

'And then what?'

'We respond with a letter of defence.'

Sandra shakes her head. 'Why are we defending a piece we know contains factual errors?'

'Why did this piece even run in the first place, Sandra?' I say. 'You told me you'd changed it on the system!'

'Oh,' she says, eyes wide, looking at Roger. 'This again? This is my fault?'

'Ladies, please,' says Roger. 'Let's take it offline.'

'The article or the catfight?' says Heather.

'The piece. Draft a letter of response today.'

'But what if they reject it?' I say. 'How can I *prove* something looked or tasted horrible when my word is my only proof? I don't have photos.'

'Whatever happens, you do not want a protracted to-ing and fro-ing. We absolutely cannot justify resource on *this*,' says Sandra.

'Sandra's right,' says Heather, looking at me with concern. 'Their pockets are substantially deeper than ours – if they wanted to make life difficult for us, they could. We can defend the facts, but it's the subjective stuff we'll struggle to verify. If they can make a case the review harmed their business financially—'

'But the place is packed with high rollers every night,' I say.

'Now it is, yes, but if they drag this out long enough and trade declines they can claim your review is partly responsible. So I agree – the key is a swift resolution.'

'Roger,' I say, turning to him directly. 'Please, let's not fight this. I'll apologise and we'll publish a correction. I don't want to cause any more harm.'

Sandra smiles her first sincere smile at me in four years.

'Nonsense!' says Roger. 'We've seen it all before, they're doing it for headlines, don't let them cow you so easily.'

Heather shakes her head. 'I'd tread softly in the first instance, it's not worth riling them with a belligerent response.'

'I disagree,' says Roger. 'I say we bite back.'

44

Roger Harris
Editor in Chief –The Voice
108 Clerkenwell Green
London EC1

Coombs & Forthmere
134 Brook Street
London W1

11 April

Dear Mr Coombs,

Further to your letter of 10 April, we reject your client's inter-
pretation that the outlined article is defamatory – and we further
advise you of the following in our defence.

Justification
Points 49 – 55.
Allegation of taking ideas from other chefs: (cf. Redzepi,
Matsuhisa, Tosi, Keller, Blumenthal), attached documentation
referencing origins of these dishes.

56 – 59
Allegation of frozen ingredients used when claimed as fresh
/seasonal. Attached documentation from the National Farmers

Union detailing UK seasonal harvest charts for produce detailed in Appendix I.

89

Allegation of passing off instant coffee as single estate fresh coffee. Our correspondent is a Licensed Q Grader, accredited by the Coffee Quality Institute and has professional expertise in coffee analysis.

Honest Comment
80 – Pea and tetragonia soup – tepid
81 – Sourdough pretzel croutons – stale
83 – Boudin blanc hot dog – congealed and cold
86 – Cod ice cream – liquid

Our correspondent and their guest pointed out the organoleptic quality issues to staff throughout the meal.

Vulgar Abuse
18 – Comparison of house white wine to battery acid. It is our contention a reader would understand our correspondent has not previously imbibed battery acid directly and is merely using hyperbolic language to demonstrate a poor quality product.
77 – Eels Flottante. 'A mouthful of horror' – again, this is not intended as a literal statement as horror cannot be consumed orally.
78 – Our correspondent has not, to date, eaten a squash ball.
79 – Nor put their tongue in *fictional character* Dot Cotton's mouth.

In relation to your client's claim we accept the following:

76 – Scallop Sriracha Kiev – inedible.

The scallop did – in truth – make it as far as our correspondent's stomach. However, once ingested, the aforementioned mollusc induced severe cramps and violent nausea.

On the basis that point 76 is no longer in dispute, we are willing to print a brief paragraph of apology regarding the scallop, online, in terms approved wholly by ourselves. And as a gesture of our goodwill, we have removed the main article from our publication's website.

Yours sincerely,

Roger Harris

45

'The brownies are two pounds each, the blondies are a pound – and if you're going to stand there eating all my samples, I'll have to charge you a tenner,' says Sophie to the two customers who've been circling her stall, snaffling freebies for the last three minutes.

'Shameless!' she says under her breath, as they walk away, showing no signs of embarrassment at all.

'Shall I restock the Black Forest and the Peanut Butter Caramel?' I say, doing a quick count.

She checks her watch. 'Yeah, go on – and maybe the dark chocolate and coconut – it's doing better than I thought it would, I should add it to the list for Celina Summer's party.'

'How many flavours do you have so far?'

'She wants six, but one has to be gluten free, one has to be Paleo. I had no idea cavemen were quite so neurotic about their brownies.'

'You should sign up Amber to help. She doesn't have a real job, and she won't eat all your stock while your back's turned.'

'Hell freezing over, Laura. Hey, if you're going to the van, on the way back can you take Dominic half-a-dozen triple chocolate to trade for two steak sarnies, and swap some raspberry ones with Mauro for coffees? You know you really should be selling coffee on the stand for me.'

'It's too much like hard work, Soph. I'm not a morning person, and I haven't got the patience when it's pissing down with rain.'

'Nonsense, you do it for me.'

'It's fun when I'm helping you – I wouldn't want the responsibility on my own.'

'I'm not saying it's easy – but being your own boss is the greatest luxury in the world. When I think about having to work for anyone else, ever again—'

'But you hated Devron – Roger's a great boss . . . ' I say, my face creasing with anxiety as I think about the trouble I've caused him, and Adam. 'Oh Soph, none of this would have happened if I'd just been happy with a bloody jam doughnut.'

'That's not true, you'd still have the law suit, you just wouldn't care what happens at the Adam end.'

'Roger thinks they won't take it all the way to court,' I say, picking at a corner of the banoffee brownie I'm taking as today's wages.

'He knows what he's talking about.'

'But he can be so gung ho; Sandra wants me to confess to killing JFK.'

'And what about Adam?'

'What about him?'

'Have you spoken to him?'

'Since he called me a lying bitch?'

'But you are a bitch,' she says, laughing. 'I mean – from his point of view. You've royally screwed him at work. I know you didn't mean to, but you've put him in a very compromised position.'

'You've changed your tune!'

'No – think about it: if they were relying on him to back up their legal threat, he can't do that. So either he has to lie and cover for the guy who messed up—'

'I don't think he'd lie for Max.'

'Right – so he'll get aggravation from his team if he shafts the guy below, and the fact he left the pass in the first place makes him look unprofessional, so he'll get grief from above too.'

'Yeah, but he did leave the pass, didn't he?'

'That's a bit harsh, Laura.'

'It's the truth.'

'You should call him.'

'I'd rather wait until he's calmed down.'

'Face up to it, Laura – you're in this together. Anyway, he's got so much stress on at the moment.'

'I am not unstressed myself.'

'If you want to be in an adult relationship with him, be the bigger person and apologise. Oh my God, look!' she says, pointing towards

305

the artisan cheese stall opposite. 'Those two are actually sneaking back for more freebies!'

'Ah, now if you watched *Game of Thrones* you'd know how to defend this cake stall to the death.'

'I cannot believe the cheek of it!' she says, grabbing the two trays of samples from the front of the stand and stashing them behind us: safe from the freeloaders, but not safe from me.

To his credit, he picks up on the second ring. I wasn't expecting him to answer so quickly, and I apologise so rapidly, because of nerves, I get lost in my sentence. 'Adam – I'm sorry about Thursday I said some stupid things I didn't mean I was just reacting without thinking what was coming out of my mouth and it all got a little heated but anyway, I'm sorry . . . I am, very.'

There's a pause on the other end of the line. 'I'm sorry too,' he says, slowly. 'Particularly the coffee thing . . . when I thought about it afterwards I realised how out of order I was.'

'That's OK . . . ' I say, relaxing. Gosh, being the bigger person is so the way forward!

'But I was angry,' he says. 'Very angry.'

'Yeah, I understand that. Did you tell your mum?'

'She was hoping to see you yesterday, for pastry class . . . '

'Apologise for me would you?'

There's another pause, so long it's like a long-distance call. Eventually he makes a small noise of agreement.

'So . . . Have you made any progress with Katie?'

He sighs. 'I've spoken to a solicitor, and I'm going to apply for a Declaration of Parentage, it's the first step. The magistrates can then authorise the birth certificate being re-registered.'

'That sounds like a positive start.'

'Katie seems to be coming round to the fact I can make her life easier. She's an idiot but she isn't stupid.'

'So does that mean you might be able to have access quite soon?'

'Maybe, as an extra pair of hands every once in a while.'

'What do you think "every once in a while" might mean?'

'Look, Laura – I have no idea at this stage. I have no idea if she'll change her mind tomorrow. She hasn't exactly behaved reasonably in the past.'

'Well, let me know if there's anything I can do.' I mean it sincerely but it sounds so hollow over the phone. 'Listen, about work . . . I hope you haven't got into a load of trouble because of me, it's just—'

'Laura,' he says, cutting me short. 'The lawsuit is nothing to do with me, I've told them I can't be involved – I absolutely do not want to discuss it with you.'

'OK, fair enough – but I'm just saying I hope it doesn't cause you extra stress.'

'Right.'

'I mean, I understand what's happening now is rough – but I never anticipated any of it. I was only trying to do my job properly . . . '

He lets my sentence hang in the air – the longer it does, the more pathetic it sounds.

Eventually he speaks. 'When I first told you where I worked, that very first time we met, did you not think it would have been easier just to tell me then?'

I think back to camping out in the toilet in the Chinese restaurant, panicking. My gut was to tell him – and then I bottled it.

No, that's not true: my gut was *not* to tell him – partly because I was being professional, but also because *even then* I wasn't willing to risk him rejecting me.

'Adam, I'm genuinely sorry this is hurting you, but I did what I thought was right at the time.' I catch myself as I realise I now sound exactly like my father trying to justify himself.

'So you *still* think you did the right thing?' he says, the edge in his voice sharp as a knife.

'I'm not saying I don't regret all this mess, but I made the decision based on the facts I had, and the way my mind thinks – how *could* I do it any other way?'

'I cannot believe the arrogance of that statement! So in spite of everything – you're still defending what you did?

'I care about my anonymity enough to want to protect it – yes.

I know it's not the Coca-Cola recipe of secrets, but it *really* matters to me.'

I can sense his anger bristling over the line.

'But if I'm being brutally honest, Adam, the other reason I didn't tell you was because I was scared you would walk away. I could easily give you a story right now about how I'd have done things differently, been more honest upfront – but it would be a lie. I know it's not what you want to hear – but I'm being entirely truthful with you.'

'Laura? You're about six weeks too late for that,' he says, and leaves me listening to the dial tone.

46

It's not been the best start to the week. My boyfriend of five and a half seconds (now ex) thinks I'm a lying bitch, but that's OK because he has a baby with another woman who's also sparing with the truth. My first lawsuit is ticking along nicely. And when I walk into the office on Monday, there's a highlighted copy of the *Telegraph* on my desk:

Restaurant Critic in the Soup

The anonymous critic behind The Dish is being sued by the owners of celebrity hotspot LuxEris. The restaurateurs allege the review, which has since gone viral, was defamatory and are applying for an undisclosed six-figure sum in damages. The scathing attack is at odds with otherwise unanimous acclaim from the capital's reviewers who have praised LuxEris's exquisite cooking and glamorous decor. Allegations of malicious intent have been denied by the paper's Editor in Chief.

To: Heather, Sandra, Laura
From: Roger
Subject: Publicity whores!

I told you they were doing this for the headlines. Bloody PR company, leekier (Ed!) than a Welsh sieve.

To: Roger, Sandra, Laura
From: Heather
Subject: Next steps

We need a catch up asap – just been on the phone to their lawyers – this is not just going to go away.

'This is so entirely infuriating,' says Roger, as we're walking up to Heather's office.

'What is?'

He pauses to catch his breath, his knuckles taut as he grips the stair rail. 'Having to pander to rich bullies and their lawyers,' he says, irritably. 'It'll get to the point where you can't say boo to a goose without Goosey Gander's solicitors issuing a writ for traumatising one of the flock.'

'You've done quite enough to upset the poultry community for one month,' I say, putting my arm out as he stumbles on the top step. 'Are you all right?'

He takes a deep breath and puffs it out. 'Legs are a bit stiff that's all . . . shouldn't have done that triathlon yesterday,' he says, winking.

Heather hands us each a copy of the solicitor's letter as we walk in. 'VanRek have rejected our defence,' she says. 'I counter-proposed an offer to make amends – we'd print the second review in full in May, with an introductory paragraph explaining there were two distinct visits.'

'And?'

'No dice. The way I see it, we have two options,' she says, spreading the rest of the paperwork out on the boardroom table. 'If you look at the substantiation documents, I've highlighted the areas I'm confident we can argue in court.'

Roger and I move in for a closer look. At the bottom of a long list denying all my claims about the food is a signature: Max's.

'This is ludicrous,' says Roger. 'I was at the bloody meal! I'll stand up in court and swear to these. Bloody ridiculous!' His face has turned red and I slide a glass of water towards him.

'That is one option, you can escalate – but in my opinion there's a reasonable likelihood they'll call our bluff and take it to court.'

'Which would be a disaster,' says Sandra.

'Or you can apologise in May,' says Heather. 'But it would need to be a general apology, an acknowledgement the food is high quality.'

'I can do that,' I say.

'And you're going to have to back down on the coffee point. It's inflaming VanRek above everything else. False sale of goods, makes them look very shoddy indeed.'

'But I'm right.' And I know it now for a fact.

Heather shrugs. 'How are you going to prove it? VanRek have submitted delivery notes, clearly showing the Single Estate coffee was delivered to the premises the week before you ate there.'

I turn to Roger who's looking ashen-faced.

'Whatever you decide, Laura, you have to do it before next Thursday's deadline,' she says. 'If we don't call it in May's issue, it'll cost us.' She gathers the papers back into a neat pile. 'Roger – do you want to go straight on to the SunFarms documentation or do you want a break?'

'Let's have a five-minute breather before TurkeyGate. Laura, we'll spare you the feathers.'

'Roger, I feel terrible,' I say, as we're heading out of the room. 'I had no idea it would cause this much grief – I want it all to go away.'

'We'll talk about it tomorrow. I may go and get some fresh air,' he says, loosening his shirt collar. 'It's a little warm in here today.'

Funny, that. I was just thinking it had turned rather cold.

47

'You're definitely not going to like this one,' says Azeem, beckoning me to his desk on Tuesday morning with a face I've only ever seen when Arsenal lost 6–3 to Man City.

'What now?'

The toilets have reached new levels of ridiculousness in the last twenty-four hours. The latest is two toilets with two of Five Star's heads (two-star review) singing 'Cistern Addict', and there's been an extensive Lou Rawls back catalogue.

'Your bezzie,' he says, nodding at Fergus Kaye's headshot grinning from his screen – Fergus currently sporting a Bethnal Green hipster beard. 'Same beard as that dude in *The Twits*, what's he called?'

'Mister Twit?'

'One letter out.'

THE DISH IN HOT WATER – ANONYMOUS HACK SHAMES JOURNALISTS' PROFESSION

Why Anon should be gone

On my graduation from Oxford in 1981 I took my father's Morgan down to Cannes with Belles Montague. There, one blistering July day, I first discovered Pierre Lachaise's 'Oeuf de Moujins dans un Jus de Truffes Noires' and was transported to high ecstasy. While others remember where they were when man landed on the moon, I remember where I was when I first supped Koffmann's croustade; nibbled Marco's trotter.

I have been writing about restaurants for nigh on 30 years – I have some small claim to pedigree. Is it too much to ask of today's critics that they know their onions?

Fine talk, coming from a man who doesn't know his halibut from his sea bass!

This is not a lament over The Dish's under-developed vocabulary, their inability to use words of more than three syllables. It is merely an imploration that amateurs should not be given a voice in print media. As the great Clint Eastwood once said, 'Opinions are like ***holes. Everybody has one . . .' To which I'd add: But we don't need to see it.

I'd wager this 'critic' went to a second-rate provincial red brick and lacks formal credentials. I'd hazard a guess they're female. How else to explain their livid over-reaction to the charming, tongue-in-cheek sanitaryware in the little boys' room? And far be it from me to provoke the feminists' ire, but perhaps this critic without portfolio used certain feminine wiles to ingratiate herself with an ageing male editor? How else to explain such a dilettante being given free rein to pontificate about subjects of which she knows nothing?

Hurling vituperative abuse from behind the sofa of anonymity is an act of cowardice. If this critic is worth half their Himalayan salt, they should have the guts to criticise a man in their own name. 'The Dish', come out, come out, wherever you are . . .

'Don't look so disturbed,' says Azeem. 'Fergus writes for a paper you get free on the Tube.'

'That's the only type anyone reads nowadays. Don't let Roger see this, he's still pissed off after yesterday.'

Azeem's eyes flick towards Roger's door. 'Too late.'

'It's fine, Roger – I don't care what Fergus writes about me.' Such a huge fib, but I just want Roger to calm down, he's looking so agitated.

'How dare he!' he says. '"Ageing editor"? After the amount of second chances I gave that pompous arsehole. He's never got over being replaced by a woman.'

'How about we run a full page in May's issue: "Fergus Kaye Puts the Ass in Sea Bass"?'

'You're being very forgiving – but I'm not having it.'

'Roger – I know you don't want me to, but it's just easier if I do what Heather says and write a full apology.'

He shakes his head. 'Your mother would not have lain down like a doormat. She'd have fought back.'

'I guess . . .'

'And who's to say VanRek wouldn't be trying to sue us if we'd printed the second version? They'd probably have taken umbrage at something else – people tend to get upset about the truth, Laura, but putting it on the page is our bread and butter.'

'Roger, I know that.'

'I am willing to fight this in court.'

'And I don't think it's worth this paper's time and money. Maybe if the turkeys weren't kicking off simultaneously.'

'If you say you're wrong about the coffee, not only will you be lying but it dents your credibility. Think through the consequences of that. Our readers are not very forgiving.'

'I know that too – I do read their letters!'

'So: I don't want you sacrificing your reputation because of these cretins,' he says, taking a hanky from his top pocket to wipe the sweat from his brow.

I don't want to sacrifice myself for them either – but I'm not sure I have much choice.

'I will be deeply disappointed if you roll over and let them win,' he says, his face darkening. 'Now, I've got to go and see more bloody lawyers with Heather – do *not* make a decision until we've spoken again tomorrow. I mean it – sleep on it!' he says, pointing a finger at me.

'OK, OK.'

'Think about what your mother would have done. I'll see you in the morning.'

'Come on, Laura – you're normally the one forcing me into it.'

'Can't we just go to the pub?'

'I've been eating Celina Summer's brownie recipes from eight a.m. and if I don't do some exercise I swear, I will have one more reason to hate that woman on top of the fact she keeps calling me Sylvie.'

'Fine,' I say. 'Roger's not coming back to the office today – we'll do the six p.m. class?'

'Katja's pulled her hamstring, so apparently we've got Chet for Total Body,' says Sophie, pointing to the poster of a steroid-pumped man mountain doing a one-armed push-up. 'Do you think Chet's been retouched?'

'That arm is a wall of orange muscle,' I say. 'What is Chet short for anyway?'

'It's bound to be a made-up name, like Wolfgang Wolf . . . '

'Like you'd take Wolfgang seriously if you knew his real name was Larry,' I say, sitting on the bench and resting my head in my hand.

'You OK?'

'Bit of a headache . . . '

'No word from Adam?'

'Nope,' I say. 'And to be honest I'm so stressed about work this week I can't cope with his tantrum too. He's conveniently forgotten he was the one begging me for forgiveness two weeks ago, so as far as I'm concerned, we're quits.'

'Quits as in *over*?'

'No – quits as in I'm done apologising.'

'Do you know what will cheer you up?' she says. 'Investing in some heavily branded merchandise. Would you prefer the racer back T-shirt or the all-terrain water bottle?'

'Decisions, decisions . . . The blue T-shirt's all right, but thirty-eight pounds? That's blatantly a Camden market four-pound T-shirt.'

'How about these?' she says, holding a pair of tiny white Lycra shorts up to my waist.

'Got about fifty classes to go before I attempt those,' I say, hanging them back on the rack. 'Come on, let's go dump our bags and get this over with.'

As we're heading to the lockers, my phone rings. I have a sixth sense it's Adam, but when I reach into my bag I see Heather's name. I'd better take it, you never know, it might be good news.

'Work call – back in two secs,' I say to Sophie as I take my phone outside.

A minute later I walk back in.

'You're not ducking out already are you?' says Sophie. 'What's wrong, Laura? Laura – what's wrong?'

48

The familiar prickle of panic infects me like tiny needles as I walk through the doors to the waiting room and see Heather sitting, eyes fixed on the doors to the resuscitation area.

'Heather – what happened? Is he all right?'

She shakes her head. 'We had a tricky round table with SunFarms' lawyers – Roger seemed very distracted; then in the cab after, he went the most terrible grey colour, sweating and complaining of a pain in his jaw.' Her hand moves to soothe her own cheek at the memory. 'I thought it might be something with his teeth, maybe an abscess but then it moved down into his shoulder . . . And then he stopped talking altogether . . . '

'Heather – are *you* OK? Can I get you a cup of tea?'

'The cabbie was brilliant, brought us straight here – by which time Roger was making no sense at all. I don't think I've ever seen a person go that colour . . . really, the most awful colour . . . and his lips . . . almost blue . . . '

'What have the doctors said?'

'Oh Christ, go in!' she says, pointing to the door. 'Yes, go in and tell them you're his daughter! They wouldn't let me through but there's a nice nurse with a beard looking after him, Graeme, his name is – I told him you were on your way.'

'He was conscious though, when he arrived?'

She nods distractedly.

'Are you sure you're OK, Heather?'

'I'm fine, yes, absolutely.'

But I can tell she's not, because in her mind she's still in the back of a cab with Roger.

* * *

Roger's sitting up in bed in one of the bays in a blue gown and socks, surrounded by a team checking his blood pressure and heart rate, a bag of saline slowly dripping into his right arm.

'Oh, hello you!' he says, giving me a strained smile. Heather's right – he is the most terrible colour and his hand, when I reach out to hold it, is wet with sweat. 'What a bloody fuss over nothing, hey? Stuck polka dots all over me like a ladybird,' he says, waving his hand feebly down at the paper discs monitoring his chest.

Graeme, the nurse, reaches over to check the probe on Roger's finger is properly attached, checks the monitor again, then turns to his colleague and says in a low voice, 'We're struggling to keep his sats up to eighty-eight per cent, can you let the Reg know – and try beeping cardiac again?'

'Roger?' says Graeme 'Has your physician given you a GTN spray for angina in the last few months?'

'G and T spray, perhaps?' says Roger, laughing weakly. 'No! I don't think so, Laura – you're Nurse Ratched – tell my lovely nurse – or are you a doctor, Graeme?'

'Nurse!' says Graeme, smiling.

'Tell the lovely nurse what I take, I can't think of the bloody names,' he says, rubbing his head in confusion.

'He's just on a statin, er, Simvastatin? And Rampirel?'

'Ramipril,' says Graeme, making a note of it.

'What's wrong with him?'

'Are you next of kin?'

'She is!' says Roger, hoarsely.

Graeme takes another look at the monitor. 'We're just waiting for the chest bloods to come back. I think he's had an NSTEMI, a heart event – well, he's definitely had some kind of event. He's struggling to breathe. We're giving him some oxygen but unfortunately he's COPD as well, so we can't give him too much. I'm concerned that his—'

'Can I go home yet?' says Roger. 'I'm going to miss *The Archers* at this rate.'

'I believe you can get it on podcast nowadays,' says Graeme, his eyes flicking back up to the monitor. 'Roger, do you have any pain in your chest?'

Roger shrugs, guiltily.

'That's a yes,' I say, as Roger lies back on the bed and closes his eyes.

Graeme keeps checking the monitor, one eye on Roger's fluids, one on the wiggly lines glaring from the defibrillator. Two minutes later, the registrar arrives and briefly observes Roger's chest, heaving up and down. The registrar mumbles something to Graeme, something I can't hear. My own heart starts to pound.

The registrar's eyes stay fixed on Roger's chest as it struggles for air. I look to Roger but his eyes are firmly shut. He seems to be asleep but he's frowning, his lips moving silently. In his hand, the registrar holds a piece of paper like a till receipt. His eyes glance briefly at it before he turns back to Graeme.

'OK, his troponin level's up at zero point zero four five, and his serial ECGs show worsening ST elevation, I've spoken to the cardiac team, they've accepted him – the nurses need to transfer him to ACW.'

He turns and addresses a navy blue uniform this time. 'Sister, can we get a transfer over to Heart please, priority, as in yesterday?'

'What's going on?' I say. 'Has he had a heart attack or is he about to have one?'

'He's had an event of some kind and he's at risk of another if we don't find out what's going on. They'll do an angiogram—'

'What's that?'

'A scan – when he gets there. You might want to call whoever you need to call – your mother, maybe?'

'My . . . my *mother*?'

'Or Roger's current partner?'

'He – he has an ex-wife . . . yeah, I should go and call her. What should I tell her?'

'Just say we're transferring him for further investigation.'

'And then what? What will the scan show?'

'If he has a blockage in one of his arteries.'

I take a breath. 'And if he does?'

He shrugs. 'He may need surgery – a stent or even a cabbage.'

'A *what*?'

'Sorry, a CABG, otherwise known as a heart bypass.'

My eyes are drawn again to the bed. Roger's looking worse than he did five minutes ago, his brow creased in pain, his breath increasingly laboured. I lower my voice and turn from him. 'Is he going . . . is he going to be OK?'

The doctor looks at me as if to say: *Do you actually think I'd commit – verbally – to saying he won't die?* 'Your father's not in good shape at the moment – but if he needs some kind of intervention, the work we do with the heart nowadays is quite routine.'

'OK,' I say, relief flooding my veins. 'OK, thank you. Thank you very much.'

'But obviously,' he says – an afterthought as he turns to go – 'as with any operation, there's always the risk of complication.'

And the minute he says that word, my heart sinks and all I can think about is Roger's daughter – and how quickly she can get herself on a plane back home.

49

I'd forgotten what ITU is like. Maybe I hadn't forgotten, maybe I'd just tried to, because sitting here next to Roger's bed feels horribly like I'm straight back in my worst nightmare.

I remember when Mum was ill – I'd thought this type of ward was called Intensive Care – so when people referred to it as ITU, the IT part made me think of computers. Which is a reasonable connection to make, really, because ITU is full of technology. Technology, doctors and nurses, and patients who hover in a too-narrow space between life and death.

It's not like a normal ward. It's not just the light – bright and white, with a sickly green sheen; a light that never goes off because in ITU it's perpetual day or perpetual fluorescent night. It smells different – it doesn't smell of much. Missing are the normal ward smells of over-boiled vegetables and indecipherable creamed soup, of vomit and flowers – there's just the faint smell of pink anti-bacterial wash, mixed with a lot of anxiety.

And there isn't much in the way of human sound; generally people aren't in a talkative mood – certainly not the patients. Many can't breathe on their own, so they're intubated – big, plastic ventilator tubes rammed ungraciously down their throats. When Mum was in, there was a young man next to her for ten days who'd been stabbed in a gang fight. His friends made a racket and his mum and girlfriend would row over his comatose body, but he survived and they moved him down to High Dependency and replaced him with a 48-year-old man who'd had a heart attack and lay in his own silent world, his wife beside him sobbing constantly until they read him his Last Rites, and then there was peace – for him.

The ventilators make a constant background noise – hissing and suctioning like a cheap hoover. And the monitors beep a lot – alarms going off every time a vital goes in the wrong direction. That noise that just went off is because Roger's blood pressure, his BP, has fallen too low.

I know about BP. I know about BiPAP. I know that two days ago during Roger's angiogram, the cardiologist discovered a constricted artery and performed an ablation to stretch the aorta, via the femoral artery. As a result of a bacterial infection in the wound, Roger developed indicators of sepsis: tachycardia, a temperature of 39.9, chest pain and shortness of breath. And given his weakened state, the medics deemed it in his best interests to protect against further heart and brain injuries; so he has been overdosed on barbiturates and his body cooled to 32 degrees – to induce the coma he is now in.

I also know that knowledge is irrelevant. It doesn't protect you, or those you love, from their fate.

Knowledge is not power. It is the illusion of control.

50

To: Heather, Sandra
From: Laura
Subject: Thursday update

Still no progress I'm afraid. The consultant, Mr Dawson, hasn't been round yet today – or if he has, he managed to avoid me. By all accounts he's brilliant medically but his people skills leave something to be desired.

Sandra – visiting hours at the weekends are the same as weekdays – come whenever you like (don't worry about bringing flowers.)

I'll be back in the office tomorrow morning, provided things stay stable here.

To: Laura
From: Sandra
Subject: re: Thursday Update

Don't worry about tomorrow – there's not much for you to do here in his absence, although I do need you to decide about May's column asap. Given the current circumstances it would be appropriate to issue a full apology. Therefore I'd appreciate it if you could draft something over the weekend and show it to Heather and myself first thing Monday.

To: Sophie
From: Laura
Subject: Tonight

Sorry I didn't pick up earlier – you're not meant to use your phone on the ward, although Arthur's wife (Arthur's on Roger's right) is shouting into hers constantly. I have no idea what's wrong with Arthur – he's conscious – but they keep on drawing the curtains round his bed, then emerging five minutes later looking most perturbed.

Thanks for the dinner invite but I'm going to stay here till they do handover, then head home and crash. I forgot how entirely exhausting it is, waiting around all day. Besides, you'll be seeing me plenty over the weekend . . .

To: Elizabeth Harris
From: Laura
Subject: Friday Update

Just to let you know there's not much to update you on – which is no bad thing in this ward. His kidneys are still functioning and his numbers are stable.

I hope I wasn't too pushy on Tuesday but I feel it's far better to be safe than sorry about these things – you have to live with the consequences either way for rather a long time.

I've spoken to my flatmate and Gemma's welcome to have my room over the weekend – just let me know when she's landing and I'll meet her at Paddington.

To: Laura
From: Elizabeth Harris
Subject: Update

It's all still a bit of a shock – when my neighbour had a stent put in I remember it was reasonably straightforward.

You weren't pushy – if you hadn't had the foresight to call it on the spot, Gemma would have had to wait another day for her internal flight. She's in Bangkok now – so will be landing tomorrow morning. I'll drive down on Sunday and then she can stay with me in the hotel. I won't come to the ward immediately. I have a terrible chest infection and my doctor said it would be unwise.

Do you think Roger is aware of what's going on around him? Is it true they can hear music? If so, could you possibly get hold of a record called 'A Bushel and a Peck' please – from the *Guys and Dolls* soundtrack – and play that to him? I'll give Gemma some money on Sunday.

To: Elizabeth Harris
From: Laura
Subject: re: Update

Some doctors say the patient picks up on sounds, some say they don't – I always thought on that basis why wouldn't you try? I've bought the record on iTunes and am playing it to him now. For what it's worth, he looks peaceful and content.

To: Sophie
From: Laura
Subject: Friday update

Today's nurse, Tim, is lovely – very gentle. He's been talking to Roger. A lot. In fact I'm sure Roger was blinking with boredom earlier when Tim was telling him about his caravan-ning holiday – though they do say blinking is just a reflex.

Roger's consultant is still avoiding me, though I tracked down the sister and she said not to worry about his BP. She said some days good, some days bad. That's the worst thing – when you think you're making progress and then something else goes wrong.

With Mum, it was like a vicious game of dominoes – once things started to fall . . . Anyway, am keeping a close eye on all his signs, and his ECG and JVP are looking OK at the moment.

To: Laura
From: Sophie
Subject: re: Friday update

Is the nurse on her tea break? You should think about re-training.

To: Sophie
From: Laura
Subject: re: Friday update

I couldn't do it in a million years – hardest job in the world. They're monitoring him 24/7, but they do occasionally have to leave his bedside – and I just feel he's safer when I'm watching too.

To: Laura
From: Dad
Subject: Any news?

Are you OK? I'm worried, I've tried calling you and can't get through. Any developments?

To: Dad
From: Laura
Subject: re: Any news?

No news. Sorry, my phone is off when I'm in the ward and then I keep forgetting to turn it on.

To: Laura
From: Dad
Subject: re: Any news?

Make sure you get some rest. It's important you look after yourself. Surely you don't need to be there every day – where's his daughter? Please Skype me tomorrow.

To: Dad
From: Laura
Subject: re: Any news?

I'm not there all the time, Dad. I just don't like the thought of him being alone if anything were to happen. May not have a chance to Skype tomorrow – have to do laundry, meet Gemma at Paddington, drop her stuff at the flat, then take her back to the hospital, etc.

To: Sophie
From: Laura
Subject: Saturday Update

Thought I'd pop in to see Roger early – en route to meeting Gemma – and guess who was sitting there holding his hand? Sandra. She must have arrived at 7.00 a.m.! I thought she was going to get all King Lear on me but she behaved herself (well, in my direction at least.)

She started being horrendously officious to the nurse, who was having none of it – then demanded to 'talk to an actual doctor'. I had to leave her to it – not a fan of the bedside squabble, had too many of those with Jess, back in the day . . .

Gemma's in with Roger now. Even though the doctors have told her he's not in pain, and he doesn't look like he's in pain, I can see it hurts her so much she can hardly breathe. She looks and dresses so much more sophisticatedly than I did at nineteen, I forget she's still so young. I'll take her for dinner afterwards – I suspect she'll want to talk about it. I remember with Mum I was OK when I was with her or with other people but when you're on your own it moves from being a surreal bubble you feel bizarrely protected in, to something extremely real.

To: Sophie
From: Laura
Subject: Sunday Update

Sorry again about last night – I owe you big time. Gemma refused to eat any of her pizza, and I didn't realise until too late that she'd ordered and drunk a second bottle of wine. I couldn't send her into Amber's flat in that state.

It's weird – when someone else is even more scared than you, it forces you to be the brave one. I always wondered why Jess seemed so calm about Mum – but maybe it's because she had to be.

Roger's had a pretty good 24 hours according to Anne-Marie, today's nurse. She's my favourite so far. She's entirely optimistic and says she's seen far worse than him pull through.

Also, she gave me the lowdown on his bedside neighbour. There but for the grace of God! Something reversible but dodgy happened to Arthur's brain during his lung operation and now he swings between punching the poor nurses, and compulsively *beating his old man* (Anne-Marie's expression, not mine). I wondered why they kept drawing the curtains. Poor man/poor nurses. They've had to wrap his hands in bandages, and now they've put giant mittens on him, too. It doesn't stop him punching, but I suppose it makes the other more of a challenge . . .

To: Laura
From: Sandra
Subject: Your column

Just a reminder that we need to see your column tomorrow so we can release it on Thursday. Heather will obviously need to go over the exact wording with you thoroughly. I've attached a standard apology template you might consider following.

See you in the morning.

To: Laura
From: Sophie
Subject: Oy, you!

I'm pretty much insisting you come home, eat something and have an early night. You are running on empty – and that won't do Roger, you or Gemma any good. Plus I want to talk to you about stuff.

To: Sophie
From: Laura
Subject: re: Oy, you!

Sorry – I know I've been totally absorbed in this bubble since Tuesday. Is everything OK?

To: Laura
From: Sophie
Subject: re: Oy, you!

Yes, of course – I meant talk to you about *your* stuff – your column, Adam, etc!

To: Laura
From: Dad
Subject: Phone

Please could you call me later. I know you're busy but I'd like to talk.

To: Laura
From: Jess
Subject: Dad

Could you stop ignoring Dad? He's worried about you.

To: Jess
From: Laura
Subject: re: Dad

Will the pair of you just leave me alone for five minutes, I've got stuff on – *as you know*. I'll call him tomorrow.

On the Tube home on Sunday night I find myself staring at the man opposite me – specifically at his feet. He's sitting, legs spread wide, a Nike shopping bag on the floor next to him and he's wearing his brand new Air Max Ones. He's telling his girlfriend why they're such a design classic, and she's nodding, her arm entwined in his, looking down at his trainers in appreciation.

They are nice trainers, I think: clean design, bold colours, currently box fresh so they look as good as they're ever going to. But they're making me dizzy. The thought anyone could ever care about trainers, care about shoes, care about things you buy in shops when Roger's lying there, tubes piercing his bruised body . . .

Roger's only been in hospital for six days and yet the world of hospital has swelled like a balloon inside my head, taking over entirely.

The only reason I feel OK leaving him now is because Gemma's still at his bedside – keeping guard. Someone has to keep guard.

ITU is a world that breeds superstition. If I don't walk up the staircase to the ward, rather than take the lift, something bad will happen. If I don't dispense exactly three full squeezes of antiseptic handwash on my way in – and out – something bad will happen. If I leave the bedside for longer than twenty minutes to get a coffee – something bad will happen. The ward is full of people like me, who share a belief that while our eyes are fixed on the patient, nothing bad can happen. We tend to ignore the fact something bad has already happened.

It occurs to me, on the Tube, as a waft of my neighbour's McDonald's assaults my nostrils, that I haven't eaten since last night's pizza. I have no appetite – just a general sick, panicky feeling I used to have when Mum was ill, fed by the belief: hospitals are the worst place in the world for someone who's ill; the fear that every day Roger is stuck in that prison of superbugs, there's a chance of further infection – and there's nothing I can do to help him escape.

At the 24-hour mini market, I force myself to buy a floppy tomato sandwich – the best of a soggy selection. I'm going home to have a hot bath, and hope some of this adrenalin pulsing through me will dissolve in the bath water so I can sleep. I don't want to speak to anyone, definitely not Dad, not even Sophie. Sandra will go mad, but I'm entirely not able to write my apology tonight.

But lying in bed, with my eyes shut, I still have business to take care of. I've been working through the details for days – and now I have an offer to put to the Lord Almighty. If he lets Roger pull through, reasonably unscathed, then I promise to do the following:

- Start believing in him again (in God, not Roger – I never lost faith in Roger).
- Stop having uncharitable thoughts about Sandra.
- And Tom.
- And Tess.
- (Scrap those last two – unrealistic.)
- Stop writing bitchy emails about Sandra with Azeem and Kiki.

- Buy *The Big Issue* every single fortnight, not just when I'm interested in the cover story.
- Improve myself as a human being in all the usual ways: exercise more, drink less, swear less, be more compassionate, blah, blah, blah.
- Speak to Dad about Mum calmly, without reverting to being a bitch.

51

Sandra's not exactly Roger's natural replacement in terms of charisma. She's been running this meeting for all of four minutes and she's already lost the crowd.

'OK . . . ' says Sandra, looking at the glum faces round the table. 'May's issue, the cover story is on the Tanquine art collection. Heather – how are we looking?'

'Yep,' she says wearily. 'We're not exposed to much risk on this one, famous last words . . . '

'What's going on with the turkeys?' says Jonesy. 'Fletchers have pulled May's ad from the plan; are we going to apologise over the shed space allegation or what?'

'We are not going to apologise, Al-is-tair,' says Sandra, with an exasperated huff.

Kiki looks at me with a small grin, and mouths 'Al-is-tair!'

'We're now looking at alternative dispute resolution as the next step,' says Heather. 'Hopefully we'll settle out of court.'

'What's going on with The Dish?' says Azeem. 'I'm getting all the stats from the affiliated sites – we're still seeing heavy traffic, it's gone bigger than when Bruni at the *NYT* dissed Guy Fieri – and the viral numbers on that were huge.'

'We're in the process of drafting an apology,' says Sandra tightly. 'That will hopefully be the end of it. Any other business?'

'Er – are you actually going to talk about Rodge?' says Jonesy, looking appalled.

Sandra drops her chin to her chest. 'I was – of course – coming to that, thank you.'

'Is he all right?' says Kiki.

'Is he going to die?' says Azeem.

'He's not going to die,' says Jonesy. 'He's not the type.'

'Should we visit him?' says Heather.

Sandra turns and gestures for me to speak. 'Laura – do you want to give the team an update on Roger's status?'

Around the table ten pairs of eyes turn my way, willing me to deliver a smidgen of good news. 'Well – he's stable, which is a very good thing,' I say, trying not to give anyone too much hope.

'How's his liver?' says Jonesy. 'I'd have thought that'd be the first to go.'

'As far as I know, all that stuff is fine.'

'Is he conscious yet?' says Kiki.

'Not yet. He's still in the coma . . . '

'But it's a good coma, right?' says Azeem. 'Not like a real one?'

'Well, it is pretty real. But yes, it's one they've put him in to try to heal his body as effectively as possible.'

'How do they do that?'

'They give you drugs to sedate you, and they cool your temperature,' I say.

'Put you in a fridge, like Walt Disney?' he says.

'Walt Disney is not actually frozen,' says Kiki. 'That's an urban myth.'

'Like Jonesy buying a round,' says Azeem.

Sandra quivers with irritation. 'I'm sorry but I find joking at a time like this in poor taste.'

'Come on, Sandra,' says Jonesy. 'We're all worried about him, we all want him to get better, but sitting around moping isn't going to help, is it?'

'Laura,' she says, shifting to turn her back on him. 'Do you have any more helpful information for the team?'

'The nurse yesterday mentioned hopefully trying to get him off the ventilator this week.'

'So they wake him up?' says Azeem.

'They'll see if he can breathe for himself – and then they'll slowly try to bring him out of the coma, but things go back and forth all the time in ITU.'

'What about visiting, then?' says Heather.

'I think having positive people around him can't hurt,' I say.

'We mustn't overwhelm him,' says Sandra.

'You can only have two at a time in there anyway. I'll do a rota if you like?' I say.

'You should do a rota,' says Sandra, as if it's her idea.

'Hey, Laura – why don't you do a rota?' says Kiki, winking at me.

'That's what I just said, Katrina,' says Sandra.

'I'll speak to Gemma to check she's OK with it all,' I say. 'And guys – if you do visit, try not to stare at the man in the next bed along: you might get an eyeful more than you bargained for.'

After the meeting, Sandra asks me to stay behind with Heather for a catch-up. At the thought of the impending bollocking, my body tenses for a fight.

'I know you've been at the hospital a lot, but I'd have thought – out of respect for Roger – you'd have drafted your apology?'

'Laura, I'm sorry but we don't have much time,' says Heather. 'Have you at least decided what angle you'll take?'

I've been swinging wildly between Sandra's forelock-tugging mea culpa, and going full-on Erin Brockovich. I'm not going to tell Sandra I wrote a draft apology first thing – because I can't bear to print it out. I'm sick of apologising for things that aren't really my fault.

'Roger's last words to me a week ago were that I shouldn't roll over.' And the fact he said Mum would've had the balls to fight doesn't help.

'Roger has a far more bellicose attitude than serves our interests at this point,' says Sandra.

'I know we're all hoping for the best,' says Heather, her gaze shifting from mine. 'But if you think about what might play out . . . '

Of course I've thought about it, relentlessly. Roger's not around; Sandra's in charge; I do what Roger wants anyway; a lawsuit cripples us; Roger spends immeasurable time in hospital, finally comes back to work and discovers his magazine no longer exists due to my bankrupting, gobshite response. Whoopee!

'I just need a little more time.'

'As you well know, Laura – you don't have that luxury.'

'You know what, Sandra? I can have a few more days.'

'I'm not having you file late again.'

'I'll file on Thursday.'

'Not after last time you won't.'

'Sandra – you clearly didn't bother authorising the copy swap with the printers last month – which is why we're in this mess in the first place.'

'*Ut-ter* nonsense!'

'No – it is not utter nonsense because I rang PrintPro last week and they told me so.' I feel my face blazing with fury – and hope to God she can't tell I'm bluffing.

'Do you have *any idea* how busy we were at the end of that week? With the Bechdel case and filling the extra ad pages? I had to prioritise – and you have to learn to do the same: write the apology today.'

So it's true! I knew it. Why did I even give her two per cent benefit of the doubt?

'And are you going apologise to *me* in the mean time?' I say.

'Whatever for?'

'You've just admitted this lawsuit is because you didn't check the supply detail on my *fluffy copy*.'

'I've done nothing of the sort.'

'You just said you didn't follow through because you were *prioritising*.'

'How could I possibly have foreseen this debacle happening?'

'*It wouldn't have!* If you'd supplied the right copy!' I say, trying – and failing miserably – to keep my voice calm.

'Listen you,' she says, jabbing her finger at me. 'You wrote the original review in the first place – don't go blaming other people for your mess.'

Urgh, I hate it when she's slightly right.

'And!' she says, pointing at me again, 'do you think Roger needed *more* stress last week?'

'What?'

'What do you think tipped him over the edge?'

I can feel fury running through my veins. 'What, Sandra?'

'Do you not think *you* contributed to his current condition?'

'Are you actually saying Roger's heart attack was my fault?' I know she'd like to say yes but even she wouldn't dare.

She looks at Heather, finds no encouragement, then turns back to me, her eyes narrowing in fury. 'Yes,' she says, jubilantly. 'Yes, Laura – I am saying that.'

I stop for a moment, my breath taken clean away.

Then I count to ten. And then fifteen. And then I say one more thing I'm going to have to apologise for.

Even if I'd counted to a hundred I don't think I could've stopped myself.

'I've never stormed out of a meeting before,' I say to Heather, who's joined me on the pavement outside for a fag.

'I didn't know you smoked?'

'I don't,' I say. 'I mean clearly I do – but I don't – I have one roughly every seven months, when I'm profoundly drunk or stressed.' I take a deep drag and feel the familiar comfort of filthy tobacco. I vowed to quit when Mum was in hospital. One of her neighbours'd had two clear, curly pigtail catheters slowly draining murky treacly fluid from his lungs. If you're willing to risk lung cancer after watching that for five days, your brain's wired differently from mine.

'Heather – you don't think I put Roger in a coma do you?'

'Don't be ridiculous,' she says, putting her arm around me. 'The man eats saturated fat three times a day and leads an almost entirely sedentary lifestyle. I'm surprised it's taken this long to catch up with him.'

I take another deep drag and blow it out slowly. 'And you don't think Sandra's going to do me for libel for calling her a stupid bitch?'

'If it's verbal it's actually slander, not libel,' she says. 'But either way, it's not defamatory if it's true.'

I can't help but laugh. 'Heather – can I ask you a favour?'

'Do you want me to play mediator between you and Sandra?'

'Not particularly. No – can I at least have another day to write this column?'

'Tell you what – if you give me something first thing Wednesday, I'll pencil time in my diary to go through it with you then.'

'Thank you,' I say, stubbing my cigarette out. 'And I do have one more small favour.'

'Another fag?'

'That big fat textbook you brought to the first meeting with Roger?'

'The *Halsbury's*?'

'Does it outline defamation law in a way that someone like me can understand?'

'The language is straightforward enough.'

'Then please could I borrow it?'

'Babe, it's for you,' says Amber, taking one look at the chaos in my bedroom, then walking straight out again.

This had better not be Adam turning up in one of those romantic gestures to apologise – my hair is greasy, my face exhausted, eyes tinged with red, I could pass for a wildling, were it not for the Jolen bleach on my upper lip and my old Guns N' Roses T-shirt.

'Stop avoiding me!' says Sophie, steaming into my room carrying two glasses of wine. 'Your phone's off and I want to talk. What are you doing?'

'I'm thinking . . . ' I say, moving the copy of *Halsbury's Laws* to the floor, along with my notepad and pen.

'Oh my goodness, I'd forgotten how tiny it is in here,' she says, crab-stepping round the edge of the bed, then lying on top of the duvet next to me and handing me a glass. 'I brought white, I didn't think Amber would let me over the threshold with anything that could stain. How's Roger doing?'

'I popped in after work – he's stable but Gemma was there and Heather was on her way, so I didn't stay.'

'Have you decided what you're doing about your work bollocks?'

I shake my head. 'It's the proverbial rock and hard place. If I say I was wrong – it makes me look unreliable. If I stand my ground, it's too big a financial risk.'

'Have you spoken to Adam?'

'I've had a couple of missed calls but he hasn't left any messages.'

'Why haven't you called him back?'

'I've been kind of busy!'

'Don't you want to hear what he has to say?'

'Of course. But if he's forgiven me, it can wait. And if he hasn't, I don't need to know about it right now.'

'You haven't told him about Roger?'

'What – so he'll be nice to me out of sympathy?'

'Oh come on, Laura – I'm sure he'd want to be there for you.'

'I'm not so sure.'

She frowns. 'But haven't you at least talked to him about the lawsuit?'

'He said he's keeping out of it entirely.'

'But aren't you going to tell him about the coffee thing? He knows the truth, he can't let them do that to you.'

'He probably doesn't know the details of the legal stuff, but how could I ask him to put himself on the line for me? It would be career suicide.'

'He's their star chef, they wouldn't fire him.'

'They sound like total wankers – I have no idea what they'd do.'

'But he might be able to get them off your back?'

'I can't ask him for that kind of favour – not anymore.'

'Why, because you've had a row?'

'No, because he needs that job.' I look down into my glass, then take a large gulp. Even now, the thought that Adam has a perfect little boy with this woman makes me feel pathetically jealous. 'And suppose he was inclined to make some heroic gesture, I wouldn't want that on my head.'

'Laura – there's nothing wrong with making Adam aware of the specifics.' The look on her face suggests she's plotting something. 'If he doesn't know, then someone ought to tell him – it's the right thing to do. Then he can decide for himself how he handles it.'

Oh God – she's got his bloody email address because of the pecan nut supplier.

'Soph,' I say, reaching out gently to touch her wrist. 'If you're even thinking of doing something stupid like contacting him – *please* don't. You wouldn't be doing me a favour. I've got us all in enough trouble because I didn't have my boundaries in place – I'm not fudging the lines again.'

'But he could help you.'

'Sophie – I don't need a knight in shining armour. I need to fix this myself.'

52

'How was his night?' I say to Anne-Marie, as I stand by Roger's bedside on Tuesday morning, analysing his monitor. The numbers are all looking OK – I know his healthy ranges by heart. 'Sats back up to ninety-four?'

'He's doing grand,' she says.

I look at him, lying there so calmly. He has a small smile on his face and I can't help but think he might actually be able to hear us. Although if he could, he'd also hear the racket Arthur next door is making, swinging a bandaged fist wildly and fruitlessly at his nurse.

'Arthur's a little lively for eight in the morning,' I say.

'Sweet Jesus, if he doesn't stop punching, we're going to have to tie those paws to the bed,' she says. 'Poor soul – must be exhausted!'

'What time's the delightful Mr Dawson doing the rounds?'

'He's always so busy, it's hard to judge,' she says, diplomatically.

'I saw him sneaking through reception on Sunday and I cornered him – he looked like he wanted to throttle me.'

'I'm not sure he's a fan of actual living, breathing people.'

'I asked him when he might extubate Roger – and he literally sneered and said, "Do you know what extubating is?" I felt like asking, "Do you know what a bedside manner is?"'

'The man's a patronising old langer,' she says, then quickly corrects herself. 'But a highly skilled doctor.' She pauses, then looks at me with an awkward smile. 'How *do* you know the word extubate?'

'My mum was in ITU for a while.'

'Ah, right . . .' Her eyes ask the question; I shake my head, feeling the familiar tightening in my throat.

I turn back to Roger. Were it not for the tubes and machines, it almost looks like he's having a lovely dream, a nap after too many Fortnums' Scotch Eggs and a bottle of Chablis at the cricket. I move closer and watch as his chest moves gently up and down, the ventilator filling his lungs with oxygen, then emptying them for him.

I take his hand. It is cool and dry but heavily swollen from all the fluids they're pumping him with. 'Roger, I'm not sure whether you can hear me – especially not over the din next door.' I look up to see the nurse in the next bay drawing the curtain round Arthur's bed again. 'Now Anne-Marie's your boss today and she says you'll be fine and she knows what she's talking about; but I'd appreciate it if you could hurry up and get better sooner rather than later because we miss you. The office is not the same without you: Jonesy has no one to spar with, Azeem looks like a lost kitten, even Lumley seems a little flat.'

I look over to the nurses' station, where there's a huddle of low-level activity. I remember the first days when Mum was unconscious, I felt embarrassed talking to her if anyone else was nearby – worried they'd think me foolish for having a conversation with someone who wasn't really there. But then I stopped caring what anyone else in the world thought because she *was* there – I knew she was.

There was something I was going to tell Roger, what was it now? Oh yeah, that was it! 'I tried to find an Elbert Hubbard quote to cheer you up – though you probably know them all already but anyway, this one struck me: "Live truth instead of professing it." It reminded me so much of you. It doesn't matter what a person says – the only thing that matters is what they do.'

I look at his hand in mine and catch sight of the deep purple bruises that make me weak every time I see them.

'Roger,' I say, smoothing down the bed sheet by his arm. 'I promise I'll do my best with this column, but I need you to promise one thing in return: don't leave. Not yet, you're nowhere near ready. I've got your to-do list and there's so much on it: the Saints and Sinners issue, golf at Gleneagles, maybe Dollywood in the autumn?'

My eyes fix again on the plastic ventilator tube in his mouth and with all my might I will his lungs to get stronger.

'Oh, and another thing – you have to have a word with Gemma,' I say. 'Her boyfriend sounds perfectly OK and all, but I don't see her, longer-term, with a man who does six hours of yoga a day. *Six hours.* To be honest, she seems a little lost – I think she needs your advice, if only so she can go in the opposite direction. And at some point in the future I'm sure there'll be grandchildren . . . and you have to stick around for them, Roger: you can't leave before that fun even starts. So yes . . . I know you don't like being told what to do . . . But please just do this one little thing for us all? Get better. Your heart is strong, I know it is – and it wants to live.'

53

May's issue is currently being finalised up in our studio. The whole office is so quiet compared to a month ago. It's not simply because we're running less controversial stories, or because we're all privately worrying about Roger. It's because Roger is the life force of this paper, he's the heart of it.

As for Sandra, it's not as though we used to do daily water cooler chat, but as of yesterday at 11.34 a.m., she's developed a proxy superpower – the ability to pretend I'm invisible. I wonder if I streaked over to Azeem's desk whether her pupils would even dilate.

There is literally nothing, officially, for me to do today apart from write my column, but instead I sit at my desk and google 'post-stent ITU – chances of recovery' and '62-year-old male – mortality rates – medium to heavy cheese-eater'.

God, I hate the Internet! After five minutes of googling Roger's chances of survival, I've developed cold sweats, an increased heart rate, a dry mouth and a tense, nervous headache – which means *I'm* now having a heart attack. I decide my time might be better spent doing some admin, like tidying my inbox. I click on the last email Adam sent me. It was the day after we came back from Italy – a lifetime ago. He'd sent me a photo of a Selfree – his take on a Selfie – a photo of his face, but made entirely of food: blueberries for eyes, baby Chantenay carrot for a nose, a curve of fettuccine for his smile.

I am so desperately tempted to call him back. Tempted to apologise and tempted to tell him he's an idiot. I'd like to know how things stand with Katie and the baby, if he's seen Josh yet. But every time I start thinking about it, it overwhelms me, and if I think about Adam, I feel guilty – because I should be focused on Roger.

So even though the thought of hearing Adam's voice makes my heart expand a little – I won't call him. And I'm going to try my damnedest not to think about the sound of his voice, his face, his smile; how happy I felt when I was with him; how much less happy I feel right now.

But there is a call I can't put off any longer and as I'm walking home, I take out my phone and dial the number I know by heart.

Dad picks up on the second ring – his voice anxious. 'Finally! I've been worried about you. How's Roger doing?'

'He's doing well, fingers crossed. They're hoping to start weaning him off the ventilator in the next few days. You know what it's like though, they say one thing and the next day everything changes . . . '

'I know this must be very hard for you, Laura. Seeing him like that . . . I can imagine what's going through your mind.'

'Dad,' I say, softly. 'Please, I'm really sorry, but can we not talk about that . . . '

'Oh. OK then.' He sounds hurt – and I wish he didn't because it makes me feel worse.

'But I do want to ask your advice? I have to write my column tonight. And I'm stuck. Sandra says do one thing, Roger told me to do the opposite, I'm damned either way . . . '

There's a pause on the line. 'Laura – I'm not a huge fan of your ex-husband, but do you know the worst thing he did to you?'

I'm pretty sure I never told Dad about the threesome Tom, Tess and her friend had in our marital bed.

'Er – he made me lose faith in other people?'

'No, darling.'

'Then what?'

'He made you lose faith in yourself.'

There is silence as Dad waits for my reaction. When I give none, he carries on. 'Over the last four years, you've asked mine and Jess's opinion about everything from what flavour Ben & Jerry's you should buy, to what word you should use at the end of a sentence.'

'Because I care what you think.'

'That's flattering sweetheart – but you're a grown up. You have opinions, you always used to have strong ones, so stop asking everyone else's advice.'

He's right. Even at lunchtime I texted Sophie asking whether I should buy a Chunky Kit Kat or a regular one.

'Dad – this is bigger than Phish Food, this is my life. Roger said Mum would have gone full steam ahead into battle. He said she wouldn't have been a wimp.'

There is another pause on the line.

'Dad – are you still there?'

'I am.'

'Oh good, I thought it might have cut out.'

'Laura. Roger knew your mother very well. And he's right, she was a fighter.'

'So you think I should let it go to court?'

'But with all due respect to Roger – I knew her pretty well myself.'

'Dad.'

'In fact I would go as far as to say I might even have known her a little better . . . '

'Dad . . . '

'And while she was one of the bravest people I've ever known, she was also someone who carefully weighed up the consequences of her actions with regards to how they'd affect those around her.'

'What are you saying?' *Just tell me what I should do!*

'Your mum picked her battles. She strived to do the right thing – but her primary goal, always, was to protect the people she loved.'

'So I *should* sacrifice myself?'

'Laura! I'm not saying be a martyr. You have to find the balance between doing the right thing by others – and doing the right thing for yourself. All she ever wanted was for you girls to be happy. My point is – you have to trust your own voice.'

'But Dad – I'm so confused I don't even know what I think anymore.'

'Then you'd better get off the phone pretty quickly and figure it out.'

54

I hold my breath while Heather reads my piece. Her brow creases as she nears the end. She looks up at me with a frown, then finishes and carefully puts the paper down on her desk.

'What do you think?' I say. 'I read the Halsbury's pages twice over – but they were starting to make me feel thick, and quite dizzy.'

'I need to have a closer reading – but I have to tell you, I'm not impressed.'

'You think I've overstepped the mark legally?'

'No. I meant your final paragraph.'

'The "PS" bit about Fergus Kaye?'

'No – the bit before you sign off.'

'Oh. That bit.'

'It's not what Roger would want,' she says. 'And I'm not particularly happy with it myself.' She picks up the article again and looks at it with irritation.

'OK. But it's what I want.' Sort of.

She shakes her head in resignation. 'Then leave it with me.'

To: Dad
From: Laura
Subject: Thank you

I did what you said. I found my voice. It's not necessarily a great one – but it's all my own.

To: Laura
From: Dad
Subject: You're welcome

She would be so proud of you. I am so proud of you.

To: Laura
From: Kiki
Subject: Your nemesis

Have you spoken to Sandra yet?

To: Kiki
From: Laura
Subject: re: Your nemesis

No – life is so much nicer this way. Anyway, I'm not sure I'll need to speak to her ever again.

To: Laura
From: Kiki
Subject: WTF?

Or are you just being over-dramatic/an optimist?

To: Laura
From: Heather
Subject: Your May column

OK, I have double-checked in *Halsbury's* and am confident you're clear of the line in terms of the law.

In terms of what LuxEris's lawyers are demanding you're

following the letter, if not the spirit of their demand, but I can't see how they can actually come back at us – you've done a great job of hopscotching neatly between the lines.

Re: your final paragraph – I believe you've written this column under stress, and at the last minute, so apologies if I sound like a broken record, but are you quite sure you want to say this?

To: Heather
From: Laura
Subject: re: Your May column

Yes

To: Laura
From: Heather
Subject: re: Your May column

Then fine – you don't need to change a word.

To: Kiki
From: Laura
Subject: May column

Can you give this a quick sub, my dear?

To: Laura
From: Kiki
Subject: :-(

You KNOW I would never use any sort of smiley face – nor caps – if I didn't mean them.

To: Sandra
From: Laura
Subject: May column

Sandra, please find attached May's column – which Heather
and the subs are now happy with.

And five minutes after I've pressed send, and for the first time in
recorded history, Sandra comes over to my desk, looks me in the
eye, and says thank you.

55

My phone rings as I'm heading to the Tube. I look at the caller ID and my heart leaps, then sinks, then tries to restore itself to the middle ground. Please, please, please.

Her voice sounds tearful – but they kind of sound like good tears. 'Laura,' she says, sniffing loudly down the phone.

'What is it, Gemma?'

'Mr Dawson's just been in to see Dad . . . '

I hold my breath, say a silent, urgent prayer.

'They're ready to bring him round.'

When I walk into the ward the following morning I notice something's different. Not Roger – he's still lying on his back, unconscious – but there's a strange absence of noise in the surrounding area.

'Where is he?' I say. The bay next door is now empty, not even a bed. 'He didn't . . . did he?'

'What, Arthur? Oh no, he's fine, he's graduated: they moved him down to High Dependency last night. We've got an incoming,' she checks her watch. 'Some poor chap, run over, texting while crossing the road – severe head trauma.' She sighs, she sees it too often. 'Ah, but Roger's had another great night. You know we've started to wean him off the anaesthetics?'

'How long before he's awake?'

'It's a gradual process, every patient's different – but he should be what you'd consider awake in a day or two.'

'Not talking though?'

'I have a feeling, from what you've said, he'll be trying to talk before we get that tube from his throat.'

'Anne-Marie – do *you* think coma patients can hear what's going on around them?'

'Depends on their GCS – but I believe they pick up on their

loved ones' voices and there's plenty of research suggesting that's the case.'

'Even if they're one of the ones that don't make it?'

'Oh love,' she says, putting her arm around me. 'Are you asking because of your ma?'

The memory of that missed phone call resurfaces like a shark – and though I try again to push it back below the surface, how am I ever going to win against a flipping shark?

'Have a seat,' she says, pulling a couple of plastic chairs over. 'I'd get you a cup of tea but we're not allowed.'

'Thank you. I don't know what's wrong with me, I have these moments . . . '

'You don't need to explain.'

But I do. If I tell Anne-Marie, maybe I can stop feeling these feelings. I never want to stop thinking of Mum, when I think about her she's alive again. But I want to be at peace with this.

'Anne-Marie, the day after my mum's operation, she was in recovery,' I say, staring at the floor. 'She rang but my phone was charging. I saw the missed call but thought I'd call later, and by the time I got round to it her phone was off.' I feel the ache as if it were yesterday. 'But if I'd known she was in hospital, of course I'd have called straight back. I would give anything to have spoken to her just one last time.'

'You didn't know though?' says Anne-Marie.

'But I feel like it's my fault – I should have known. I should have picked up on something that was said, the way she was acting before . . . '

Anne-Marie looks at me with confusion. 'Why would you be so hard on yourself?'

'Because those precious hours were wasted with Tom. I took them from Mum and gave them to him and that makes me sick with guilt. And after Mum died I was angry with everyone – angry with the doctors, angry with a God I stopped believing in, angry with *her* for dying . . . '

'But that's a very common feeling, you know that?' she says, gently rubbing my shoulder.

I shrug. 'That doesn't help me much,' I say, smiling softly. 'The thing is, I know it's unfair to still blame Dad for keeping it a secret. But I guess it suits me better that way.'

'How so?'

'Well . . . because if I blame Dad . . . then I guess I don't have to blame myself.'

Sometimes it's easier to be completely honest when you're talking to a stranger.

Anne-Marie looks at me kindly. 'You do realise you don't actually have to blame anyone? Life's a lot less painful when you don't create your own stick to beat yourself with.'

'I should have called her back, Anne-Marie, I wish I'd called her back.'

'Oh love,' she says. 'In this job I hear people talk about the things they regret all the time. Things they wish they'd said or hadn't said, done, or hadn't done . . . And I always tell them the same thing: don't hold on to regrets you can't do anything about. Focus on the ones you can still fix.'

56

The Dish

Mistakes, I've made a few . . .

In April's issue, due to an administrative error, we published an incorrect review of LuxEris: wrong in tone, wrong in content. I apologise wholeheartedly to my readers for this – and to the owners and staff of the restaurant. Journalists make mistakes, the same way chefs make mistakes – we're all fallible. The ability to apologise makes us human.

Had the correct review run it would have said head chef Adam Bayley's food is fantastic – flavours, textures and execution were on a par with the best in the business. I'm sure whatever he does in his career, his passion, dedication and respect for his customers will shine through.

New restaurants rely heavily on good reviews. Critics are given a short cut to power: power is open to abuse – hence why I write incognito. Money is another short cut to power: hypothetically a rich business can intimidate a poorer one with the threat of years of litigation through sheer financial might. I think that's bullying, and my mother taught me not to stand for it. So while I'll apologise for an administrative error, I refuse to apologise for my opinions on eating out, which are these:

1. A great restaurant should make every customer feel equally welcome when they walk in – and when they walk out they should feel even better, *not* done over. I'm happy to pay a fair

price for quality but I personally feel ripped off being charged £24 for a Heritage Carrot. At that price the carrot should have gone to Eton and dated a Middleton – even if it was Carole.

2. The restaurant business is called Hospitality for a reason. Yes, technical mastery is important, but so is a generosity of spirit and attitude. If you're serving a £45 burger – even a foie gras and bone marrow sous vide deluxe £45 burger – throw in the chips too, because potatoes are not expensive. Besides, some things belong together: burgers and chips. Waiters and eye contact. Service and a smile.

3. Great restaurants create a sense of conviviality. If you look around them, people are relaxed and having a good time – not just rubber-necking to see if that really is Sir Elton over in the corner booth.

4. Having a menu that's a checklist of trendy ingredients – yuzu, Tiger's milk, sea buckthorn – is tiresome. What customers truly crave – pleasure, nourishment, delight – never goes out of fashion. The best meal I ate this year had four ingredients – none of them foraged from a ditch outside Copenhagen. Give me a simple dinner made with love, over a Kimchee-Lobster Shiso-Ramen Steamed Bun made with nothing but cynicism, any day of the week.

5. For me, the definition of luxury is not drinking a £600 bottle of Krug out of a £134 wine glass, then peeing it into a golden toilet. Luxury is the sheer splendour of sitting on a garden chair on a hilltop eating a bowl of beans with someone wonderful.

6. At the end of a great meal, coffee should not be an afterthought. Coffee, like service, like bread, is a reflection of the care a restaurant takes in every part of the experience. One of my criticisms in April's review was regarding the quality of

coffee served. LuxEris maintains it was fresh – I was convinced it was instant and the reason I felt confident in my judgement was because I spent ten years working in coffee – at Union Roasters and Bean To Cup. During my career I visited fifty-three farms in eleven countries, I've tasted literally tens of thousands of cups. If you're after proof of my coffee credentials, you can find me on Google – my name's Laura Parker. However, what I cannot prove is what the liquid in my bone china cup was two months ago – and on the basis the law requires proof: I am wrong.

Sometimes people have good reasons for keeping secrets. Sometimes those reasons fade or are surpassed by a greater responsibility – in this instance to the truth. This column has been a privilege to write. I've eaten at many great restaurants, run by talented people, with heart and soul. I have loved sharing the highs – and occasional lows – with you. For now, it's time to hang up my knife and fork.

Bon appetit,

Laura Parker

PS Fergus Kaye – 'Conviviality' has s-i-x syllables, I've counted them out on my fingers and opposable thumbs.

And I hope you enjoyed my halibut – it isn't the French name for sea bass – it isn't even close.

57

It's Sunday, a week and a half later. I'm sitting by Roger's bedside in a normal ward, reading my horoscope – 'Full moon in Aquarius, a time of great change' – when he opens his eyes. He's been coming back to life slowly but surely. Nine days ago they took away the tube in his throat and now he's breathing entirely unaided. Last Saturday, he said his first words – Gemma said they sounded something like 'bloody buggeration'. Since then we've celebrated him sitting up in a chair and his first foul steamed cod and watery mash dinner. He's planning on celebrating the removal of his catheter any day now – we'll let him do that one in private.

The human body can be amazingly resilient – as can the mind. Roger can't remember anything about being in the coma and when I point out Arthur, who's walked past our ward a few times while he's doing physio, Roger can't believe it. 'I slept through all of that? Bribe one of those nurses quick, and get me some propofol for the next board meeting!'

Roger's probably in here for one more week, but he's doing so well. He's asked to see May's issue, and I keep pretending I've forgotten it – but I'll show him tomorrow or maybe Tuesday. I'm here every day, even if only for twenty minutes. Jess made some stupid comment about how empty my life must be that I can find the time to visit Roger every day. She said, until you have kids, not only do you not grow up but you have no idea what 'busy' means. I did point out that Dad does almost all her childcare for her – and then I hung up on her – but anyhow, I have wanted to be here every day. I feel grateful I've had that time.

'Roger – I'm going down to get a posh coffee, well, a foul, over-brewed one, but still . . . can I get you anything from the shop?'

'You can sneak me back a bottle of Glenfiddich? The twelve-year will suffice, don't worry about finding the eighteen.'

'I was thinking more like carrot sticks or some prunes?'

As I'm walking, head down, through main reception, I hear my name being called, twice. I freeze at the sound of his voice. I cannot believe Sophie told him I'd be here: I am pissed off she did that.

I stand on the spot and he moves toward me, kisses me awkwardly on the cheek. I can't believe five weeks ago we were in Italy, in bed, and now when his lips briefly touch my face it feels like we barely know each other.

'I've tried calling you. I had no idea,' he says, his eyes sad, his face confused. 'Why didn't you tell me about Roger?'

I shrug. 'There's not much anyone can do in these situations . . . It's fine, he's doing well, back to his old self, almost.' I smile softly.

Adam looks down at the ground, then back at me. 'Why didn't you tell me about the coffee? I would have helped, Laura – there's no way I would have let that happen.'

'And that's why I didn't tell you.'

'I don't understand?'

'I wouldn't want you putting yourself on the line for me with some noble gesture.'

He thrusts his hands in his jeans pocket and his gaze shifts to the floor. 'It would have been about doing the right thing, Laura – not about doing it for you. And now you've gone and quit, and that makes me think your decision had something to do with me.'

I laugh at the irony. 'Well, Adam, believe it or not, you big-headed fool, I didn't do that for you! I did that for myself.' I smile, but his face is filled with sorrow.

'Laura – I read your column in May's issue.'

I feel my face colour. I wrote it in such a rush, and the minute I saw it in actual print I felt silly, having put that personal stuff in about him and me, on top of the hill.

'And I finally got round to reading the review you left in my kitchen,' he says.

'Oh. I thought you'd have thrown that away.'

'Look – I was angry. And I overreacted. And I was a dick, and I'm sorry.' He shakes his head slowly. 'You did me proud, Laura.'

'Well, I didn't write anything that wasn't true; I didn't make up how good I think you are, Adam.'

'Laura – you can't just walk away from something good – ' He checks himself. 'From something you're good at – you have so much potential. My mum said the same.'

'Adam, don't worry about it. This was my best solution to a shitty problem – it's not the end of the world.'

He chews the inside of his lip, then glances at his watch.

'Anyway,' I say, 'how are you? You look exhausted.' He looks like he's lost weight, though he still looks entirely gorgeous. I'd forgotten how perfect his mouth is, that bottom lip, that beautiful strong jaw.

He shrugs. 'More insane than ever . . . '

'How's Katie? How's Josh?'

At the mention of the baby's name, he visibly relaxes. 'Yeah, no, that's good, we've made a lot of progress.'

Adam's world has very much carried on without me. Why on earth wouldn't it have, just because mine's been on hold?

'I looked after him last Sunday night, round at hers,' he says.

I smile, though I fear the twitch at the corner of my mouth gives me away.

'Katie and I have been getting on a lot better in the last fortnight – '

What does that mean? What does that lead to?

'And I've got him for the afternoon – probably why I look so tired.'

'You've got him *today*?'

'Mum's round the corner with him, we didn't want to bring him into a hospital.'

'No, of course not . . . '

He looks at me intently and I hold his gaze. My body's so confused. It's exhausted from all the recent stress, and right now it feels nervous – my arms are slightly tingling. My brain feels unsure of what's going on between Adam and me, but I do know I feel a definite physical longing, and a slight sickness in my stomach at the thought of Katie.

Adam looks like he's trying to remember something at the end of a long list – then his face relaxes again, and he nods. 'Come and say hi. Come say hi to Mum, come and meet him.'

I shake my head.

'Come. She'd like to say hi. He'd like to say hi, too, or maybe he'd like to sick up on you, which is his way of being friendly.'

'I don't have time . . . '

'Laura,' he says, reaching for my hand. I look down at his fingers entwined in mine, and my body stops being confused. Adam standing here, holding my hand, makes my heart feel calm and it's as simple as that. 'Please?' he says. 'Just for one minute – we're literally around the corner.'

Anna Bayley is sitting at the back of the quiet coffee shop with a small white bundle wrapped up in her arms, gazing at the baby with adoration.

'You forget how perfect they are when they're asleep!' she says, gently rocking him, peering more closely at his sleeping face and then smiling all over again.

'It's so nice to see you,' I say. 'I'm sorry I didn't get to see you after all the stuff that's been happening . . . '

She waves the comment away. 'Times like this you realise what actually matters. How is he? Adam said he's out of Intensive Care?'

'On the mend.' I watch, as Adam comes over to his mother and the two perform a gentle, already deft handover. Adam stands, cradling Josh in his arms – his face lit up, transformed. Since I've been out of the picture, he has fallen in love.

Adam proudly holds the baby up for me to see. Josh is dressed in a super-cute blue and orange stripy Babygro, grey trim at the cuffs. He's fast asleep, his left arm curled over his body, nestling into his father, his right hand spread out slightly across his left cheek, as if really, he's just had *the most* tiring of days. He is tiny. Perfect. New hope. A blessing. I'd like to reach out and touch his cheek, feel the softness of his skin, hold those adorable little fingers in my own.

Adam asks if I'd like to hold him, but I hesitate as my mind spins off to its own peculiar place. I hadn't fully imagined what seeing Adam with Josh for the first time would feel like; I thought I'd be fine, but now they're in front of me I feel utterly unsettled. This should all be a big Athena poster dream – the gorgeous hunk nursing the even more gorgeous baby. But I feel like I'm a long shadow cast across the picture. This tight, happy unit isn't mine to waltz into – it belongs to someone else.

When I look at this beautiful child, my heart starts to open like a flower. But a moment after I see the baby's perfection I see my own imperfect thoughts. I wish this baby was mine and Adam's – not only Adam's. And I wish it was ours – not today, not now – but perhaps in two years' time, or even three, when I'm a little more ready for it. And these are blemished and selfish thoughts, and they've been quick to rise to the surface – and from a sense of deep shame I blatantly look at my watch and pretend I didn't realise it was already nearly four o'clock.

'I'm so sorry but Roger will be wondering where I've got to.'

'Give him a call, say you'll be five minutes?' says Adam.

'They never answer the phone on that ward. Anyway, the doctor should be doing his rounds and I wanted to speak to him directly. Anna, so nice to see you again.' I do my best at a smile, but I can tell she's not buying it. 'Thank you, Adam, for coming by. It was great to see you . . . really, it was.'

And I drift out of the coffee shop, carrying a world of regret on my shoulders: I regret all of it. I regret the way I've just behaved, I regret not being a bigger, better person, but most of all I regret ever meeting Adam because I have realised I am in love with him – but this isn't going to work out for me, I don't think I can do it.

I think back to Anne-Marie's words. If I'm going to be adding a few more significant regrets to my list, I'm really going to have to clear out the backlog.

* * *

'Dad, it's me, can you talk?'

'Are you at home, shall we Skype?'

'Let's stay on voice call.' This is going to be hard enough, without having my own foolish face looking back at me from the screen. 'Dad, I can't speak for long but I wanted to tell you something important.'

'What is it darling?'

'I needed to say I'm sorry.'

'Why, what have you done?'

'I mean I'm sorry for giving you such a hard time over the years, about Mum.'

'Oh,' he says, quietly. 'Oh, you don't need to apologise for that.'

'I know I've been harsh with you about it, I know you did what you thought was right, and I should have just accepted that.'

'I've been thinking about it, with Roger's situation,' he says. 'How different a heart attack is, how hard it must be to have no warning, when death is not even on your radar. When your mother and I were in the consultant's room and he told us the news, my heart sank,' he says, softly. 'The timing of it was so terribly cruel. Of course, we wanted to tell you – but we talked it through endlessly and truly, we could not have done it differently. If we'd told you about the operation, you'd have wanted to postpone the wedding.'

'But Dad – I would rather have done that and been there for her, been there while she was still conscious, been there to support you guys.'

'Of course. If any of us had known, but we didn't know what would happen either . . . ' He lets out a long sigh. 'I don't suppose you ever look at your wedding photos do you, Laura?'

'Not much.'

'There's one I took, of you and your mother sitting in the garden, just before the car came to pick us up.'

I remember it well – us laughing about how Dad wasn't exactly Muswell Hill's answer to David Bailey. Jess standing behind Dad, fussing with the strap of her dress, Mum holding both my hands in hers, giving my left hand an extra big squeeze, then lifting it to touch her cheek. She'd insisted that photo was taken without her beautiful new hat on; I remember her being quite adamant, placing it carefully down on the grass and saying, 'Oh, but it hides too much of my face. Better without.'

'Your mother was as happy as I've ever seen her, as happy as the day you were born,' he says, his voice heavy with sadness. 'That wedding was the best gift you could have given her; so, regardless of what came later, how can I regret our decision? Whenever I do, I think of her face in that photo – the way she was smiling . . . ' His voice trails off, then comes back. 'And the way you were smiling too.'

That's the other reason I didn't want to do this on video call – I didn't want to see Dad in any pain.

After a long pause, he clears his throat loudly. 'So you forgive me?'

'Dad – you should be the one forgiving me.'

'There's nothing to forgive you for.'

And when he says these words I feel something in my mind shift ever so slightly; because if he can forgive me, then maybe I can finally start to forgive myself.

58

Roger's sitting up in his striped pyjamas with a copy of the *New York Times* crossword, a copy of *Gourmet* magazine and May's *The Voice* on the trestle table over his bed.

'How are you today, Roger?' I say, ignoring the fact *The Voice* is open on my column.

'Very much ready to leap out of bed and wring your neck.'

'Oh, come on! I didn't roll over totally.'

'No – I liked the Fergus part, bolshy. But I did not appreciate your resignation without consulting me.'

'Roger, they were smashing a hammer on your legs and you were out for the count, I wasn't quite sure how to reach you!'

'You shouldn't have done it.'

'Roger – the world is not going to stop spinning if I don't write that column.'

He leans forward for his cup of water, his hands still shaky. I move to help but he bats me away. 'So have you started to think about what you might like to do now?'

'About what?'

'Oh.' He looks surprised, then slightly shame-faced. 'Have you not spoken to Sandra?'

'Roger?'

'Ah. I thought she'd have sent the email already. Oh well, we only discussed it this morning, I suppose she'll do it tonight.'

'You are going to come back to work eventually, aren't you?' I say. The magazine won't be the same without him – he is the magazine.

'After close consultation with my bossy daughter, and my equally bossy doctor who looks the same age as my daughter, it might make sense to take it a little easier, a "staggered" return to work – maybe one day in the office, spend more time on my Elbert Hubbard biog.'

'OK . . .' Don't say it – I know it's coming, I know it's inevitable but not yet.

'Which leaves Sandra Acting Chief,' he says.

'Oh right, OK,' I say, swallowing a lump of dread as fast as I can, and layering on a smile.

'Oh, Parker, you'd make a God-awful actress, that's the least convincing performance I've seen since Nicole Kidman in *Grace*.'

'So . . . I guess Sandra's said she doesn't want me to be her secretary.'

'Be honest: would you want that job?'

He is, of course, right, but that's so not the point! 'Couldn't I do one day a week for you and—'

He shakes his head.

'But the systems I've set up are quite complicated; I'm kind of the only one who knows how things work.'

He suppresses a small laugh. 'I know you're irreplaceable and all that, but the world is also not going to stop spinning if you don't book my cabs.'

'Roger,' I say, shifting in my seat as I try to figure out what this means for me. 'Is this a friendly firing?'

'Not in the slightest. Parker, do you know who first came up with the concept of turning the lemons life gives you into lemonade?'

I'm sure this one came up in the charity pub quiz, it's on the tip of my tongue, I know it, I do. 'Wasn't it in some Billy Wilder movie?'

'Tut tut, Parker. Have you been paying no attention whatsoever?'

I stare at him in disbelief – he gives a small, amused nod.

'For goodness' sake, Roger, is there anything Elbert Hubbard didn't say? Next you'll be telling me he wrote *The Collected Works of Shakespeare*.'

'I've always rather liked lemons myself. Sharp. Acidic, but at least you know where you stand with a lemon. You're rather a lemon yourself.'

'Oh, cheers!'

'I mean it as a compliment.' He looks at me a while, then nods abruptly. 'You like a good pastry, don't you?'

'That is clearly a rhetorical question.'

'And you know where to get one in London?'

I think of asking Adam to make a batch for Roger, then think: bad idea for a number of reasons. 'Roger – I don't want to bring you in anything unhealthy, the nurses will confiscate it if they find it—'

'How would you feel about doing five thousand words on the quest for the perfect croissant, in the home of the perfect croissant?'

'I take it you don't mean Greggs on Peckham High Street?'

'Parker – has your brain turned to jelly while I was out for the count?'

'But—'

'Do the article for July's issue, I'll pay you the same per-word rate as we give any other feature writer. Jonesy will drum up some more food advertisers, if it means more lunches for him. Have a look at the longer length piece on Singapore laksa in here,' he says, handing me the copy of *Gourmet*. 'Make it part travel piece, part food description, all Parker.'

'Roger – are you sure?' I feel slightly overwhelmed with excitement about the idea of writing a piece all about croissants; slightly terrified at the thought of having no permanent job; and slightly conscious that Adam is floating around at the back of my thoughts, an unresolved source of anxiety all of the time.

'Parker,' he says, with a smile both gentle and sad. 'When you joined us, you were a different person. Don't you think now might be a good time to go out and see what you could do if you truly set your mind to it? I can clearly see what you're capable of. It would be marvellous if you could see it too.'

59

'Write one sticker for each flavour,' says Sophie, placing her fingers to her temples as she surveys the brownies piled on platters on her kitchen counter. 'From the left: cream cheese and raspberry jam; butter salted caramel; toffee; Paleo with dates; gluten-free cherry and chocolate fudge and finally,' she says, pointing to the last plate with a troubled expression, 'Campari.'

'Campari?'

'Celina insisted; her "people" want to pitch her to some drinks brands as "the face of fashionable summer cocktails".'

'I thought she was AA?'

'She's NA.'

'But I thought they were all sort of connected?'

'Not when she's after a sponsorship deal, they're not.' She picks up one of the brownies, sniffs it and takes a small bite. 'The balance of bitter and sweet actually kind of works, now I've added the orange zest. OK, stick one label on the lid of each box and I'll pack.' She checks her watch. 'The courier's picking them up at ten p.m. so we've got loads of time.'

'They're shooting these tomorrow?'

'Bloody Fletchers glossy in-store magazine has to go to print end of May for September. Celina fakes her party tomorrow, the ad agency send along a bunch of catalogue models to pretend they're her multi-ethnic best mates, and they do a *Hello*-style spread: "Celina's Sparkling Fortieth". I have to do stunt-double brownies for the background shots.'

'Three months before the actual party?'

'They probably need three months for all of Celina's retouching. Three months, and I've done nothing about getting anyone in to help,' she says, rubbing her face wearily. 'I've been so flat out on the day to day – the made-to-order's picked up massively – and now I'll end up having to pay some agency person double—'

'It's four weeks of help you need in August?'

'Five – from twentieth of July.'

'Could I do it?'

She laughs. 'Don't you think Roger might notice you're not at your desk after a day or two?'

'He won't mind – I'll be a free woman, a week on Friday.'

'*What* are you talking about?'

'I'm leaving my job,' I say, raising my eyebrows.

'When the fuck?'

'About three hours ago.'

'Because of your piece?'

'Nothing to do with it,' I say. 'Roger's not back for a month, then he'll only be doing one day a week. I'm going to help line up my replacement – and then I'm off.'

'Are you OK about it?'

'I guess I'm still just celebrating the fact he's alive. In a way, he's done me a favour. Jess said a while back, about the day job being a comfort zone.' It does feel a bit like a warm bath which has started to get cold, and Sandra in charge is like a tonne of ice cubes being poured in, straight down my back – the thought alone makes me shiver.

'So you could help out with Celina's! You know, I could use a hand one day a week, even before then? Lisa from Fletchers has asked me to cater her engagement party. Did I tell you she went on a date with a guy from Soulmates – sixty-five but claimed he was forty-five, and when she called him on it, he claimed forty-five was his "biological age"?'

'And she's getting engaged to *him*? Jesus, times are hard . . . '

'No. She walked out on the date and met a lovely man on the train home – turns out they grew up two miles down the road from each other.'

I smile, though the story reminds me a little of meeting Adam after I stormed out on Russell – and the memory of that first encounter makes my heart throb like one large bruise. If only he'd told me on day one. If only I'd told him . . .

'What do you reckon?' she says. 'Fridays – you could help out with shopping, prep and managing the website?'

'Great. I wouldn't be able to do anything for the next month or so though . . . '

'Are you going on holiday? I would, after the amount of stress you've had this month.'

'Roger's given me a dream assignment – five thousand words on the perfect Parisian croissant. I'll go out and spend a bit of time with my family. I'll need the holiday *after* a month with Jess.'

'And dare I ask what's happening with Adam?'

'What – so you can play fairy godmother and email him again?' I say, shaking my head.

'You couldn't just leave him hanging like that, it's not fair.'

'It wasn't deliberate but you're right. And seeing him the other day helped. It made me realise I can't do it. The baby, his mum, this whole happy families thing – it's too much too soon. It's too messy and it's too complicated.'

'Laura – so is life.'

'It's more than that. With his hours it was hard enough seeing him before, but he's going to want to take any access Katie gives him – he's just not thinking through how he'll have any sort of personal life. He won't. And I don't want to feel like I'm in constant competition with the baby for his time.'

'People make time for the things they want to.'

'Not with that job. And it's more than logistics, Soph. The way Adam looks at that little boy is with pure love – you'd be worried if he didn't. But I don't think I could ever look at a kid that way if it wasn't mine. And now this has happened with my work, I have to sort my life out, not hover around playing part-time step-mum.'

'But don't you want to be with him?'

'Yes, I do – but not enough.'

She looks at me with complete disbelief.

'Soph, it's fine, honestly. It's absolutely fine.'

There I go again – saying it's fine, when in fact I mean it's not.

60

To: Dad
From: Laura
Subject: News

Dad – am doing my first full-length feature for *The Voice* –
specialised subject: croissants! If I come to Paris for a month,
I can help take care of the girls, if you want some time off?
Or does Jess have you locked in a cage?

To: Jess
From: Laura
Subject: Get your 'I TOLD YOU SO' T-shirt out of the ward-
robe

If you haven't already heard from Dad, you'll be delighted to
know the PA job has given me up, and the chef who works
unsociable hours is toast.

To: Laura
From: Jess
Subject: Zzzzz

Sorry about the man. Re: the job – does this mean you're going
to go back into coffee? Latest industry figures v. buoyant, year
on year.

To: Jess
From: Laura
Subject: Don't yawn at me

No – it means I'm coming to scrounge off you, a week on Saturday, eat a load of baked goods and work out what the hell to do with my life.

PS Reckon it might make a good Judd Apatow movie, two sisters – one, an uptight Alpha, one, a failed divorcée, one very long month in hell . . . no? Bagsy Kristen Wiig to play me.

To: Laura
From: Jess
Subject: I do not have time to change my subject headers on every email!!

Fine – you can do school runs, shopping, laundry and we can work on a brand plan together.

There is a difference between being mature and being uptight. Once you have children, you might reach maturity yourself.

PS Bagsy Gillian Anderson to play me.

To: Jess
From: Laura
Subject: Clearly you do have time to change your headers . . .

Cinderella will report for duty as per the attached agenda. I'll bring Parmesan biscuits.

And don't try to set me up with any French bankers – I want to be alone.

To: Laura
From: Jess
Subject: NO I DON'T

All right, Greta Garbo/Cinderella/a royal pain in the arse.
We'll meet you at Gare du Nord.
   Plus ça change . . .

To: Jess
From: Laura
Subject: ?

What is *plus ça change* supposed to mean? And don't give me a
smart-arse translation, I know what the phrase literally means
– what do *you* mean?

To: Laura
From: Jess
Subject: French lesson

I mean: you're getting very good at fleeing town every time
you break up with a guy.

To: Jess
From: Laura
Subject: French dictionary

Jess, there are many rude French phrases I could insert at
this point – luckily for you, there are far too many to choose
from.

To: Adam
From: Laura
Subject: News

Hey – it was good to see you last week, and your mum – and Josh – he's absolutely gorgeous.

Listen – I'm leaving my job and going to Paris for a month, Saturday week, so I wanted to say goodbye. I'm not good at goodbyes. I'll keep it brief. The time I spent with you made me properly happy. I felt something big. I'm very glad I met you – and I'm sorry again about all the bullshit. But anyway – I hope things work out exactly how you want them to with Josh and Katie and your job. I think it's best if we kind of call it a day – you have a lot on – and so have I.

To: Laura
From: Adam
Subject: re: News

Wow. You're actually doing this on an email? Ouch. Are you seriously planning on leaving town without talking about this face to face? Is this about everything that's happened in the last month?

To: Adam
From: Laura
Subject: re: News

I'm sorry – but I am super-busy tying up loose ends at work before I head for Paris. Also, I'm not sure it would be helpful to see each other – cold turkey, dare I say it.

And no – it's not about what has happened. It's about what happens now – I'm not sure I can do it.

But I really hope we can be friends at some point down the line?

To: Laura
From: Adam
Subject: re: News

Laura – I'd like to say I can be your friend – but I can't. We're not friends – we're more than that, and you're lying to yourself if you think we could make a friendship work.

To: Adam
From: Laura
Subject: re: News

I'm sorry you feel that way. Well, then I guess this is goodbye.

To: Sophie
From: Laura
Subject: urgh

Sophie – he asked to see me and I said no – it's just too hard.

To: Laura
From: Sophie:
Subject: You're being an idiot

The reason it's too hard is because you don't mean it/it's the wrong decision!

To: Sophie
From: Laura
Subject: Maybe

I can't explain. I just feel I have to break it — before it breaks me.

61

The last ten days have been hectic. Gemma flew back to Thailand last Sunday, so we went out for a meal on Saturday to celebrate. The minute she boarded the plane, Roger caught a stomach bug that was going round the ward, which set him back temporarily. But he's doing OK now, still in there and crotchety as hell.

Sophie and I spent most of Sunday baking double-layered cheese-cake brownies to take to Anne-Marie and the nurses, though there aren't enough brownie layers in the world to begin to express every-one's thanks.

And this week has been busier than I expected. Kiki and Azeem have forced me down The Betsey three times already; if I even say the word Jägermeister out loud I now retch. And it turns out I'm not quite as replaceable as Roger said – well, bizarrely, not in Sandra's eyes. Every PA I've selected for interview, she's found glaring fault with: 'skirt too short', 'hair too long', 'far too casual – she didn't even bother wearing a jacket!' She's chosen Maisie – because she's posh and sweet (and, I suspect, seems the most . . . malleable, although that should probably read bully-able).

I've been so busy I haven't had much time to think about things – but now I do, as I'm packing my bag the night before I'm due to leave. I don't want to leave Adam like this; I want to go back to the way things were, and I know I sound like a giant baby, because all this boils down to is: I want things to be different to the way they are.

I'm lying on my bed, staring up at the ceiling, one hot silent tear running down my left cheek into my ear. I wipe it away, then do the same a moment later on the right.

I force my brain to switch back to Roger: I am profoundly grateful he is OK. That's enough for me. That is this year's silver lining.

There's a gentle knock at the door, and Amber comes in, holding

Annalex. She plonks the dog down by my side, then sits on the end of the bed.

'Babe – are you OK?'

I prop myself up on my elbows and nod.

'Are you upset about this guy?'

I nod silently and feel the soft, silky part of Annalex's ear between my fingers. If I bought Amber a new Mulberry bag on my credit card, would she let me borrow Annalex for the month?

'You know what my therapist would tell you?'

Buy a magic £200 crystal from her and she can magic away all my sadness? 'What, Amber?'

'She'd say it's not the actual person you miss – it's only the idea of him. Falling in love is almost entirely about projection. Or is it transference? Either way – the thing is – it's not about him, he's a concept. It's about what he represents. I forget if it's Freud or Jung, but it's one or the other.'

I let out a deep sigh. 'Amber – while I'm away, please could you water my basil plant?'

'Sure, babe. But seriously – I totes know what I'm talking about: you don't actually miss *him*, it isn't about him.'

When I first moved in to Amber's flat I used to have a recurrent dream. In this dream I'd walk into my bedroom, turn left and find a secret door to another, much larger bedroom where I could actually move around, spread my arms and dance! There was space in this room and light, streaming in from a huge bay window. God, I loved that room.

Being with Adam felt like being in that room. I could be myself, I could breathe, I could be free. That space, that time was there in my life, waiting to be discovered – but I didn't know about it so I didn't use it, I didn't live in it fully.

So perhaps I should be glad Adam showed me that my life could be bigger – end of story.

When I used to wake from that dream, there'd always be a moment where it still felt real, a moment where I didn't want for anything.

And then I'd always fall back down to my smaller life with a bump.

62

To: Sophie
From: Laura
Subject: Bonjour

I can't believe I've been here almost a week. The first three days were a write-off – you know what it's like when you're running on empty, it's when you finally stop that you fall over. Much to Jess's annoyance, I was forced to take to my bed. Rose and Milly were looking after me – not vice versa. They gave me new, directional hairstyles daily, and buttered me umpteen rounds of crumpets (thank heavens for M&S on the Champs Élysées).

I've been back on my feet since Wednesday – hot on the croissant trail. I've learned that one of the secrets of a happy croissant is allowing the dough plenty of time to rest in a cool place – I'm hoping the same will work for me. The last month was so dominated by Roger being ill, everything seems to be hitting me now – I hadn't processed what I've given up: the job, Adam . . . Still, for the best, I'm sure.

Anyway, I have to go, Milly says she needs help with her computing homework – though frankly, she knows way more than I do already. It's amazing how quickly they learn, how much info they can absorb. I love watching her while she's figuring out the answer to something tricky – she gets the cutest little frown.

I've promised her if she does all her work without protest, she and Rose can have an extra ten minutes playing Minecraft (they're completely addicted to this game – you build houses, farms, cities, etc. It's kind of educational, I suppose).

To: Laura
From: Azeem
Subject: Come back, all is forgiven!

Laura – it's 4.15 p.m. and you're not at your desk and it's caaaaake run time.

Oh yeah – that's right – you've fucked off and left me here with Jonesy out to lunch, Sandra in a strop, and no one to moan about her with!!!

Now get on the next Eurostar home and buy us cakes. (We miss you.)

To: Laura
From: Kiki
Subject: Schoolboy error

Couldn't you have sourced a male PA as your replacement? I've run out of men on Tinder within a 20km radius – and I am not yet desperate enough to date outside the M25.

To: Laura
From: Maisie
Subject: Help needed!!!

Hiya, Laura – Maisie here!

Two things – firstly – there's a clear tube thingy in the kitchen cupboard Azeem says you used to make coffee with. I don't know how it works – could you help please?

Oh – can't remember the second thing but I'm sure I wrote it down somewhere . . .

To: Maisie
From: Laura
Subject: re: Help needed!!!

It's called an AeroPress – there are demos on YouTube. Don't let Sandra throw it away!

To: Laura
From: Maisie
Subject: Ah!

Oh yes, that was the second thing! What's the best way of handling Sandra? Is she always a bit . . . I don't know what the word is?

To: Maisie
From: Laura
Subject: re: Ah!

I do know what the word is but it's NSFW. Never figured out how to handle her myself. I guess keep your head down and ignore the death stares. Best of luck!

To: Laura
From: Roger
Subject: Bonjour, Parker

Am back home and bored rigid, though also feeling rather exhausted – like I've had a bad dose of the flu. Still, a bloody sight better than being stuck in that ward.

To: Roger
From: Laura
Subject: re: Bonjour, Parker

Roger – you had a touch more than flu. Does it count as being bossy if I'm in another country and doing it via email? No. So – take it easy, please.

PS Have found the best coffee shop in Paris, Le Caféothèque by the Seine, and it's next to a good wine bar too, Lot Of Wine (I think that's a French pun, though hard to know – these guys are not Europe's biggest jokers).

To: Sophie
From: Laura
Subject: Week deux – update

Have settled into a routine, of sorts. In the mornings I take the twins to school. I thought my French accent was passable but the twins can't stop giggling every time I open my mouth.

After drop-off, I do four hours of research. (The French are *so* French – they have a *boulanger* law: there has to be a bakery open every day in every village, even if the baker doesn't want to work!)

After the morning gorge, I grab a coffee and walk to La Grande Épicerie in St Germain to buy dinner. I could spend all day/all of Jess's money in there – amazing new potatoes from Île de Ré today. I drop the groceries back at the apartment, do some tidying, then take a sandwich over to the park.

At 4.00 p.m. I pick the girls up from school and we do homework – they are teaching me Mandarin. Today's phrase: *Wǒ gǎndào nánguò.* (I feel sad.)

To Laura
From: Sophie
Subject: Why sad?

Haven't you spoken to him yet?

To: Sophie
From: Laura
Subject: No

He said he doesn't want to be my friend. And actually when
I type that, it makes me feel a bit sick – the thought we won't
ever speak again – so it's easier if I pretend he doesn't exist.
On which note – I think we should stop talking about him,
full stop.

Besides, this city is not the worst place to be miserable – it
is exceptionally pretty (apart from the dog poo and graffiti
everywhere). Actually – it *is* possibly the worst place to be
miserable when you're being paid to comfort eat – I should
have gone to Germany or somewhere the food was crap.
Yesterday I was speaking to an old lady who runs a bakery in
the 4th, and she told me a perfect croissant is one third butter.
It's only a matter of time before I am too.

It's warm here, and all the women are in chic shorts; literally
none of them has cellulite. (Though I actually never see them
eat carbs – they're very into 'Bio' and salads. Meh.)

To: Laura
From: Sophie
Subject: German lesson

Don't knock the Germans for comfort eating! They even
have a word for 'flab gained due to comfort eating':

Kummerspeck translates as 'grief bacon'. Wonder if they have a word for 'flab gained due to testing brownies for B-list celebrity who is poor man's Gwyneth Paltrow except no man is that poor – and who *still* can't make her flipping mind up about flavours'.

(This is the last thing I'll say about Adam – but it is my prerogative as your friend to say it: you're being an absolute idiot about the whole thing – you made a mistake, admit it to yourself, email him and sort this nonsense out.)

To: Sophie
From: Laura
Subject: re: German lesson

And it is my prerogative to be an idiot. Now enough, please – or I will have Bobby Brown playing in my head all day.

To: Laura
From: Sophie
Subject: German Lesson – Part II

You know that's called *Ohrwurm* in German – ear worm, a song that you can't get rid of.

To: Laura
From: Kiki
Subject: Le Fitness?

What are the men like? Have you seen any Vincent Cassel lookalikes?

To: Kiki
From: Laura
Subject: I haven't been looking

I only have eyes for croissants.

To: Sophie
From: Laura
Subject: Double trouble

Just had to tell you what the girls did earlier. After dinner, they took themselves off to their room mysteriously. All was quiet, but when I put my ear to the door I could hear the occasional muffled burst of giggling. Good God, when I walked in I found they were – of course – playing Minecraft and were busy turning a bunch of sheep bright pink.

So far, so girly/harmless/innocent – but then they were exploding the poor little lambs with fireballs, to turn them into meat to sell at a supermarket they were building. Maniac seven-year-old capitalists! Have told them no more computer games – and have promised to teach them some old-fashioned card games tomorrow.

To: Laura
From: Roger
Subject: Readers' feedback

Still at home, even more bored, as I'm too tired to concentrate on anything for more than half an hour. I am feeling my age for the first time in my life, terribly depressing. However, have been immensely cheered by the letters in response to your May column – they're still coming in. Thought you might enjoy this one!

So it was a woman after all! I had a bet with my husband that The Dish was female – she didn't employ that patronising, know-it-all tone Fergus Kaye used to have – and she noticed small details. My husband thought it was a man because 'he' made him laugh, and my husband is one of those men who think women can't be funny! Gosh, I enjoy spending his money.

And this (possibly from your papa?)

I can't believe The Dish has left – that column was the only reason I still buy your mag – everything else in it is boring as ****. I might as well read the Economist *now! Bring her back, pay her double!*

And this, Angry *Daily Mail* reader from Cheltenham . . .

Carole Middleton is the future King of England's mother-in-law, and to make a joke at her expense is tantamount to treason. I always knew your magazine was subversive but I didn't know it would stoop so low. Shame on you!

One thing I forgot to mention – for June's issue, Sandra had a last-minute panic (never seen the woman drop a ball before in fourteen years). She had to fill your space with something – so I told her to take your Second Helpings pieces off the system. I hope you don't mind – they're rather charming; will of course pay you accordingly.

Now how are my croissants coming along?

To: Amber
From: Laura
Subject:Reminder

Hope all is well. Please don't forget to water my basil plant, and give Annalex a cuddle from me.

To: Laura
From: Amber
Subject: re: Reminder

Babe – hope you're feeling better about the boy. Remember
– it's not actually him you just miss, just the idea of him.

To: Amber
From: Laura
Subject: re: Reminder

Amber – I do not miss *the idea of him*. I miss *him*. I miss him
in the morning, like nobody's business, and I miss him at night
even more. I miss him very specifically – his smile, his sense
of humour, the way he gets embarrassed when he makes a
crappy joke. I miss his body, particularly his mouth. I miss who
he is – and I miss *what* he is too: a grown-up. Hard working.
A man who is ready, willing and able to be in a relationship
– a rare beast. And I miss what he and I might have been.

To: Laura
From: Amber
Subject: re: Reminder

Babe – you sound like you need some major therapy! Do you
want me to give you my therapist's number?

To: Amber
From: Laura
Subject: re: Reminder

Sorry for going off on one, and thank you – but I don't need
therapy – I've been here before. Heartbreak is part of life –
you have to take the pain, work through it, and it fades.

To: Roger
From: Laura
Subject: Croissant update

Week three, 36 croissants in, and have struck gold – stumbled across a ludicrously perfect *boulanger* in the backstreets of Canal Saint Martin, exceptional croissants, paper-thin golden crispy flaky exteriors, soft, fluffy multi-layered insides. Think it is the frontrunner for this year's Grand Prix at the Concours du Meilleur awards (please can I attend?!). I interviewed the owner – she's third generation of the family to run the place, recipes handed down, etc. She told me the store's history – all the ingredients for a great story – love, heartbreak, a cheating husband, and vast amounts of Brittany butter.

Will obviously keep eating my way through the city to check I haven't missed a trick – but I'm pretty sure I've found The One.

To: Sophie
From: Laura
Subject: The horror

Shocking day today! I was getting quite a few looks from cute French guys – that never normally happens to me. Decided I should spruce up a bit, so I went along to this cool vintage clothing store where you buy clothes by the kilo. In the changing room, I realised why I was getting so much attention: large dark chocolate smear across my upper lip from eating warm chocolate and pistachio swirl in the street. Worse to come: I forced myself into weird, polyester 1960s dress I'd taken an irrational shine to and got stuck – cheap zip! I had to be cut out by unimpressed owner who obviously made me pay for it, though luckily it was not Big Fat Gypsy Wedding style.

Thought for the day: all-you-can-eat pastry assignment should come with free gym membership. (Will be going to

Wolfie's daily on my return. Wonder if they do an all-you-can-sweat package?)

To: Laura
From: Kiki
Subject: Your number one fan!

You won't believe this but The Laminator might actually be missing you. The other day poor Maisie messed up the agenda for conference and Sandra said, 'Laura would *never* have made such a basic mistake.'

To: Sophie
From: Laura
Subject: Aunty Tourettes

Have now got the girls hooked on cards – we've been playing every night. Their favourite seems to be Shithead – though I panicked when they asked what the game was called and told them it was called Shiphead, and now they keep asking what it has to do with boats. I would make such a terrible mother, I didn't realise how often I swear.

PS Thought I'd found two French female carb-eaters in Le Marais, lunch plates piled high with couscous, but when I hovered near their table I heard them speaking Dutch.

To: Laura
From: Sophie
Subject: re: Aunty Tourettes

I reckon women with children swear just as much, if not more, than women without.

To: Sophie
From: Laura
Subject: May kill sister any minute.

Jess had a go at me this morning for not making her tea to the correct Pantone – it was like that scene in *Zoolander* where Will Ferrell throws latte in his assistant's face because the milk is too frothy.

Then this evening, she insisted on talking about my career. I told her I'm in the middle of writing the piece for Roger, and helping you out, but she pointed out that's not the most convincing long-term plan . . . Then! While I was cleaning my teeth she sneaked into my room and left a huge presentation about the coffee industry on my pillow.

And I'm not going to talk about him, but Jess and I did talk about him – and she said that men aren't worth getting worked up over, which is easy to say from the shores of a secure marriage. She thinks you just have to flick a switch in your brain, on or off.

And I am trying, Soph, I am. I'm trying to pretend he doesn't exist. Most of the time I can push him out of my mind, but occasionally I'm hijacked by a thought of him – doing something mundane, like laundry, or cleaning his teeth. And when I think of him as a real person, very much alive and getting on with it – ouch – those thoughts make my heart hurt and I just have to sit and wait while the feeling passes, or at least gets dimmer.

To: Sophie
From: Laura
Subject: Change of plans

Filed copy yesterday and am waiting for Roger to come back to me.

Am feeling rather lost. Strange – even though the girls are exhausting and quite naughty, and have to be nagged incessantly to tidy up after themselves, when I say goodbye to them every morning I miss them before they're even through the school gates.

Was meant to be coming back to London this Friday but have decided to stay out here another fortnight to hang out with them.

To: Laura
From: Sophie
Subject: Weirdo

It's quite peculiar you're so fond of those two little girls – I mean, it's not like they're your kids or anything, is it? When you write about them, it almost sounds like you love them . . . ?

To: Sophie
From: Laura
Subject: What?

What do you mean?? Of course I love them!

To: Laura
From: Sophie
Subject: Der!

Oh, silly me. I thought you were incapable of loving a child that wasn't your own . . .

To: Sophie
From: Laura
Subject: Yeah, yeah, very good.

Meanwhile, I took Dad for dinner last night to his favourite bistro (amazing creamy mash, and they serve chocolate mousse in a giant soup terrine – you're allowed to help yourself, though if they catch a whiff of an English accent, they whip it away instantly). The food was amazing, but their coffee was crap. It got me thinking, and I've had an idea – I reckon it might be an OK one. In the last five years there's been a huge boom in restaurants in London, and also in specialty coffee – both have upped their games to New York standards, but the two aren't aligned. So customers expect better coffee at cafés – but they don't often see it on restaurant menus. Restaurant owners don't invest in coffee because it can seem intimidating – but if someone could advise them, they could improve their coffee, charge a bit more, give the customer a better experience and everyone's a winner, right?

Freelance Coffee Consultant to the restaurant trade, three days a week. Jess is helping me with the numbers and it looks like there's a real opportunity. You can earn decent money as a consultant. What do you think?

To: Laura
From: Sophie
Subject: Love it

It's a great idea. (Would you still do one day a week with me – and Celina's horror party?)

To: Sophie
From: Laura
Subject: Breaking news . . .

Of course I'll help.

   Meanwhile, I have finally found a French woman with cellulite! – in the Jardin du Luxembourg. Admittedly she is a statue, but still – she's called La Femme aux Pommes and the sign by her feet praises her 'sensual grace'. Every time I look at her and feel as though I'm looking in a mirror, I think *sensual grace* and it makes me feel slightly better.

To: Laura
From: Roger
Subject: Encore!

Love the piece. We should think about syndicating it to food or travel mags internationally. Now pitch me some ideas for the rest of the year!

To: Laura
From: Sophie
Subject: The one who cannot be named

Are we really not allowed to talk about Adam? That's a shame, because he emailed me yesterday. But presumably you wouldn't want to hear anything about that . . .

To: Sophie
From: Laura
Subject: re: WHAT?

. . .

To: Laura
From: Sophie
Subject: re: Yup!

He said he was interested in doing a farmers' market and could I give him some more info.

To: Sophie
From: Laura
Subject: Oh

How come he's interested in doing a farmers' market? Did he mention me at all?

To: Laura
From: Sophie
Subject: re: Oh

He asked if you were back yet. And he said to say hi. He used a standard font so I can't read much more into it than that.

Re: farmers' markets – ask him yourself! I swear, the pair of you are as bad as each other.

To: Sophie
From: Laura
Subject: Again, WHAT?

Why do you say that? Did you speak to him about me?

To: Laura
From: Sophie
Subject: Not in detail

But I'm sure he'd appreciate you reaching out, that's all.

To: Adam
From: Laura
Subject: Hi

I hope you're well and that everything is calmer at work.

All is fine in Paris. I am now a world expert on croissants –
have eaten many you'd love (pain au chocolat with banana?) – but
none quite as good as yours.

How's everything with Katie? How's Josh?

Are you thinking of doing a farmers' market? Nothing to
do with the restaurant, presumably?

Let me know how you're getting on.

PS I miss you.

To: Sophie
From: Laura
Subject: I feel sick

Four days, no reply, nothing. Why do people nowadays think
it's perfectly acceptable behaviour to ignore an email? People
you have been really quite intimate with?

He told me he didn't want to be friends – I shouldn't have
pestered him. I shouldn't have told him I miss him.

Four days ago I may have felt miserable and lonely, but at
least I didn't feel miserable and lonely and rejected and exposed.

To: Laura
From: Adam
Subject: re: Hi

Sorry for the late response – been unbelievably busy. So, I have some news . . . You'll be pleased to hear I've handed in my notice. Speaking to Mum and my solicitor, if I'm going to make a decent case for any sort of part-time access to Josh, I'm going to have to dramatically rethink my set-up. I'll never be able to do head chef hours and build a meaningful relationship with him. Or anyone else.

Besides, not sure my soul would have survived much longer at LuxEris. I've been focusing my energies into savoury pastries – made one last week with white beans and rosemary, Italian style – you would have liked it.

To: Adam
From: Laura
Subject: Wow!

Congratulations – that's fantastic news. They didn't deserve someone as talented as you. What will you do instead? If you're thinking of the Breakfast on a Bike idea, I could be your coffee consultant – I'd give you a mate's rate – haha.

That bakery with the banana pains au chocolat also sells delicious escargots – snail shape, not snail flavour. They do a fantastic strawberry one – if you're not working and fancy popping over to Paris for a day trip, I could take you there?

To: Laura
From: Adam
Subject: re: Wow!

Strawberry snails – what a very Jonn idea. I'll make sure not to mention it to him.

Nice thought re: Paris, but I'm working out a month's notice and getting my own stuff together in the few hours I can grab in between. Anyway, I wouldn't feel right taking advantage of a mate's rate – we're not mates.

Cheers.

To: Sophie
From: Laura
Subject: Cheers?

He leaves me with *Cheers*?

And seriously, what is up with the bitchy point scoring? – *We're not mates.* Yeah, well, next time I won't bother trying to be friendly.

To: Laura
From: Sophie
Subject: re: Cheers?

You dumped him by email – you have no right to get the hump about any of this.

And when he said 'you're not mates' – don't you think he might be holding out for more than mates??

To: Sophie
From: Laura
Subject: Adam

Right, so when you emailed Adam last week, did you tell him I'd be back this Friday?

To: Laura
From: Sophie
Subject: re: Adam

Yes, I told him – when I saw him – yesterday . . .

To: Sophie
From: Laura
Subject: ?!?

Oh, come on!

To: Laura
From: Sophie
Subject: Yeah

We had a quick coffee – he didn't realise the farmers' market was so competitive. I think he thought he could just turn up and get a stall, so he wanted to chat. Anyway, he did me a favour with the pecans, so I've offered to trial a couple of his flavours on the stand this Saturday – they'd better not outshine mine, though I guess they're complementary.

But why are you even asking about Adam? If it's over it's over . . .

To: Sophie
From: Laura
Subject: Sophie!

I'm just curious what he's up to. It's not like my feelings for him have stopped overnight. Anyway, I didn't end it because I wanted to end it – I ended it because I had to.

To: Laura
From: Sophie
Subject: Laura!

Just get in a room with him and talk about it, for God's sake
– you're both as stubborn as each other. Right – when exactly
are you back?

To: Sophie
From: Laura
Subject: Friday

Train gets in at 10.35 p.m. on Thursday night so shall I pop
in for breakfast Friday? No more croissants, no more toast,
even. Grapefruit, every day for a month.

To: Laura
From: Sophie
Subject: re: Friday

I'm in Clerkenwell on Friday at lunch, looking at packaging
for goody bags. (Seriously, it's a '40th' – the way Celina's carrying
on, it's bigger than Kim and Kanye at Versailles.)
    Meet me at Fabrizio's at 11 a.m. I haven't been for ages,
and I could do with pitching some new flavours to him. Why
have I not done a dark chocolate espresso brownie before?
Do you reckon he'd go for it?

To: Sophie
From: Laura
Subject: re: Friday

I'll just see you in the flat, it's easier.

To: Laura
From: Sophie
Subject: Fabrizio's!

No can do – I'm at Borough first thing. See you at 11 a.m. at Fabrizio's.

To: Sophie
From: Laura
Subject: re: Fabrizio's!

Fine – I'll bring you some Jean Clement praline millefeuilles – if I don't eat them on the train.

63

Amber is asleep by the time I arrive back on Thursday to find my basil plant a month dead, shrivelled brown leaves curling on my window ledge. She's been in my room, though, because she's left a pastel-covered self-help book on my bed: *Raging Angels – Silencing Your Inner Saboteur and Finding Compassion on the Road To Healing*.

I could probably write a self-help book myself now: *The Paradox of Pastry on the Road To Recovery: How Stuffing your Face with Proper French Croissants Can Make You Feel Better – Yet Worse*.

At least Annalex is pleased to see me – you can see the delight in her eyes, aided by the velvet Alice band keeping the fur from her face. If this coffee consultancy works out, in six months' time I might be earning enough to rent my own flat. It would be nice to have more toast in my life – more toast, more space. But poor Annalex might feel lonely without me – or perhaps the other way around.

I give her a quick cuddle, chuck the basil plant in the bin, put Sophie's pastries in the fridge and I'm asleep a moment after my head's on the pillow.

There's a strange stillness in the flat when I wake the following morning. Amber must be out walking the dog. I lie for a minute, listening to the sound of my breathing. I forgot how quiet a home can be when you're the only one in it. Outside it's a grey, heavy sky – great British summertime. It was easier in Paris – a different country, another life. Two little faces every morning, sometimes covered in jam or Marmite – two faces that brought sunshine in, regardless of the weather.

The thing to do when you're feeling down is get straight out of bed and up to standing position before the sadness can creep under the covers with you. I take a quick shower, then search my wardrobe for something to cheer me up. My blue polka dot dress always does the trick. As I hold it up to the light I notice a tiny mark on the front – either from a potato scone or French toast – and a twinge of memory, of riding in a lift, sears up through my chest. I hang it back in the wardrobe and put on my jeans.

I'll call Kiki and Azeem after I've met Sophie, and see if they fancy lunch, and I can get the gossip. Now Roger's on the mend, I think it's OK if I listen to them bitch about Sandra – as long as I don't actually join in, I reckon God will forgive me.

On the way to the station I buy a copy of the *Big Issue*, and flick through it on the Tube over to Fabrizio's. Peculiar, doing my normal commute without my job to go to, I feel like a confused corporate homing pigeon who's lost its way. Come Monday morning, the hard work starts. Jess and I have mapped out a plan. I'm going to call Doug and some of my old contacts; I reckon I can be up and running within a month. There are things, good things, to look forward to.

When I arrive at Fabrizio's there's a small queue at the counter, just spilling on to the street, and as soon as I walk through the door I notice something's different. Finally! After years of my nagging, and at the exact point I've stopped being a regular, he's started selling food. I peer past the man in front of me's shoulders, and see on the counter two platters stacked with savoury pastries: Parmesan and bacon brioches, and leek, shallot and Gruyère spirals. They're perfectly beautiful and somewhat familiar.

Fabrizio is in the middle of taking payment from a customer but as soon as he finishes he comes round to hug me. 'Where the fack you been? I thought you were away for one week?'

'I said a month, Fab.'

'But now is nearly two whole months!'

'You've missed me?'

'I wanted you to see this,' he says, waving his arm towards the pastries. 'Your friend is a genius.'

'Yeah, and my other friend is going to be well pissed off you're stocking Adam's stuff and not hers! She'll give you a bollocking herself in a minute.'

'She coming here too?' he says, looking surprised.

'Meanwhile, how long have you been seeing Adam behind my back?'

'Only for one week so far – I make the Tweet of the flavours in the morning, sell out by noon,' he says, gesturing with both hands in a game-over sign.

'So . . . did Adam drop these off this morning?' I ask, trying to sound nonchalant, but feeling a flutter of nerves when I mention his name, feeling a mild throb of anxiety when I picture him standing where I'm now standing, just a few hours ago.

'He didn't already tell you the plans?'

'Well, you know . . . he's been very busy . . . '

'He's not busy now?' he says, looking confused.

Fab clearly knows more about Adam's work schedule than I do, and I'm not in the mood to go into detail with him about my failed relationship, especially not when the woman behind me is tutting impatiently. 'Listen Fab, you're busy – I'm going to head to the back and wait for Sophie. I'll order when she gets here.'

'I'll give you a minute to catch up,' says Fabrizio, and lets out a small sigh of contentment, before turning snappily to the next customer.

I head towards the back room, pull the curtain to one side and catch my breath because there's already someone in the room – sitting at the corner table, looking grumpy and exhausted but still entirely gorgeous. His eyes are fixed in my direction, those beautiful blue eyes, and when he sees me he smiles the most wonderful smile – a smile of forgiveness and new beginnings. I cannot believe Sophie told him I'd be here. I am secretly delighted she did that.

I take a seat next to him and try to calm myself, though I feel like my heart is having a minor event.

He looks at me with a mixture of affection, amusement and a slight edge of holding back.

'Laura – I'm glad you're here . . . '

'Adam, I'm glad you're here too . . . ' I say, trying to conceal quite how overjoyed I am to see him.

'I'm glad you're here – because you still owe me for that doughnut, and I've come to get my fiver.' His face is serious, but he's struggling not to smile.

'Oh right, your money . . . ' I say. 'Of course . . . You know what? I'll double-check but I think I've only got about two pounds on me.' I open my handbag and reach for my wallet. There's a pound coin, some shrapnel and the rest is left over from France. 'Is it OK if I give it to you in euros?'

'Actually – I need it in sterling. I need every penny I can lay my hands on,' he says, looking mildly panicked. 'Unemployment beckons, a week from now.'

'But you're doing your own thing, right?'

'Starting to,' he says, looking up to the ceiling, as if for reassurance. 'I've got half a dozen delis and coffee shops lined up and a few high-end restaurants who buy in their bread. I need more than that – but I have to keep enough time free for the rest of my life. It's do-able. Other people do it – I guess I can, too.'

'Don't worry, Adam – you'll be great. Your pastries are like crack.'

'Do you mean that as a compliment?'

'Of course! Why?'

'Well, I've been doubting myself recently . . . since some foul old man in *The Voice* wrote rather a lot of brutal things about me.'

'Oh, that old man is clearly an idiot. Besides, you shouldn't believe everything you read in the papers.'

He smiles gently, then his smile fades and he stares at me intensely. I imagine he's doing what I'm doing: replaying in fast-motion the highs and lows of us. God, I hope he's feeling what I'm feeling because I feel it now more than ever – but it stops my heart, it scares me so much.

I can't figure out what to say to him, there is so much I want to say: I've missed you. I want you. Do your best not to hurt me and I promise I'll do the same. Let's be one of those couples who are happy – not Facebook happy but truly happy. I look into his eyes, hoping to find a watertight guarantee that together we will make this work – what I see there is as close as I think a person can get.

We've been sitting, contemplating each other for a full minute when he finally breaks the silence. 'Laura, why did you leave town like that, without even seeing me?'

If ever there was a time to tell the truth it is now: a time to stop running from the fear of pain, a time to be brave.

'Adam – I feel so much for you, and I have done since the day we met. If I'd seen you before I left, it would have made me feel worse, it would have hurt more and I already felt pretty beaten up. So if I'm honest I was being cowardly.'

He nods. 'And that's why I said we can't be friends,' he says, shrugging his shoulders.

I feel it like a punch in the gut. 'You don't want to be my friend because you think I'm a coward?'

He tuts loudly. 'I don't want to be your friend because you and I are way more than friends.' *Are* way more than friends – not *were* – *are*.

I take a deep breath and carry on. 'And I have to be honest about the baby. I can't pretend to be this amazing, unfazed type who takes it all in her stride. My instant reaction was to freak out. A situation can be rational in your head, but you don't know how you'll feel about it until it's there in front of you.'

He rubs the back of his shoulder slowly. 'So . . . the thing is, I still don't know yet how it's going to pan out with Katie. I'm asking for access every other weekend and one night a week but he's so young it might not be practical till he's at least a year old. I might just get once a month till then – I don't know. And she could so easily turn round at any point and say I can't even have—'

'Look, don't bother explaining,' I say, biting my lip as I summon up all the courage I can muster. 'It doesn't matter what access you end up getting. It makes no difference at all.'

His face falls. 'But Laura – surely if I can—'

'Adam, what I said just now – about having things worked out logically in my head . . . ' I pause and take another deep breath. 'When I saw you with Josh, my overwhelming thought was: I can't do this. But sitting here with you now – I know in my heart I can't *not*.'

He reaches out slowly and takes my hand, and his thumb gently rubs mine. We sit quietly, neither of us moving. I feel almost dizzy with the possibilities of what might yet be. After a minute he glances at his watch and tips his head back in irritation.

'You've got to go back to work again?' I say.

'Only one more bloody week, I swear.' He sighs apologetically.

'Adam – are you looking after Josh this Sunday?'

'I'm not sure yet – if I do, it'll be in the afternoon. Why?'

'Well, how's this for a plan? I'll give you the fiver – in sterling – on Sunday morning and the two of us can sew ourselves a little white flag out of the bread in a bacon sandwich?'

'Now you're talking. At yours?' he says, grinning, and edging his chair closer to mine.

'Nope, no bread allowed. But I know this great little place where they do a mean bacon sarnie, and if we get there early enough they might even have a custard doughnut left . . . '

'A bacon sarnie, a custard doughnut and a new beginning?' He strokes his chin as he considers it. 'Hmm. I'm not entirely sure I can do that . . . '

'Why ever not?'

'Well, it's nothing personal, Laura, but I think I know the place you mean, and the last time I went there I was accosted by a lunatic who stole half my breakfast.'

'Is that so?'

'It is! In fact I think this woman was borderline insane – she actually pulled her own tooth out in a pub.' He clicks his fingers, 'Like that – didn't even flinch.'

'Why would she do that?'

'I believe just for the hell of it. And then she rained down a world of pain on me at work, and she slightly broke my heart,' he says, lifting my hand to his lips, softly kissing my wrist, and then moving my palm to his chest. He places his other hand on top of it and holds it close.

'It's still beating, Adam. They're stronger than you think.'

'And the worst part,' he says, resting our hands back down by his side, 'is that in spite of all those things – or perhaps it's because of them – I've grown rather fond of this creature.'

'You have?'

'I have.' He stares at me with an expression full of hope, then shakes his head in wonder. 'In fact I can't imagine being quite this fond of anyone else in the foreseeable future.'

He looks back down at our entwined fingers, then turns to me and smiles, and I know with my whole heart, whatever happens next, whether we make it or not, it won't be because we didn't try.

Acknowledgements

For starters, many thanks to the fabulous Victoria Hobbs, Pippa McCarthy and Jennifer Custer for good humour, wise counsel and all round brilliance.

I am immeasurably indebted to Mari Evans for insight, ideas and gentle guidance. And über thanks to the magnificent team at Headline – Vicky Palmer, Frances Gough, Frances Edwards, Katie Bradburn, Katie Corcoran and Frances Doyle.

This book was so much fun to research, thanks in no small part to the supremely talented chefs who shared their time, passion and knowledge with me: Pete Begg, Marianne Lumb, Dan Doherty, Shams at Patogh, Frankie at Fiendish and Goode, and the greatest baker in the world, creator of *The* Custard Doughnut, Justin Gellatly at Bread Ahead.

Thanks to all my friends, always, for love, comedy, fun and games – in particular my early readers – Joy Cotterell, Kathryn Finlay, Belinda Kutluoglu, Felicity Spector, Michelle Grose, Dalia Bloom, Susie Aliband, Bobby Sebire, Phil Thomson and Anna Hayman. And also to Adam Polonsky for Italy and beans, car-aoke, illegible notes and letting me win at Trivial Pursuit that one precious time. Ali Bailey – inspirational beauty and provider of dodgy wasabi peas. Andrew Hart, always there in my many hours of need. Rachel Swift, burger-partner extraordinaire. Gerry Katzman for putting up with my writer's block grumpiness. Jenny Knight for infinite wisdom and patience. Ann Farragher and Massi Passimonti for Italian lessons, Nima Amjadi for Persian lessons, Baykar Tafi for your nafas. Dominic Fry for advice about a dog, Andy Pullen for your charming bedside manner, Simon Doggett for bringing editorial meetings back to life. Graeme Dunn, superstar, man of many hats, medical-guru extraordinaire, James Harris for bike advice and sartorial inspiration, Eli Dryden for generosity and kindness.

Clive Jones, curry partner on those dark winter nights and the hot summer ones too,

Lexie Emerson-White for saving me from my bad self over and over, and for coming to Wolfies with me. Cassie Suddes, canapé-chaser extraordinaire, for helping me research more than a few of the meals in this book – I'm still not mentioning *The Notebook*. Laura John for schooling me in the finer points of libel law, Elizabeth and Laura Watkins and David Staples, for giving me a room with a fabulous view. Dan 'Zvuv' Simmons, for that loving slap in the face, Keren Levy for the date-from-hell story and more, Russell Hardiman – restaurateur extraordinaire – for insider info, Toby Finlay for your helpful feedback, Mum and Dad, for pretty much everything.

And finally – a huge thank you to my readers for your support and kind words – the icing on my cake.